The Terran Consensus

By Scott Washburn

Zmok Books

The Terran Consensus
By Scott Washburn
Cover by Jonathan Cresswell-Jones ©Jonathan Cresswell-Jones

Zmok Books an imprint of
Winged Hussar Publishing, LLC, 1525 Hulse Road, Unit 1, Point Pleasant, NJ 08742

ISBN 978-0-9903649-8-6
Library of Congress No. 2015918275
Bibliographical references and index
1.Science Fiction 2. Space Opera 3. Action & Adventure

For more information on Winged Hussar Publishing, LLC, visit us at:
https://www.WingedHussarPublishing.com

The Terran Consensus

Prologue

The crew recreation chamber aboard the starship *Nightpiercer* was designed to be a place of peace and relaxation, but it brought no comfort to Expedition Leader Keeradoth. A tasteful selection of living plants, combined with clever holographic projections, made it appear to be a forest glade of dark blue-green vegetation. Huge tree-like growths stood at intervals and gigantic ferns grew in clumps between them. A waterfall splashed musically in the distance. The small sounds of wildlife could be heard above and all around. Blue and green flowers on hanging vines filled the air with pleasant odors. It all seemed very real, so much like the home world, and more realistic than the similar chamber on Keeradoth's own vessel, the much older, *Seeker of Truth*, which orbited a short distance away. Many improvements had been made since their departure so long ago. In truth, it did seem like home. And now they were to return there.

To go home. How wonderful. I can feel it calling to me. What will it be like after so long? To feel the ground beneath my feet, to breathe the air and feel the sun on my face. To know the warmth of the clanmind. Will it be home? Or is my home just a memory now?

But before they could depart for home, one last thing remained to be done, and it would not be a pleasant one. The thought of the coming confrontation with Dalranor, the commander of *Nightpiercer*, was very disturbing. It would be so tempting to just let it be; go home and leave the problem to others. But Keeradoth could not do that; too much was at stake.

Keeradoth walked toward a mass of ferns and passed a hand before them. The vegetation vanished and was replaced by a large window looking into the blackness of space. In the distance a blue and white ball floated in the void, and beyond it was a smaller gray-white orb. Keeradoth could not escape from the knowledge that the upcoming meeting could well decide the fate of the nine billion sentient beings which lived on that planet.

I have watched this world for so long. I should be tired of it. Why do I fear leaving? Much of what Dalranor had said in earlier discussions was true: times had changed and they must adapt. And Dalranor carried the orders of the Council. *How can I oppose them? But they are wrong. They know not this world or its people. I fear disaster—and not just for us.*

"Expedition Leader Keeradoth?" A disembodied voice spoke without warning, startling Keeradoth.

"Aye?"

"Respected One, Senior Expedition Leader Dalranor awaits you," said the voice.

"Thank you, I come." Keeradoth turned and strode through the glade and into a corridor. The transition from glade to ship was done in a tasteful and elegant manner; tall wooden doors swung wide, opening to a corridor lined with carved paneling and lit by traditional lanterns. The corridor might have been in an ancient clan lodge instead of a space vessel. But step by step the traditional features were replaced by the more utilitarian décor of a spaceship. A few dozen more strides brought the expedition leader to a metal door, which opened automatically. Within was the public chamber of the Senior Expedition Leader. Dalranor stood behind the workstation and looked up as Keeradoth entered.

"Greetings, Expedition Leader," said Dalranor. "You leave for home soon, do you not?"

"Indeed, Honored One." replied Keeradoth. "A day from now we depart."

"To go home! What a glorious thing! How I envy you!" said Dalranor, radiating good will. "Only a short while have *Nightpiercer* and I been here, and already we yearn for home."

Dalranor was clearly trying to delay what was coming, but Keeradoth refused to be distracted by pleasantries. "I have come to speak of the mission."

Dalranor was silent for a moment and then spoke without the earlier congeniality. "So I assumed. Must we again debate this? I now command this expedition; your job is done. The orders of the Council are clear and I will obey them."

"The Council is wrong in this matter." Keeradoth was amazed that such words could come so easily.

The senior expedition leader was plainly startled. Waves of color passed across Dalranor's face before subsiding. They had discussed the matter several times but never had Keeradoth made so bold a statement. Few anywhere had made so bold a statement about the Council!

"Wrong?" exclaimed Dalranor, leaning forward across the workstation. "The Council speaks for the Race and you dare declare them *wrong*?"

"The Council is far away," said Keeradoth, trying to remain calm. "Their information is outdated and incomplete. I do not question their wisdom, but in this case they are wrong."

Dalranor's shock and alarm could be clearly sensed. *Were our places exchanged, I might think me mad.* Could it be true?

"You and your crew have been here too long," said the senior expedition leader warily. "You have been kept from your clanmind. Discord fills you instead of harmony. Go home Keeradoth! Take your ship and go! Leave this world to others."

"I wish that I could," replied Keeradoth who paused for a long moment as doubts began to grow. "Perhaps you are right. I have been here too long. Perhaps I should go." *No! Do not give into the Consensus! It dulls your anger and saps your will. You are right and they are wrong. See it through!* "But I cannot without trying to make you see the Council's error."

Dalranor was silent for a long time, but at last said: "Very well, convince me."

Keeradoth took a deep breath. There was still hope.

"The program, as first envisioned, has proceeded satisfactorily. For seven-dozen cycles we have guided these people toward our goal—and with minimal interference. Another two-dozen cycles could bring us to fruition. To attempt to take direct control now could lead to total disaster."

"Disaster?" said Dalranor. "How?"

"These people are not like us..."

"Of course they are not!" interrupted Dalranor. "They are savages! Barbarians! More the reason to take direct control!"

"More the reason to *not*," countered Keeradoth. "They know neither the clanmind nor the Consensus. They are suspicious creatures. Everything they question. Ill will they expect from all. Were they to learn of our presence prematurely, were our agents to be discovered, they would become our enemies. All our hopes would be undone and our labors turned against us."

"That could still happen with the first program," replied Dalranor, obviously trying not to become angry. "You say another two-dozen cycles, yet your own people predict they may discover us within a single dozen. When their new ship, whose construction you did not stop, travels to the fourth planet, how will you then hide our presence?"

"That is true," admitted the expedition leader. "But we would not be discovered in a hostile act, and still, our goal could be reached. These people are strong and inventive. With proper guidance they will be of great value."

"Proper guidance!" snorted Dalranor. "Your 'proper guidance' nearly destroyed them as I recall! They are *too* strong and *too* inventive; they need control, not guidance!"

Keeradoth's head nodded sadly. "Truth. We made serious mistakes at first. We did misjudge them. They are not like us. But we have learned much since then. Control rankles them. They will rebel."

"Not if we control their leaders," said Dalranor.

"The risk is too great," said Keeradoth, almost pleading. "Sooner or later they must learn of us to be of use. If they even suspect we control their leaders, a bloody revolt will be inevitable. Their history shows that no consensus is reached even with many cycles. Docile they lie for generations and then explode given the merest cause."

Dalranor's head bowed and the senior expedition leader was silent for a very long time.

"Keeradoth," Dalranor said at last. "The matter is out of our hands. I begin to see your concerns and I promise you I will study the situation fully before we act. But for too long you have been gone. Things have changed at home. The people tire. We must move faster and bring an end."

"An end?" said Keeradoth in surprise. "This world and these people can be of great value, but they will not bring an end."

"But it will be a change," continued Dalranor. "The first change in a dozen-dozen cycles. The Council wishes it, the people wish it, it must be so. I am sorry."

This was not going well, but before Keeradoth could think of a reply, an urgent voice intruded.

"Senior Expedition Leader! Please come to central control at once!"

They shared the same look of surprise as to what could possibly have happened to prompt such urgency—and such a breach of protocol?

"This is the Senior Expedition Leader," said Dalranor, turning away from Keeradoth. "What do you require?"

"Honored One! Long range sensors have detected a drive source!"

Both of them were shocked beyond words. There were only a few possible explanations and none of them were good. After a long moment, they turned and rushed out of the chamber toward central control. *Nightpiercer* was a bit larger than *Seeker of Truth*, but they were both relatively small ships and it did not take long for them to arrive. A babble of voices met them at the portal, but cut off as they entered. A dozen crewmembers stood at control consoles but all eyes were on the sensor display floating at the far end of the chamber. A three dimensional diagram of the solar system showed the central sun, the orbiting planets, and various other objects. Data on each of them was displayed nearby. But none of that was what had the unwavering attention of the crew. A flashing yellow icon had appeared beyond the orbit of the sixth planet, and well above the plane of the ecliptic. The sight was one Keeradoth had feared all of these long cycles. Too soon! This was far too soon! The two leaders stood and stared like the others for a few moments before the senior expedition leader stirred.

"Report status!" commanded Dalranor.

"Singularity detected, bearing three-seven point four-twelve," reported the sensor operator. "Distance, one-eight point three-nine, speed nine-two-eleven, decelerating at nine point four gravities, Honored One."

"Course?"

"Honored One," said the operator. "I must report the target is headed directly for our position."

"Time until arrival?"

"One point four days, Honored One; they will cross the ComBarrier in one point two-four days."

"Analysis of drive signature?"

The operator paused a moment as if reluctant to utter what everyone there already suspected. "The drive is consistent with *Brak-Shar* technology, Honored One."

A silence engulfed the Command Center. No one said a word. They all simply stared at the sensor display where the single yellow icon blinked fiercely. Even as they looked, the display updated to draw in the intruder's course. A thin yellow line connected the blinking icon with the third planet. Finally, Keeradoth turned to the senior expedition leader.

"It seems that the desires of both the Council and myself have just become irrelevant."

Chapter One

Lieutenant-Colonel Kathryn Youngs rested her hand on the throttles with the sure touch of a seasoned veteran, and yet her face shown with a barely concealed excitement. Takeoff was her favorite part of flying and she could hardly wait any longer.

"Ready, Gerry?" she said to her co-pilot.

"Everything's green, Colonel," said Major Gerry Messier.

"Edwards Control, this is *Lewis and Clark*, ready for takeoff," said Youngs on her com.

"Roger, *Lewis and Clark*, stand by," replied the Edwards Air Force Base control tower.

As she waited, Youngs thought about what was soon to come: all that power, the roar of the engines, the takeoff, and the climb to orbit, it was just great. Of course, being up there was great too; the stars, that beautiful Earth down below. And the re-entry! The ionization glow, she loved that. Okay, she loved all of it, but takeoff was still the best!

"*Lewis and Clark*, you are cleared for takeoff."

"Roger, Edwards."

"All right. Let's do it!" said Youngs and she pushed the throttles forward.

The faint rumble of the idling aerospike engines at the rear of the spaceplane grew to a muted roar. A moment later, the ship began to move forward down the enormous desert runway.

"And we are rolling."

As the thrust continued to build, Youngs was pressed back in her seat. The runway was rushing toward her faster and faster. Fortunately, her helmet hid the silly grin on her face from her co-pilot. The speed indicator reached the proper point and she eased back on the control yoke. The nose came up so she could no longer see the ground. There was the gentlest of bumps, and they were airborne.

"Liftoff; wheels up, Gerry."

"Roger that, wheels coming up."

"*Lewis and Clark*, this is Houston," said a new voice. "We now have control."

"Roger, Houston," said Youngs. *The hell you do! I'm flying this crate, not you!*

There was a small thump and instrument lights flashed to indicate that the landing gears were fully retracted and their doors closed.

"That was sweet, Colonel," said Major Messier. "They told me you make the smoothest take-offs around."

"Wait until you feel the landing, Major," grinned Youngs. "I'm even better at those."

"Altitude 5000 meters, speed 650 knots," reported Messier.

"Roger that. Throttling back. Houston, this is *Lewis and Clark*. Request rendezvous course for refueling. That you down there, Harry?"

"*Lewis and Clark*, this is Houston, course information uploading now. We estimate rendezvous in ten minutes. Yeah, that's me, how you doin', Kay?"

"Just fine, Harry," answered Youngs. "A beautiful day to be flying! You got that course, Gerry?"

"Yes, Colonel, steer 225, rate of ascent 200 meters per minute."

"Roger. Coming to 225." Youngs moved the yoke slightly to the left and the spaceplane swung around onto its new heading.

Yeah, it's a beautiful day to be flying, thought Youngs. *But then any day's a beautiful day to be flying.* She looked over the cockpit with deep satisfaction. She was piloting the most sophisticated vehicle ever built by man and it was all hers. *Not too shabby for a simple country girl from Ohio!*

Youngs had been one of four girls growing up in a small town in western Ohio. Her three sisters had all gotten married and had kids before they reached their mid-twenties, but Kay had other ideas. She knew she was headed somewhere, she just had to figure out where. Stories her grandfather had told her about the Cleveland Air Races had stirred something in her. Kay never quite believed him when he told her that her great-grandmother had actually known the Wright brothers when she was a small girl in Dayton, but it was still neat to think about. And there was that slightly run-down museum just down the road in Wapekeneta—that museum for Neil Armstrong. The teenage Kay Youngs had decided she wanted to fly.

The Junior Air Force ROTC program in high school had gotten her started. Her grades weren't the best, but she made up for it with her zeal. A scholarship to Ohio State followed, then graduation and flight school. That was when her dream almost came to an end. While she had a natural feel for flying, she couldn't navigate worth a damn. Numbers made her head hurt and her natural sense of direction was definitely second rate. A lot of hard work and some tutoring helped her squeak by. And, although she still hated to think about it, she had cheated—just a little bit.

Just that one test! It was only that once. Was I supposed to let it all slip away because of one navigation test? That's what computers are for! I wanted to fly, dammit! Not crunch numbers!

She won her wings and her natural flying skills had gotten her posted, a few years later, to one of the first co-ed fighter squadrons. She flew twenty-four combat missions over North Korea in '26, with one confirmed kill (and one unconfirmed, dammit!). Later, it was back to school for some graduate work, then test pilot school, and finally the Astronaut Corps. Kay at last realized where she had been headed all this time: to the stars.

I won't get there, but I'll blaze one more mark along the trail.

"I have a visual on the tanker, Colonel," said Major Messier.

"Roger, I see it; commencing approach."

To permit the maximum payload, the space planes took off with the minimum load of fuel. By refueling after takeoff, *Lewis and Clark* could boost fifty tons of cargo into orbit. Youngs maneuvered her craft behind the lumbering tanker aircraft and matched speeds.

"We're in position; activate auto-refueling sequence," ordered Youngs.

"Roger, auto sequence engaged," replied Messier.

Kay removed her hands from the control yoke as the computer took control of the plane. She kept a watchful eye as her ship slowly closed in on the refueling line streaming back from the tanker. Youngs had refueled manually many times when she was flying fighters, but she had to admit that this was one time when she was perfectly happy letting the computer do the work. The refueling line had a locational transponder in the end, as did the probe that now extended from the nose of *Lewis and Clark.* The computer, in its idiot-savant fashion, moved the ship so the two transponders occupied the same space.

"Hook up complete, fuel transfer commencing," reported Messier.

The huge fuel tanks of the spaceplane took nearly fifteen minutes to fill. During that time, Youngs and Messier double-checked that everything was green for going to orbit. And all the while, Youngs kept an eye on the plane in front of her and never moved her hands far from the controls. When the transfer was complete Kay took control back from the computer and pulled her ship away from the tanker.

"Houston, this is *Lewis and Clark*, refueling complete, request a go for Earth Orbit Insertion," reported Youngs.

"Roger, *Lewis and Clark*, you are go for EOI," replied the controller in Houston.

"All right!" grinned Youngs. "Next stop: outer space!"

Kay pushed the throttles forward again and the thrust began to build, pushing them back in their seats. Then, reluctantly, Youngs activated the auto-pilot. A display lit up on the control panel showing the pre-planned flight corridor. The dot representing *Lewis and Clark* settled precisely into the center of the corridor. *Hmph! I could do that! Well, at least this way I can enjoy the ride.*

There was a slight vibration that quickly faded. "Passing through Mach One," said Messier, his eyed glued to the instrument readouts.

The nose of the spaceplane tilted up again and the bright blue sky above them slowly changed to indigo.

"Passing sixteen thousand meters, speed two thousand four hundred meters per second," reported Major Messier.

"Gerry," said Youngs, smiling, "you only make your first trip to orbit once, loosen up and enjoy it!"

"Okay, Colonel," said Messier sheepishly. "I'll listen to the sage advice of a veteran just this once."

They both stared out the cockpit window as the sky turned from indigo to black and the stars came out.

"Damn, that's pretty," whispered Messier. "Thanks, Colonel; I would have missed it."

"Nothing else like it, Major," said Youngs quietly. "And you're welcome."

There was another faint thump and Major Messier reported: "Air scoops retracted, we are now on internal oxidizers." The spaceplane used air like a conventional jet to burn its fuel in order to save weight, but now the air was too thin and they were using the liquid oxygen stored onboard.

"Roger that. Houston, this is *Lewis and Clark,* requesting final go for orbit," said Youngs.

"*Lewis and Clark*, this is Houston, you are go for orbit—have a great flight, Kay!" said the controller.

"Roger Houston, we are go for orbit. See you when we get back, Harry!" answered Youngs.

The two astronauts watched in silence as their craft continued to gain speed and altitude. The roar of the engines could still be heard faintly, the noise being transferred through the fabric of the ship. The nose came down enough that they could see the Earth below them. The curvature of the planet was plainly visible.

"Columbus was right," said Messier. "The world is round."

"I think someone else has already said that, Major," replied Youngs. "You are going to have to come up with something more original to get in the history books."

"Right," grinned Messier. "I'll work on it."

"You do that. We are coming up on main engine cut off in fifteen seconds," said Youngs.

The time counted down, and on the mark, the aerospike engines shut down. The faint roar died away and the cockpit of *Lewis and Clark* was silent.

Well, almost silent. There was the whir of the ventilation fans and a host of other small noises from the equipment—half of which Kay had never been able to identify. Actually, it was not very quiet at all…

"ETA until rendezvous?" asked Youngs.

"Thirty-seven minutes, Colonel."

Kay nodded. For once their takeoff time and the target's orbit matched up perfectly and they could make a direct approach without even a single orbit. She unfastened her helmet and took it off. Then she leaned back in her seat and smiled.

"How are you doing, Gerry?"

"Me? Just fine, Colonel," he replied, removing his own helmet.

Kay looked at her co-pilot and had to admit that he did look fine: none of that greenish complexion that a lot of astronauts exhibited their first few times in zero-G. A lot of astronauts like Kay Youngs. She thought back to her first mission. She had spent the first few hours after reaching orbit with her face glued to a puke bag. The mere memory made her a little queasy and she turned her thoughts away from that.

"I think I'll unstrap and take a look at the cargo bay, Skipper," said Messier.

Youngs grinned and watched him head aft. There was absolutely no reason to check the cargo bay; it was obvious that Gerry just wanted an excuse to bounce around in the micro-gravity for a while. Apparently, he was one of those lucky types that would have no trouble with drop-sickness. Kay envied him.

While Messier was off floating around, Kay checked in with Houston and confirmed that everything was going according to plan. That only took a few minutes and then she realized she had nothing to do. Crews of the earlier space shuttle program, or even the short-lived *Constellation* series, would have been scandalized: on those ships there had *always* been things that had to be done. The spaceplanes of the newest generation, though far more sophisticated, were much easier to actually operate. That was the way of technology: things start off very simple, but then they get more and more complicated as the boundaries are pushed. As the techniques are refined, things become simpler again—at least for the people using them.

Kay was immensely proud that she was a spaceplane pilot. It was the culmination of all her work.

Or she had thought it was.

Kay frowned. *Why hasn't Jennings gotten back to me with an answer yet? I know they have a lot of factors to consider, but I should at least have heard something by now!*

All through her flight training, all during her fighter-jock days, and right on into the Astronaut Corps, Kay had always been pushing and pushing to reach the next step. Each accomplishment was just a springboard to the next level up. When she had first started, being a spaceplane pilot was the top of the heap—it didn't get any better than that. But now that she was finally here, that was not quite true anymore.

And the reason it wasn't was coming into view now—the reason for this supply mission.

A brightly glowing star had detached itself from the horizon of the planet below. As Kay watched, it slowly rose until it was almost directly ahead. It grew bigger by the minute. She twisted around and opened a small storage locker next to her seat to withdraw a pair of binoculars. Putting them to her eyes, she focused in on the growing star.

Under magnification, she could see that the single bright blob was made up of several smaller ones. One was the familiar shape of the International Space Station. Its ungainly collection of solar panels, labs, and habitation modules made it look like some child's tinker-toy creation.

But it wasn't the station she was looking at. Just beyond, and slightly to the side of the station, was a huge shape that made Kathryn Youngs' heart beat faster. It was long and narrow. At one end was a cluster of shapes that looked like a more compact version of the station, without all the solar panels. Then a long girder stretched back to another structure at the far end.

It was a spaceship.

Not just some cargo and passenger shuttle like Kay was piloting. Not some spam-in-a-can, throw ninety-five percent of it away, one-shot probe like the Apollo missions. A *spaceship*. A real spaceship. A ship that could go places and do things and then come home, refuel, and go someplace else.

It had been under construction here for the last eight years and now it was nearly finished. Kay could see smaller shapes scattered around the ship, but she was still too far away to pick out any of the space-suited construction crew. It did not look much like the spaceships of fiction, but it was the most beautiful thing Kay Youngs had ever seen.

And when it made its first voyage next year, she was absolutely deter-mined to be aboard.

She lowered the binoculars and sighed. The odds were against her, she knew that. Despite her years of experience, there were other astronauts with more years and more rank and more fame ahead of her. She knew there was no chance of her being named the commander or pilot of the ship—and certainly not the navigator! But there were other slots available, slots she had been training herself to fill. She had worked and sweated and pushed herself, and she was nearly finished with a doctorate in environmental engineering. It wasn't something she was terribly interested in, but it might be her ticket aboard the ship. They would need an engineer to keep the life support systems running and wouldn't it be great to have one with hundreds of hours of space experience who was a damn good pilot to boot?

At least Kay was hoping they would think that way. At least that was the way Kay had presented her case to Samuel Jennings, the man who would be making the final crew recommendations.

She'd been boning up on nuclear engineering, too. There was no time to become a full-fledged nuclear engineer, but she figured every little bit would help. Assuming they ever got the fuel to actually fire it up!

That was the big sticking point just at the moment. The ship was propelled by a nuclear engine—the only way of making the ship practical, as no chemical propulsion could do the job. But people were afraid of nukes. In Kay Youngs' mind, it was an irrational fear, but she knew that many fears, though irrational, were no less real. Three Mile Island and Chernobyl were many decades in the past. Only a handful of people alive today had even been born when Hiroshima and Nagasaki had been headlines. But many people—far too many people—equated nuclear energy with terrible danger.

Youngs was still slightly amazed that the design for the ship had ever been approved in the first place. Funding for space exploration of any kind had been terribly hard to come by for decades. The ISS itself had been an orphan child that nobody wanted for years—and few people seemed to care.

Then, a handful of men and women with the vision and the will had come on the scene. They had made the case that Man's future lay in space and they had the courage to stand by their convictions. They had convinced others. Not everyone to be sure, but enough. The spaceplanes had been built and then the ship. Kay felt a thrill just being a part of it.

But the ship had a nuclear motor and that required nuclear fuel. That, in turn, required nuclear fuel to be launched into orbit. Many had protested and tried to block the launch in the courts. It was only a few short months since they had been cleared for the launch. The *Lewis and Clark* was not shuttling the fuel, but rather the equipment needed to handle it once an unmanned rocket brought it to them. That all, of course, was if the damned protesters didn't find some other way to delay it.

Kay ended her musings and looked out again. The station and the ship were much closer now.

"Gerry," she said into the com, "you might want to come up here and have a look at this."

"Roger. On my way," came back the reply. It was just a minute before her co-pilot floated back into the cockpit.

"Holy cow, will you look at that!" he said upon catching sight of the ship.

"Sorry, Gerry, that one's been used, too—although you won't find it in the official histories," grinned Kay.

"What? Oh!" said Messier with a startled laugh. But he was not paying attention to her. His eyes were glued to the sight through the window. "God, I've seen the pictures, but they just don't do it justice, do they?"

"Nope. Hell of a thing, isn't it?"

"Sure is."

"*Lewis and Clark*, this is Houston," said the radio, startling both of them slightly. "Your overtake velocity is twenty-two meters per second. Course is right in the groove. Begin final orbit insertion in one minute."

"Roger, Houston," said Kay. The initial boost given to the spaceplane had lifted them to an orbit just slightly lower—and hence faster—than the station and the ship. This allowed them to catch up with their destination. Now, a few small bursts of thrust were all that was needed to put them in the same orbit. The seconds ticked away and the thrusters fired on schedule. Once again, it was all automatic, but Kay kept a close eye on what was happening. The computer did a good job—almost as good as Kay could have done—and shortly, *Lewis and Clark* was drifting alongside the station, about three hundred meters away.

"ISS, this is *Lewis and Clark*," said Kay into the radio. "We are here with the goodies."

"Roger, *Lewis and Clark*," came back a heavily accented voice. "Good to see you again, Kay."

"That you, Sergei?"

"Yes, I am here."

Kay smiled. She had gotten to know the Russian engineer very well while taking her courses on environmental engineering. In spite of the mess that the Russian space program was in—hell, the whole country for that matter—they still knew more about the life support systems of space vehicles than anyone else.

"Have they decided where they want all this stuff yet?" she asked.

"Yes. Mister Ericsson wants it at the construction site immediately."

"Roger. We'll head over there right away. Talk to you later, Sergei."

Kathryn Youngs smiled a broader smile. She got to do this part manually. "Okay, Gerry, we've got a load to deliver. Let's get to work!"

* * * * *

Commander Robert Hancock, United States Navy, turned off the main highway leading from Frederick, Maryland and navigated the smaller country roads to his house. It was a relief after the madhouse of Washington traffic on a Friday afternoon. He glanced at the man sitting in the passenger seat; a rather short, stocky fellow wearing a captain's uniform.

"It was really great that we bumped into each other, Ed," said Hancock, smiling at his old friend. They'd been roommates at the Naval Academy twenty-odd years earlier, but they'd taken different career tracks and didn't see each other much anymore.

"Yes, it has been a while, hasn't it?" replied Edward Osborne, smiling in return. "What's it been? Three years? Four?"

"Closer to five, I think." He turned into the driveway and saw another small car already there. "Oh, good, Lissa's home. I was afraid she might be out somewhere."

He parked the car and the two men got out. Almost immediately there was a loud barking and then a large, gray shape came bounding across the yard. The dog had a happy look on his face, but he suddenly skidded to a halt at the sight of Osborne. He began to bark again with an entirely different tone.

"Hey, Cedric! Don't you remember me?" There was a mock tone of hurt feelings in Osborne's voice.

Hancock walked over to the Irish Wolfhound and carefully began rubbing his ears. After a few reassuring words and some cautious sniffing, the big dog reacquainted himself with Hancock's friend.

"Hi, Dad!"

Hancock looked up and saw his daughter coming out of the house. She was smiling, but hesitated for a moment when she saw that her father was not alone.

"Hi, Melissa!" said Osborne.

"Captain Osborne?" the girl replied uncertainly.

"Hey, what's this 'captain' business? I used to be your Uncle Eddie—but you've grown up a bit since those days! Look at you! What are you, now, twenty?"

The young woman nodded and her smile grew broader again and she came forward and exchanged hugs with Osborne.

"Ed's boat is in dock for a while and I've asked him to stay the weekend, Lissa," said Hancock.

"That's great! Well, why don't you guys come in and relax? Have you eaten yet?"

"Yes we did; stopped at *Chuy's* on the way here."

"Okay, can I get you something to drink?"

"That would be fine."

Shortly, the four of them were on the screened-in back porch. Melissa and Osborne exchanged news while Bob scratched Cedric's back. He looked at his daughter with pride and satisfaction. She was such a good kid. She had survived the messy divorce between him and her mother with hardly a scratch. Or at least it seemed that way to him. The fact that she had decided to follow in his footsteps and go to Annapolis probably had a great deal to do with his feeling about her and he was honest enough to admit it to himself.

As they sat there, the evening softly became night. Clouds of fireflies imitated the stars that were shinning in the darkening sky. The heat of the Washington day was scarcely even a memory now.

"Well, if you two can keep yourselves amused, I'm going to get out the telescope and do a little stargazing," said Melissa.

"It's a good night for it," Osborne smiled as he nodded to her. "If you see anything interesting let us know."

"Will do."

She went into the house and after a few minutes came back with the bulky telescope and tripod in her arms. A set of powerful binoculars were hung around her neck. Osborne held open the porch door for her and Cedric followed her out into the backyard. The two men watched her set up.

"Still got her head in the clouds, I see," said Osborne.

"Yup. Just like her old man."

"She planning to go to flight school?"

"I'm not sure. I don't think she is either. She wants to fly, but she's really into the engineering aspects of it—especially computers. I think she's looking at the astronaut corps."

"A chip off the old block, eh?"

"I guess so."

"I still remember what a big space buff you were at the academy, Bob. Hell of a shame about your leg. How's it doing anyway?"

"The leg's not too bad." Bob looked down at his leg; the trousers covered the scars, but nothing could erase the memory of what had happened. "My golf game's still shot to hell, but the leg itself doesn't really bother me anymore."

"That's good. But you should have gone into the Boomers with me, Bob. On *Tennessee* we don't care if a man walks with a limp. Another advantage over those carriers you were always raving over. Damn hard break, though, if you'll excuse the pun."

"Not sure if I will or not, Ed." He smiled, but it was just a mask. His leg. His damn leg. Seven years ago, Robert Hancock was second in command of the Air Wing on *USS Ronald Reagan, CVN-75*. Another year and he'd have the Wing for his own. Then it was only a matter of time until he got one of those carriers that Osborne was always griping about. Captain and eventually flag rank. The future had been bright.

Then, a stupid mistake, a wrecked car, and a crushed leg and that future was gone. It was clear immediately that he would never fly jets again. Sea duty was out of the question, too, until the lengthy rehabilitation was finished. Somehow, even now he wasn't quite sure how, he had ended up with a desk job in Naval Intelligence. They put him to work monitoring space activities—probably because his boss had heard about his interest in it back at the academy. After all this time he was still there.

He looked down at the sleeve of his jacket. He was in civilian clothes, but he could almost see the three gold rings of a commander's uniform there. Not the four gold rings of a captain—like his friend was wearing. Like many of his friends were now wearing. Oh, he'd make captain one of these days, but it would be a prelude to retirement instead of flag rank.

"It wasn't supposed to storm, was it?" asked Osborne suddenly, startling Hancock out of his musings.

"I don't think so, why?"

"There have been some flashes like lightning."

They could not see much of the sky because of the porch roof, but what they could see was still clear.

"Heat lightning?" suggested Hancock.

"Maybe. See? There's another one."

This time Hancock saw what his friend was talking about: a brief flash that momentarily lit up the yard. He could also see Melissa looking up with her binoculars. Cedric was at the porch door with his tail between his legs.

"Dad…" she said without looking away.

"Storm coming, Lis?"

"Uh… Dad," said Melissa with a strange catch in her voice. "I… I think you better come look at this."

Chapter Two

"Okay, easy now," said Doctor Usha Vasthare. "Bring it a little to your left; now forward."

Usha twisted her diminutive body around in the micro-gravity so she could observe the alignment of the control rod assembly. She was glad the latest model space suits were far less bulky than the old ones she had trained on—she never would have fit in here wearing one of those things. Even so, her instructors would have been appalled by where she was. The assembly massed nearly twenty tons and she was directly between it and the even more massive reactor housing. If the assembly moved in the wrong direction now, she would be crushed. That particular danger never even entered her mind.

The alignment looked good, but she knew that it had to go in exactly straight or it would jam. The tolerances were exceedingly fine. She moved again to look from another angle. She took a laser-leveling tool from her belt and placed it along the side of the assembly. She pressed a button on it, waited a moment, and then placed it on the guide track. She compared the figures on the display and then did some quick calculations in her head.

"Howie, move your end about a centimeter to the left."

"Right, boss," came the reply from one of her technicians.

She checked again and was finally satisfied. "All right, it looks good. Lock it down and we'll get ready to retract."

A chorus of acknowledgments came back over her suit radio. Usha slowly pulled herself out of the cramped space she had been in, being very, very careful not to bump the large assembly. Once she was clear, she drifted up to the top of the compartment and grabbed a handhold. She watched her crew tighten down the bolts that held the control rod assembly to the retraction guides. After a few minutes, they had all floated back and announced they were ready.

Usha had her hand computer ready and tied into the control unit for the reactor. A part of her brain marveled at how easy the latest generation of computers was to use. Without any hard connections, she could tie into any device on the ship and it was like being right there at the control console. The rest of her attention, however, was on the current job. She double and triple-checked all the readings and then hit the 'retract' command.

Immediately, the huge assembly began to move. It did not move quickly, perhaps a centimeter per second, but it was moving. Usha's eyes flicked back and forth between her computer readout and the assembly itself, checking the progress. It took nearly twenty minutes for the twelve-meter long piece of equipment to slide into its proper position, but it did so perfectly. Usha took a deep breath and let out a long sigh when all the lights turned green on her display. Her crew all gave a cheer when she gave them a 'thumbs up' gesture.

"Great job, everyone," she said with a smile. "Now all we have to do is get the control connections hooked up to all the rods."

This produced a groan just as loud as the cheer had been, but Usha knew they were just kidding. Morale in her crew was literally sky-high. The prospect of fueling the reactor on the great ship had everyone excited.

"Hey, there are only a thousand of them," she said brightly. "You'll have them all done by dinner, right?"

"Dinner sometime next week!" said Howie Crawford, her chief technician.

Usha laughed. "Seriously, get as many of them done as you can and then turn things over to the next shift."

"Right, chief," said Crawford.

Usha watched for a few minutes and then turned and headed for the exit. As she neared the hatch, she noticed someone there, also watching. After a moment, she recognized Lieutenant Colonel Youngs, the spaceplane pilot who had brought up the assembly they had just secured.

Usha frowned. She did not particularly like the colonel. Part of it was simply the fact that she was in the military. Usha was not happy at how much control of this project the military seemed to have. Most of the key people were either current or ex-military. She did not have anything against the military *per se*, but she did not feel they had any business with the ship. It was an exploration vehicle and the military should keep their hands off it!

The other part of her dislike for Youngs was the colonel's personality. She was just a bit too loud, a bit too forward for Usha's taste. She was always poking her nose into things and asking questions. It was obvious to Usha that Youngs desperately wanted to be named to the crew of the ship. *Well, she's not getting this position! That's already taken!* Usha Vasthare was the chief nuclear engineer on the project and when the ship made its maiden voyage next year, she would be aboard to oversee the function of the nuclear motor.

"Hello, Doctor," said Youngs as Usha neared her. "All the new junk fit properly?"

"Hardly 'junk', Colonel," said Usha a bit sternly. "It's the heart of the motor. Without it there's no propulsion—and no ship!"

"True. But it did fit?"

"Yes, it fit."

"Good. Hate to think I'd have to fetch up another one for you. Are you heading back to the crew compartment?"

"Yes."

"Me, too."

Usha frowned slightly, but said nothing. She pressed a button and the heavy, shielded door of the reactor containment vessel slid open. She and Youngs floated into the airlock and shut the door behind them. The main reactor control room on the other side was not pressurized yet, so the other door could be opened immediately. Usha stopped and pretended to check a few of the control panels in hopes that Youngs would go on ahead, but she did not. She floated up and hung there looking over her shoulder and asking questions about the reactor. Usha tried to answer politely.

Eventually, she realized that Youngs was not going to go away, so she sighed and headed forward with Youngs in tow. Another airlock took them out of the engine module and into the central keel of the ship.

Usha caught her breath even though she had seen the sight a hundred times. A three hundred-meter long framework of trusses and girders stretched away from her. In the distance was the crew module. When the ship was complete, dozens of huge fuel tanks would be attached to this keel. A network of pipes connected the tanks to the reactor. In the reactor, the fuel—or reaction mass as it really was—would be heated by the reactor to a high temperature and expelled from the stern of the ship to produce thrust. Not a great deal of thrust compared to something like the colonel's spaceplane, about a tenth of a G. But instead of providing thrust for a few minutes like the spaceplane, this motor could operate for hours or days and attain velocities higher than anything man had ever constructed. Earth to Mars in six weeks; Usha got giddy just thinking about it.

At the moment, none of those fuel tanks had been attached. She could look out through the open framework and see the Earth. She pushed herself over to one of a set of cables that ran the length of the keel and attached her suit belt to a hook on the cable. Colonel Youngs did the same. Usha pressed a button set next to the cable and it began to move. It accelerated smoothly to a quick walking pace, about two meters per second, drawing her forward with it. It took about three minutes to make the journey from the engine module to the crew module. As they neared their destination, the cable slowed and eventually stopped a few meters from another airlock. This led into the crew module and there was pressure there. Once inside, Usha removed her helmet and clipped it to her belt.

"I'm going back to my quarters for a while, Colonel; it has been nice talking with you."

"Thank you for your time, Doctor," replied Youngs. "I'll see you later."

Usha breathed a sigh of relief as the pushy American astronaut finally left her alone. She floated along the main corridor in the ship, past the large cargo holds and the hanger pockets that would hold the landers—if they ever got them completed. Eventually, she reached the modest cabin that was hers. She carefully took off her space suit and stored it in its locker along with the helmet. Then she closed her eyes and just drifted in the zero-G and the blessed silence.

She was tired. The pace had been grueling since they got the final go ahead to assemble the reactor and motor. The permission could be revoked at any time based on the fickle winds of public opinion and they desperately wanted to get it finished before it was. But once the fuel was up here, there would be no stopping things—and they had to be ready for the fuel.

They would be; she was sure of it. Her crew was performing wonders and they were ahead of schedule. The fuel rods would be boosted into orbit in a month's time and they would be ready.

Doctor Usha Vasthare was young for a position of such responsibility. She had left her native India ten years earlier to come to the United States. Partly it had been in protest of her country's continued attempts to build a nuclear arsenal in spite of world opinion. But mostly it was because of opportunities she had heard of in the United States' renewed space program. Usha was a brilliant nuclear engineer, but her dreams were in space. Mankind's future lay there, of that she was utterly convinced. She had followed the results of the myriad of unmanned robots dispatched to the planets with great interest, but she had always thought they were ultimately pointless unless people eventually followed.

She knew that many felt differently; felt that the cost of manned missions was too great. She had friends at the Jet Propulsion Laboratory who believed that their robots could do it all. They had been scandalized by her statements that all their data was of no use except to pave the way for human explorers. She could respect their views, but she knew in her heart that they were wrong.

And so, through hard work and perseverance, she had become involved in the project to build the ship.

The Ship.

It did not have a name yet—that was being argued over just like every-thing else. Usha secretly favored 'Agni', the Hindu god of fire. She felt it would be appropriate considering the nuclear fire they would soon kindle inside it. But she knew that it would inevitably be something like 'Discovery' or 'Explorer' or—*the gods protect us*—'Enterprise' which would suit the tastes of the Western public. It really did not matter what they named it, she supposed—just so long as they let her finish it!

She knew she should rest, but the nervous energy inside her was too great. She left her cabin and pushed herself forward. She looked into the unfin-ished lab modules that took up a great deal of this part of the ship. She forced herself to admit that these were really what the ship was all about. Even if her precious motor could take them to Mars or Jupiter or beyond, this was a science ship and the scientists needed places to work. The labs would not be completed for quite a while, but there was no great rush. Once the fuel was aboard and the motor completed, there would be many months of testing before the first long voyage—plenty of time to complete the labs.

Usha poked her head into the main environmental and recycling module but quickly backed out again. Colonel Youngs was there and she had no desire to resume their earlier conversation. Instead, she went to the fabrication module. This was their machine shop. Several people were there working with the au-to-fabricators. She drifted over to one of them and watched.

The fabricators were about the size of an automobile and they never ceased to amaze her. When she had been going to school, the 'rapid prototypers' were all the rage. They could take a three dimensional computer model and cre-ate an actual object from it. The objects were made of a thermoplastic or some similar material and were very limited in size and strength. Even so, they were useful in testing concepts for new mechanisms. The fabricators took it one step further. They used lasers and magnetic fields to manipulate streams of vaporized metals and other elements to form finished parts that could actually be used. They were still too slow for use in mass production, but for one-of-a-kind projects like the ship, they were invaluable. Operating in a micro-gravity environment, they could create alloys that were stronger and lighter than anything that had been possible before.

And they could create parts quickly that would take months to make by older processes. Usha looked through the polarized window into the center of the fabricator. She recognized a piece of her reactor taking shape. There had been a minor improvement made in the design and several components had to be re-placed. In the old days, that would have been out of the question. Once a design was finalized it was virtually impossible to change it without massive delays. That was why big projects like this used to have technology twenty years out of date by the time they were finished. That was not going to happen this time!

Usha nodded to the technician and pushed herself toward the other fab-ricator. Before she got there, however, there was a loud tone from the ship's PA system and then an urgent sounding voice:

"All department heads report to the bridge! Repeat, all department heads report to the bridge at once! This is an emergency!"

Usha jerked herself around, nearly colliding with the fabricator before she could stop her motion. This had never happened before! An emergency? What sort of emergency? After a moment's hesitation she was scrambling out of the fabrication module and toward the bridge. The ship was huge by any prior standard, but it was still not really that large. In less than a minute she flew through the hatch to the bridge and had to quickly grab a handhold to keep from plowing into the other people already there. Everyone seemed to be talking at once and then John Ericsson, the construction manager, bellowed for silence.

"Quiet, everyone! Please!"

The noise subsided and Usha then realized that the others were crowding around one of the main communications monitors. She pushed herself up to the ceiling until she could see past the others. In the monitor was Angela Prescott, one of the NASA flight controllers. To one side of her was a man in an Air Force uniform. People seemed to be running around in confusion in the background.

"I'm sorry, Angie, could you repeat that?" said Ericsson.

"I said that we are tracking three large, unidentified objects approaching Earth," said Prescott in a strained voice. "Currently they are coming in at about sixty klicks per second but they are decelerating."

A stir went through the group of people on the bridge. Usha was as stunned as the rest of them. *Decelerating!* But that could only mean...

"We have to assume they are spacecraft of some sort," continued Prescott.

"How large?" asked Ericsson.

"How far away?" added someone else. Several others began to ask questions before Ericsson angrily waved them into silence.

"Big," said Prescott. "Damn big. We've got radar and visual tracking from the ground. We're only guessing, but they are all several hundred meters long at least. They are currently about a hundred and fifty thousand kilometers away and almost directly on the opposite side of Earth from you. But they are headed in your direction. They will be in your vicinity in less than an hour."

For a few seconds, Ericsson did not have to tell anyone to be quiet. Everyone was speechless as they tried to digest this incredible news.
Spacecraft! thought Usha. *They can't be from Earth! Aliens? It can't be! It just can't!* Then, some of the others found their voices.

"What's the rate of deceleration?"

"If they're that big, why weren't they spotted sooner?"

"What do they want? Have you tried contacting them?"

Ericsson shouted for quiet again.

"They are decelerating at about three gravities—say thirty-five meters per second squared," continued Prescott, trying to answer the barrage of questions. "I don't know why we didn't spot them earlier. They just showed up about twenty minutes ago. There are no exhaust plumes visible, so we don't know what kind of drive they are using. As for contacting them..." She trailed off and glanced at the officer standing next to her.

He stepped forward. "I'm General Douglas Vanderhei. Colonel Youngs, are you there?"

"Yes, sir," said Youngs, moving forward slightly to get closer to the camera pickup. Usha frowned. Who was this general and why was he involved? Surely he wasn't assuming the unidentified ships were hostile already!

"Colonel," said Vanderhei, "I'm placing you in command of all personnel up there; both on the station and in the ship. Get everyone suited up and into the storm cellars. I'll have more information for you later."

"What?" said someone.

"Hey! Who do you think you are?"

"Quiet!"

An angry babble of voices filled the bridge for a moment before Ericsson's shout cut them off. He seemed a bit upset himself. Usha was silently fuming, but she held her tongue.

"General," said Ericsson, "I'm sorry, but you are going to have to give my people more explanation than this if you want our cooperation. Is there some reason why you believe that we might be in danger?"

General Vanderhei did not look pleased, but he bit back any sharp reply he may have had and took a deep breath. "Mister Ericsson, I am not a paranoid fanatic as some of you are probably thinking. I have no reason to believe that these ships are approaching with specific hostile intent toward you or us. However, I believe that they do represent a real danger to you up there."

"And why is that?" asked several people simultaneously.

"Because they are shooting at each other." There was a hesitation in the General's voice before he continued, his tone grave. "With nukes."

"What?!" Usha was startled that one of the chorus of voices that had made that exclamation was hers. It had just been pulled out of her.

"We have currently registered at least forty nuclear detonations. Our visual observations show that these are not part of some Orion-type drive system. They are clearly tossing nuclear missiles at each other. We believe that other types of weapons are in use as well, but we can't confirm this. The EMP from the explosions is already affecting satellites. As they get closer to you, the radiation bursts could pose a threat. Colonel Youngs, this is now a military situation and you are the ranking officer present. I want your people in the shelters immediately."

"Yes, sir! Right away!"

"Good. Contact me when you are all secure. Vanderhei out."

Usha and most of the others were still gaping, but Youngs was suddenly all business.

"Mister Ericsson, get all of your crew into the shelter. Miss Tewari, contact the station. Doctor Vasthare, please contact your team and get them up here."

A few more moments of silence ensued, then people began to react.

"Colonel," said Usha, "as you know, the engine module has substantial shielding—even heavier than the shelter—perhaps they should stay where they are."

"Wait a minute," said Paul Allbrook, the head of the lab construction team. "What about all the computers in the labs? If we are dealing with EMP, they could be fried! We need to move them!"

"And what about all of my equipment?" asked someone else. Other joined in. After a few more seconds Youngs pushed herself up to float in front of everyone.

"Quiet!" she called. It was not a particularly loud shout, but it cut through the babble and got results. "There is no time for debate! Doctor Vasthare, the engine module is unshielded to the rear and partially on the sides; it is not a safe refuge. As for the rest of you, your equipment can be replaced, but you and your people cannot. Now, get your teams and yourselves into the storm cellar—and I mean right now!"

* * * * *

Thirty minutes later, Usha and the last of the construction crew squeezed into what the Americans quaintly called the 'storm cellar'. It was actually a fairly apt name. Space was full of potentially harmful radiation and the ship was adequately shielded against the levels it would normally encounter. There were times, however, when the Sun would put out unusually high levels of radiation—solar storms. During those periods, astronauts could be exposed to unhealthy—possibly even fatal—doses of radiation. The risk was less in close orbit to Earth, since the planet's magnetic field provided some protection. For deep space voyages, the ship needed a special, heavily shielded, refuge in case it encountered such a storm far from home. That was what the 'storm cellar' was for.

Solar storms could last for several days, so the 'cellar' had been made comfortably large, with toilet facilities, food storage and preparation, recreation equipment, and a small control station. During normal times it would function as a crew lounge.

Unfortunately, the construction team was nearly four times the size of the normal crew for the ship. As a result, the 'storm cellar' was packed. Usha slowly wiggled her way toward the control station, wary of flailing feet and elbows from the people around her. Her small size helped and she eventually got close enough to see what was going on. Youngs was talking to that general again. Usha was slightly irritated with Youngs, but even more so with herself. Her suggestion that her team remain in the engine module had been idiotic. She knew it was as she said it, but somehow she had instinctively rebelled against the colonel's authority. *What's the matter with me? This is the most important thing that's ever happened and all I can think about is my own turf rights?* She shook her head.

"General, everyone here and on the station is in the shelters," said Youngs. "We are buttoned up as well as we can. All pressure doors are sealed and unnecessary equipment shut down. What's the situation look like now, sir?"

"Good job, Colonel," replied the general. As he spoke, there was a burst of static that momentarily disrupted the picture. "We have better reads on the bogies now. There is one large one and two smaller ones, although even the small ones are at least two hundred meters long. The two small ones seem to be fighting the one big one as near as we can figure. They are currently about forty thousand kilometers away and their speed is down to about twenty-five KPS. They are continuing to fire nukes and it is damaging a lot of the civilian satellites." As if in confirmation, there was a prolonged burst of static.

"Fortunately," continued the general, "the MILCOMSAT network is functioning with flying colors, just as we'd hoped. We project that their course will take them about ten thousand kilometers from you at closest approach. From what we have seen so far, you should be all right where you are."

"Roger, sir," said Youngs. "Not that we really have the option of going anywhere else, sir."

"No, I suppose not. The bogies should be coming into sight around the curve of the planet in just a few minutes. Do you have your 'scopes trained?"

"Yes, sir. The sixty-centimeter here on the ship and the two-meter on the station are both tracking based on your data. We should be able to get some pretty good pictures. Assuming the nukes don't fry the electronics."

"Very well. We'll just keep our fingers crossed down here. Good luck, Colonel—and to all of you. Vanderhei out."

Youngs drifted a few centimeters back from the com panel and bumped into someone else. Carefully she turned around.

"All right, everyone. Things should get interesting very shortly. I know you are all going to want to see what's going on. I'm going to put the images from the 'scopes on the two biggest monitors. Let's try to get ourselves sorted out into rows so everyone can get a look."

It was not easy establishing order out of the chaos in the compartment but Youngs did so. Usha grudgingly admitted that there were times when a military background might come in handy. Eventually, everyone could see the screens. Usha, as a team leader, got a position near the front. Diane Hartley, one of the astronomy technicians, was controlling the ship's telescope from a control console.

"Okay, heads up!" said Hartley. "If that data we got from Houston was correct, we should see something just about... now!"

Usha stared at the screen with the image from their 'scope. For a moment there was nothing, but then a bright blur darted into view and veered around wildly. Then another one followed it. On the second monitor, a single blob appeared.

"All right, got a fix," said Hartley, her eyes glued to the controls. "Stabilizing the image and focusing."

The two blurs stopped jerking around and slowly came to rest near the center of the screen. Second by second the image sharpened. There was complete silence in the compartment. Everyone seemed to be holding their breaths. The images were still badly blurred, but it was possible to see a few details, although they made little sense. Suddenly the whole image went white in a dazzling flash.

"Damn!" exclaimed Hartley. "I have the auto-filters in place, but that still almost fried us!"

"Was that a nuke?" asked someone.

"What the hell else?"

The image slowly came back. The two shapes looked just as before: lumpy ovoids. Parts of them seemed to be bare metal that reflected light, other sections were much darker and could be barely seen. From time to time smaller flashes of intense light, like huge flashbulbs, burst around them.

Without warning, a host of bright yellow lights leapt away from the two ships and off the screen. Usha's eyes flicked to the other monitor. The third ship was shaped pretty much like the first two, but its coloring seemed to be primarily a deep red. As she watched, a scattering of flashbulbs popped all around it.

"Missiles!" said someone else. "Those must have been some sort of missiles!"

"But without nukes; those bursts were too small to be nukes."

"Even so, those were big explosions! How are they surviving all this?"

Usha had no clue, but her mind was not on the weapons. She kept looking and looking as the images grew bigger, but there was no sign of any engine nozzles or exhaust plumes. *And yet they are decelerating! They move like the chariot of Surya! How? How? How are they doing it?*

She realized they had some sort of drive system beyond anything mankind had managed yet. With that realization came an indescribable emotion deep inside her. It was like that first time, back in school, when the miracle of quantum physics suddenly made sense to her. Then, it was like looking into the mind of God and seeing some small part of creation unfolded. Those beings, those people in the ships, they had looked deeper and seen more of God's mind.

An incredible need, a longing, filled her soul. She had to know! She had to know how it was done! They could teach her! She could learn from them! She could…

With a start, she suddenly remembered that those same beings were unleashing incredible energies in an attempt to destroy each other! *Vishnu the Merciful! Why are they doing this? And why are they doing it here?*

She wasn't sure how long she had been staring at the screen, but the images seemed to be getting smaller again. She looked around.

"What are the readings now?" Youngs was asking one of the technicians.

"That last burst brought the outside readings up to about four hundred millirems, Colonel. Not that bad for a short exposure, but I'm glad we're in here. It's still barely above normal background readings here."

"Good. Looks like we got off lightly."

Usha looked back at the monitors and was startled when a large, bright shape moved across the screen, blotting everything out.

"That's it," said Hartley. "They've gone beyond the edge of the planet. They're gone for now."

Everyone sighed. "Can we get out of this can now, Colonel?" asked someone.

"Just hold on, everyone," said, Youngs. "I'm going to check with Houston."

In a moment that general was back on the screen. He was still frowning.

"How are you doing up there?" he asked.

"We are A-Okay, General," said Youngs brightly. "Radiation levels hardly got above normal in here and they are falling fast in the rest of the ship. We'll have to check for damage, but most systems seem to be responding. Do you think it is all right to come out of the shelters, sir?"

"Hold on, Colonel," said Vanderhei. "The bogies are down to about eighteen KPS. That's way above orbital velocity for their altitude, but they are still slowing and they are bending their courses around the planet. They may be attempting to get into orbit and that could bring them right back toward you. So sit tight for now."

"Yes sir," said Youngs. She turned to face the rest of them. "You heard the general: stay right where you are—this isn't over yet!"

Chapter Three

Far above the planet that the local inhabitants called Earth, three space-craft were locked in a deadly duel.

Seeker of Truth shook slightly as the enemy laser blew another hole in the hull. Expedition Leader Keeradoth was thrown against the safety restraint with enough force to cause mild pain. An enemy missile's nuclear warhead had exploded close by and had drained the shield capacitors on a part of the hull sufficiently for the follow up laser attack to penetrate. The *Brak-Shar* had managed to do that a number of times to both *Seeker of Truth* and *Nightpiercer,* but they had also managed the same feat in return with their own lasers and kinetic missiles. None of the damage inflicted by either side had been vital—so far.

"Honored One," said the shield controller, "capacitors in sections eight and ten are at two-dozen and four percent."

"Steersman, roll the ship eight-dozen degrees left," commanded Keeradoth. "Engineering, give those capacitors the highest recharge priority."

"Aye, Honored One. Rolling left," answered the steersman respectfully. The engineering controller did the same.

Keeradoth looked at the main display in hopes of gaining inspiration, but nothing came. The battle had already gone on far longer than any had expected and no end was in sight. The *Brak-Shar* vessel, tentatively identified as a *Vipunen* class long range cruiser, was half again the size of *Seeker of Truth* or *Nightpiercer*. But like the two smaller vessels, it had sacrificed weapons for range and endurance. All three ships had appropriate defensive systems for their size, but all were light on offense. As a result, the battle had gone on and on with no advantage to either side.

The planet was very close now: less than its own diameter away. Much to Keeradoth's relief, the *Brak-Shar* had directed no weapons against it. That had been the great danger and it had dictated their tactics. Senior Expedition Leader Dalranor, aboard *Nightpiercer*, had feared—and Keeradoth had agreed—that the enemy might do this. In spite of cycles of conflict with them, the *Brak-Shar* remained unpredictable to the Race. At times they would act with unimaginable aggressiveness and violence, and at others they would flee at the mere hint of battle. This time, their actions had taken a middle course. They had pressed relentlessly forward, toward the planet, but thus far they had not fired upon it. Both *Seeker of Truth* and *Nightpiercer* were standing ready to intercept if they should suddenly change their tactics.

"Missile tubes reloaded, Honored One," said the weapons controller. "*Nightpiercer* signals ready."

"Launch on their command," said Keeradoth.

A few moments later, the ship shuddered as it salvoed off a flight of missiles. Keeradoth could see a similar group coming from *Nightpiercer* on the main display. The two groups merged and headed toward the enemy with gathering speed. The *Brak-Shar* lasers began destroying the missiles almost immediately.

"Stand ready with main laser," said Keeradoth.

"Standing ready, Honored One," answered the weapons controller.

Most of the missiles were destroyed by the enemy defensive fire, but three or four struck home against their shield.

"Shoot!" commanded Keeradoth.

"A hit, Honored One!" said the weapons officer after a moment. "*Nightpiercer* has struck as well."

"Damage?"

"No noticeable decrease in capabilities, Honored One," answered the detection controller.

Keeradoth felt the frustration building inside. They had expended nearly half of their missiles to little effect. The tactics the enemy had forced them to adopt had robbed them of their best weapon's effectiveness. The Race, unlike the *Brak-Shar,* favored kinetic missiles over ones with nuclear warheads. They were less costly to build, easier to maintain over long periods, harder to detect or destroy, and they were smaller, so more could be carried. Unfortunately, for them to have their greatest effect, they had to strike the target at the highest velocity possible.

A closing attack was always the best. Drive toward the enemy at high speed and fire the missiles as you near. Adding the relative velocities of the vessels to what the missiles' own drives produced could result in a devastating attack. Unfortunately, the launching vessel would then be rushing past the enemy and it could take a very long time to turn around and come back.

In this situation, that was unacceptable.

If *Seeker of Truth* and *Nightpiercer* had accelerated toward the enemy vessel and then failed to destroy it, the *Brak-Shar* could have proceeded to the planet and done whatever they wished for many twelfths of a day before they could have returned.

Thus, they had been forced to attempt a parallel course and ended up closing on the planet alongside their enemy. Their relative speeds had been low and the kinetic missiles correspondingly ineffective—unlike the enemy's.

"Enemy missile launch," announced the detection controller. "We are the target, Honored One."

"Defensive fire on automatic," commanded Keeradoth.

"Aye, Honored One," said the weapons controller.

The enemy's nuclear missiles were slower, easier to detect, and easier to hit, but they had huge damage potential no matter their relative velocity to the target. All they had to do was get close. *Seeker of Truth's* four defense lasers went to rapid fire and began picking off the incoming missiles. *Nightpiercer's* weapons joined in. Some of the missiles detonated when hit and others did not. But once again, the last one was close enough when it exploded to weaken the shields, and again, the enemy's laser lashed out to gouge another piece from the hull.

"Capacitor one-twelve-eight has been destroyed, Honored One," reported the integrity controller. "Switching reserve capacitor to active."

It was not a critical loss, reflected Keeradoth, but a bit at a time the ship was being hurt.

"Communications, connect me to Senior Expedition Leader Dalranor."

"At once, Honored One." A moment later the connection was made.

"Aye?" said Dalranor from the vision screen. The lack of courtesy showed the strain the commander was under.

"We gain nothing by this exchange, Honorable One," said Keeradoth. "Perhaps a change in tactics is in order."

"What do you suggest, expedition leader? The *Brak-Shar* have a more powerful drive and match our moves step for step. We can neither draw ahead nor drop behind to give our missiles a greater chance to accelerate."

Dalranor was using the clipped tones of the command tongue rather than the more formal speech proper between near equals of middle rank. Keeradoth had noted that many in *Nightpiercer's* crew spoke in this fashion—much had changed at home, apparently. It rankled Keeradoth slightly, but he thrust it aside. There were more urgent matters!

"I see no option but to divide our forces, Honorable One. We are now orbiting the planet and no longer decelerating. If one of us were to reverse course and double upon the foe, perhaps a decisive blow could be dealt."

"To divide bears great risks, Expedition Leader!" said Dalranor hotly. "Our combined defenses can fend off the enemy's blows as you have seen. While one of us doubles on them, the other may be overwhelmed."

"Truth, Honorable One," replied Keeradoth. "But our reserve of missiles will soon be expended. What then? Our lasers alone can do little hurt to the foe. They have more missiles to expend than we that may overwhelm us in the end anyway."

Dalranor was silent and considered Keeradoth's words. Another salvo of missiles was sent toward the *Brak-Shar* and another was received while the senior expedition leader pondered. This time, the enemy fired on *Nightpiercer* and Keeradoth could see the image on the screen shudder slightly. The blow seemed to shake Dalranor awake.

"Very well, Keeradoth. I believe you are correct. This battle may well be pointless now, but we must still triumph. One of us must double back. The most dangerous task is for the one who remains engaged. *Nightpiercer* is the more capable ship and as the senior, I claim that honor. We will keep the *Brak-Shar* occupied while you set up the killing blow. Is this understood?"

"Perfectly, Honorable One. All glory to you and *Nightpiercer!* I will reverse course under the cover of our next salvo." The thought occurred to Keeradoth that the enemy might just as easily follow *Seeker of Truth* as continue to fight *Nightpiercer*, but no matter, it would work either way.

"Steersman, prepare to reverse thrust at full power on my command."

"Aye, Honored One. I stand ready."

The missile tubes were reloaded and presently another salvo streaked from Seeker of Truth.

"Initiate!" commanded Keeradoth.

There was no perceivable sensation, but the drive field, which had been pulling the ship forward and down to maintain a circular path around the planet, was now dragging the ship backward at an acceleration nearly four times the gravity of the home world. The enemy ship and *Nightpiercer* slowly began to draw ahead; then faster and faster as the ship's speed fell. The enemy flicked a few lasers in their direction, but to no effect. Moment by moment the distance increased and presently the ships were lost to sight around the curve of the planet.

Keeradoth could still track the enemy ship because of the cloud of observation satellites that englobed the planet. The *Brak-Shar* continued to fight *Nightpiercer*.

Keeradoth checked the astrogation board and saw that if the enemy did not change course, *Seeker of Truth* could deliver its attack in less than half a twelfthday. The expedition leader did expect the enemy to alter their course, but was not sure in what manner. *Surely they realize what we attempt. They are not stupid. But their options are limited. No matter how they might dodge, unless they simply try to escape, we shall have our chance to hurt them.*

There was a considerable time before they could act and Keeradoth's thoughts were drawn away from the immediate task. The battle must be won, but then what? The Plan was in ruins. Concealment had been lost. The Terrans could detect them now—indeed this battle must be visible to their unaided eyes! *They will know we are here—or at least that someone is here. How will they react? What can we do to save the Plan?*

Keeradoth had no immediate answer. Perhaps the contact scenarios could be modified and still used. At the very least, Senior Expedition Leader Dalranor's new version of the Plan must be abandoned. The Terrans would double and triple their watchfulness! No direct attempts at control could now succeed. *But will Dalranor see that? I must remain here until I know how the senior expedition leader will proceed.*

While Keeradoth pondered, *Seeker of Truth's* velocity dropped to zero and began to increase again in an orbit opposite that of the other two ships. Faster and faster the ship went and the distance to the enemy dropped rapidly. Strangely, the foe did not alter course. This puzzled Keeradoth slightly, but it was known that the *Brak-Shar* were rigid and literal minded creatures. Perhaps they had orders to survey habitable planets in this region. Perhaps the commander of this vessel was determined to carry out the survey even in the midst of a battle! Keeradoth did not know.

"Honored One! A communication from *Nightpiercer!*" said the communications controller. The viewing screen activated and Dalranor was there. To Keeradoth's dismay, the commander seemed to be injured and smoke was visible in the background.

"Expedition Leader, we need your help quickly! As I feared, the enemy's strength is too great for one ship alone. We are badly damaged."

"Hold fast, Honorable One! We come!" replied Keeradoth.

"Come quickly, then. We shall await..." In the midst of Dalranor's words the screen went blank.

"Detection Controller, report!"

"Honored One, I am reading several warhead explosions in close proximity to *Nightpiercer*. I cannot estimate damage, but their drive still registers."

Keeradoth consulted the astrogation board again. It was still a significant time until they could launch.

"Steersman! Can we increase our speed?"

"Nay, Honored One. Our drive is at maximum."

All they could do was wait and watch the purple icon for *Nightpiercer* twist and squirm like a fire slug pursued by a drathla.

But the Brak-Shar are intent on their victim! They make no attempt to parry our blow! But a few moments more...

"Stand ready to launch!" commanded Keeradoth.

"Standing ready, Honored One!" exclaimed the weapons controller. A feeling of courage and determination seemed to fill the control chamber with a desire to strike at the foe that was hurting their comrades. It came from each person, growing and strengthening as each added to it. Keeradoth was tingling with energy. For so many cycles they had pursued their lonely task at this world. They had forgotten what it was to be a warrior!

For a moment it seemed like the torrent of emotions sweeping through them might grow out of control, but then Keeradoth spoke:

"Steady, my friends."

That was all it took. The torrent became a stream. Strong and deep, but under control. The time continued to pass and the range dropped...

"Launch," said Keeradoth.

The missiles sped away from *Seeker of Truth*, accelerating over ten times faster than the ship that launched them. When the tubes were reloaded, a second salvo followed the first. At last, the *Brak-Shar* seemed to realize their peril. They began accelerating directly away from the incoming missiles. They could not hope to outrun them, but they might lower the relative velocity at impact. Gallant *Nightpiercer* followed the movements of the enemy, as best as its crippled drive would allow, and continued to fire.

The missiles entered the range of the enemy's defensive lasers and the *Brak-Shar* began to destroy them as rapidly as they could. The missiles were closing much faster than any of the previous salvos, but there were only half as many. Consternation swept the control chamber of *Seeker of Truth* as the first salvo was destroyed short of the target. But the second salvo was much closer before the enemy could shift their fire to it, and now a third salvo was also on the way.

More missiles were destroyed, but this time they were simply too close and closing too fast to all be stopped. Three of them struck the Brak-Shar shield and exploded in a dazzling fireball that rivaled the nuclear warheads of the enemy. The majority of that blast was directed harmlessly away, or was used up in draining the enemy shield, but enough got through to inflict great harm. Hull plates were vaporized or torn to fragments. The equipment sheltered by those plates was destroyed or rendered inoperable. All the previous damage that the ship had taken was but a scratch compared to this.

The ship was alive, but still in deadly peril. The third salvo was even closer than the second before the *Brak-Shar* could try to deal with it—and the shield was terribly weak facing the attack. The ship twisted around to try and interpose an undepleted section. They succeeded, but in the end it made no difference.

Four missiles struck this time. The weapons controller on *Seeker of Truth* had been clever and one missile had trailed slightly behind the others. The first three took down the shield and inflicted heavy damage, just as the three from the second salvo had done. But then the fourth struck home and there was nothing at all to stop it. It was heated to white hot as it passed through the fireball of its cohorts, but then it actually struck the *Brak-Shar* ship while still intact.

Another fireball lit up the skies of the planet below. The missile was vaporized on impact, of course, but almost its total kinetic energy was imparted to the target and that was enough to blow completely through the *Brak-Shar* ship and out the other side. The strike was nearly amidships and it almost tore the enemy in two.

Then *Seeker of Truth* flashed past at many times the orbital velocity of the planet. Lasers stabbed out to punch more holes in the now shieldless enemy. It was only moments before they were out of range again, but the job had been done.

"The enemy's shield and drive have failed!" said the detection controller on *Seeker of Truth* excitedly. "I believe their power plant has failed as well!"

"Excellent," said Keeradoth with great satisfaction. "Steersman, reverse the drive and plot a rendezvous with *Nightpiercer*. My compliments to you all."

The speed of the ship was taking them rapidly away from the other two vessels. Even with the drive at maximum, it would take a considerable time to slow and match course with their compatriots. Then, after a short while, the navigation controller spoke up:

"Honored One! Observe the path of *Nightpiercer*!"

Keeradoth did so and was alarmed. Dalranor's ship had attempted to match the last evasive move of the *Brak-Shar* vessel and in doing so had lost orbital velocity. The drive readings from *Nightpiercer* were extremely faint and its projected course intersected the planet's atmosphere not long from now. The remains of the enemy vessel were also tumbling out of orbit, even more quickly.

"Communications Controller, contact *Nightpiercer*," said Keeradoth.

"I have been attempting to do so, Honored One. I am receiving no reply."

"Continue the attempt."

"Aye, Honored One."

Keeradoth's alarm continued to grow as the attempts to communicate remained unsuccessful. *Seeker of Truth's* course was curving around the planet, but its velocity forced it to take a very elongated path. They could not hope to assist *Nightpiercer* until long after it entered the atmosphere.

"I have a reply from *Nightpiercer*, Honored One!" said the communications controller, at last. "Voice only!" A distorted and barely audible voice came from the speaker.

"This...this is Assistant Power Controller Ralnar. We have been seriously damaged, *Seeker of Truth*. I cannot contact the control chamber. My own superior is dead. We need immediate assistance!"

"Power Controller Ralnar, do you have control of your vessel?" asked Keeradoth anxiously. "Your path will soon strike the planet's atmosphere."

"Nay, Honored One," came back the reply. "The main and secondary drives are non-functional. Main power has also failed. We are operating on emergency batteries. The gravitational nullifier is only capable of twelve-eight percent power. We have attitude control and minimal shields, but we cannot alter our course."

"Have you hope for repairs?"

"Small hope, Honored One. Many are dead or injured. Damage is heavy. We shall do the best we can, but I have faint hope for speedy repairs."

Keeradoth again checked the astrogation panel. On its current course, *Nightpiercer* would enter the atmosphere above the ocean known by the Terrans as the North Pacific. With its nullifiers at their present levels, the ship would overfly the North American land mass, the North Atlantic Ocean, and impact in Western Europe. This was not desirable for several reasons. The *Brak-Shar* ship would land in the Pacific and could be dealt with later; *Nightpiercer* was the problem. Keeradoth entered some numbers and observed the options.

"Power Controller Ralnar, I desire that you reduce the nullifier's output to twelve-two percent. This will bring your ship down in the Atlantic Ocean, rather than on land. Do you have functional escape pods or small craft?"

"Our small craft are destroyed, Honored One. Several escape pods still read as functional. I do not believe there are sufficient for all living personnel."

"I understand," said Keeradoth. "Adjust the nullifiers as I have instructed and then have all who may do so abandon ship. We shall pick them up. I regret that this must be so. We will also dispatch small craft to assist those who may survive the landing." Keeradoth gripped the control station with head bowed; so many dead, Dalranor likely among them, and this last command had probably doomed even more. A costly victory indeed!

"I understand, Honored One. It shall be as you say."

The communications ended and all in the control chamber of *Seeker of Truth* watched the flashing purple icon of their comrades' ship drop nearer and nearer the planet. Time passed and they observed the *Brak-Shar* ship, amidst a cloud of debris, enter the atmosphere and fall toward the ocean below.

They were heading back toward *Nightpiercer* now, but they were still too far away and moving too fast to be of immediate help. Two new icons appeared on the display as the escape pods were launched. Their nullifiers and modest drives would easily carry them clear of the atmosphere and to safety. One good thing, at least. Suddenly the detection controller spoke up:

"Honored One! *Nightpiercer's* course has altered! They are descending more rapidly!"

Almost immediately, there was another communications from the stricken ship. "*Seeker of Truth*!" said the power controller. "Our nullifier has partially failed! It now operates at only six percent. There is nothing which we can do!"

Nothing they can do. The words rang in Keeradoth's brain. *Nightpiercer's* course would now lead to an impact on the eastern part of the North American land mass. A densely-populated region. This was a disaster of the first order. There could well be Terran casualties and property loss. These Terrans were so possessive about their property. And the ship itself would be there for them to see. Not out of sight beneath an ocean (although even that was no security) but out in the light of day. Disaster.

"Honored One!" exclaimed the detection officer again. "A small vessel has detached itself from the wreckage of the enemy ship! It is regaining orbit!" Survivors? Some of the enemy still live?

"What is their course?"

"They appear to be heading toward the Terran space station, Honored One!"

The Plan was in ruins. Would there even be any pieces left to pick up?

Chapter Four

"Two hundred channels and there's still nothing on!"

It was a common enough complaint, but for once it was almost literally true. Robert Hancock flipped through a dozen more stations on his TV and then gave up. There was just static. "Nothing but 'Cartoon Network' and 'The Weather Channel'!" he said in disgust. "Anything on the radio, Ed?"

"Same stuff as before: 'We don't know what's going on, but stay calm and stay tuned for more information when we have it'," said Edward Osborne, a small hand-crank radio from Bob's supply of emergency gear pressed to his ear.

Hancock flopped down in a chair and watched his daughter pick up the remote and continue switching through television channels. More static. The satellites were obviously still out of commission from whatever it was they had seen four hours earlier. *A battle, it had to have been a battle. A battle with nukes. But between whom?* He had been asking that question since Melissa called them out from the porch to look at the lights in the sky.

With the naked eye, all that could be seen at first was a series of bright pinpoints of light. But they were very bright. They lit up the whole landscape. Through the binoculars, they were even brighter. Hancock still had a faint afterimage in his eyes and he hoped there was no permanent damage. But in addition to the flashes, he had seen the three objects. He was trying not to call them ships, but he was losing that fight. What else could they have been?

He had watched them through the binoculars for several minutes. Melissa had tried to train her telescope on them, but could not keep them in the view for more than a second or two. Hancock had seen satellites pass overhead on many occasions. These objects seemed to be moving slower than most satellites, but they were still reflecting sunlight more than an hour after sunset, so they had to be in a fairly high orbit. He was not sure what that said about their speed...

"I've got something here, Dad," said Melissa. Hancock looked up at the wall screen and saw that the local cable station was on the air. They had a ground fiber-optic line feeding them information from a bigger network and were passing the information along.

"...we still have no official word from any government source about the amazing phenomena being seen in the skies above our planet," said an attractive young woman with an expression of nervousness on her face. "However, the spokesman at FEMA, the Federal Emergency Management Agency, is urging everyone to remain calm and stay in their homes. There have been some reports of panic, but these cannot be confirmed. The greatest reaction seems to be confined to those areas in the Northern Hemisphere where it was night and clear weather. The phenomenon was most easily visible in those areas although the bright flashes of light were seen in daylight as well.

"We have now received a report that several top scientists believe that the objects sighted are spacecraft of extraterrestrial origin..."

"Ha! I wonder what 'top scientist' would go out on a limb like that this early?" spat Bob Hancock.

"But what else could they be, Dad?" asked Melissa. "You saw them. So did you, Uncle Eddie."

"Well, as much as I could see with your dad hogging the binoculars," said Osborne. "I thought rank was supposed to have its privileges."

"But you both saw!" insisted Melissa.

"Yes, we did, Squirt," said Hancock. "I don't know what to say. I can't think of anything else they could be either, but still..."

The threesome fell silent.

They had watched the lights move from west to east, passing nearly overhead. They had faded a bit when they went into Earth's shadow, but those flashes of light were just as bright. Finally, all the lights had been hidden by the line of trees to the east. At that point, they had rushed into the house. Hancock had called his office first, but was told to sit tight until he got new instructions. Then they had sat and tried to get something—anything—on the television. That had been three hours ago...

The communicator on Hancock's computer beeped loudly. He jumped up and hit the accept key. Immediately, his superior, Captain Janice Pescatore, was on the screen.

"Bob, I assume you've been following this?" she said without preamble.

"Yes, ma'am. Do you have any information on what's happening?"

"Some, but more questions than answers," she said. "The Military Communications Satellite network is mostly still up, thank God, so we have good communications. Our friends up there seem to have been having quite a little fracas, Commander! But, apparently, it is over now. The two little ones were fighting the one big one and the little guys have won. Here, let me transfer a few images we took from our ground stations."

The screen split and a fuzzy image appeared, showing two oval-shaped blobs.

"These are the two little ones," continued Pescatore. "I say 'little', but they are still damn big—over two hundred meters long." The picture changed to a single reddish blob. "This is the big guy, maybe three hundred meters. The three of them were chasing each other around the planet and tossing nukes. Then one of the little guys doubled back. Damn, those bastards can move! We tracked it doing at least three Gs. It put itself on a reciprocal course with the big one and launched a swarm of missiles. About forty minutes ago our station on Iceland caught these images."

The screen showed the red blob. After a moment a bright flash filled the screen silhouetting the blob starkly. "That was the first hit," said Pescatore. "Now watch this." The initial flash had barely faded when a second one replaced it. Then, an instant later, another dazzling light came from the center of the blob, whiting out the whole screen.

"Blew right through them!" exclaimed Osborne. The image disappeared and Captain Pescatore was on the whole screen again.

"So it seems," she said. "Even so, it did not destroy it completely. What's left is coming down. We project an impact site somewhere in the Gulf of Alaska. We already have ships and planes dispatched to the area."

"You really believe these are spaceships, Captain?" asked Hancock.

"What the hell else, Bob? They sure aren't meteors, comets, or swamp gas! They changed their course a number of times and they were shooting nukes, for God's sake! Ninety percent of the commercial satellites are still out from the

EMP. And unless the Air Force is a lot better at keeping secrets than I think they are, they certainly aren't from around here!"

"Yes, ma'am. So what do we do?"

"All right, there's still more to this. One of the little ones seems to have been badly damaged. We observed a lot of nukes bursting close by just before the big one got zapped. It's coming down, too. It's not on a true ballistic trajectory, so they must still have some power, but they are coming down. Right now we have a tentative impact site in the North Atlantic. Ships are on their way there, too.

"I've talked to the Chief and he wants an investigation team put together. You are on it and so are Sam and Esther. I'll be back to you later on just where and when you'll be meeting and what your directive is. So for now, just sit tight."

"Yes, ma'am," said Hancock. Pescatore broke the connection.

Robert Hancock, his daughter, Melissa, and Edward Osborne sat in silence, digesting what they had just seen and heard. Finally, Hancock stirred.

"Where's the dog?" he asked.

"Oh, he's in the bathtub," said Melissa.

"The bathtub?" asked Osborne.

"Yeah," laughed Hancock. "Our huge, fierce, wolf-killing doggie is terrified of lighting, thunder, loud noises, and just about anything else out of the ordinary. For some reason he seems to think the bathtub is the safest place to be. We were looking all over the place for him the first time he did it."

"I'm halfway tempted to join him there," said Osborne. "Sounds like a smart beastie to me."

"Spaceships, Dad!" said Melissa, recalling what was happening. "They really are spaceships!"

"So it would seem," admitted Hancock.

"But what are they doing here? And they were fighting a battle! Why?"

"How should I know, Squirt?"

"You're my dad, you're supposed to know everything."

"Someone has grossly misinformed you, sweetheart."

"You're just being modest again," said Melissa, getting to her feet. "More coffee anyone?"

"Sure, why not?" said Osborne. "Not like we're going to get any sleep, anyway."

"I guess not," said Hancock. "Make that two." He yawned and stretched and then sat down again.

"You certainly know how to entertain a guest, Bob," said Osborne with a grin. "You shouldn't have gone to all this trouble. An earthquake or volcanic eruption would have been fine, really!"

"Oh, no problem! "I just wanted to…"

The communicator buzzed again. Hancock had it in an instant.

"Pescatore here again," said his superior briskly. "We've had a major change in the situation, Bob. The small one is coming down faster. Still not a true ballistic, but definitely faster. We are now projecting the impact site somewhere in eastern Pennsylvania."

"Good God!"

"Somewhere west of Philadelphia, but that's just a guess. Impact should be in about twenty-five minutes. Bob, I'm sending a chopper for you. I want you to get up to Willow Grove ASAP. Set up a command post and contact me once you are in place. I'll get Sam and Esther there when I can."

"Yes, ma'am," said Hancock, a bit stunned. "But why me, ma'am?"

"Because you're the space nut, or so I'm told! Look, Bob: by morning, the FBI, CIA, NSA, and probably the DAR will be swarming all over the wreck—assuming there is one. Not to mention the Air Force, Army, and Coast Guard! The Chief wants to be damn sure the Navy has got its own claim staked—and you are the one who's going to do it! Understand?"

"Yes, ma'am," said Hancock. His eyes swept over to where his friend was sitting. "Can I take along an assistant?"

"Take whoever you need. Just be ready: that chopper will be there in forty minutes!" She broke the connection.

Hancock stood there shaking his head slightly. Then he looked to Osborne.

"Want to come along?" he asked with a twisted smile.

"Try and keep me away!" said Osborne.

"Count me in, too!" Melissa was fairly bouncing on the sofa.

Hancock frowned. "Now wait a minute, Squirt..."

"Why the hell not, Bob? She's as qualified as anyone else for something like this. And a young perspective could be valuable to a couple of old fogies like us."

"Thanks, Uncle Eddie," said Melissa with a grin. "I'm starting to remember why I liked you so much."

"Okay, I've got no time to fight this—and you're probably right, anyway. Let's get packed. I need to get into a uniform and so do you, Lissa. Your cadet uniform isn't going to carry much weight, I'm afraid. See if you can find something of mine in the closet. You're not that much shorter than me..."

"But considerably thinner," interjected Osborne.

"...but considerably thinner," finished Hancock with a scowl. "Just about like I was when I was a lieutenant."

"Do you think I should, Dad?" asked Melissa hesitantly. "I mean, I don't have my commission yet or anything. Wouldn't I be impersonating an officer or something?"

"Temporary field commission by my authority as the US Navy's Official Representative to the Little Green Men from Planet Mongo. Satisfied? Now let's get moving."

Twenty minutes later they were dressed, packed, and going out the door. Hancock's uniform fit Melissa like a sack, but at least she was recognizable as a naval officer.

"What about Cedric?" asked Osborne.

"I called a neighbor and they'll look after him," said Hancock. His gaze shifted to his daughter. She was staring intently toward the northeast.

"Ready to go, Squirt?"

"Sure, Dad," she answered, but her stare did not waver. "I wonder what's happening up there?"

* * * * *

It came out of the west. At first it was just a fuzzy star on the horizon, but it rapidly grew bigger and bigger as it drew near. It had thundered across Washington State, Idaho, Montana, the northern plains, and the Midwest, trailing a window rattling sonic boom behind it. By the time it had crossed the Appalachians, its speed had dropped to subsonic. Shortly after that, it had picked up several Air Force jets, which paced it the rest of the way.

As its speed fell and its altitude declined, the impact point was localized more and more accurately: Eastern Pennsylvania; about twenty miles northwest of Philadelphia. Urgent messages went out to police and emergency personnel. There was no time for any evacuation, but they were to do whatever they could. The State Police shut down traffic on the four major highways that all converged in the area. Fortunately, it was now almost three A.M. on Saturday morning. A few hangers-on from the Friday night crowd were still about, but most people were in their homes. Some were sleeping, but most were still trying to get some sort of news on the strange happenings. A few others were outside, hoping for another glimpse of whatever it had been.

Radio stations broadcasted urgent instructions to those in the impact zone: Stay in your home! Get down to the basement and stay there! Police directed anyone in vehicles away from the danger site. Helicopters with loudspeakers buzzed the area urging people to take shelter.

Some obeyed, but quite a few went outside to watch. Most of those who did got the sight of their lives. For a few—mercifully few—it was their last.

It came out of the west, growing bigger, but not rising any higher in the sky. It glowed a dull red, still hot from the friction of entering the atmosphere. The ship's weakening shields had protected it from the worst of that friction, but it was still red hot. The Air Force jets had their landing lights on and they were dazzling specks on either side.

The ship fell lower and lower and the jets had to pull up. The ground was rising too fast. Just ahead was the Valley Forge National Park. Important and historic ground, to be sure, but of far more immediate interest it was nearly *empty* ground in a crowded suburban district. The pilots of the jets saw the dark patch in the carpet of lights below and tried to will the huge mysterious thing down into it.

Almost, but not quite.

The ship hurtled past Mount Misery, its speed down to about three hundred kilometers an hour. Directly in its path was neighboring Mount Joy. It was not much of a mountain as such things go, but in this particular case it was about five meters too tall.

The ship plowed into the peak with a deafening crash of shattering rocks, tearing metal, and splintering trees. Its shields absorbed a bit of the force before they failed completely, so the ship was not destroyed in that instant. Several hundred cubic meters of rock and dirt, along with dozens of large trees, exploded away from the ship as it sheared off the top of the mountain.

The blow deflected the ship upward slightly and it soared over the park. Small groups of watchers were there, but they were too busy dodging the sudden shower of boulders and splintered tree trunks to get much of a view. The ship's momentum carried it over the deserted Pennsylvania Turnpike and toward another bit of high ground just east of the tollbooths at Exit 326.

It slammed down for the last time on that high ground. Ironically, there had once been a General Electric plant that built satellites in that spot, but now it was just another parking lot for the huge King of Prussia shopping mall that lay directly ahead.

The ship's speed was a mere hundred kilometers an hour now but it careened down the gentle slope like a metal avalanche. Light posts were snapped off and the few vehicles still in the lot were crushed or flung aside like toys. It skidded across Goddard Avenue and through more parking lots before colliding with the mall.

Like most buildings of that sort, they were not heavily constructed. They were certainly not built to take the blow that they now received. The ship plowed through them like a boulder through tall grass. Walls collapsed and girders snapped. Merchandise was smashed and tossed away. Glass shattered—lots of glass shattered. Several dozen small stores went first. The J.C. Penney was next.

Each impact robbed the ship of some of its momentum and an impressive mound of debris was being piled up in front of it. The speed fell and fell with every meter forward it moved. Finally, the ship, which had traveled farther than any of the mall's patrons could truly imagine, came to a rest, imbedded in the Neiman Marcus store.

The noise, which had been so loud that it hardly even qualified as mere sound, died away. Or it seemed to by comparison. In fact, there was still quite a lot of noise. Some parts of the building were still collapsing from the impact. Innumerable objects were still tumbling about, looking for a resting place. And in the distance was the rumble of circling jets and the thumping of helicopter rotors. Nearer—and coming nearer still—were sirens and more sirens.

Slowly, a new sound was added. Much of the ship was still very hot. Small fires started almost immediately from the wreckage. The mall buildings had sprinklers, of course, but many of the pipes had been broken by the crash. The working sprinklers kept the fires from spreading far, but the crackle, and then roar, of the flames joined the other sounds. Smoke mixed with the cloud of dust the ship had raised. Soon, the smoke was greater than the dust, and it drifted away into the dark sky.

Dawn was still two hours away.

* * * * *

Lieutenant Colonel Kathryn Youngs stared at the man in the communications monitor.

"It seems to be over for now, Colonel," said General Vanderhei. "The big one splashed down in the Pacific and one of the smaller ones just hit in the Philadelphia region. We have teams heading for both locations."

"What about the third one, sir?" asked Youngs.

"We lost track of that one, I'm afraid. We had it on radar and visually, but about twenty minutes ago it just blinked off radar and a few minutes later it disappeared from sight. They must have some sort of stealth equipment in operation."

Youngs heard someone behind her mutter something about a 'cloaking device' and suppressed a grimace.

"Can we get out of this sardine can yet?" said someone else, much more loudly.

"General, some of my people are asking…" began Youngs.

"Yes, I heard," interrupted the General. "What are the radiation readings now?"

"Just about normal, sir."

"Very well, you can come out of your 'can', Colonel. I think everyone should stay in their suits for the time being, however."

"Very good, sir," said Youngs. "We've got a lot of checking to do for possible damage, so that is a good idea anyway."

"All right then. I'll talk to you later, Colonel. Vanderhei, out."

Youngs closed the connection and turned to face the mob of people around her. "All right, everyone. You all heard the news. We can get out of here now. All department heads should do an immediate check for damage. And stay alert! If anything else happens we may have to get back in here on the double!"

With a lot of muttering, the crowd turned toward the hatch. It took a moment to get it open, and considerably longer than that until the people made their way out.

"Mister Ericsson," said Youngs, snagging the construction manager. "I am going to have a look at my ship. If you need any help, or if there is any serious damage reported, please contact me."

"Sure thing, Colonel." The man moved away shaking his head. "Heluva day! Heluva day!" he was muttering to himself.

"Can't really argue with that!" said Youngs to Major Gerry Messier. "C'mon, Gerry, let's go see how *LC* weathered this storm."

Thirty minutes later, Kay Youngs was smiling in satisfaction. All the important systems on her ship seemed to be in good order. They would have to run a more thorough check before they actually tried to operate it again, but at first glance everything seemed good. The reports coming from the ship construction crew and the space station indicated only minor damage to some of the electrical systems.

Once the immediate task was finished, Kay leaned back in her seat and sighed. The demands of her job had forced her to keep her mind on business and not allowed any real thought on the incredible events of the last few hours. But now, those events were finally demanding her attention.

"What do you think of all this, Gerry? You've hardly said anything."

"Not sure what to say, Colonel," said Messier. "Words don't quite seem adequate for what's happening."

"I know what you mean," said Youngs with a small laugh. "Alien spaceships fighting a battle just outside the window! Not exactly a normal day at work!"

"I still can't get it, though, Colonel," said Messier, his face very thoughtful. "Why the hell would they be fighting *here*? I mean with all the space out there, what are the odds that these clowns just bumped into each other in our backyard?"

"Doesn't seem too likely, does it?" said Youngs, nodding her head. "There's got to be more to it—a lot more."

"An interstellar war," said Messier shaking his head. "I'd always dreamed of heading out there someday. Seems like it might not be a very friendly place."

"I don't know," said Youngs. "We can't draw any conclusions just from…"

The radio in her suit suddenly came to life, interrupting her:

"Colonel Youngs! This is Sergei, on the station! Come in please!" said a familiar and heavily accented voice.

"I'm here, Sergei, what's up?"

"Colonel! We have an object on radar! It is closing on us, bearing two-two-eight, by four-one. It is very close!"

"I see it!" exclaimed Gerry Messier, who had looked out the window immediately. "It's above us and to starboard, Colonel! Hell, it's nearly as big as the *LC*! Not moving too fast though."

Kay moved over to where Gerry was and looked past him. She caught sight of a reddish, egg-shaped object. She toggled her com switch.

"Houston, this is *Lewis and Clark*. We have a visitor! Repeat, an unidentified spacecraft has just rendezvoused with us! It is the same color as the big ship that got zapped, but much smaller." She cut her connection briefly and spoke to Messier. "Gerry signal the ship personnel and tell them to stand by!"

"Right, Colonel."

"*Lewis and Clark*, this is Houston. Are you sure? We are not reading anything on our scopes."

"Yes I'm sure! The thing is parked right outside! Do you want me to take down the license number?"

"Stand by *Lewis and Clark*…"

"Yeah, like I can do anything else."

"Colonel! Look!" exclaimed Messier.

Kay looked out again. A large door or hatch was opening up on one side of the alien vessel. A moment later, a swarm of small figures began to emerge. They were obviously spacesuits—or something. There were so many of them and they were moving quickly enough that she could not establish what sort of shape they really had. They seemed to have arms and legs, but it was hard to tell.

They split into two groups. One headed toward the ISS in the distance and the other moved toward the unfinished ship.

"Heads up, everyone! I think we are about to be boarded!" shouted Youngs.

An instant later there were bright flashes of light from some of the figures and Kay felt a slight vibration. A gust of air, ice crystals, and metal fragments came into view. There was a cacophony of noise over the radio.

"Holy shit!" exclaimed Messier.

Kay Youngs stared out the window as the figures moved toward the ship.

"Gerry, I think that war just escalated."

Chapter Five

"Houston, we have a problem—a *big* one!"

Lieutenant Colonel Kathryn Youngs was shouting into her radio and trying to look out the canopy of her spaceplane at the same time.

"What's happening, Colonel?" came the reply. Youngs wasn't sure if it was the normal fight controller, or General Vanderhei, or someone else.

"The ship is being fired on! Space suited...*things* are blasting their way in! Another group is headed for the station. I don't think they've noticed *Lewis and Clark* yet, but they're blowing the hell out of the ship!"

"Uh, roger, *Lewis and Clark*, stand by."

Youngs clicked off the connection in frustration. *Stand by!* She switched to the Station's frequency.

"Sergei, this is Kay! They're headed your way, too. They're shooting their way in over here! I don't know what you can do, but be ready!"

I don't know what you can do! What the hell can *we do?*

"They're getting in, Colonel," said Gerry Messier.

Youngs twisted around to get a look. Messier was right: she could see the attackers moving into a gaping hole in the side of one of the lab modules.

"*Lewis and Clark*, this is Houston. How many of them are..." The message was suddenly cut off.

"What happened?" asked Youngs.

"I think they shot out the ship's antenna. You want me to switch over to ours?"

Kay thought furiously. They had been hooked up to the ship's communications system...

"No, they'll pick that up and it may draw them over here. Houston can't help anyway."

"What are we going to do, Colonel?" Her rookie co-pilot looked close to panic—just about the way she felt, too.

"Warm up the engines and get ready to move! We can't fight these things so the only hope is to escape."

"Just us?"

"As many as we can get aboard." She switched to the ship's internal com system. "Mister Ericsson—anyone on the ship—this is Colonel Youngs! The aliens are getting aboard at lab module six! Try to get to the shuttle as fast as you can!"

All she got back was an unintelligible babble of shouts and screams. She moved around to one of her control stations and tied into the network of cameras mounted inside the ship. The camera in lab six wasn't working. The one in the passageway outside showed several of the attackers. They *did* have arms and legs and, to her surprise, a long tail. The helmeted heads were just...*wrong* somehow. Strangely elongated and oddly placed on the body. Some of them were different: much bigger than the others. They were all carrying things that had to be weapons. No more time to look, she switched to another camera...and froze.

It was lab module four. There were a half dozen of the crew in there and, as Youngs watched, the aliens burst in. The humans were against the far bulkhead, floating there, not moving and with their hands out in front of them.

The aliens raised their weapons and shot them down. There were flashes of light and then patches of the human space suits erupted outward.

There was no hesitation, no attempt to communicate that Youngs could see. They just shot them. It only took a moment and then six bodies were slowly tumbling there, spouting air and blood from their punctured space suits.

"Oh my God," hissed Youngs.

"What is it, Colonel?" asked Messier from his control station.

"They...they're killing everyone!"

"What...?"

Youngs switched on the communicator again. "Get out! Everyone get out! The aliens are shooting anything that moves! Get out any way you can!"

It was no use. All she got back was more noise. She switched cameras again. Most of them showed nothing, but some showed aliens moving down corridors or through compartments. A few showed drifting bodies.

"Anyone on board, answer! This is Colonel Youngs!"

Still no answer. Just noise.

"Gerry, are we ready to move?"

"Almost; another minute."

Kay Youngs took one more look at the monitors and then twisted around, a snarl on her face. She grabbed her personal bag from the rack next to her chair and unzipped it. The bag was exactly like the bag carried by every shuttle commander for the last thirty years. NASA provided them and they came with a very special set of instructions.

Youngs fumbled with her gloved hands for the hidden zipper inside the bag. She found it and pulled. The inside flap folded back and revealed what she was looking for.

She drew out an automatic pistol. It was a very special pistol with an enlarged grip, trigger, and guard to accommodate a space suit glove. Kay had been trained how to use the weapon, but she had never thought she would ever need it. Messier's eyes grew wide when he saw it.

"Where the hell did you get that?"

She didn't answer. Instead, she stuck the weapon into a pocket of her space suit and turned back to the monitors. She switched to a camera covering the corridor that led to the umbilical connected to *Lewis and Clark*.

There was an alien there.

It wasn't looking in the direction of the boarding hatch, but there was no way anyone was going to get by it. With a chill, Youngs realized the thing was only a few meters away. In spite of the urgency of the situation, she continued to stare at the creature. It seemed to be smaller than a human and its legs were jointed backward like the back leg of a dog or horse. And that head...

"We're ready, Colonel," said Messier.

They might be able to get out. She had no idea what the alien vessel or any of the aliens that might be out there would do when the spaceplane started to move, but there was no hope in sitting here.

"Close the hatch and detach the boarding collar," commanded Youngs.

"Roger."

The thought of running away while her friends were being slaughtered burned inside her, but what else could she do? A single pistol wasn't going to beat that army out there. Still…one more try.

"This is Colonel Youngs! Is there anyone aboard? Answer!"

She didn't expect any answer, but she got one.

"Colonel…this is Usha Vasthare… What should we do?"

"Doctor? Where are you?" exclaimed Youngs in sudden hope.

"I…we are in the engine module. My whole crew. The aliens have not come this way yet…but I have been…watching on the monitors…"

Kay didn't have to ask what she had been watching.

"Hold on, Doctor! We're coming to get you!" Inspiration suddenly came to her.

"Gerry! Open the cargo bay doors!"

"Right, Skipper!"

"Doctor, I am going to move the shuttle aft. Get all of your people to the far stern of the ship—right by the exhaust nozzles. I'll maneuver back there and you can all make a jump into the cargo bay. We aren't going to have much time! Get back there and get ready!"

"Yes, Colonel, I understand. We will move now."

"See you in about two minutes!"

Kay turned to her flight controls. The spaceplane was now floating a few meters from the side of the ship. She quickly double-checked her position. She had a clear path leading directly aft.

"Firing bow thrusters—now!"

A blast of flame burst from the nose of *Lewis and Clark*, driving her backward. Kay wanted to hurry, wanted to keep burning those thrusters, but she couldn't. She had to halt the ship by the stern and she could not get moving too fast. She cut the thrust and her ship coasted. She looked out the cockpit windows trying to see if the aliens were reacting. The keel of the ship was moving past at what seemed like a snail's pace, but there was no sign of any…

"Colonel!" exclaimed Gerry Messier. "The cargo bay!"

She jerked her head around to look at the monitor that Gerry was indicating. It showed the interior of the cargo bay and she saw a half-dozen of the aliens floating down into it. One of them was one of the bigger aliens she had seen earlier. They all seemed to have some sort of maneuvering unit built into their bulky space suits. She stared in horror as they started forward. A few seconds and they would be at the hatch leading to the command deck.

What could she do? Her pistol wasn't going to stop all of them. Instinctively, she flipped down the visor on her suit helmet, while her mind raced frantically. They were still coming; drifting closer to the camera pickup…

Drifting!

Kay Young turned back to her controls. With adrenaline-quickened fingers she typed in a series of commands. Several warning lights came on and Messier choked off an exclamation. Kay was telling her ship to do something it wasn't supposed to do. But Kay knew what it could do—not just what it was supposed to.

"Hang on!"

She punched one more button and the aerospike engine at the stern of the vessel suddenly came to life—at full power. Zero to four gees in a tenth of a second. It played hell with the engine, but not as much hell as it played with the aliens.

Kay and Messier were slammed against their seats. She watched in the monitor as the rear of the cargo bay leapt forward to smash into the aliens. The cargo bay was twelve meters long. For the aliens it was like being dropped out of a ten-story building onto concrete.

After a few seconds, Kay shut off the thrust. She still hoped to get back to pick up Doctor Vasthare and they were heading the wrong way. As the thrust died, the aliens were propelled forward slightly.

"Hell! They're still alive!" exclaimed Messier. Kay looked at the monitor in consternation. It was true, several of them, including the big one, were still moving. Two of them were not, but the others were at least twitching. Their momentum was bringing them closer and closer.

"All right! Let's do it again!" She activated the main engines and the rear of the cargo bay came up to swat the enemy again.

This time, the 'fall' wasn't quite so far, but the big alien hit a cargo container secured at the stern and crashed right through it. Kay cut the engine and observed her handiwork.

The big one was still moving, but it seemed to be trapped in the cargo container. Arms and legs flailed, but it was stuck for the moment. Two of the other ones weren't moving and tumbled out of the cargo bay into space. She wasn't sure about the others.

Then one of them fired a weapon.

It wasn't fired at the command deck or the humans in it; it was fired aft—at the engines. A small explosion blew away a piece of the rear bulkhead. Kay could feel the thump.

"Hell!" she snarled. She reached up and fired the bow thrusters. The ship lurched backward and the alien correspondingly moved forward. Not very quickly, but it drifted forward for a few seconds. Then the creature activated the thrusters in its suit and matched the motion of the shuttle.

But it was now six meters from the rear bulkhead and that would just have to do. Youngs killed the bow thrusters. Before the alien could react, Youngs cut in the main drive and the rear of the bay claimed another victim.

She reached out to cut the thrust, but before she could do so a dozen lights started flashing on her control board and the engine died of its own accord. She had pushed it too far.

"Shit! The fuel pumps have shut down!"

Kay looked at her controls, but there was nothing she could do at the moment. She might be able to get it running again, but it would take some time. Did she have it? She checked the monitor and the alien in the cargo module was still moving, but still stuck. Maybe she could...

Without warning, the hatch leading from the command deck to the cargo bay blew open.

There was pressure in the command deck, but only for another instant. A hurricane tugged at Youngs and Messier and sucked every loose object out. The straps on their chairs held the two humans in, but everything else not secured was gone.

"What the..." said Messier in a dazed voice.

Youngs twisted her chair around.

There was something coming through the hatch. Another alien. *One we missed! It must have been clinging to the forward part of the bay!*

Youngs clawed at her suit for the pistol. "Gerry! Look out!" she cried.

But Major Gerry Messier needed no warning. It had only taken him an instant to realize what had happened. He hit the release on his seat harness and flung himself at the intruder.

The alien shot him.

The weapon, whatever it was, went right through his torso and blasted a panel behind him. The impact threw him backward.

Kay had the pistol out. She thumbed off the safety and fired. The thing was only two meters away and she couldn't miss. She fired once, twice, three times. The pistol jerked noiselessly in her hand and the alien was flung against the bulkhead.

But it was unharmed.

Kay could see that its space suit was covered in thick pads. The bullets—the special bullets designed not to penetrate the skin of the spaceplane—had pocked several of them, but had done nothing else. *Body armor!*

The thing swung its weapon around toward her and she knew she was dead.

But she was not quite dead—neither was Gerry Messier.

Her copilot had bounced off the console behind him and drifted toward the alien again. His right hand suddenly darted out and grabbed the alien's weapon and wrenched it aside. A blast of something flashed past Kay's head and blew out a section of controls above her.

Now the two of them were grappling. Kay could see vapor and blood spurting out of the holes in Gerry's suit. The latest suits had some self-sealing properties, but it clearly was not helping much here. In spite of his wound, Messier had hold of the alien and its weapon and he would not let go. The creature wrapped its tail around a handhold and tried to throw the human off. But Messier was considerably larger than his opponent and held on like a bulldog.

Kay gaped at the pair. She still had the pistol, but what use was it? She'd probably just hit Gerry by mistake. She looked around wildly, was there something heavy she could hit the thing with? Nothing.

The alien now had Messier pinned up against the ceiling in the zero-G. Its legs were braced against the deck and its arms were over its head.

Then Kay saw it: *just like a medieval knight!*

The armored pads covered the alien's body. Arms, legs, torso. *But not there!*

Kay hit the release on her safety harness and lunged forward. She grabbed the thing's left elbow, rammed the muzzle of her gun into the creature's armpit, and pulled the trigger. The pistol bucked, but she held it in place and fired again. And again. The alien jerked violently and its tail whipped around to hit her in the ribs. But then, with one last twitch, it was still. Dark brown fluid covered the pistol and her hand, and more droplets floated about.

Kay pushed herself away from the creature, breathing hard. It had let go of its weapon and Gerry Messier was drifting slowly away, still clutching the alien device.

"Gerry!"

She quickly found a handhold and then dragged her copilot over to her.

She frantically rummaged around and found a package of emergency patches for the space suits. There seemed to still be a little bit of vapor puffing out of the holes as she slapped the patches in place on his chest and back. She kept calling his name, but there was no response. Kay pulled the suit around until she could look into the helmet.

There were ice crystals on the inside of the visor, but she could still see his face. He had blood on his lips and his nostrils. But his eyes moved slightly as she stared at him. One eyebrow moved up a half centimeter. It was the tiniest of gestures, but Kay instantly knew what it meant.

"Yes, Gerry, we got him. We got the bastard!" she said, nodding vigorously.

The face moved another tiny bit and Gerry Messier was smiling.

"Hang in there, Gerry. I've got the holes in your suit patched. We'll get you back home soon and everything will be fine."

They both knew it was a lie.

Gerry's lips began to move. There was no sound, but he deliberately mouthed out each word. Tears filled Kay's eyes. Major Gerry Messier had found his quote for the history books. It wasn't really printable, but Kay Youngs vowed that it would get in the books anyway. She wouldn't forget.

For a moment she closed her eyes and clenched her fists, but she knew she could not stay that way. She pushed herself over to the control panel. The alien's shots had smashed a number of controls, but the monitor was still working and the camera in the cargo bay was still there.

Before she could even strap herself back into her chair, the whole ship jerked suddenly.

Again.

She looked into the monitor and saw that the larger alien had finally gotten out of the cargo container. It was firing its weapon into the rear of the ship— into the engine compartment. As she watched, a large piece of the bulkhead went flying away.

Hell! If it hits the fuel tanks for the thrusters with those hypergolics, it'll blow us all to bits!

Her ship was being damaged beyond repair and she knew it. It was probably too late already, but she had to try and stop that thing. She turned away from the controls and went back to Gerry Messier. Gently, she pried the alien weapon out of his hands. She examined it quickly, but carefully. It was about the size of a carbine and was very oddly shaped. Even so, there was no doubt which was the business end and a little more looking revealed what had to be the trigger.

She pushed herself over to the hatch leading to the cargo bay. She slowly edged up to it and peered out. The alien was still blasting away. It seemed to have anchored itself to the deck of the bay somehow. As she stared at it, Kay suddenly realized that she had been wrong about what it was. It was not a bigger alien. It was an alien wearing some sort of powered exoskeleton. She could make out the shape of one of the 'standard' aliens inside.

She brought up the weapon. There were no sights for aiming on it, so she lined up her shot along what seemed to be the barrel. Then pressed the trigger.

There was no recoil, just a flash of light and a small explosion on the rear bulkhead. She had missed. She shifted her aim slightly and fired again. This time she hit it dead center and she thought a small piece of something went flying.

But now the thing was turning. She fired again and hit it again, but it was still turning. One last shot and then she instinctively shoved herself back from the hatch.

There was a dazzling flash right in front of her and the edge of the hatch frame exploded into fragments. Something hit a ringing blow against her helmet. She pushed herself further back, blinking her eyes from the dazzling light. There was another blast and more of the hatch and bulkhead was blown out.

She turned and scrambled to the front of the cockpit to escape the shrapnel that could puncture her suit. Fortunately, the flight deck was about a meter above the hatch opening, so no shots could come directly through to hit her. She slammed down the sun visor on her helmet and cursed herself for not thinking of it before. There were still spots floating in front of her eyes.

Youngs could feel several more chunks being blown out of her ship, but then it stopped. She looked into the monitor and saw that the alien was slowly advancing down the cargo bay toward the front of the ship.

Toward her.

She gripped the alien weapon and positioned herself so she would have a shot when it came at her. Maybe she could hit something vital. She didn't have much other hope left at this point.

"Youngs' Last Stand coming up," she muttered.

She waited, her heart pounding in her ears.

She continued to wait—what was taking it so long?

Just as she was building up the nerve to edge forward and take a look, the ship shook again and a swirl of debris came in through the hole in the bulkhead.

Kay twisted around to look at the monitor. She saw the alien tumbling down the cargo bay with one of its arms drifting in the other direction. As she watched, there was a very bright flash and the alien blew apart in a cloud of wreckage.

What the hell?

She floated there for a moment, completely indecisive, then she pulled herself up and looked out the cockpit windows. The spaceplane was tumbling slowly after all it had been put through and the stars wheeled across her view. She caught sight of the Earth and then, in the distance, the ISS and the ship. They were easily ten kilometers away now and still receding.

Then she saw something else.

A silvery disk was hovering a short distance away. Since she had no clue how big the thing was she couldn't judge the distance, but it only seemed a few hundred meters. The object was definitely saucer shaped.

As she continued to stare, a hatch opened up and five figures emerged. They were not like the aliens she had just been fighting. They were much more humanoid in shape. No tails, a more normal head. Skinny arms and legs. They wore silvery space suits with large helmets.

The other side in this war? Are they here to help, or were they only interested in finishing off their enemy?

Well, that didn't matter right now. Kay needed to tell Houston what had been happening. She clicked the communicator but quickly found that the transmitter or the antenna wasn't working. She was cut off. Alone.

The new aliens floated down into the cargo bay and came toward the ragged hole where the hatch had been. Kay braced herself against the control console and held her weapon ready—not pointed directly at the hole, but just off to the side.

A shape appeared in the opening a few meters away. It advanced very slowly and it had its empty hands raised. Kay remained motionless and it came all the way inside. The alien was short, maybe a hundred and thirty centimeters tall. It was built like a human, but with spindly arms and legs. The helmet seemed much too large. It was reflective like a mirror and Kay could not see inside.

"Lieutenant Colonel Kathryn Youngs?" said a voice in her helmet radio.

Kay jumped in spite of herself. The word 'Youngs' was printed on the chest of her suit, but how had it known the rest of her name and rank? The voice was in perfect, unaccented, English.

"Y… yes. Who are you?"

"I am a friend. We mean you no harm. Your attackers have been destroyed. You are in no danger now."

"Really? Oh, good," said Youngs in a daze.

"Is Major Gerald Messier injured?" said the creature, indicating Gerry with its hand.

"He's dead."

"We grieve with you."

"What…what about the others?"

"We regret that there have been many casualties among your comrades. We have found fifteen alive aboard the spaceship under construction and eight more on your space station. We are saddened that we could not arrive sooner to save more."

Kay gritted her teeth. There had been almost fifty people working on the ship! And another sixteen on the station. Why had those bastards tried to kill everyone like that?

"What happens now?" asked Youngs.

"I fear that your space craft is too badly damaged to function at this time. Both the ship and the station are also badly damaged. I do not believe you or your comrades can remain here for long and you have no way to return to Earth. We offer you assistance. We invite you back to our ship and then we can make arrangements to return you to Earth."

Kay Youngs floated there without replying. It was almost too much to take in all at once. But this person was right: She could not stay here and they were the only ticket home.

"All right."

"You can follow me. We shall also bring the body of your comrade…" There was a slight hesitation. "…you will have no need of the weapon."

Youngs stared for a moment. The weapon felt very reassuring, but it clearly wasn't going to give her any great bargaining power with these people. On the other hand, it was a priceless bit of alien technology—paid for in blood.

She slowly pushed herself over to Messier's body. She used a velcro strap on his suit to secure the weapon to it.

"This is his," she said and her voice grew stern. "It belongs to him and you make sure it stays with him! You understand?"

A long pause. "We understand. It will be as you say."

She looked around and spotted the automatic pistol, still floating in the compartment. She snagged it and flipped on the safety. NASA had issued the pistols because of the terrorist threat. No one had ever had to use one until now and it had remained one of the few secrets NASA had been able to keep. Kay doubted that anyone had ever expected it to be used the way she'd used it today!

Her eyes drifted over to the body of the first alien. It had been an intelligent creature and she had killed it. She had killed someone else, long ago, but he had just been a blip on the heads-up display of her fighter. This one was right here in front of her and its blood was on her glove. The nausea of weightlessness that she had overcome years before returned and threatened to overwhelm her.

Then her eyes went to Gerry Messier. *He was an intelligent creature, too.*

She very deliberately pushed the pistol into the pocket of her space suit and zipped it closed. She was staring into the helmet of the alien standing in front of her. All she could see was her own distorted reflection

"All right," she said. "Let's go."

Chapter Six

Melissa Hancock sat in the passenger compartment of the helicopter and tried not to look as excited—or nervous—as she felt. The chopper was sitting on the tarmac at Willow Grove Naval Air Station, about ten miles north of Philadelphia. The sun was just peeking over the trees to the east. It had the promise of being a warm and humid day.

Her father and Captain Osborne were off conferring with some people and she had been instructed to stay where she was for the moment. She was happy enough to do so. She felt extremely conspicuous in her borrowed uniform and wanted to stay out of sight as much as possible. At the same time she was incredibly excited to be there.

An alien spaceship! Right here, only a few miles away!

It still seemed too impossible to be really true. But there was no doubt that something had happened. The helicopter had approached Philadelphia while it was still dark. They had swung around to the west and passed a few miles from the crash site before continuing east to the air station. From above, they could see the flashing lights of an enormous number of emergency vehicles clustered around a smoldering site of fire and smoke.

Her father had wanted to come in for a closer look, but the helicopter was low on fuel and had to proceed to the base after only a few minutes. It had not been possible to see much in that short time.

She looked out through the window and saw that the refueling was complete. The fuel truck and its crew were driving off to service other aircraft.

And there were plenty of other aircraft.

Willow Grove was the only military air base in the vicinity. Officially it had been closed down years earlier, but due to local politics it had never been quite abandoned completely. Now the government was glad of that fact: the next closest were over in New Jersey or down at Dover, Delaware. Helicopters and aircraft of all sorts had been landing at regular intervals the whole time she was sitting there. Others had been taking off and heading toward the crash site. The base was not all that large, and it would soon be packed at this rate.

Melissa was not sure just what she hoped to do on this strange mission, but she was grateful to be a part of it. She supposed she would end up as her dad's assistant. That would probably mean fetching coffee, running errands, and taking notes, but she did not mind. Her father was not old fashioned as far as the role of women in the military; far from it. But she knew he would be protective toward her and, in truth, she was just a midshipman with no practical experience, so what else could she expect?

Of course, *no one* had any practical experience with what was happening. The truly unprecedented nature of it was still just sinking in. What were they going to do next? Check out the crashed ship, to be sure, but then what?

As she pondered those questions, she looked up and saw her father, Captain Osborne, and another officer hurrying toward the helicopter. They got in and plunked down in their seats. Her father told the pilot to take off and head for the crash site.

"This is Lieutenant Sokol," he said, indicating the new officer. "He's our liaison with the base. Lieutenant, this is my daughter, Melissa."

"Pleased to meet you...Lieutenant," said the young man. He smiled as he looked at her baggy uniform.

"What's happening?" asked Melissa, not sure what to say to Sokol.

"Well, it seems that Captain Pescatore left out a few acronyms when she told us who would be swarming around the wreck," said her father with a wry grin. "The EPA, FEMA, NASA, and the NTSB are here, too—along with a few more agencies I've probably missed. They are all demanding facilities and support services from the base. We are seriously lucky that this is a Navy base—we're getting top priority so far."

The blades on the helicopter were spinning rapidly now and a moment later they lifted off and headed southwest.

"The EPA?" asked Melissa in surprise. "Is there a threat of contamination, do you think?"

"Apparently so. That ship is hot—I mean radioactive. Not surprising considering it got nuked during the battle. Not as hot as you'd expect, but not exactly safe, either. It scattered debris all over the place after it hit the mountain. That is all going to have to be collected and tested."

"Fat chance of that!" snorted Osborne. "Souvenir hunters are swarming all over Valley Forge Park gathering up pieces."

"Yes, sir," said Sokol, "we're trying to keep them out, but it's a big place and there'll be no stopping them for a while."

"Silly twits," said Osborne. "They'll be convinced it's just a 'government plot' to seize all the evidence, so they'll hide the fragments under their beds and then wonder why they get cancer five years from now!"

"Not much chance of hiding any evidence on this one!" said her father, shaking his head.

The helicopter was speeding along and crossed over the Schuylkill River. A faint cloud of white smoke was rising in the distance.

"The souvenir hunters are the least of the problems right now, sir," said Sokol. "The smoke from the fire was radioactive, too, and it's been blowing east toward Philadelphia. And all the water they sprayed on the fire. That's been running off into storm drains. Those empty into the Schuylkill down there and that flows down past the city before it joins the Delaware."

"Hell," muttered Osborne. "Just how are they going to deal with that?"

"A state of emergency has been declared," said Sokol. "They are trying to evacuate the immediate vicinity. At first they wanted a ten mile radius but when they realized that would mean nearly a million people, they cut it down to three. You can see all the traffic moving away down there. Everyone else is ordered to stay inside. Any water works that draw from the Schuylkill have been shut down and EPA teams are being posted all along the rivers to monitor radiation levels."

"What about biological contamination, sir?" asked Melissa. "Is there a possibility of that, too?"

"Good point, Squirt...err, Lieutenant," said Hancock. "There certainly could be a danger but no one has any ideas yet what to do about it. If there was anything harmful aboard, it could be spread all over the place by now."

"Great," said Osborne.

"Were there many casualties from the crash itself?" asked Hancock.

"Surprisingly few—that we know about. A few serious injuries from flying debris to some of the people watching in the park. One woman was killed when a tree trunk came through her bedroom window. There were more injuries and two known fatalities to people that were around the mall area. Unfortunately, anyone who may have been right in the ship's path is buried under tons and tons of rubble. It may take a while to account for those. Still, we were awfully lucky: I was stationed here years ago and this area is as congested as Washington. If that thing had come down in the middle of a work day we could have had thousands of casualties."

"Is there any more word on what's happening to our people up in space?"

"Not a thing since that first message that they were under attack. I'm afraid it doesn't look good for those poor devils."

"There it is, sir," said the pilot, breaking in to their conversation. They looked through the forward canopy and could see the crash site. Melissa noted the usual collection of suburban houses and strip malls and the larger blocks of office complexes, but her eyes were drawn to a very large group of buildings, surrounded by parking lots, which had a white cloud drifting out of its center.

"We're going to have to swing around to the west again, sir," said the pilot. "We need to stay upwind, just in case."

"Very well, carry on," said her father.

They watched intently through the left side windows as they moved past the site. There seemed to be an incredible number of other aircraft, mostly helicopters, in the vicinity.

"We're having trouble keeping the news helicopters at a safe distance, sir," said Lieutenant Sokol. "There are so many of them—and swarms of drones, too—we may have to declare some sort of 'no-fly' zone."

"Then they'll scream that we're trying to cover up the whole thing," said Osborne.

"We'd have a hard time covering up that," said Robert Hancock, pointing out the front canopy.

Melissa looked and saw the small mountain in the distance where the alien craft had first hit. The whole top had been sliced off leaving a wound that shone brightly in the morning sun. It was in glaring contrast to the dark woods around it.

"Wow!" she said. "Do we have any good estimates on how big that thing is?"

"No one's really had a chance to work on that yet," answered her father. "But here we are, maybe you can make a guess of your own."

The helicopter was now approaching the wreck. They could see where the ship had hit the ground and then slid into the mall buildings. There was a deep gouge in the pavement showing the path it took. Where it had hit the buildings it looked like...what? Melissa struggled to find an analogy. A snowplow through deep snow? An icebreaker through sea ice? A bulldozer through soil? She finally decided that it looked like an alien spacecraft that had smashed into a shopping mall.

The ship itself was sitting in the midst of the crushed buildings. Those closest to the ship had collapsed or burned, some both. A large pile of rubble was in front of the ship and smaller mounds along its sides. Some of the debris was on top of the ship. All around, the area was blackened and burned. Water was standing in a number of places and a white mist continued to rise from the hot areas.

Melissa thought the ship was around two hundred meters long and about a hundred wide. It was sufficiently battered that it might have been longer or wider before the crash. It was considerably taller than the mall buildings and it stuck up well above the roof. The shape was a simple ovoid, like a flattened egg. She could see all sorts of small features on the hull, but nothing large.

"Kind of plain, isn't it?" said Osborne. "I was expecting big fins or warp pods or something like that."

"You can see some damage on it," said her father. "I mean which wasn't caused by the crash. See toward the rear, there? That hole punched in the hull. It must have been made in the battle."

"Yeah, there are several of those," agreed Osborne. "And that whole section near the stern looks melted. Maybe that was from the nukes."

"Has anyone gone inside, yet?" asked Melissa.

"I don't think so, but why don't we go down and ask?"

A forward command post had been set up in a nearby motel. The helicopter set down in the parking lot and they got out and went inside. All the guests and staff had been evacuated, of course, but the place was swarming with officials, both in and out of uniform.

"Who's actually in charge of all this?" asked Melissa, looking around.

"That is still being fought over at the highest levels," answered her father with a frown. "For the moment, NTSB is in charge of the actual crash site; they have more experience with that sort of thing than anyone. The Pennsylvania National Guard, working with the state and federal emergency people, are in charge of the evacuation and ground security. The Air Force and Navy are handling air security. Naturally, everyone wants to get a look inside."

After a bit of confusion, they managed to secure a room for their own use. Melissa's father reported in to his superior. She still did not have any definite orders for him except to keep an eye what was going on and report anything important. After some discussion, they decided to split up to look around and then get back together to compare notes later. Melissa walked off toward the crash site. She soon discovered that Lieutenant Sokol was staying with her.

"Hello," he said with a smile when her eyes fell on him.

"Hello, Lieutenant. Weren't we supposed to split up?"

"Commander Hancock asked me to keep an eye on you. I hope you don't mind."

"I'm not sure if I do or not, Lieutenant," answered Melissa. "I don't really need a chaperone—or a baby sitter." Her tone was friendly enough, but she actually was a bit angry.

"Oh, I'm sure he didn't mean that you did…Lieutenant."

Melissa decided not to pursue it any further. It didn't really matter. It was no time to be making waves! She was lucky just to be there.

They reached the set of barriers that had been erected and looked over. Soldiers with rifles stood at short intervals all along the perimeter. Some of them glanced in their direction, but the uniforms—even an extremely baggy one—seemed to satisfy them. They were still a good four hundred meters away and could see far more of the mall than the ship.

"Strange name for a town: 'King of Prussia'," said Melissa, gesturing to the sign above one of the buildings.

"It goes back to colonial days," said Sokol. "During the French and Indian Wars, England was allied with Prussia. Old Fritz won some big victory against the French and the local tavern owner named his tavern after him. The name stuck."

"Do you think we can get any closer?"

"Well, I don't know..." said Sokol uncertainly.

"I promise I won't try and sneak off and get into the ship on my own, Lieutenant. I'm not that stupid."

"Wasn't suggesting you were," said Sokol. "I just don't think they'll let anyone much closer. Look at those guys over there: full environmental suits. We're not exactly dressed for it."

"I suppose not," admitted Melissa. "But how long is it going to take them to get inside? Suppose some of the aliens are still alive? They may need medical assistance. They might die if we delay too long—and who knows how the others that are still up there will react to that?"

"That's a good point. But we have to think of the potential dangers to ourselves. If we go poking around in there and let out something nasty—radioactivity or bio-hazards—thousands could die."

Melissa nodded but did not say anything. The pair worked their way along the barriers trying to find a better angle to get a view. Unfortunately, there really was not much more that could be seen from that distance.

"It's still so hard to believe," said Melissa. "Aliens coming from God knows where to fight a battle right here."

"It does seem pretty unlikely," said Sokol.

"Yes!" said Melissa, warming to the subject. "The odds of both sides just arriving here at the same time are incredibly long. Now what can we do to lower those odds to something manageable?"

"What do you mean?"

"What other factors could have worked to bring the aliens here at the same time?"

Sokol frowned and was silent for a moment. "Uh, I suppose there could have been something that drew them here. Maybe transmissions from our TV or radio?"

"Good! That's a possibility. It could account for them coming here instead of all the millions of other stars out there. But getting both sides here at the same time is still a reach. We can't assume they started the exact same distance away so they would not have gotten the signals at the same time or have had the same travels times."

"Maybe, but they might not have reacted to the signals at the same rate," suggested Sokol. "Side A gets the signal ten years before Side B, but Side B sends a ship right away, while Side A waits a while to send theirs. Or Side B's ships are faster. Too many unknown factors here, Melissa. Uh, you don't mind me calling you 'Melissa', do you?"

"No, that's fine." She hardly even noticed; she was fixated on the problem. "We're assuming that both sides showed up at nearly the same time. But what if they didn't? What if one side was already here—maybe for a long time?

Then if the other side shows up at any point, they will meet!"

"Well, that would certainly increase the chances," said Sokol, clearly impressed with her reasoning.

"Yes!" said Melissa, getting really excited. "If one side were already here for years, then the timing issue becomes a lot less critical. Whenever the other side shows up, there could be a battle. That makes a lot more sense!"

She paused and a frown slowly grew on her face as the meaning of her statement began to sink in. She looked up at Lieutenant Sokol.

"They've been here, watching us, for a long time."

"We don't know that, Melissa. We don't know anything about their technology. If they do have some sort of faster-than-light drive, both sides might just stop in every now and then and this is the first time they were both here at the same time. Or maybe it just is a fantastic coincidence."

"Maybe, but I don't like fantastic coincidences."

"Still, I think your idea is an important possibility," continued Sokol. "It doesn't look like we are going to see much here. Why don't we contact your father and tell him about it?"

"Okay," she said with a faint smile. She pulled out her phone and flipped it open but then grimaced. "I forgot, the satellites are still out. Guess we'll have to look for him."

"Here, try mine. It's linked to the military network." Sokol handed her his phone.

"Thanks!" She smiled and he smiled back. Melissa blushed and had to dial the number twice before she got it right. Her father answered right away.

"Dad? It's Melissa. I..."

"I was just going to call you," interrupted her father. "Get back to the motel right away."

"Why? What's happening?"

"Big stuff, Squirt. There has been a communication from the other alien ship!"

"We'll be right there!"

Chapter Seven

Doctor Usha Vasthare clutched her hands together in her lap and tried to keep from fidgeting. It wasn't easy. Most people would have understood her nervousness. After all, she was aboard an alien spacecraft, the existence of which, no one on her planet had even suspected until a few hours earlier. In addition, she had seen dozens of her comrades mercilessly slaughtered and only escaped death, herself, because of the intervention of these same aliens. Most people would have understood—but most people would have been wrong about why.

Usha Vasthare was fidgeting because a very great part of her wanted to leap up and start tearing up the deck plates to try and get a look at the mechanism that was making this thing work! It was not that she wasn't afraid. She was. It was not that she did not grieve for her lost friends. She did. But she was also in shock. Nothing had ever prepared her for the events of this day and she found herself falling back on the reassuring and comforting habits of the engineer that she was. Later, she would chastise herself for acting in so callous a manner, but right now it was do that or go mad.

She took a deep breath and forced herself to calm down. She looked around and saw the survivors of the ship and the station sitting all around her. She took comfort from their presence; knowing that they were all together, sitting on the deck of the strange alien ship. She supposed it was just a shuttle or some other form of small craft. It was not the main ship—but they had been told they were on their way there.

The mere fact that they were sitting rather than floating had Usha incredibly excited. Artificial gravity! Something was holding them down to the deck and it was not acceleration! It was only about a quarter of a G she supposed, but it still felt strange after weeks of weightlessness. There were no chairs or seats of any sort in the vessel; they were forced to sit on the deck. It was probably just as well, because the ceiling overhead was very low. Usha, shortest one of the whole crew, could just stand up without brushing her head. All the others had to bend over.

All the other humans, that was. The aliens were even shorter than Usha and had no trouble with the low overhead. There were a number of the beings all around them and they did not appear to sit down at all. She had caught a brief glimpse through a hatch into the control room and everyone there seemed to be standing as well.

The aliens were short and spindly and had large heads. Or she assumed they did; none of them had removed their reflective helmets yet. Some wore silvery space suits while others wore coveralls of various colors. Many of them were carrying devices, the purpose of which she could only guess, but they did not seem like weapons.

But they certainly had weapons. Usha had watched two of the amazing vessels approach the ship. She had been watching in the monitor as the first group of aliens—the attackers—had floated down the length of the ship's keel toward the engine module. There had been no more word from Colonel Youngs and she had to assume her plan to pick them up had failed. She was quite certain she was going to die.

Then, without warning, the aliens had begun to explode. Bright flashes of light seemed to tear them apart. Two ships approached and dozens of this second group of aliens had spilled out. The battle had been brief and one-sided.

Not too long afterward, she had been ushered into one of the ships. The fact that these creatures even knew her name was the least of the surprises this day had brought. And now that ship was taking her and her companions to the main alien vessel. Or so she assumed. There had not been the slightest sensation of acceleration and that had sparked her interest again. A reactionless drive of some sort. The artificial gravity proved that they could manipulate that most fundamental of forces; the drive must work on that principle, too!

She wished she could see out to confirm that they were moving, but there were no windows. Or there were no windows right now. When they had first entered the ship, there had been rows of windows along the walls. But the aliens had done something and they had vanished. Where they had been was now just a smooth and blank section of wall.

Usha contained her frustration and continued to look about. The interior of the ship was very surprising in itself. It was highly ornate. The structural members and bracing were all intricately shaped and decorated. Some areas actually looked like carved wood, but she supposed it was really some sort of synthetic material. The deck was covered with something like carpet that had strange patterns. The colors were all very blue. Blue-green, blue-violet, and deep purples. It was kind or eerie but at the same time beautiful. The fact that the aliens had artwork and valued this sort of thing was reassuring to Usha. They couldn't be *that* different!

She glanced over to where Colonel Youngs was sitting. Usha had been happy to see the colonel unharmed, but she had noted the absence of her copilot and seen the grim look on her face. Youngs had made a number of requests—demands really—for information, but their hosts had politely deflected all of them, stating that their commander would soon receive them and try to answer all questions.

Some of the other humans appeared to be in an even deeper state of shock than Usha. They had seen their friends shot down before their eyes, but somehow survived. At least all of Usha's team had escaped unharmed. But Mister Ericsson and Diane Hartley and a lot of other people she had known were not here. She started to shake slightly and felt tears forming in her eyes. *No! I will not disgrace myself in front of everyone!*

Suddenly there was a small jolt and the aliens began to move about. Usha suspected that they had docked with the main alien ship. One of the creatures stood in front of them.

"We have arrived at our destination. Our commander desires that Lieutenant Colonel Kathryn Youngs, Doctor Usha Vasthare, and Doctor Burr Eichelman come and confer. The rest of you may remain here." The voice was the utterly textbook English they had heard earlier.

Usha nodded to herself. The three people named were the commander of the spaceplane and the senior members of the crews for the station and the ship. The senior *surviving* members—Usha felt a chill when she realized that honor had fallen to her. Colonel Youngs got to her feet, hunching over considerably to avoid the low overhead, and Usha got up as well in anticipation of following the alien. But the colonel had other ideas.

"No, we will remain together," she said. "Either your commander comes here, or you take all of us."

The alien was silent, but Usha was stunned and then suddenly furious. *What is she doing? Is she going to pass up a chance to look inside the alien ship! That idiot!* She was on the verge of trying to strangle Youngs when the alien spoke again.

"Very well," it said. "Our commander will come here."

"No!" cried Usha in frustration. Every head turned toward her.

"Is there a problem, Doctor?" asked Youngs. The friendly tone the American had always used with her was missing and Usha suddenly realized that if it came to a real test of wills, she didn't have a chance. *Gently, Usha! Gently! Don't lose your temper!*

"I…couldn't we compromise, Colonel? We are guests here, after all. Perhaps we could all meet halfway somewhere?" She was grasping at straws.

"I have no objections, Doctor, as long as we all stay together." She turned and looked expectantly at the alien. The creature was silent and Usha assumed it was conferring with its superior.

"There is a chamber where a meeting could take place that is approximately halfway between this place and where the commander is now. Would that be satisfactory?" asked the alien. Again, there was no inflection to the voice, but Usha felt sure there was a slight tone of puzzlement—or was it amusement?

"Doctor?" asked Youngs.

"Yes! Fine! That would be wonderful!" Usha felt like she was babbling.

"Very well," said the creature. "Please follow me."

A hatchway opened up in the side of the vessel and the alien walked through it. The humans began rising to their feet and followed. Usha hurried to be among the first out. She went down a short ramp and nearly stumbled. The gravity had increased abruptly. It was still only about a half of a normal G, but the change had taken her by surprise. Their guide immediately noticed her misstep.

"My apologies. Please be aware of the change in gravity here." The alien made sure each person safely made the transition. While it was doing so, Usha looked around.

Their small vessel was now resting inside a large chamber which Usha assumed was a hanger bay on the mothership. Several of the smaller vessels were there. Each was a circular disk shape, about twenty meters in diameter and perhaps six meters high at the mid-point. There were numerous small details to be noticed on the skin of the vessels, but no major projections—or obvious drive mechanisms—were visible. Usha realized she was lagging behind the group and hurried to catch up.

The hanger had a high ceiling, so her taller companions had no problem there, but they soon entered a corridor. The ceiling here was higher than in the shuttle, but still too low for most of the humans. They walked hunched over and looked anxiously from side to side. All of them still had their space suits on with the visors closed. Usha noticed that the elaborate decorations she had seen earlier were continued in this vessel, too. It vaguely reminded her of temples she had seen in Thailand.

Eventually, their guide brought them to a large compartment that was filled with growing plants. Usha was quite surprised to see this, but she was delighted as well. It did not appear to be a hydroponics garden for growing food or recycling air. It looked to her like an arboretum—something done for beauty rather than function. The plants were a deep blue-green for the most part—just like the colors on the shuttle.

As they entered, Usha saw several of the aliens standing in another doorway on the opposite side of the chamber. As soon as the humans were fully inside, these aliens started toward them. With a thrill—or was it a chill?—Usha realized that these aliens were not wearing helmets or spacesuits, just some sort of coverall.

She stared at them as they drew nearer. Their basic shape was no surprise since it followed what they had seen in the spacesuited aliens: Very thin arms and legs, small body and rather large heads. It was those heads that had the humans' attention right now. Their most obvious features were two large dark eyes. There were no whites or irises visible, just a large, dark orb. The 'face' had hardly any nose, just a breathing orifice. The mouth was a horizontal slit. No obvious ears, either, just a small hole on either side. The round skull was hairless and the skin a blue-gray color. Usha stared with the others and was stunned.

They look exactly like those awful pictures in the American tabloids!

She couldn't believe it. They really did look like that. Almost exactly. There were a few differences, to be sure, but not enough to dispel the shock of what she was seeing.

Have those cranks been right all along? Have these creatures been visiting us and abducting people for all these years? It can't be! It just can't!

All the other humans were gawking as well. The aliens approached to within a few meters and halted. One of them raised a hand—a hand with two opposing thumbs and four fingers, Usha noted.

"Welcome aboard the vessel *Seeker of Truth*," came a voice over the speaker in her helmet. "I am Commander Keeradoth. You may open your visors if you wish. The air here is completely compatible with your biology and I assure you that it contains no pathogens harmful to humans." Usha had seen the alien's mouth moving, but it was hard to imagine that mouth making the sounds she had just heard. She was so intent on studying the alien she hardly realized what it had said. When she did, she was filled with sudden doubt.

But Colonel Youngs took the lead immediately. She opened up her visor without hesitation and stepped forward.

"Commander, I'm Lieutenant Colonel Kathryn Youngs—but then you people already seem to know that. First, I want to thank you for your assistance. Next, I've got about ten thousand questions I want answered."

"Yes, I am sure that you do, Colonel," said the alien. "I will try to answer as best I can. However, I do have urgent matters that must be discussed as well."

While the alien spoke, Usha was studying Youngs. She did not seem to be having trouble breathing the air, so Usha opened her visor, too. The smell that entered her nostrils was unlike anything she had ever experienced. Not unpleasant, but very, very different. She wasn't sure she'd want to be breathing it for very long, but it was tolerable for the moment.

"All right," said Youngs. "First off, why were we attacked and by who?"

"The beings who attacked you are called the '*Brak-Shar*' by my race. We are at war with them and I fear that they mistook you for our allies. I deeply regret that our conflict has caused you so much harm."

With her visor open, she could hear the alien actually speaking. It was a strange, musical sort of sound—and completely unintelligible. And yet the language coming through her helmet speaker was perfect English. Somehow, it did not surprise her a bit. There also seemed to be a sort of echo and after a few moments Usha realized that the voice was not only coming from her helmet speaker but also from a kind of medallion hanging around the alien's neck. Some sort of translation device? The three overlapping 'voices' were a bit distracting, but she forced herself to focus on just one.

"Right," said Youngs, frowning. "And just who are you people and what are you doing here?"

"Our name for ourselves is not easily translated. However, you may call us 'Somerans'. It is what we call our home planet and you can think of it as our version of 'Earthling' or 'Terran'."

"And where is this home planet? How far away is it?"

"Our home world's sun is approximately a hundred and fifty light years away in the direction of the constellation Cygnus. I can give you the exact right ascension and declination if you wish."

The alien's words caused a notable stir among the humans. *A hundred and fifty light years!* thought Usha in amazement. Had they come all that way at less than the speed of light? If not, how had they managed to cheat Einstein? And not only do they know human language, they know about the human constellations and coordinate systems! What else do they know and how did they find it out?

"Perhaps later," said Youngs, apparently impervious to the wonder of this situation. "But what are you doing here—and what are your intentions?"

The alien paused for a few seconds. "We are here on a…scouting…mission," it said. "I assure you that we mean no harm to you or your people. We were here collecting information on your world when the *Brak-Shar* attacked. As for our intentions now…" the creature paused again. "We had intended to make open contact with your world when we felt the time was right. That plan is, in light of recent events, obviously, obsolete. You know of our presence now and contact cannot be delayed. We wish to open peaceful and friendly relations with the people of Earth."

Usha sucked in her breath. This was wonderful! She had been fearing that the aliens would simply return them to Earth and then leave. But they would stay! There would be a chance to talk with them and learn from them. She looked to the colonel and was surprised to see Youngs still frowning.

"This is quite a lot you are throwing at me, Commander," she said. "Any sort of formal relations will have to be arranged through people with a whole lot more rank than I have! For now, I'm chiefly concerned with the safety of my people here."

"I can understand that, Colonel. In fact, that brings us to the urgent matter I need to discuss with you. As you may be aware, the other ship of our expedition has crashed on Earth."

Youngs nodded. "We had just received word of that when your friends attacked."

"I assure you, Colonel, that the *Brak-Shar* are not our friends!" said the alien leader hurriedly. Usha wasn't sure, but there seemed to be ripples of blue coloring moving across the alien's face. Was it angry or alarmed? After a moment the colors faded. "Oh! That was one of your jokes. My apologies, Colonel. We sometimes have trouble following your speech patterns accurately."

"Sorry, I'll try to be more careful," said Youngs. "You were talking about your crashed ship."

"Indeed. The ship has crashed near one of your cities: Philadelphia. I fear that there was considerable damage to property and some small loss of life among the inhabitants."

"I am sorry to hear that," said Youngs.

"As are we, Colonel. We realize that we must make reparations for what we have caused to happen and we are prepared to do so."

Usha twitched. What were they talking about? Reparations! What reparations? These beings represented a priceless treasure trove of knowledge. What were a few smashed building compared to that? The deaths were another matter, of course, but surely everyone would recognize that it was accidental!

"That's also a bit outside my authority to discuss, Commander," said Youngs. "I'm sure it can be handled at the appropriate time."

"Yes, of course, Colonel. Of most urgency to us is the possibility that some of our people may still be alive in the wreck."

The colonel was clearly startled. Usha was, as well. "Is there a possibility of that?"

"We do not know. There has been no communications since the crash, but the impact was not so severe to rule out the possibility of survivors. And clearly time is of the essence if any of them are going to continue to survive."

"Yes, I can certainly see that, Commander," said Youngs. "I would imagine that our own emergency people on the ground are making efforts to help."

The alien commander made a strange motion with its head and shoulders; not exactly a shrug, but Usha didn't know how else to describe it. "Many emergency personnel have converged on the area, but sadly, Colonel, they are hesitating to enter the ship. We have monitored some of your communications and it seems they are concerned about the threat of radioactivity or biological contamination."

"Well, I can see that, too."

"The danger is slight. While there is some residual radioactivity, it is not severe and I can assure you that there is no biological threat of any kind."

"I see," said Youngs. "Perhaps you should contact someone down there and tell them that. While you are at it, I would appreciate you telling them what's happened to us."

"That is exactly why I wished to speak with you, Colonel," said the alien. "We are somewhat reluctant to simply make an open broadcast to your people. We do not know what sort of confusion or panic such a thing might cause. I would request that you make the initial contact and explain what has happened and what we wish. It will make for a smoother beginning to our relations."

"Well, anything would be smoother than what we've had so far," said Youngs with a slight smile.

Usha was not smiling. She had been willing to let Youngs take the lead in what was clearly an emergency that she was better trained to handle than anyone else. But now! This was a delicate diplomatic situation. They didn't want some ex-fighter-jock setting the tone! The aliens had clearly chosen to talk to Youngs because of her military rank, but that wasn't right. Usha fidgeted. She was no diplomat either. She scanned the faces of the other survivors and tried to see someone else who could take the lead. But there really wasn't anyone... The alien leader was speaking again:

"Colonel, would you be willing to make such a broadcast? Time may be very critical."

"Sure, why not?" said Youngs. Usha winced. "Take me to your communicator and let's do it."

Chapter Eight

Commander Robert Hancock inched along the wall of the crowded conference room and tried to find a position with a good view of the main wall screen. The motel that had been chosen as a forward command center had been close to the crash site, but it had little else to recommend it—certainly not an adequate conference room! More people were trying to crowd into the already over-crowded space. He saw Melissa and Lieutenant Sokol at the entrance and he waved to them. Eventually they spotted him and began working their way through the throng.

"What's going on?" asked Melissa once she finally got near.

"About twenty minutes ago NASA got a message on one of their normal mission frequencies. It just said that at 0830 we would be getting a further transmission from the alien ship," replied Hancock, almost shouting to make himself heard.

"0830? That's only a few minutes from now! Are we tied into the right frequency?" Melissa gestured to the screen.

"We're supposed to be. They've certainly had enough technicians scrambling around."

"Where's Uncle—I mean Captain Osborne?"

"He said he couldn't stand the mob. There are a couple other, smaller meeting rooms that are tied in, too. He said he was going to try one of those. Funny: I thought those sub-drivers were used to crowded conditions."

Melissa smiled at him, but then her eyes were drawn to the front of the room. A man had forced his way to the front and was calling for everyone's attention.

"Please! Quiet down everyone!" he called. It was obvious how many military personnel were in the room just by how quickly the man got what he wanted. The room was suddenly still and every eye was on him.

"The transmission is scheduled to start very shortly. I want you to know that there will be several other groups tied into this in Houston, the Pentagon, the White House, and probably a few others. To prevent chaos, all replies will go through the flight controllers at Houston, so don't bother shouting questions at the screen. Those of you with hand computers can hook into any discussion that may follow at the address on the screen now."

Hancock looked up and saw what the man had indicated and quickly got out his computer; Melissa and Sokol did likewise. He typed in the indicated address—somewhat awkwardly with one hand—and saw that it was a fairly standard tele-conferencing format, except with an unusually large number of participants.

"Okay, here we go." The man—Hancock had no clue who he was—ducked out of the way as the large screen came to life.

A woman appeared on the screen. A human woman, who looked vaguely familiar to Hancock. She was wearing a space suit, but had the helmet off. A tag on the front of the suit said 'Youngs'. She was wearing a nervous smile on her rather attractive face.

"This is Lieutenant Colonel Kathyrn Youngs, commander of the spaceplane *Lewis and Clark*," she began. "I am speaking to you from a spaceship called *Seeker of Truth*, which is, I'm told, currently about fifty thousand kilometers over the South Atlantic. *Seeker of Truth* is one of the ships that was observed from Earth last night. As we deduced, there was a battle being fought between those ships. Some of the survivors of the opposing ship later attacked the space station, the ship under construction, and my spaceplane.

"I regret to report very heavy loss of life aboard our ships and station. We would all have been killed were it not for the intervention of *Seeker of Truth*..."

Hancock listened in growing wonder as Youngs recounted what had happened to her and her comrades and told what she knew about the aliens and what they wanted. It took almost fifteen minutes, but his attention was completely riveted on the woman. Finally, Youngs paused for a moment and briefly glanced away from the camera.

"The most critical matter is the issue of possible survivors aboard the crashed ship," continued Youngs. "The 'Somerans', as they call themselves, request permission to send down a rescue party. At the same time, they would return me and the others to Earth. We will stand by for your reply."

The display went blank and a long moment of silence ensued. Then, everyone seemed to be talking at once. It quickly became impossible to hold any sort of conversation. Hancock looked at his computer to see if anything useful was happening there, but inputs were coming so rapidly it was little better than gibberish.

It went on for several minutes and then that same man was at the front of the room shouting for quiet. Eventually he got it.

"I've just gotten instructions from the top. We are going to set up a four-way conference with Houston, the Pentagon, the White House, and here. For our end of things, they want one representative from each agency or military branch. Everyone else please leave!"

Hancock looked at Melissa and Sokol. "Well, for the moment I'm the Navy's representative, so I guess I'll see you two later—try to stay out of trouble, will you?"

"Some people get to have all the fun," said Melissa. "I'll expect a full report later on, Commander!"

"Aye aye, ma'am."

It took about ten minutes before all the people who no longer belonged there were completely ushered out. At least there were places to sit now. During that time, cameras and several additional display screens were set up. Hancock noticed that there were now armed sentries outside the conference room.

Finally, things were ready. The screens lit up again and Hancock could see the other three groups involved in the conference. The screen from the White House showed the President and most of his cabinet. The Pentagon screen had many of the Joint Chiefs, including his boss' boss in naval intelligence. He did not recognize anyone in the NASA group.

The President, wearing his customary dark blue suit, cleared his throat and began. "Ladies and gentlemen, I don't need to tell you that we are in the midst of something truly amazing in the history of our country—hell, the whole planet for that matter. We've got a lot of important decisions to make. But for right now, we need to make a response to the aliens' request to land a rescue party. Should we allow them to do this?"

The Secretary of the Air Force stood up. "Mr. President, my department has been accused of covering up evidence about UFOs for years, so this might be a case of the pot calling the kettle black, but I don't think we should allow the aliens inside that ship. They could very well scoop up everything in there as well as any casualties. That wreck represents a priceless technological resource and we should do everything in our power to hang on to it."

"What if the aliens don't agree to that?" asked the Secretary of State. "We have to consider how our actions could affect future relations with these people. If some of their injured should die because of our refusal it could have the worst effect possible."

"From a legal standpoint, things are rather vague, Mr. President," said the Attorney General. "Obviously, the aliens are not signatories of any existing agreements or treaties. Typically, in the event of an air crash on foreign soil, any survivors are repatriated to their own countries as quickly as feasible. The owner also has first claim on any salvage rights to the wreck—and responsibility for any damage caused by the crash. There is also the question of belligerency and neutrality. This ship crashed here as the result of a war between the two groups of aliens. We can rightly claim to be neutrals and therefore have a right to intern anyone or anything violating our territory. I'm not recommending that we do this, but it would be an option."

"Mr. President." Hancock saw that someone from the NASA group had stood up. "I'm Doctor Bettendorf of the Advanced Propulsion Unit. From what Colonel Youngs has told us, the aliens are looking to establish relations with us. That would almost have to include the opportunity to buy or trade for their technology. As part of that exchange, we could expect to receive instructions on how to build and use their devices. Anything we might get from the wreck will be a mystery we have to puzzle out and that could take years without help. Perhaps it would be best to cooperate with the aliens now rather than start things off on the wrong foot."

"And what if they just strip the wreck and leave, Doctor?" asked the Secretary of the Air Force. "By the time you add up the damage to the satellites, the space station, the ship, *Lewis and Clark*, and all the damage on the ground, those people have done about a hundred billion dollars of damage. What if they just say: 'Thanks very much and we'll see you around sometime,'?"

"And what if we seriously piss them off by refusing to let them save their injured comrades?" asked the Secretary of State. "General O'Connell, if these beings decided to turn hostile, what sort of threat do they represent?"

Henry O'Connell, the Chairman of the Joint Chiefs, stood up and his expression was not pleasant. "Mr. Secretary, I've had my people looking at that very question ever since we first detected the alien ships. Obviously, we don't have as much information to go on as we would like. However, based on our observation of their performance during the battle, I would have to say that they could represent a very serious threat indeed."

There was a bit of muttering and uneasy shifting in seats in the room where Hancock was sitting. Although he could not hear the muttering, he could see that the reaction was the same in the other three rooms as well. He just nodded his head. *Of course they could be a potential threat! It's up to us to make darn sure the potential doesn't become actual!*

"The alien ship is far in advance of anything we have," continued General O'Connell. "It can accelerate so quickly that no weapon in our arsenal would even have much hope of hitting it. Any ground-launched missile would take so long to get out of the atmosphere that this ship could just thumb its nose at them and move out of range. That is to say nothing of any sort of active missile defense. In addition, our observations indicate that these ships may have some sort of protective shield—right out of science fiction, I know. Both the crashed ship and the surviving one withstood nuclear explosions at very close range—ranges that would have destroyed anything we are capable of building. This indicates either a shield or incredibly strong materials. Considering the damage the crashed ship took from its impact on landing, I would think the shield is the more likely answer."

O'Connell sighed. "What this means is that the aliens are pretty much invulnerable to anything we can throw at them. We could probably destroy their ship if they were obliging enough to let us hit it with a few dozen nukes, but they are unlikely to do that.

"As far as the aliens' offensive capability, we are less certain. Some of our readings indicate that only the other side in the battle was using nuclear warheads, but we cannot confirm this. We suspect they have some powerful laser or particle beam weapons and some other sort of non-nuclear missiles. Even these conventional missiles could do considerable damage to a ground target. And since we really can't hurt them in return, they could just hang out of range and drop things on us as long as they like."

"What's the bottom line, Henry?" asked the President.

"The bottom line, sir, is that we better think very carefully before we do anything to piss these folks off."

There were a few chuckles, but they were strained. The full meaning of the general's words was hard to take. All the world's military might, all the incredibly expensive machines and technology stockpiled for the last century, were virtually useless.

"So you are recommending that we allow them what they ask?"

"I'm saying that from a strictly military view, there is almost no way to prevent them from taking what they want, sir. Although if they wanted to actually come down here and go through the wreck, we could make things a lot more difficult for them than we could if they just stayed out in space."

"Mr. President." Hancock looked and saw that Roy Hertwig, the head of the National Security Council, had stood up. "I must agree with General O'Connell on the alien's threat potential. However, the Secretary of the Air Force also makes some valid points. These aliens have barged in here and have done a great deal of damage. In addition, from what Colonel Youngs has told us, they may have been here, watching us, for some time. Long enough to learn our language, certainly, and probably a great many other things. We only have their word that their ultimate aims are not detrimental to us. Now they are requesting that we cooperate in letting them come down and mount a rescue mission.

"While this is certainly a reasonable request, we would probably wish to grant it on humanitarian grounds." Hertwig paused with a slightly startled expression. "I guess that's not exactly the proper term, is it? In any case, you know what I mean. But getting back to my point: the aliens have made a request. If we agree to it without reservation or condition, we may be setting an unfortunate precedent. Who knows what they may 'request' next? Then the requests may become demands. I believe that we must begin our relations with these people from as strong a position as possible. If we show weakness it may set the tone for all future relations."

"Then you believe we should turn down their request?" asked the President. "Even if their injured die as a result?"

"Is it possible for us to enter the wreck at this time and care for their injured ourselves?" responded Hertwig. "We could then give them back at a later date. Right now it seems too much like a hostage exchange for the return of Colonel Youngs and her people."

The President turned and looked out of the screen at the people at the wreck site. "How about that? How soon could you folks get in there?"

The leader of the National Transportation Safety Board team stood up. "Michael Traskan, here, Mr. President. The radiation levels are within acceptable limits for people with protective gear. Colonel Youngs tells us that there is no biological hazard. If I get the order, I can have teams inside in fifteen minutes."

"But what about the alien injured?" asked someone from the NASA group who did not bother to identify herself. "Can we hope to give them any real medical aid?"

"A good question," said the President. "What do you think Catherine?" He turned to the Surgeon General.

"Mr. President, I have to be frank with you: the chance of us being able to help these people is almost nil. We know nothing about their physiology, we have no drugs that we can safely use on them, the problems go on and on, sir. Minor injuries we might be able handle to a degree, but anything serious and we would probably do more harm than good."

"Perhaps we could get instructions from the aliens up in space," suggested someone.

"That would not be enough for critical injuries. And I must remind everyone that with every passing minute, the chances for any survivors grow less."

"If there *are* any survivors," interjected the Secretary of the Air Force.

"The aliens may just be using that as an excuse to come down here."

"Now we have no way of knowing that..."

A number of people began adding comments all at once and the discussion became general. There seemed to be a nearly even split between those favoring granting the alien's request and those against. Perhaps a few more in favor, but those against were more vocal. Bob Hancock sat and took it in. He, like most of the junior members of these groups, did not say anything. They all knew enough to stay out of the path when the Big Wheels were rolling!

And yet there seemed an obvious compromise solution that no one had raised. Hancock looked around at the others in the room. He felt sure they saw it as well as he did and yet no one had brought it up. He sat there struggling with indecision. It was always best not to draw attention to oneself in things like this. But still...

He looked down at the three gold rings on his sleeve.

What the hell do I have to lose?

"Mr. President."

Hancock stood up and spoke loudly enough to be heard. After a moment everyone was looking at him and he wondered if he had done the right thing.

"I'm Commander Robert Hancock, sir. Perhaps we could try a compromise: our people go in and bring out the alien injured. Then we turn them over to their comrades who can give them proper aid. The aliens do not get near the crash site, so we get what we want and the aliens also get what they want."

There was a moment of silence and then the President began to nod. "Yes, Commander, that is just what I was thinking myself. It is a good compromise and that is what we'll do. You folks up there get your teams into the ship at once. Also set up a site where the aliens can land to pick up their injured and give us back our own people. It shouldn't be too far from the crash site, obviously, but not too close, either. Meanwhile, we can contact their ship and tell them what we propose.

"Let's get moving people!"

* * * * *

"Let's get moving people," said Kay Youngs. The humans, who had been sitting comfortably in the arboretum, picked themselves up and slowly headed for the small craft hanger. Youngs almost had to drag Doctor Vasthare along with her.

"Colonel, we must make arrangements for future visits!" she said earnestly. "And to allow information and technology exchanges! We can't just leave now!"

"Doctor, I sympathize and believe me: I'm as interested in what they have to offer us as anyone—but first things first!"

"Colonel Youngs is correct, Doctor Vasthare," said the alien leader, as it walked along with them. Kay hated thinking of the alien as an 'it', but she had no clue if it was a 'he' or a 'she' or neither—or both for that matter! And in spite of having heard it several times, she was not entirely sure she could pronounce its name properly.

"There will be many opportunities for future exchanges. We hope that this will be the start of a long and mutually beneficial relationship."

"But Commander Keeradoth," persisted Vasthare, "there is no immediate need for all of us to return to Earth. I—and anyone else who wanted to—could stay to begin the exchange. Why send us down and then have to bring us back up?"

"An interesting idea, Doctor Vasthare, but I do not believe it would be practical at this time. In truth, we shall be so busy tending our injured—assuming there are any—and making repairs from the battle, we will have little time for anything else for a few days. In addition, I fear that unless we return all of you there may be some suspicions raised with your fellows on Earth about our good intentions. Forgive me, but our observations indicate that many Terrans are quite suspicious about such things."

"Suspicious! Paranoid you mean!" said Vasthare angrily. "This is the greatest event in our history; the greatest opportunity to learn we have ever been presented with, and those idiots down there can only see you as a threat!"

"Doctor..." said Youngs.

"It's a disgrace, Colonel, a disgrace!" continued Vasthare, in spite of Kay's attempts to calm her down. "To refuse the Somerans the right to mount a rescue operation! Their people may be dying and we are preventing them from being saved! I can't believe you did not argue harder to gain permission."

"Doctor, we all have our duty to carry out," said Kay, trying not to become angry in turn. "You have a very admirable devotion to your science and the quest for knowledge. I, on the other hand, am a serving officer in the military of the United States. I have a duty to carry out my orders—whether I personally agree with them or not."

"Doctor, Colonel, please," said the alien. "We are sure your people on the ground will make every effort to find our people. You need not fear that we will be insulted or provoked by the action of your government. After all, we are the trespassers here and it is only proper that we abide by your wishes."

"I'm glad you can see things that way, Commander," said Youngs. She smiled at the strange being. It made some odd motion with its head and its skin color lightened a shade. Was that a smile in return?

They reached the hanger and the humans began to board one of the small ships. Kay continued to stare at her host. The initial shock that these beings looked like the aliens on supermarket tabloids had mostly faded, but she was still amazed. It was too long a coincidence for Kay's tastes. Clearly, these aliens must have been visiting earth for quite some time and some people must have seen them. But all that stuff about abductions—was that true, too? There was going to be a lot to talk about!

Then another thought struck her. It had been growing in her since the fight in the spaceplane. There was something strangely familiar about the other aliens—the *Brak-Shar*. She could not place what it was, but she was sure she had seen something that looked like them as well.

But that's ridiculous! Where could I have seen things like that and not remember it?

"Colonel Youngs, thank you once again for your efforts on our behalf. I wish you a pleasant journey home and I look forward to speaking with you again."

Kay looked around and saw that everyone but her was now aboard the ship. She looked back to the alien commander and was startled to see it standing with an out-stretched hand. With a smile, she slowly reached out and took it—very gently. It was about the size of a ten-year old child's hand and seemed very fragile. Youngs gave it a gentle squeeze.

"Thank you, Commander. For saving us and for getting us home again. I hope that we will meet again."

Youngs released her grip and then stepped back and saluted.

"Permission to leave the ship, sir?" asked Youngs. The alien seemed startled and did not answer for a moment.

"Granted, Colonel," it said, finally. It made no attempt to return the salute. Kathryn Youngs boarded the alien craft and did a quick head count. Everyone was there—even Doctor Vasthare.

"Okay, folks, let's go home!"

Chapter Nine

Expedition Leader Keeradoth looked at the people standing around the meeting chamber. They were mostly the senior staff from *Seeker of Truth*, but several key members from *Nightpiercer's* crew were there as well. It was fortunate that two life pods had managed to escape before the ship crashed. That had been two local days earlier and there was now much to discuss.

"The Terrans have returned seventeen of *Nightpiercer's* personnel," said Keeradoth. "They say that there is little hope of finding more alive."

"Honored One, I am quite amazed that even that number reached us alive after seeing images of the wreck," said Nabrado, the senior medical officer. "The Terrans have expended every effort and extended us every courtesy."

"Except allowing us to attend them ourselves," said Valnadar, the senior survivor from *Nightpiercer*. Keeradoth could sense the anger. "Had we been allowed to, how many more of our comrades might have survived?"

"Some, perhaps," answered Keeradoth. "But the Terrans' caution is understandable: they are suddenly made aware that they are not alone in the universe. Their first impression of us is made during a desperate battle. Their people are attacked without provocation in orbit and death and destruction is rained upon them from the skies. Can we wonder at their reluctance?"

"And these Terrans put a very great importance on 'face' during negotiations," said Tandalin, Keeradoth's second in command. "Did you notice how Colonel Youngs and Doctor Vasthare insisted on a halfway meeting point when they first came on board? The Terran leaders now do the same thing. They insist we meet them halfway."

"They have not returned all of the bodies of our fallen as they agreed to," stated Valnadar.

"No, that is true," admitted Keeradoth. "They have secretly kept a few for study. Again, that can scarcely be wondered at. And considering the loss of life among their own just from the crash, they can hardly be condemned for thinking it justice."

"It dishonors their spirits, Expedition Leader. Forgive my impertinence, but you should have insisted."

"Our comrades died attempting to carry out this important mission, Valnadar. Do you suppose they would want the mission jeopardized for the sake of their mangled remains?"

"You mean 'further jeopardized', Honored One," said Tandalin. "The mission hangs by the barest thread—we should do nothing to fray it further, Valnadar!"

"The mission!" snorted Valnadar. "The thread has already broken! It is now just a matter of waiting for it to smash to bits when it strikes the ground!"

"You believe we have failed?" asked Keeradoth.

"You know my belief, Expedition Leader! We should have secured the wreck of *Nightpiercer* or, failing that, destroyed it. If the Terrans are allowed free access, they shall learn too much, too soon, and all will be lost."

Keeradoth noted the agitation in Valnadar. It had been like this since the survivors boarded *Seeker of Truth*. At first, Keeradoth had assumed it was because of their ordeal and the grief over lost comrades. But now... *Is there something Valnadar is not telling me?*

"Destroy the wreck? Not only would that destroy the remains of our comrades that you seem so concerned about, but it would kill many twelves of the Terrans who cluster about it. That would certainly destroy any further hope for the mission!"

Valnadar radiated anger, but said no more. Keeradoth felt pity for the senior survivor of *Nightpiercer*. The crew of that vessel, as was so often the case, had all been drawn from the same clan. Valnadar had not just lost friends and comrades, but kin.

"It is yet too soon to judge if the Plan has failed completely," said Keeradoth. "Until we know that for certain, we must proceed with the assumption that it may still succeed and shape our actions accordingly. First, what is the status of *Seeker of Truth?*"

"Honored One," said Tandalin, "the ship is fully functional although some damage remains to be repaired. Our spare parts were sufficient to replace the damaged mechanisms and we are now fabricating new spares. I regret that several of the hull breaches are too large to be patched properly. They can be sealed, but will not have the full strength of a proper repair. We have also expended nearly two-thirds of our missile supply. We are manufacturing more, but it will be many twelvedays before they are finished. We are also running short on certain raw materials and may have to dispatch survey parties to the outer system to find what we may need. Fortunately, we are unlikely to be engaged in combat again soon."

"Perhaps we can obtain what we need from the Terrans," suggested Nalorom, the Chief Technician. "They are eager to trade for our technology."

"It is a possibility," said Keeradoth. "As you know, I will descend to the planet to meet with many of the Terran leaders in only a few twelfthdays. It is likely that nothing of import will result from this. The Terrans spend much effort on ceremony and protocol but true progress takes place in smaller meetings. Still, as you say, Tandalin, we do not urgently need replacements for the missiles, so that may come later."

"We hope there will be no need," said Valnadar. "What certainty do we have that there are no more *Brak-Shar* on the way to this system?"

"None, of course, and we dare not become overconfident. But the nearest *Brak-Shar* base is nearly three-dozen light cycles away. Other ships may be in the vicinity, but even they would likely take cycles to reach here. The enemy ship certainly did broadcast messages announcing our presence before it was destroyed—messages that were powerful enough to penetrate our ComBarrier—but it may be many cycles before they reach anyone."

"So we may hope, Honored One," said Tandalin. "But even so, the enemy will eventually know of this world and our presence here. No doubt they will mount a major attack when they do. Many twelvecycles in the future that may be, but can this world be ready to face such an attack when it comes?"

"That is the task that lies before us," said Keeradoth. "*Seeker of Truth* was scheduled to return home and leave this mission to the crew of *Nightpiercer*. Obviously, we shall have to remain until the next ship arrives from home. Fortunately, that will be in only ten cycles. We will not have to wait here for another eight-dozen to be relieved. We shall attempt to carry out the mission until we can turn over our charge."

"And how will you do that, Honored One?" asked Valnadar. "I know that you disagreed with the new instructions that Senior Expedition Leader Dalranor had brought from the Council. What are your intentions?"

Keeradoth was silent for a moment. It was true that there had been a major difference of opinion between the new expedition leader and the old. Keeradoth felt that the Council's decision, based as it was on information five-dozen cycles out of date, could lead to a major disaster. But it was impossible to challenge the Council's will—and Keeradoth had no longer been in command. Now the situation was dramatically changed. Keeradoth was in command again—and the Council's instructions were entirely obsolete.

"Clearly the Plan as first envisioned can no longer be carried out, Valnadar," said Keeradoth. "The Terrans are aware of us and will be very watchful. The Council's instructions to attempt to take direct control of them is now impossible. Likewise, the original plan to gradually prepare the Terrans for meeting us and forming an alliance is obsolete. We had hoped to bring the Terrans forward slowly to this point, but contact has been thrust upon us both without warning. Now we must decide what to do. How can we best gain their trust and prepare them for what will come?"

"From the standpoint of their technology and industry, Honored One, they have not so far to go," said Naloram. "The key items are in place as we had planned. Still primitive, to be sure, but now merely a matter of upgrades rather than creation from nothing. With full cooperation, a single twelvecycle may be all that is required for them to have meaningful military potential."

"Full cooperation, you say, Naloram," interjected a new voice. "But that is the key, is it not? It has always been the key, these many long cycles. So much effort we have expended to assure that cooperation, but now all is chaos. We cannot predict what these Terrans will do now that they have learned of us."

All eyes turned to the speaker, Hablajin, the Chief Xeniologist.

"Truth, Hablajin," said Keeradoth. "This is indeed the key: can we win the trust of these Terrans? They have agreed to return our injured and now they agree to meet with us. Clearly, they hope to take advantage of the situation and learn of our technology. They do not suspect that the technology would have been theirs in any case. Can we use this hope of theirs to further our cause?"

"For a short time only, Honored One," answered Hablajin. "Perhaps a few cycles. Their greed and desire for knowledge and power will lead them on, but with each new thing they receive, their dependence upon us will grow less. We cannot hope to base an alliance on this alone."

"And their suspicion will taint all that we hope to do," said Tandalin sadly. "They will deduce we have been watching them for many cycles and they will suspect the worst."

"And well they might!" said Keeradoth. "For it is truth that we have greatly interfered with them over the cycles. Much of what we have done of necessity—and let us be truthful: out of ignorance and even foolishness—they would find repugnant. I fear greatly their reaction if they should learn the truth."

"Then we must prevent their learning or delay it as long as we might," said Hablajin. "I believe that our primary goal must be to instill in the Terrans a fear of the *Brak-Shar.* If we can convince them of their danger and focus that fear, we may be able to divert their attention from our... manipulation. Failing that, we may convince them that their only hope is in an alliance with the Race—no matter how they might feel toward us."

"Yes, Hablajin, you speak wisdom," said Keeradoth. "The Terrans know much about self-interest. They have nothing like the Consensus to temper their actions, but they will cooperate if they feel themselves to be in danger. It may be the key to salvaging this situation."

"Honored One?"

Keeradoth looked up in mild surprise, for it was Yitsaban who had spoken. Naloram's mild-mannered assistant rarely spoke at these meetings, although Keeradoth had much respect for the technician's ability.

"Yes, Yitsaban?"

"Honored One, I have been conferring with Pagnarath, the senior surviving technician from *Nightpiercer*. I have a matter of some urgency to discuss regarding the computers on the fallen ship."

"Yes?"

"As you know, Honored One, our efforts to guide the Terrans' computer technology was far more successful than we had anticipated and we are far ahead of schedule. We had hoped to take a more measured pace, but the Terrans started anticipating some of the advances and we had to move quickly just to keep them on the desired path. It was difficult sometimes and..."

Keeradoth remained patient. Yitsaban rarely spoke at meetings, but once started the technician could prattle on for a twelfthday if not stopped.

"Your pardon, Yitsaban," interrupted Keeradoth. "But you said there was a matter of some urgency?"

"I beg pardon in return, Honored One," said Yitsaban, clearly embarrassed. "I was trying to explain how the Terrans' quick progress forced us to take certain precautions. I was working with the chief computer tech on *Nightpiercer* to be assured that they took the same precautions. Unfortunately, the battle intervened and I'm not sure if...if... "

Yitsaban stopped speaking. Keeradoth and everyone else in the chamber was suddenly looking at Valnadar and one of the other *Nightpiercer* crew. They had been talking quietly together, but now they were radiating such hostility it was impossible not to notice. The other, Kantaval, suddenly spoke loudly and angrily:

"I say that they must be told!"

"Silence!" hissed Valnadar. "Dalranor did not wish it revealed!"

"Dalranor is dead!" retorted Kantaval. "This is a matter of the greatest import and Keeradoth must know!"

"I must know what, Kantaval?" asked Keeradoth. Every eye was on Kantaval and Valnadar. The latter was clearly furious but made no more attempt to stop the other from speaking.

"Expedition Leader Keeradoth, I must inform you of something that could have the gravest impact on the mission."

"And that is?"

"Honored One, *Nightpiercer* was carrying twelve Tadath-Belind aboard."

"What?!" Keeradoth's shock was so great it was nearly a tangible thing.

"It is true, Honored One," said Kantaval sadly.

"But how can this be? Senior Expedition Leader Dalranor said nothing to me of this!"

"When Dalranor discerned your opposition to the new direction the mission was to take, it was decided to withhold the information. Since you would soon be leaving for home, it was not considered urgent that you should know."

Keeradoth's thoughts were in turmoil. *How can this be?*

"Expedition Leader," said Valnadar. "The Tadath-Belind were in the lower part of the ship. It is unlikely any could have survived. It is even possible that their bodies would have been destroyed in the crash. The Terrans may never..."

"They will be found!" exclaimed Keeradoth. "And when they are, the Terrans will be enraged as nothing else we might do could!"

"As I urged, Expedition Leader: we should have seized or destroyed the wreck," said Valnadar.

"And now I see why you urged it so strongly! Disaster! This is a disaster of the first order!"

"We are monitoring the Terrans' communications, Honored One," said Tandalin. "There is no indication that they have found the Tadath-Belind. Perhaps they will not."

"You grasp at the wind, Tandalin. They will be found."

"What will you do, Honored One?"

"For now, I must go and meet with the Terrans. Pray to the Ancestors that they do not make this discovery while I am among them or you will have to select a new leader!"

Chapter Ten

"Congratulations, Bob!" said Captain Edward Osborne.

Robert Hancock looked up from his bagel and coffee and saw his friend standing next to the table in the motel's restaurant. He smiled.

"Thanks, Ed. Sometimes it pays to stick your neck out, I guess."

"Well, you deserved to get this a long time ago. Looks good on you, too," said Osborne, gesturing to Hancock's sleeve. The four gold rings of a captain shone there. "Ordained by the President, no less!"

"I don't know about that," protested Hancock. "The Army and Air Force coordinators here are both colonels. The Navy didn't want me to be outranked. But don't just stand there, sit down and have some coffee."

"Okay, but I can't stay long."

"You're really going to leave in the middle of this?"

"No choice. *Tennessee* will be ready for sea tomorrow. I have my command to think of, Bob—not that the boomers much matter anymore."

"Or the carriers, either, I'm afraid," said Hancock with a grim smile. "Obsolete dinosaurs, every one of 'em. 'The World Turned Upside Down'."

"It sure as hell is! And not just with the military!" said Osborne. "Have you been watching the news or reading the paper? People are just going nuts!"

"I know. It's been four days since the wreck and a day since the alien commander visited the UN and it's just getting worse."

"Hell, we may need the carriers and boomers just to keep order—even if they are dinosaurs."

"I hope it doesn't come to that, but you could be right. Riots all over the place. The people don't know what to make of it and it's driving some of them to violence. Religious fanatics and just plain wackos. Even the more sensible folks are pretty stirred up. The stock markets have stayed open for what? About twenty minutes total the last two days?"

"About that. The tech stocks are going berserk and the Feds keep shutting it down."

"Well, I'm not going to lose any sleep about the market," said Hancock. "I'm more worried about what the other countries are going to do. They're all demanding access to the wreck and making threats if they don't get it."

"The alien commander promised that everyone would benefit from the technology they had to offer," said Osborne. "You'd think that would satisfy them."

"Not a chance! They want to be here and get their own hands on the stuff."

"Any likelihood of that happening?"

"Don't know," replied Hancock. "Not my call, thank God. For the moment, I just have to do my job."

"And what is that job now?"

"Well, I'm officially a member of the 'Ship Investigation Committee'. For the moment our primary task is to do a complete survey of the wreck and inventory every item we find. We'll only try to figure out what it all means after we've done that. You sure you want to leave, Ed? I could use the help."

"You'll get along fine without this old dinosaur driver," laughed Osborne. "Besides, you have Melissa to help out. You did get her situation straightened out, didn't you?"

"Yup. She was scheduled for a summer training cruise after her leave. I had a little talk with the Academy and they agreed that this would be far more valuable experience. She's assigned as my assistant with the temporary rank of ensign."

"Bet she's glad to be out of that uniform of yours."

"Yes! She managed to get one that fits her—with the right rank, too," chuckled Hancock. "She's going to be a lot of help."

"Where is she now?"

"Actually, she's just about to go into the wreck."

"Really?" said Osborne, obviously surprised.

"Yes, the top priority right now is that survey. Frankly, I think it's because of all the outside pressure to get at the wreck. The NTSB doesn't want anything removed until the survey is complete, and the brass wants everything portable removed as soon as possible."

"That could take a while," said Osborne. "That thing's as big as a bloody aircraft carrier!"

"I know. The NTSB teams are being stretched thin, so Melissa volunteered to help out."

"Isn't that pretty technical work? She isn't trained for that, is she?"

"True, but they have some laser surveying tools that are mostly computer controlled—and you know how Melissa is with computers."

"Right," said Osborne with a smile. "She never met a chip she didn't like. But aren't you a little worried about her going in there, Bob?"

"She's a big girl now, Ed. She'll have all the proper protective gear and I sent Sokol along with her."

"Like I said: aren't you a little worried?" said Osborne with a grin.

"He seems like a good kid, Ed, and I know that Melissa is. I'm not worried."

"Okay, you're the boss, but I'd keep an eye on Sokol—he's definitely keeping an eye on Melissa!" said Osborne, and his grin grew larger. "Well, I've got to shove off, Bob. It's been great seeing you again."

"I'll walk you out," said Hancock, getting up from the table.

As they exited the motel, their ears were assaulted by the roar of a convoy of tractor-trailers heading toward the wreck site. Some were loaded with long metal tubes, while others had pallets loaded with building materials.

"What's all this?" asked Osborne.

"We're going to build a roof over the ship," answered Hancock. "Sort of a light-weight geodesic structure. The official reason is to contain any residual radioactivity—especially run-off from rain. The unofficial reason, of course, is to keep spying eyes—anyone's spying eyes—off the wreck."

"Sounds reasonable." Osborne stuck out his hand. "Good luck, Bob. If you get a chance, I'd sure like to hear from you."

"Will do, Ed. Good luck with your boat and a safe voyage." Hancock shook Osborne's hand firmly and smiled.

Hancock watched his friend walk toward a waiting shuttle-bus and then turned back to the motel. He already had a half-dozen reports he needed to complete but his eyes drifted over to the crash site. Melissa was over there now. In spite of his comments to Osborne, he was a bit worried about his daughter.

I wonder what she'll see in there?

* * * * *

Acting Ensign Melissa Hancock shifted the respirator so the straps did not pinch quite so much and then consulted her computer.

"Okay, we have to go this way about thirty meters and then there is a cluster of six compartments we need to survey."

"Right—ouch!" said Lieutenant Stephen Sokol, bumping his head yet again on the low ceiling. "I wish these guys had been a bit taller!"

"You and me both," agreed Melissa, who was stooped over as she headed down the corridor. "At least most of their lights still work."

"For what they're worth—too damn blue!"

It was true: the lights had a very blue tint to them. It added an eerie feeling to what was already an eerie place. Melissa had been eager to get in here and it had been fine near the entrance where there were plenty of other people around. But now that they were away from the others it was definitely a bit creepy.

Don't be silly! Teams have already been through all of these levels. The only unexplored parts are way down below. Get a grip on yourself and get the job done!

They reached the area indicated on her computer layout. This part of the ship was in good shape. There was hardly any wreckage at all in the corridor, unlike many of the other parts of the ship which were in much worse condition. The strangely shaped and ornately decorated door had already been opened by the rescue teams. Melissa ducked her head even lower and stepped through.

She had no idea what the function of this compartment was, but it seemed to be loaded with all sorts of equipment. Much of it was incomprehensible, but there were also things that looked very much like computer workstations. Some had broken loose from the deck and were piled up against the forward bulkhead, but others appeared to be intact. Several actually had symbols glowing on the video displays. They had strangely shaped keyboards, too. She took a moment to examine those. There were perhaps a hundred odd looking keys with various symbols on them. Letters, numbers, and special functions, she supposed—just like a human computer. Suddenly the place did not seem quite so strange any more. She reached out a finger toward one of the keys to see what might appear on the screen…

"Hey, no time for sightseeing, Ensign," said Sokol. "We have a job to do."

"Aye, aye, sir," said Melissa sheepishly. "May as well get with it. If you would be so kind as to set up the scanners, sir?"

"Right." Sokol took the pair of objects he was carrying and unfolded sets of tripod legs. It took a few minutes to get it set up properly but eventually they had two black globes about fifteen centimeters in diameter sitting atop slender poles several meters apart. Each one was just about a meter off the deck.

"Okay, all set," said Sokol.

"Well, hit the button and then stand back."

He did so and the pair retreated outside the compartment. After about ten seconds, lights came on at the base of the spheres but nothing else visible seemed to be happening. In this case, appearances were deceiving. Melissa knew that dozens of invisible lasers were rapidly scanning the compartment. This equipment was a standard tool for surveyors and engineers. It could create a three-dimensional computer image from the information it was collecting. When downloaded, the data would give them a perfect record of the compartment and everything in it. Every item and every bit of debris—as well as the walls, deck, and overhead—would be on file.

After about five minutes, the lights went out on the globes. "Okay, that should be it," said Melissa, stepping back inside. "Now let's see if I can do this right."

She had been instructed how to do the download with a handheld computer. She had run through it several times before entering the wreck, but she was still a little nervous. Standing next to the scanners, she entered the proper commands and was relieved to see everything work just as she had been told it would.

"Got it!" she said with a satisfied grin. "On to the next one."

Sokol did not bother to fold up the scanners for such a short move. They shuffled into the next compartment hunched over like cave explorers. The new compartment was much like the last one. It only took a minute to set up the scanners this time. Sokol hit the activation button and they retreated again. Five minutes later, they went back in. Melissa swore when the glove she was wearing caused her to hit the wrong command.

"What's wrong?" asked Sokol.

"Oh nothing, I de-selected the scanners by mistake. I just have to re-select them."

Melissa moved the cursor up to the 'select peripheral' box on the small screen and hit the select key.

"What the hell?"

"Now what?"

"Oh, the damn computer has gone nuts. The selection screen is full of garbage. Great!"

Sokol peered over her shoulder at the screen, which irritated her a bit. She did not particularly like the idea of looking like a klutz in front of him. But what was wrong? The selection pull-down was filled with line after line of text that spelled nothing recognizable...

"Wait a second," she said. "There's the scanner. It is listed here, but what's all this other stuff?"

"Who knows? Can you get the scanner selected?"

She did so and had no trouble downloading the data. She was scowling as they moved to the next compartment. What had caused that to happen? While she was waiting for Sokol to get the scanners set up, she called up the 'select peripheral' screen again. The same thing happened, but there seemed to be fewer lines of garbage this time. She glanced around the compartment and there definitely seemed to be less equipment in here...

No! There's no way! You're hallucinating, girl!

It was an utterly ridiculous notion, but it refused to leave her head. They got to the last compartment on their list to survey. It appeared to be a storage compartment. A lot of the items were smashed. She checked the peripherals again and there were only a few lines of text on the screen this time.

"Damn," she whispered.

"Computer giving you problems again, Melissa?"

"No...well, yes. Steve, this is crazy, but I think somehow my computer is listing the alien equipment as peripheral devices."

"What? But that's impossible."

"I know, but I think it's happening. Since we're done with our survey, I'm going to try something."

"I don't know, Melissa, we don't want to screw anything up..."

"Hey, if I melt down the computer, I'll buy NTSB another one."

Without waiting for Sokol to say anything else, Melissa moved the cursor over one of the lines of gibberish in the selection screen and hit the key. Immediately a new screen appeared. It was entirely gibberish, but there were things recognizable as selection buttons and the overall layout was completely familiar. She hit one of the buttons and got another screen. This time it included a picture. It looked like a landscape, but it was of no landscape that had ever existed on Earth. Several of the alien creatures could be seen in the foreground...

"Oh my God," whispered Melissa.

Sokol had been watching. "Melissa, how is this possible?"

"I don't know, but we've got to let someone know about this! C'mon! Let's find my father!"

* * * * *

"Melissa, what are you talking about?" demanded Hancock.

"Dad, my hand computer just accessed one of the alien devices on the ship! I was able to call up data from it!"

"How can that be, Squirt?"

"It can't! That's just the point! There is absolutely no way something like this can happen! At least not by accident." Melissa suddenly straightened up and her eyes went wide.

"Not by accident," she whispered again.

"What do you mean?" asked Hancock. He saw his daughter's 'deep thought' expression and did not press her when she did not answer immediately. He had accepted long ago that his girl was smarter than he was—at least in some things.

"Dad," she said after a few more seconds. "This cannot happen by accident—trust me on this. There are only two possible ways to explain what's happened. One is that the aliens have deliberately built their computers to be compatible with ours. If they have been around here for a while, that's not a problem—except for the 'why' question."

"Maybe so they could access *our* computers, Squirt," interrupted Hancock. "That's a scary enough thought, but it would make a bit of sense."

"Yes, it would, Dad—and you're right, it is scary. So maybe that area we surveyed was some sort of computer lab built to interface with our computers. But maybe not. Dad, on the way out I went into a few other compartments; I even snuck up onto the bridge. Most of the stuff there is a wreck, but *I was able to access things there, too!*"

"Hell," muttered Hancock.

"Why would they build *all* of their computers to be compatible with ours, Dad?"

"I don't know, but I have a feeling you're about to tell me."

Melissa grinned slightly but was all business again. "The only other option is this, if their computers are not a copy of ours—*then ours are a copy of theirs!*"

"Now wait a minute, Melissa," protested Sokol.

"Hold on, both of you," said Hancock. "That's quite a theory you've got Squirt, but it is just a theory. For right now the critical thing is to confirm what you are saying. We have brought a few of the devices out of the ship. I'll see if I can get hold of one for a little test."

"But, Dad! If the aliens are able to access our computers, who knows what they can do? We've got to tell people!"

"If they can, then you are absolutely right, Squirt. But if they can access our computers, they can probably access our communications as well. We've got to proceed very carefully."

"But..."

"No buts! I don't try to tell you about computers. You don't try to tell me about intelligence work! Okay?"

Chapter Eleven

Melissa Hancock swallowed nervously as the car turned into the entrance to the White House. She couldn't believe this was happening.

Maybe I should have just kept my mouth shut!

The last few hours had been a whirlwind of activity that had left her breathless. They had performed a test on an alien device and she had convinced her father that what she had claimed was really true. Then there had been phone call after phone call as her father worked his way up the chain of command. It had been difficult because he refused to say anything more than he had something of great urgency to discuss and that he could not do it by phone because it was not secure.

Melissa had been afraid that they were not going to be able to convince anyone, when suddenly there was a helicopter waiting and minutes later they were speeding toward Washington. The hour they spent in the air was more than long enough for Melissa to get extremely nervous.

The car stopped and they were checked through several layers of security and ushered inside. In the foyer, they were met by a woman in a Navy captain's uniform.

"Bob! What the hell is all this?"

"Hello, Captain," replied Hancock. "This is my daughter, Melissa. Melissa, this is Captain Janice Pescatore, my boss."

"Nice to meet you, ma'am," said Melissa.

Pescatore was frowning at her. "Nice to meet you. Your father says that you have made a discovery of extreme importance, Ensign. Would either of you mind telling me just what it is?"

"Not out here, Captain," said Hancock. "This really is hot and we have to be somewhere secure."

"All right, the President is going to meet us downstairs in a few minutes. Let's go."

An elevator took them down. And down. Melissa had heard that there were supposed to be secret rooms under the White House, but she had only half believed it. When the doors opened, a short walk brought them to a comfortable conference room. Several Secret Service agents were there and they were searched again. Melissa's computer and the alien device they had brought along were set out on the table. She could tell that the agents were not happy with the presence of the device.

"Is everything electronic turned off?" asked Hancock.

"All the phones, computers, faxes, and cameras have been unplugged," said Pescatore. "I've been promised that the sound recorder will be an old-fashioned cassette tape model. Bob, this had better be good! If you've made all this fuss over something trivial you better be ready to give that new stripe back! And probably all the rest, too!"

"Don't worry, Captain. I guarantee it will blow everyone's socks off."

In spite of her father's confident tones, Melissa was sweating. This had all been her doing. What if something went wrong and she could not prove what she was claiming? He father would be in serious trouble! They sat down and waited.

A few minutes later the President arrived with a half-dozen advisors and cabinet members and more Secret Service. Introductions took a few minutes and Melissa was shaking as she was presented to the Chief Executive.

"I'm told you are the one with the great discovery, Ensign."

"Y-yes, sir. I hope you'll think it's worth the bother, sir."

"Well, let's find out! Just what have you got?"

"Yes, sir."

With trembling hands, Melissa turned on her computer and much to her relief she was able to access the alien device just as she had done back at the wreck. The President and his advisors looked on in silence as she brought up screen after screen of alien data, including pictures and diagrams of incomprehensible objects. While she was doing so, Melissa gave her theories on how this was possible. Talking about computers, all her nervousness disappeared.

"But all the text is in the Roman alphabet," pointed out the President's Chief of Staff. "Even if it is gibberish."

"Yes, sir," said Melissa. "This computer's graphics are limited to standard text fonts. It can't reproduce the alien's alphabet, so it's just substituting symbols. The same thing used to happen with us if we got a foreign language document with unique characters."

"If I am understanding you correctly, Ensign," said the President. "There is no possibility of this being a coincidence?"

"No, sir. The odds against it happening by chance are truly astronomical. The fact that our computers' Dewies can interface…"

"Our what?" asked the President.

"I'm sorry, sir. For the last eight or nine years virtually every computer made has had the Dynamic Operating User Interface—Dewey for short—as part of its basic structure. This has allowed the wireless accessing of peripheral devices as well as universal compatibility of software."

"And the alien computers use this 'Dewey' system, too?"

"Apparently so, sir. It is the only way I can account for this."

"And these two theories of yours about how this could have happened, how confident are you in them?"

"I can't claim to have all the answers, sir," said Melissa, suddenly nervous again. "But if it did not happen by accident, then one system has to be a copy of the other."

"Surely it's more reasonable to assume that the aliens have deliberately copied our systems, Ensign," said a woman whose name Melissa had forgotten. "To accept the other would mean that these aliens have been manipulating our technology for decades!"

"Yes, ma'am, I realize that. But the fact that I could access alien devices all over their vessel might argue against it. Why would they rebuild all of their computers—computers that would have no reason to ever interface with ours—rather than just a few specially built for that job?"

The woman frowned, but did not look convinced.

"Excuse me, Mister President," said Roy Hertwig, the director of the National Security Council. "While the 'whys' and 'hows' of this are certainly important, I think we need to concern ourselves with the immediate effects first of all. If what Ensign Hancock says is true—and I tend to believe her—then we have to assume that the security of every single computer, every bit of communications we have, has been compromised."

The President nodded. "Captain Hancock, I assume that is why you insisted on our meeting in this fashion?"

"Yes, sir. If Ensign Hancock is correct, the aliens could have access to all our documents and be privy to anything sent or stored electronically."

"But we have safeguards," protested someone. "All the communications are encrypted."

"I'm sorry, sir," said Melissa. "While the alien computers run on the same basic principles as our own, I believe they are vastly more capable. This small device, here, appears to contain about a million times as much data as I can store in a human computer of equivalent size. If we assume a similar ratio in their computational capabilities, that would give the aliens more than enough muscle to crack any of our codes or security systems in a matter of minutes. And if my theory about them having guided our own computer development is true…"

"They'd know every trick we had," finished the President, nodding grimly.

"My God!" exclaimed the Chief of Staff. "With their space capabilities, they could have placed taps in all of our satellites—after they were in orbit!"

"I suppose that is a possibility, sir," said Melissa, a bit startled. She had not thought of that.

"And virtually all communications are sent via satellite these days," said Hertwig.

"All right, they can read our mail," said the President. "What should we do about it?"

"Sir, for routine matters—even routine secret matters—we should leave things as they are," said Hertwig. "First off, we have no choice. There's no way we can put the entire Federal Government back to paper and pencil on short notice! Second, if we tried to do so—even in a limited fashion—it would immediately tip off the aliens that we were on to them. As of this moment, I'm sorry to say, the only secret we have left is the one we are talking about right now—and the longer we can keep it a secret, the better off we'll be."

"You mean we won't demand that the aliens cease their activities?" asked the Chief of Staff in amazement.

"Not just yet, Aaron," said the President. "Roy is correct: right now we have an advantage. We know the aliens are reading our mail, but, hopefully, they don't know that we know. How can we best use that advantage?"

"Are you thinking of some sort of deliberate mis-information campaign, sir?" asked Hertwig.

"I'm not sure what I'm thinking, Roy. Frankly, I'm not sure what sort of mis-information I would even want to feed them at this point. I'm just looking for ideas."

"Sir," said Hancock. "I believe that what we need to know now, more than anything else, is the true motives of the aliens. They have come here professing friendship and a desire to help us. That might be entirely true—but it might not, just as easily. If we assume that the ship crash and our discovery of the computer compatibility is not part of some huge deception scheme, then there may be the possibility of accessing records from the wreck that could tell us the truth."

"But they're just gibberish, Captain," said the President. "How are we going to translate them?"

"A good point, sir. It may be very difficult, but we can also assume that the aliens have software specifically designed for that purpose. If we can find it, it could be the key."

"It's worth a try," said the President. "We'll have to set up a team and get to work on this."

"Sir, security is going to be a major problem," said Hertwig. "If word of this leaks out and the aliens get wind of it, they may take steps to erase the information."

"Yes. All right people, we need some ideas here. Foreign countries are demanding access to the wreck and aliens are reading our mail. Let's try and get a handle on this before something else comes up!"

* * * * *

Philip Harvey, field investigator for the National Transportation Safety Board, wished he could wipe the sweat out of his eyes, but the respirator mask was in the way. The heat from the cutting torch was making the air very hot. The fact that the alien metal—whatever it was—was extremely tough to cut was not making matters any easier.

Finally, the cut was complete and the twisted plate that was blocking the passage could be pulled aside. Harvey crawled forward a few meters and peered ahead.

"All right, the lights are out in there. Bring up some portables."

This was done and he inched along the corridor, carefully examining everything as he went. He forced himself to keep his mind on the job because he was discovering—much to his surprise—that he did not like enclosed spaces. He was a twenty-year veteran of the NTSB and had investigated dozens of plane crashes during those years. But most of those crashes had left little more than acres of scattered debris with little of the aircraft left intact. A few times there had been substantial pieces left and that could sometimes mean crawling around a cargo hold. But none of them had been anything like this.

He was fifteen decks down in the belly of an alien spaceship. He was acutely aware that he was surrounded by thousands of tons of metal. He did not like it one bit. The fact that this latest deck had been partially crushed by the impact did not help any. The rest of the ship was cramped and claustrophobic, but here, the distance between deck and ceiling was even lower. The crumpled bulkheads squeezed the corridors to the point they were almost impassable.

Harvey moved forward perhaps ten meters and came to a door. The impact had sprung the door loose from its mounting and he could pull it aside without cutting. He shone his light into the next compartment. It was choked with wreckage. He moved inside and looked around. The ceiling of the compartment looked to have been higher than normal before it had been crushed down, but other than that it looked like the rest of the ship.

Sweeping his light around the compartment he could see that on the opposite side the damage was even worse. He knew he was nearing the bow of the ship and it only made sense that this would be the case. He probably would not be able to get any farther forward without some serious cutting…

He froze.

There was something in the beam from his light. It was something he had seen far too many times before in his twenty years with the NTSB. It was something he had forced himself to become used to seeing.

But it was something he never expected to see here.

"Get a medical team down here!" he shouted over his shoulder. "Now!"

* * * * *

"All right, people," said the President, "I believe we have the makings of a plan. Let me summarize. We shall set up several secure facilities to process and study the information from the alien computers. These facilities will be completely isolated electronically. Their… Dewies …will be disabled and everything will be hardwired. There will be no direct electronic connections of any sort between these facilities and the outside world. Information will be brought in via disks that have been downloaded elsewhere.

"Personnel to man this facility will be drawn from the active military and reserves as much as possible, supplemented by specialists who have the proper security clearances. The primary goal will be to find a means of translating the aliens' language and discovering just what they are up to.

"Okay, are there any more comments up to this…"

There was a knock on the conference room door and a Secret Service agent stuck her head in.

"Excuse me, Mister President, but there is a call from Mister Traskan at the crash site. He says it is extremely important."

The President paused and then nodded. "Excuse me ladies and gentlemen, I'll take that and be right back."

The Chief Executive left the room. The others began discussing the plan of action. Melissa thought it was a good one. She was more amazed than ever at what she had started. *But at least they believed me!* She saw her father staring at her. He smiled and she smiled back.

"You did good, Squirt," he whispered.

Her father had never been stingy with praise for her while she was growing up, but it had never felt this good. She found herself blushing.

The door opened and the President returned. Melissa was instantly struck by the change in his expression. All through the meeting he had been serious but even-tempered and confident—just like a leader is supposed to be. But now! His fists were clenched and all the color had drained out of his face. He slowly made his way to the head of the table and sat down. He was silent for several seconds. There was not a sound in the room.

"Ladies and gentlemen," he began at last. "I've received some very serious news from the crash site. Teams exploring the lower part of the ship have found additional bodies—and a survivor."

Melissa was surprised. It was nearly five days since the crash. To find another survivor now was nearly miraculous—but why was the President so upset about it?

"I suppose we'll have to inform Commander Keeradoth to come and pick them up," said the Chief of Staff. "Although from what we've been talking about here I guess he already knows."

"We will do no such thing!" thundered the President. He slammed a fist down on the table and every person in the room was frozen at the sight of his anger. "Forgive me," he said after a moment. "No, Aaron, we will not be informing the aliens and frankly I don't give a damn if they find out about it! We will not be returning the bodies or the survivor, ladies and gentlemen, because the bodies— and the survivor—*are all humans!*"

Chapter Twelve

Expedition Leader Keeradoth stared at the blue and white planet grow-ing larger in the viewscreen. The clouds were sufficiently few enough to see the outlines of the eastern North American land mass and the shuttle's destination.

The Terran cities are such nightmarish things! How they can bear to live in them I cannot see. They are truly a strange species. And this 'New York' is perhaps the worst of all of them. Would that we could meet elsewhere.

Keeradoth had been to New York only three local days earlier to ad-dress the Terrans' United Nations. It had not been as unpleasant as feared. The locals were polite and friendly and eager to talk. It seemed likely that this new meeting would not be nearly as enjoyable.

They have found the Tadath-Belind. They do not say so, but it is true. And now they will demand explanations. What can I tell them except the truth? But which truth—and how much?

"Dalranor was a fool not to tell you, Honored One," said Hablajin sud-denly from beside him. "And Valnadar as well. To conceal such vital information! Madness!"

"They expected me gone. And Dalranor carried the word of the Coun-cil. I could have argued until the stars burned out and it would have changed nothing. They wished to avoid a confrontation—and no one could have foretold these events."

"You are generous, Honored One. Had we but known…"

"Then what, Hablajin? What could we have done? Sent missiles to de-stroy *Nightpiercer* before it touched ground? Destroyed it afterward, unmindful of the Terran casualties? Landed to take the evidence despite the Terrans' pro-tests? The first only was possible and I would have shrunk from slaying our own comrades even had I known of the Tadath-Belind."

"As would any of us, Honored One," said Hablajin. "But at the least we could have planned for this."

"Perhaps. But what is done is done. What may I expect from this meet-ing?"

"The Terrans are unpredictable, Honored One, and often irrational. They will slay themselves by the millions in internecine conflicts, and yet will expend measureless grief over a single person killed in some senseless ac-cident. It is probable that they will see the Tadath-Belind as victims of ruthless exploiters. Though countless millions of their own people are held in near-slav-ery or serfdom, they will fixate on the Tadath-Belind. Explanations on our part or descriptions of the kindness we have displayed may well be brushed aside in the emotion of the moment. I fear I have little advice to give, Honored One."

"Blame not yourself, Hablajin," said Keeradoth. "None foresaw this."

"What will you tell the Terrans, Honored One?"

"I have been asking myself that question. The truth seems the best, but will it be enough—or even believed?"

Hablajin fell silent and Keeradoth mused on the events of recent days. At least not all the news was bad. Protocols had been established for exchang-ing information with the Terrans. There was a great deal of uproar among the

Terran populace, but there seemed to be no immediate threat of a breakdown in order. Most had already accepted the notion of intelligent life beyond their planet, so the shock was not as great as it would have been fifty, or even thirty, cycles earlier.

One bit of good news was that small craft from *Seeker of Truth* had located the wreck of the *Brak-Shar* ship and were in the process of salvaging parts of it. Their task was made more difficult by the presence of Terran ocean-vessels with the same aim, but hopefully some of the enemy computers could be secured. *Brak-Shar* computers were relatively simple and easy to penetrate. Keeradoth hoped that some useful information could be gleaned from them.

That thought led to another—a far less pleasant one.

"What do you think of Yitsaban's warning about *Nightpiercer's* computers?"

"I think the warning must be heeded, Honored One. The Terrans are clever—in some ways far more clever than ourselves. I only wish Yitsaban had been more forceful at the meeting and warned us sooner."

"Yitsaban is rarely forceful. The news about the Tadath-Belind overshadowed everything else."

"There has been no indication that the Terrans have discovered anything about the computers on the wreck, Honored One. I have closely monitored their activities. Is there anything we can do to purge the computers?"

"We have been unable to establish contact from space," answered Keeradoth. "I have strongly considered sending down a drone, but the humans swarm over the wreck so thickly I fear the drone would be detected."

"Aye. And that could make things even worse."

As they spoke, the shuttle came in sight of the city. The bizarre spires, huddled close together, marked the center of the sprawl that extended in all directions. Even the nearby ocean and rivers seemed clogged with floating structures. They descended toward a newly constructed landing pad near the building for their United Nations—one of the more modest structures in the city. Keeradoth considered that entirely appropriate for the nearly impotent body that claimed to represent humankind.

The landing pad was surrounded by high walls to cut off any direct view from outside. The Terrans said it was for security reasons and Keeradoth believed them. The furor caused by recent events could well produce renegade Terrans willing to direct violence against the visitors from the stars. In the few moments before the shuttle settled behind those walls, Keeradoth could see thousands of Terrans clustered around pointing and gesturing excitedly.

A slight jolt told them that the shuttle had grounded. Keeradoth, Hablajin, and two assistants walked to the hatch. They activated their gravitational nullifiers and set them for standard. The hatch opened and they stepped out into the strange too-yellow light of the Terran planet. While it was fortunate that they could cancel out the excessive pull of this planet's gravity, they could do nothing about the smell of the air without wearing a mask—and that simply could not be done.

A small crowd of Terrans was waiting for them. Keeradoth felt the familiar uneasiness at being surrounded by these giants. Their custom of shaking hands was also very unnerving. The physical strength of the Terrans was frightening.

An enclosed passageway led from the landing pad to the building. More Terrans met them in the main lobby. The formal greetings took some time, but Keeradoth did not mind. The Race had even more courtesies than these Terrans. Reading their facial expressions was something Keeradoth had not mastered even after so many cycles, but there seemed to be a certain stiffness to their actions.

"What is their mood, Hablajin?" asked Keeradoth, switching off his translator, as they were escorted toward a meeting chamber.

"Difficult to judge, Honored One," replied the xeniologist. "All seem nervous, but they were that way during the first meeting. Some of those we met before seem wary, but there could be any number of reasons for that."

"Any number, but we know of one for certain!" snorted Keeradoth.

"At the least, there have been no outright expressions of anger or hostility, Honored One."

"Not yet. But as these Terrans say: the day is still young."

They were escorted to a large meeting room. It was not the huge assembly hall where Keeradoth had addressed them days before, but it was still built to Terran-scale and seemed enormous. Once again there were chairs waiting for them and once again they had to be rolled away when they reminded their hosts that they did not 'sit down'. It was just as well that they did not, since even seated, the Terrans were still taller.

There were more introductions and pleasantries. Keeradoth had trouble following all that was said even with the translator, but the basic concept was clear: this was a special committee to clear up some important questions that the Terrans wanted answered.

"Commander Keeradoth," said the head of the committee, "during your address to the General Assembly, you assured us that your intentions toward us were not hostile and that you wanted friendship with Earth. You also expressed a desire to give us technological aid and establish close relations with us. Some of that technological help has already begun and your people have started giving us information on advanced devices and techniques.

"For that, you have our thanks. However, since then there have been some disturbing discoveries at the wreck site that have raised several critical issues. The American Secretary of State is here and wishes to discuss these matters."

"I will attempt to answer the Secretary of State's questions, sir," said Keeradoth. A Terran male who Keeradoth vaguely recognized stood up. Distinguishing individual Terrans was no easier than judging their facial expressions.

"Commander Keeradoth, I will come directly to the point. Two days ago our rescue personnel discovered the bodies of eleven dead humans and a human who was still alive inside the wreckage of your ship. Examinations have shown that these are, indeed, human beings from this planet. We have to assume that they were forcibly abducted by you and your people. I'm sorry, sir, but around here, that sort of action is not considered friendly! Do you have an explanation?"

Keeradoth hesitated. The question had been anticipated, but what answer to give? And a survivor? Was that good news or bad?

"Mister Secretary," said Keeradoth after a moment, "I can understand your great concern. We have observed the protectiveness with which you hold your fellow humans. Forgive me, but we have also observed that you are a naturally suspicious species and often assume the worst of others. I am afraid that there is no simple explanation and perhaps it would be best to give you more background on our activities and goals."

"That would be appreciated, Commander," said the Terran. "In the light of this discovery, we are going to insist on knowing a great deal more about you."

"Very well, Mister Secretary. As I had mentioned in the first meeting, my people have been watching your planet for some time..."

"How long?"

The interruption irritated Keeradoth. It was true that the Terran was of a far higher rank in the relative scheme of things, but it was still rude.

"Our first exploration ship entered this solar system in the year 1832 by your western calendar."

"Eighteen-thirty-two!" exclaimed someone.

"My God! That long ago?" said another Terran.

The head of the committee called for order. "Please continue, Commander."

"That first ship spent several years observing your planet. We were very interested in your species. Intelligent life is relatively rare and we had never encountered a civilization in the stage that yours was at that time. Before that ship left, the crew acquired samples of many life forms... including humans."

"*Acquired samples!*" exclaimed the Secretary of State, clearly angry even to Keeradoth. "Kidnapped human beings, you mean!"

"As you wish, Mister Secretary. I cannot justify our actions to you, I can only tell you what happened. The crew of our first ship did not actually snatch humans away from their homes. After considerable observation they noticed that large numbers of humans died in accidents on a nearly continuous basis. Shipwrecks, in particular, were very common. The humans that were taken were those whose ships sank in situations where there was no hope of rescue and the humans most certainly would have died without our intervention."

"That is very interesting, Commander," said the American, "but instead of returning the people they 'rescued', they carried them off to the stars. That's still kidnapping in my book!"

"With all respect, sir, our people were not here as life-guards or a rescue service. Again, I cannot hope to justify our actions to you, but what is done is done. We are hoping that this will not ruin chances for our future friendship."

"That remains to be seen. So you took our people back to your planet? What was done with them there? And who are the people we found aboard the crashed ship?"

"The original group of humans—forty-eight in number—were taken back to our home world. They were treated with care and not abused. Naturally, they were very frightened and I cannot pretend that our attempts at kindness did much to allay their fears. I can apologize to you here, but such words are meaningless at this point.

"Once they reached my planet, they were studied. Means to communicate were found. We harmed none of them. Since that time, a small community of humans has grown on our world. There are now several thousand."

"As lab animals! Humans in a zoo!" said the Secretary of State loudly.

"They must be returned! All of them!"

"That will take some time, Mister Secretary," said Keeradoth. "It would take a minimum of sixty years to bring them here and I cannot promise that they would all want to come. The humans on my world are not prisoners now. They order their own affairs. I must also tell you that the humans you found on our ship were from this community. We have committed no further abductions. Those humans had volunteered to return here in hopes of smoothing our initial contact with you."

The American Secretary of State looked as though he was preparing another angry outburst, but another Terran spoke first.

"Excuse me, Commander, but I'm a bit confused. You have told us that your initial scout ship reached here about two hundred years ago. The humans that were found on the wrecked ship are descendants of the original group that was taken. And yet you told the Assembly a few days ago that your planet is one hundred and fifty light years away and that your ships cannot exceed the speed of light. Mathematics is not my strong point, but it seems to me that if it takes three hundred years for a round trip, you are about a hundred years short of having the necessary time to do what you say has happened."

Keeradoth was glad of this interruption. While it was impossible to sense the emotions of these Terrans it was evident that many of them were highly upset. Perhaps a few moments of technical explanations would serve to calm the mood.

"Yes, if we were forced to come directly here, limited to the speed of light, what you say would be true. Fortunately, there are other ways."

"Ways of traveling faster than light?"

"Yes. While our ships cannot exceed lightspeed, it is possible to build a transfer portal—a gate—between star systems. Using these, a ship can be instantly transported great distances. One of our colony worlds is approximately thirty light years from here. Our ships need slightly over thirty years to go between here and that world, but once there, they can reach our other worlds much more quickly."

"So you control many planets?" asked the American. "Why have you not constructed one of these 'gates' here—not that I think I want you to!"

"The gates are enormous, sir, and take much resources and many years to build. We did not have the resources here to do so. And they are so large, you doubtless would have noticed the construction."

"How large?"

"A gate is almost half the diameter of your planet's moon, although not nearly as massive."

There was a silence among the Terrans. Engineering on such a scale was clearly beyond their experience.

"I see," said the Secretary of State after a few more moments. "And do you have plans to build such a gate here in the future?'

"If satisfactory relations can be established between us then yes, construction of a gate would be very desirable. It would allow rapid communications and trade between our civilizations."

"It would also allow a full-scale invasion if that was part of your plan!"

"Mister Secretary, I say again that we have no hostile intentions toward you. I might also add that had we desired to conquer your world, we could have done so long ago—long before you could have had any hope of resisting."

Keeradoth realized that the last statement might not have been wise. These Terrans were full of pride and did not like to be reminded of their weakness. The Terrans were silent for a moment and Keeradoth pressed on.

"We Somerans have no hostile intent, but I must warn you of the danger presented by our enemy, the *Brak-Shar.*"

"Yes, you have mentioned them in your earlier address. There is no doubt that they acted in a very hostile manner against our personnel in space. But how much of their action was due to your presence? You told Colonel Youngs that they probably mistook us for your allies. If you had not been here, how do we know they still would have been hostile?"

"Mister Secretary, I will not try and tell you that the *Brak-Shar* are monsters, bent solely on conquest and destruction. We have been at war with them for many of your centuries, but we do know that they have peaceful relations with other races..."

"Other races? There are more civilizations out there?"

"Indeed, sir. The network of gates allows many civilizations to have trade and communications. We currently have contact with thirty-eight other civilizations and know of many more. The *Brak-Shar* are not irrationally aggressive, but they are our enemy and I believe that you must think of them as your enemy as well."

"That is very convenient for you," said the Terran in a low-pitched voice. "What if we decide to negotiate with these *Brak-Shar* and not become their enemy?"

"That is, of course, your decision," answered Keeradoth. "I am skeptical that you would be able to reach an agreement with the *Brak-Shar* that would guarantee your security and independence, but we will not prevent you from trying."

The Terrans pondered Keeradoth's words and Keeradoth did so as well. Could that work? A neutral Earth with the strength to enforce its neutrality would not be the ideal situation, but it could still be a gain. *But they must have the strength and we are the only ones who can give it to them. Will they listen?*

"Before we go on, I have a question about this abduction business," said another human. "Commander Keeradoth, you claim that there have been no more abductions since your original expedition. And yet there are countless claims to the contrary in the popular media. In addition, there are descriptions by these claimants that are remarkably similar to your physical appearance. How do you account for this?"

"We have not abducted any additional humans," said Keeradoth. "However, you must understand that we have never attempted to make contact with a civilization like yours before. We were uncertain about the best way to proceed. It was decided some years ago to show ourselves to certain individuals. Our hope was that the rumors that would ensue would make your people more comfortable with the idea that there could be other intelligent species besides your own. In this we have been successful. However, we did not take into account the active imaginations of your species or the... unpredictable... behavior of some of your individuals. The vast majority of the claims you see in your media are complete fabrications—certainly all the stories of abduction are."

"So, let me summarize," said the American Secretary of State. "You have been watching us for nearly two hundred years. You have abducted our people and trained them to be intermediaries between our races. You have been trying to manipulate our public opinion. Now you wish to draw us into your war with the *Brak-Shar*. Frankly, Commander, I don't like one bit of this. You say you come as friends, but this is the damnedest display of friendship I've ever heard of!"

Chapter Thirteen

"Help me, Colonel!" pleaded Major Gerry Messier. His hand reached out to her, but Kay Youngs could only sit in her seat and stare, her limbs as heavy as lead. The pistol in her hand weighed tons.

The alien was bent over Gerry and its clawed hands were ripping open the front of his spacesuit. Air and vapor gushed out. Then the claws found flesh and the vapor was followed by a fine red mist. Gerry's plea became a scream even though he should not have been able to talk at all with no air left in his suit.

"Colonel! Help me—*please!*"

Struggling like she was wading in glue, Kay released her safety harness and pushed herself at the alien creature. She was slow—hopelessly slow. But the alien seemed unaware of her presence. She grabbed the thing's elbow and pressed her pistol into its armpit.

She fired. Again, and again.

A thick brown fluid covered the pistol and her glove. She floated away from the alien.

But the alien still seemed oblivious. It finished disemboweling Gerry and then slowly turned toward her. Its helmet, which had been opaque, was suddenly transparent. An eyeless skull with a death's head grin stared out at her.

She raised the pistol again, but froze as she caught sight of it. The brown fluid was bubbling and boiling. As she watched, it turned a sickly green and the pistol melted away in her hand. She just gaped. But then her glove began to dis-solve…and then her hand…her flesh was on fire…the pain…

"*Noooo!*"

Kay sat bolt upright in her bed and fumbled for the light switch. The light revealed the familiar confines of her bedroom. She sat there, breathing hard and clutching her hand. She could still feel the pain. She was soaked in sweat and the sheets were twisted around her legs.

"God, that was a bad one," she said to the empty room.

She got her breathing under control and disentangled her legs and head-ed for the bathroom. She ran some cold water and splashed it on her face. Then she stared at herself in the mirror.

Another nightmare. She had been having them at intervals in the month since she had returned from space. Not every night, but far too often. She knew that they were rooted in what had happened up on *Lewis and Clark*, but she told herself that it was really the fatigue. She was tired, very tired.

First had been the endless debriefings. Anyone with more rank than her wanted to hear her story firsthand. Then had come the awards. They seemed to think she was some sort of hero. The medal and the promotion to full colonel were nice, but everyone who had not had the opportunity to debrief her, now wanted to honor her and rub elbows with her.

And there were the funerals. The funerals for her comrades killed on the station and on the ship and on *Lewis and Clark*. Too many funerals. Far too many flag-draped coffins. It had been grueling and this was the first night she had spent in her own home since she had left for the mission, so impossibly long ago.

And the nightmares would not stop.

This one had been the worst by far. They were all similar and Gerry died in every one of them. Sometimes she managed to kill the *Brak-Shar* and sometimes not. But this one had been new. The 'face' of the *Brak-Shar;* she had never dreamed that before. The dissolving gun and her hand...

Her hand.

She stared down at her hand and then held it up. It was the same hand she had always had. Unharmed. Undissolved. Why had she dreamed that? It was nagging at the back of her mind. It has been nagging at her for weeks. Something familiar, something she should remember. But what?

Kay left the bathroom and walked to the kitchen. She was still shaking a little and she turned on every light as she went. She got a beer out of the refrigerator and then sat down in front of the TV. She groaned when she saw that it was only 2AM and she doubted she was going to be able to go back to sleep.

Most of the channels were working again and she numbly flipped through them. The top story on the news networks was still the aliens and Earth's reaction to them. But there were actually a few other stories starting to creep in. Even the greatest event in human history could not keep the attention of people forever. The flap over the humans discovered on the ship was starting to die down, too. A lot of people—a *lot* of people—were still outraged, but the furor did not seem to be leading in any direction. Much smoke but little fire, thankfully. The sole survivor was still in a coma.

What a story she's going to have when she wakes up!

Kay continued to cycle through the channels. She did not really want to watch anything in particular, but she was just waiting until she was exhausted enough to try to sleep again. Suddenly, her finger paused on the remote.

Her wall screen was filled with the image of a dark, spooky corridor. It had all kinds of pipes and conduits and hissing steam and dripping water. Several people were being pursued by a hideous monster. It was a pretty unconvincing monster and Kay wondered how long ago this movie had been made. The monster was obviously a guy in a suit and no one did it that way anymore.

She shook her head and changed the channel again.

And stopped.

The nagging in the back of her head had finally crystallized into a memory. Or perhaps a memory of a memory. It was something she had seen long ago. A movie?

She got up and went over to her desk for her computer. Returning to her chair, she linked to the wall screen and began a search: *Science Fiction, Movie, Monster.*

She hit the enter key and a few seconds later she had a listing of dozens of Internet sites. She scrolled down the list. 'The Complete Index of SF Movie Monsters' seemed like a good choice and she called it up. She winced when she saw the length of the list.

Oh well, I'm not going to get any more sleep anyway.

But it only took a few minutes before she found what she was looking for. It was under the A's. An icy stab of fear pierced her belly when she saw the image.

"My God," she whispered. "That's it."

* * * * *

"That's it," said Colonel Youngs pointing to the computer screen.

"You're sure?" asked Captain Robert Hancock.

"Yes. I remember seeing this as a kid. Scared the hell out of me. Of course, some of the details are different. The *Brak-Shar* was wearing a spacesuit for one thing. Also, it did not have the big spines sticking out of its back and the legs bent the other way. Smaller, too, but the rest of it is pretty darn close."

"Not surprising about the legs," said Hancock. "They had to fit a person into the suit."

"Yeah, but the tail and the shape of the head are almost exact. This thing seems to have six fingers, but I don't remember how many the *Brak-Shar* had."

"Hmmm," said Hancock, fingering his chin, "it could just be a coincidence, Colonel."

Kay frowned. She did not know who this navy captain was or why she was at this godforsaken army post in some Maryland swamp, and his skepticism was not improving her mood. She had first gone to her immediate superior with her suspicions and had been passed from one person to the next. Each had nodded and asked a few courteous questions and then shuffled her off to someone else. Finally she was sent here.

In spite of her irritation, her first impression of Hancock had been favorable. She immediately spotted the aviator's wings on his uniform and it only took another second to see the North Korean campaign ribbon. He was pretty good-looking, too. About her age, or maybe a few years older. Sandy-brown hair with gray at the temples, a strong jaw and brown eyes. She thought she had found a comrade-in-arms who might listen to her, but now he was doubting her just like all the others.

"It would be quite a coincidence, Captain," she said, trying not to lose her temper. "That film was considered a ground-breaker and it spawned a number of sequels and countless spin-offs and rip-offs. For a whole generation, that image defined what a space monster looked like—and it just happens to look like a *Brak-Shar*. And there is more," continued Kay before the captain could break in. "Look at these other images from the same time period." She typed in more commands on her computer. "They look remarkably similar to the Somerans, don't they? And in every one of these films, the aliens are friendly and sympathetic."

"What are you suggesting, Colonel?" asked Hancock.

"I'm not entirely sure, Captain," admitted Kay. "My suspicions are that the Somerans have been using a subtle—and very long term—propaganda program to condition us. To make us sympathetic toward them and just the opposite toward the *Brak-Shar*. Not that they would need to do much to make us dislike those creatures!"

"That's quite a theory, Colonel," said Hancock. "As I recall, some of those movies were made by the top filmmakers of that era. Are you suggesting they were in league with the Somerans? Or controlled by them somehow?"

"I'm not really sure about that either, Captain." Now she was getting annoyed. Did he expect her to have *all* the answers? "But it would not really take collusion or control, would it? Just a few suggestions dropped in the right place, perhaps. I don't know and I suppose I'm just wasting your time, too."

The captain looked at her with a thoughtful expression. "Excuse me for a moment, Colonel. I need to make a call and I'll be right back." He got up and left the shabby little room they had met in. He was gone a good twenty minutes and Youngs was fuming by the end of it. When he returned he sat down without an explanation or apology and stared at her for another minute.

"Yes, that's quite a theory you have, Colonel," he said at last. Youngs bristled. "But as it happens, you are absolutely correct."

"What?" asked Youngs.

"I said you are correct. Now come with me and I'll show you how we know."

He escorted her out of the building to the adjacent parking lot. Shortly, they were driving toward some unknown destination on the base.

"What's a navy captain doing on an army base?" asked Kay after a few minutes.

"Aberdeen was a convenient location, Colonel," answered Hancock. "It's about halfway between Washington and the crash site. Plus it has a lot of room and there is plenty of civilian traffic coming to see the Ordnance Museum, so we can have people come and go without attracting a lot of attention."

He glanced briefly over at her. "I have to warn you that what I'm about to show you and tell you is absolutely top secret, Colonel. That phone call I made was to get clearance for you. We want you as part of the Project, so if you have any reservations, now's the time to back out."

"The Project? Just what sort of project are we talking about?" Kay wasn't sure she liked the sound of this.

"I can't give you any details until we get to the facility, but I'm sure you have already guessed that it involves the aliens. We're doing some very important things here and I think you'd be a valuable member of the team."

Kay thought about it, but not for long. "Well, I guess I'm pretty much out of a job as a spaceplane pilot. I hate to think about how obsolete those things are now. But I am a pilot, Captain. That's where my interest has always been. You're a flyer, too. You know what I'm saying. I don't want to be chained to a desk forever. If we can get copies of the aliens' ships—buy 'em, borrow 'em, or build 'em ourselves—I damn well intend to be one of the people flying them!"

"I *was* a flyer, Colonel," said Hancock and there was something in his tone that made her look at him closely. "But I do know what you are saying. I can't make any specific promises, but I think you would be in line to get a crack at anything we can come up with."

Kay thought for a few more seconds. "Okay, count me in. So what's the big secret?"

"I'll tell you when we get to where we're going. For now, just enjoy the ride."

Kay frowned and looked out the car window. There were dozens of antique armored vehicles lining the road. She didn't have much interest in them and they were soon left behind as they headed into less frequented parts of the base. Kay glanced at Hancock again.

"I see you were in the NK operation, Captain. What ship?"

"I was a squadron commander on the *Ronald Reagan*. I know you were there, too, Colonel."

"Yes," said Kay. "It seems like a long time ago. But you were on the *Reagan*? I remember how some of you folks helped us out with those SAM batteries during the first week. We owed you big time for that one."

"Yeah, that was us. And it was our pleasure, Colonel."

Hancock smiled at her and she smiled back. Her earlier irritation had faded and it was hard to stay angry at someone who had saved your ass—no matter how long ago.

Another ten minutes of driving brought them to a large building that looked like a warehouse. There were a few vehicles parked around it, but nothing at all to draw attention to it.

"Here we are," said Hancock. "I'm afraid you'll have to leave your computer, your phone, and any other electronic device in the car. I'll explain when we're inside." He parked and they walked to the entrance. She noted that there were no sentries outside—rather strange for a high security location.

There was security inside the building, however. Several MPs with assault rifles watched them carefully. An officer was on duty at a desk. He looked at Hancock's ID carefully although he seemed to know him.

"This is Colonel Youngs. She's joining the team. Here's her authorization." He pulled a paper out of a pocket and handed it over. "That was sent through while I was on the phone," he explained to her.

"Okay, Captain," said the officer after a minute. "Everything checks out. We'll get an ID made up for the colonel."

"Thanks. Come this way, Colonel."

They passed through another set of doors. The inside of the building was nearly all one huge space. It was filled with hundreds of perfectly ordinary office cubicles. Each cubicle had a computer and a person bent over it.

"Well! I can see why you wouldn't want word of this to leak out," said Youngs. "What would people say if they discovered the Federal Government had bureaucrats?"

Hancock laughed. "It's not quite what it seems, Colonel. Each and every one of those people are translating computer files from the alien ship."

"What?" said Kay in shock. "But how?"

"It's complicated, but four weeks ago my... one of our people accidentally discovered that our computers are compatible with the aliens'. Before you tell me that's impossible I'll tell you that it is possible—because the aliens planned it that way."

"What? I... I don't understand."

"We've got evidence that the aliens have been manipulating our technological progress for decades, Colonel. For some reason they wanted our computers to mesh with theirs and they have managed to see that it happened."

"My God," said Kay. "And just a little while ago you were razzing me because I thought the aliens were giving ideas to film directors! This is a hell of a lot bigger!" Kay paused and then went on slowly. "But for them to have done this..." She looked at Hancock in amazement. "You're not honestly suggesting that the richest man in the world, one of the most renowned entrepreneurs of the age, was in league with aliens?"

"No, Colonel. As far as we can tell there was no active cooperation between any humans and the aliens—but we've only scratched the surface on this, we could be wrong. For the most part, it seems like they did their work electronically. Once they had the Internet in place…" Kay looked at him sharply. "Yes, that was their doing, too—apparently it was a major objective for them. Once that was in place, they could just drop e-mails into the 'inbox' of various technicians. We've found messages in the aliens' files that direct software engineers to pursue certain lines of research and even include sample code."

"But didn't those people ask where the stuff came from?" demanded Kay.

"As far as they knew it came from their supervisors. If any of those supervisors ever got suspicious, they must have kept their mouths shut because…"

"Because they could take credit for it that way," finished Kay.

"Right," smiled Hancock.

"But what about before the Internet was in place?" asked Kay. "How did they plant their ideas then?"

"We're less certain about that," said Hancock who was frowning. "We've got some clues, but frankly, they're even scarier than what I've told you so far."

"Scarier? How?"

"We've found some references to individuals being 'implanted'. The context suggests that it was an idea or data that was being implanted rather than some physical object, but we aren't sure."

Kay shook her head, trying to take it all in. She stared at the rows of people working away.

"You said they were translating the aliens' files. Even if you could access the computers, how did you crack their language?"

"Well, that was a lot easier than we expected and the Somerans gave us the clue we needed themselves."

"How?"

"Do you remember how Commander Keeradoth was able to talk to you on the ship and how he talked to the people at the UN?"

"Yes! He had that medallion around his neck."

"Exactly," said Hancock. "A translator device of some sort. We found a number of them on the wrecked ship. We could access the software in them, too. They were only set up to translate spoken human words into the aliens' language and vice versa, but by analyzing the binary code, we were able to find similar programs in other computers. A little trial and error, and a fair amount of luck, and we found a translation program that converted their written language into ours."

"Yes, they'd need that to create their fake e-mails and all," said Youngs, nodding. "So now you have access to all their records?"

"Yes, and there are too damn many of them. We're roughly guessing that we have about ten thousand Library of Congresses to translate. Their records are well organized, but finding what we really want is still very difficult."

"You seem to have found quite a lot in spite of that, Captain. You were saying that you have information about the movies and the *Brak-Shar*?"

"Yes. There is definitely some evidence that the Somerans have been influencing the media. Not just the movies, but television and the publishing industry as well. Back in the 1930's, 40's, and 50's, monsters from space were always exactly that: monsters. But starting in the 60's there was a distinct trend away from the aliens-only-as-monsters theme. One of the classic TV shows, in particular, presented a vision of the future that had humans and aliens working together as friends."

"Yes, I remember that—although it was a bit before my time," she added hastily.

"Mine, too," said Hancock grinning at her. "But the Somerans were in that up to their eyebrows, it seems."

"They don't have eyebrows," said Youngs.

"True, but anyway they were involved in a lot more than your movie, Colonel."

Kay looked around the huge room. Hundreds of people were working there, oblivious to Hancock and herself.

"I'm a fighter jock, Captain, not a computer jock. Just what do you expect me to do in this operation?"

"There's a lot to be done, Colonel," answered Hancock. "What you see here is just one part of the operation. The aliens' records are downloaded onto chips either right at the crash site or close by. Then the data is brought here on chip and transferred to these computers where it is translated. The translated data is then backed up onto chips again. Several copies are made and sent to different secure locations. Our immediate worry is if the Somerans discover what we are up to they might try to insert a virus into the data from the crash. Then, when it gets here, it could wipe out all our computers and the data. By backing it up and getting it away from here, we hope to forestall that.

"As each item is translated, the operator tries to categorize it. From there it goes to the next level of analysis. We have different teams working with different types of data. They further categorize it and tag things of particular interest. Obviously there is far too much stuff here to really look at each item very carefully, so we have to try and sort out the critical items.

"Those items are sent to the senior analysis teams who try to put it into some sort of order. Finally, the top analysts have to make sense of it all. Figure out what really is important and present it to the brass."

Hancock paused and looked at Kay. "We want you as part of that group. With your experience on the Someran ship and your general expertise in space affairs, your insight could be particularly valuable, Colonel. But be ready for some grilling: we have weekly meetings with the Joint Chiefs and the President to pass on what we have found. They want answers to their questions and they need them now. They want to establish a policy for dealing with the Somerans and they can't do that until we know what they are really up to."

Kay looked at Hancock in surprise. In spite of her suspicions about the aliens and what they had been doing with the media, in spite of the technological meddling Hancock had revealed to her, she still regarded the Somerans as friendly creatures. After all, they had saved her ass, too. Some of their methods might be questionable, but she did not think they intended any real harm. Hancock's tone indicated he felt very differently.

"You don't think they've been telling us the truth about their motives?"

"I'm not sure, Colonel. I don't think they are truly hostile, but they certainly have not told us the whole truth about what they want. They have their own agenda here and I am beginning to suspect that their whole moral outlook may be quite a bit different than ours."

"How do you mean?"

"I think they have taken the old saying of the end justifying the means to limits we scarcely imagined, Colonel." Hancock's voice was grim and his expression matched his voice. "I just hope the brass can hold off for a while longer."

"I'm not sure I'm following you, Captain," said Kay hesitantly.

"Keeping this operation a secret is vital. And we don't just have the Somerans to worry about, but other nations as well. We don't dare tell anyone about this for as long as possible. Unfortunately, some of the information we are coming up with is very disturbing. Some very important people are pressing to confront the Somerans with it and that would give the game away."

"What sort of information, Captain? Or do I really want to know?"

"I'm starting to wish I didn't know about it, Colonel. But you will need to know. C'mon, I'll show you."

Chapter Fourteen

"So, Doctor, am I making any more sense to you?"

Usha Vasthare looked at the strange creature on her monitor and smiled. "I think so, Nalorom, but I am an engineer not a physicist, so you will have to forgive my slowness."

"Not at all, Doctor, your grasp of this is very impressive. But perhaps a simpler visualization is in order. The primary maneuvering drive on our ships is gravity based, as you know. The drive creates an artificial gravity well in space-time. A sort of 'dimple' in the fabric of space, if you want to imagine a three-dimensional analogy for it. The ship will then slide 'down' this gravity well, accelerating all the time. Since the 'dimple' moves with the ship, the ship can never reach the bottom of the well and will continue to accelerate. By changing the location of the 'dimple' in relation to the ship, acceleration in any direction is possible. Naturally, since this is a gravity-based acceleration, it affects the ship and its contents equally, so the crew feels no acceleration affects at all."

"Yes, I can see that, Nalorom," said Usha. "But I'm still uncertain about where the energy for this is coming from. When I compare the amount of power needed to produce the effect with the kinetic energy gained by the ship, there is a great inequality. Perhaps I'm missing something, but it seems like you are getting something for nothing here and we are taught that is impossible from day one."

"Ah," said the alien. "I see your difficulty. No, Doctor, we are not cheating entropy or thermodynamics, but the energy is not all coming from the ship's power plant."

"But then where?"

"You are probably aware of some of the recent discoveries your own scientists have made concerning gravity. It does, indeed, propagate through multiple dimensions. We are tapping the energy from those other dimensions."

Usha shook her head. This was very confusing, but it obviously did work.

"A good analogy would be one of your earthly wind-powered sailing vessels. Such a ship has no 'power plant' at all. It borrows energy from the wind in order to move. Our drive does the same thing except we use power to create the 'sails' instead of canvas. I can assure you that for the universe as a whole, energy and momentum are conserved."

"I think I understand," said Usha. "But doesn't a gravity well of that strength have...detrimental effects on things in the vicinity—like planets?" asked Usha. "In fact, wouldn't your maneuvering drive do nasty things as well?"

"Fortunately not, Doctor," said the Someran. Usha could not be sure, but it almost sounded like the translator device was adding a tone of amusement to the synthesized voice. "The 'dimple' created by the drive does not create a far reaching gravity well the way a large mass would. Its effects only extend a short distance beyond the ship."

The alien paused for a moment and then went on. "There have been attempts to use the drive effect as a weapon, but, thankfully, with no success."

Usha nodded. She was well aware how technology could be misused. Had she not left her native land rather than see nuclear energy misused in just that way? She banished that thought from her mind. This new technology that the Somerans were showing her was not going to be misused! With their help, humanity would soon have a space drive that would open up the solar system— and eventually the stars, too. And Usha would be a part of it. The thrill of that prospect could not even be dimmed by the fanatics and terror-mongers who were denouncing the aliens.

This whole fuss over the humans who were taken away so long ago and the return of their descendants was ridiculous. Humans had done exactly that countless times in the past. Explorers carried off the local inhabitants time and again. And the Somerans had actually rescued people who would have died otherwise. Why did people always assume the worst about others? It had been two months now since the crash—time to get over the fears and on with business!

"I have been studying the plans you sent us, Nalorom," said Usha after another moment. "It appears that most of the items for the drive can be constructed using our fabricators, but there will be certain components I doubt we can make ourselves—at least not yet."

"Yes, we expected that to be the case. We will be very happy to supply you with what you need," said the alien engineer. "It will be an honor to help you join the community of space-faring races, Doctor."

The alien's words sent an excited shiver through Usha. She was part of a team of scientists and engineers who would take the Somerans' technology and put it to use. Right now they were making plans for a small spaceship. With the anti-gravity devices it would incorporate, it could be constructed right here on Earth and then go anywhere in the solar system. The time savings in construction would be enormous. In just a few years humans would be out there, exploring their universe. She scarcely even regretted that all the effort she had put into the ship up in orbit was now pointless.

"I can't begin to thank you and your people enough, Nalorom," said Usha. "But we must get back to business. One major question I had about the drive was…"

Usha was interrupted by a beeping and then an icon appeared on her monitor. She had a priority call coming in. She was irritated by the timing of it, but she excused herself to the Someran and then switched to the new message. The face of her division supervisor, Alfred Buxton, appeared on her screen and he did not look happy.

"Yes?" said Usha.

"Doctor Vasthare, I'm afraid I have to ask you to stop what you are doing and come to the main conference room."

"But I'm discussing the plans for the drive with Nalorom," protested Usha. "Can't it wait?"

"I'm afraid not, Doctor. This is coming right from the top. Please conclude your call and join us in the conference room."

Usha frowned. She could not imagine anything that could possibly be important enough to justify this. She sighed and then did as she had been asked. Nalorom did not seem upset by the interruption, but Usha was. She had come to genuinely like the Someran during their numerous discussions and she felt like she was being rude.

She left her office and walked to the main conference room. As she entered, she immediately sensed that something was wrong. The other engineers and scientists were all muttering angrily.

"What's going on?" she asked one of the others.

"I'm not sure. Some sort of nonsense about cutting contact with the Somerans!"

"What? Why?"

"I don't know. There's going to be some sort of announcement in a few minutes."

"There's got to be some sort of mistake," said Usha in a daze.

"I sure as hell hope so!"

Usha found a chair with a growing sense of dread. What was happening? Had the paranoids finally convinced someone important that the aliens were a threat? The thought of losing what the Somerans had to offer was too bitter to stand. What could she do? After a few minutes, Buxton walked to the front of the room and called for quiet.

"All right, I know the rumors are flying here, but please calm down. All I know is that we have been ordered to break off communications with the Somerans until further notice." There was a growl from the assembled people. "I don't know if this is just temporary or how long it will last or the reason for it. There is going to be a tele-conference in just a few moments with Washington. All I can tell you is to sit down and stay calm until we get some answers."

The announcement did not mollify anyone, but since there was no one to focus questions—or anger—at, the people found seats and waited. They talked among themselves, but Usha did not feel like talking. She alternately felt like crying or throwing breakable objects. Finally, the main screen lit up. It showed a room full of people, none of whom Usha immediately recognized. Far too many of them were wearing some sort of uniform. A man not in uniform stood up.

"Good afternoon, everyone. I'm Walter McCollough, Secretary of Defense. We have called this conference to inform you of some very critical matters that have arisen concerning our dealings with the aliens. There are currently eight other locations tied into this conference and in about half an hour we will be linking with the United Nations where a special session is going on.

"I'm going to begin by letting you in on a secret. For the past two months we have been downloading and translating files from the wrecked alien ship."

There was an excited stir around the room. Usha was amazed. How could that be—and why hadn't she heard about it?

"I'm not going to give you the details of how we accomplished this right now. You'll be able to get that information later. For now it is sufficient that you know we have been able to do it. There have been large numbers of people working on this. Naturally, we have only scratched the surface of the huge volume of data, but we have discovered some very important—and very disturbing—information." The man paused and scowled. "I deeply regret having to inform all of you that the President has ordered all contact with the Somerans to be severed—permanently."

"What!" exclaimed someone. "Why?" shouted another. "That's insane!" The angry babble continued in spite of the fact that the sound pickups were not on and McCollough could not hear them. Apparently he could see them, however.

His eyes darted from side to side as though he was checking a number of monitors.

"Please," he said after a moment. "Calm down and I will explain the reason for this."

It took a few minutes but eventually order was re-established. Usha just stared at the screen blankly. This couldn't be happening!

"I can understand your dismay. This is a very unfortunate situation. For those of you involved in technical exchange, I want to mention that we have every reason to believe that the records we are translating will have the same data as you are receiving now."

"But with no help to figure it out, you idiot!"

"Do you have any idea how much longer that is going to take us?"

"Quiet, everyone!" shouted Buxton. Usha shook her head. Having the data would help, but her colleagues were correct, it would take far longer to make use of it. McCollough was continuing.

"I am sure that many of you are upset by this turn of events, but I believe the President was justified in taking this action. In addition to the technical data, we have uncovered information on the Somerans' activities here on Earth stretching back many decades. Frankly, that information is shocking."

That seemed to get people's attention.

"There has been a systematic and long-term program to manipulate our technology. They have been spying on our electronic communications—I have no doubt they are listening in on us right now. They have influenced our media to precondition our opinions prior to contact. They have watched and tinkered with almost every part of our culture and society."

Usha just gaped. It did not entirely surprise her. Some of the things that the Somerans had let drop during conversations hinted at some of the things that McCollough was saying. But none of that was grounds for breaking off contact!

"If it were just these things," continued McCollough, "we might have been able to tolerate it. However, we have discovered that the Somerans have also taken more direct action in trying to control us. They have actively interfered with the political processes of virtually every nation on Earth. And they have used as their unwitting instruments, men whose policies we can only term as abhorrent." At this point, McCollough's voice became choked with anger.

"These are some of those men."

An image flashed up on the screen. It was the picture of a man. Usha recognized him immediately. Even though he had died over fifty years before she was born and had never set foot in her native India, she knew him. She sucked in her breath.

"Vishnu the Merciful," she whispered.

* * * * *

Usha was dimly aware that the United Nations session was starting. She was in as great a state of shock as she had been after the *Brak-Shar* had massacred her comrades on the ship. Betrayed. Once again, her trust had been betrayed. The government of her home country had betrayed her long ago and now the Somerans had done so again. That dismal realization wrapped her brain in a shroud. After a few minutes she heard angry voices coming over the speaker and she forced herself to look up and pay attention.

The screen was now divided into two sections. One showed the Secretary General of the United Nations, Lars Sjolander, while the other showed a Someran. It was Commander Keeradoth.

"So then, Commander, you admit to manipulating our technological development?" asked Sjolander.

"It would be pointless to deny it, Mister Secretary," replied the alien. "You have found the evidence, it would seem. But we did so only to make the use of our technology easier for you."

"And what of this so-called 'ComBarrier' that we have found references to? What is the purpose of that?"

"The communications barrier is a system of satellites circling your planet at a distance of approximately five hundred thousand kilometers," answered Keeradoth. "They use a gravity-based technology to scramble any incoming or outgoing signals of intelligent origin. They were put in place to protect you—to keep the *Brak-Shar* from detecting your radio and television broadcasts."

"And it also isolated us, isn't that true?" demanded Sjolander. "For years we have been listening, searching, for signs of intelligent life beyond Earth. But we were never going to find it thanks to your meddling!"

"It seemed the best course of action," said Keeradoth.

Usha was startled. The Somerans had been keeping them isolated? Denying them scientific knowledge? Betrayed again! For the first time, anger flared in her at the aliens.

"And what of the humans we found on your crashed ship?" demanded the Secretary General. "You lied to us about them, didn't you? You said they were to smooth initial contact with us. What you meant was they were to infiltrate our society! Your own records tell us that!"

"Then it would be pointless to deny it," said Keeradoth.

"So you have manipulated our science, kept us ignorant of surrounding civilizations, and planned to plant your agents among us," stated Sjolander. "That by itself would be a matter of great concern to us, Commander. But there is more, isn't there? You have also used some sort of mind-control—'implantation' you call it—to make humans do your bidding."

The alien was silent for a few seconds. When Keeradoth spoke, his voice was as emotionless as before. "The implantation process involves introducing ideas into the thoughts of a sleeping subject. A small drone device is used to perform the task. There is no harm to the subject and it is not actual control."

"Oh really?" said Sjolander hotly. "There is evidence of over seventy years of this activity. Hundreds of humans have been 'implanted' with your ideas! Everything from ideas for movies and television shows to…to…" Sjolander's voice grew angrier. His face turned a bright red and he sputtered to a halt. It took him a moment to recover his poise.

"Tell me, Commander, do you recognize this human?" Sjolander pressed a button on his desk and the screen split into another section. The new section showed the picture of a man in a uniform. A man with a strange mustache. It was the same picture Usha had seen earlier. It was a picture that almost anyone on

Earth would recognize. Keeradoth was silent. Everyone in the room with Usha was silent. There was an agonizing anticipation over what the alien would say—or wouldn't say—next.

"Adolf Hitler, Chancellor of Germany from 1933 to 1945," said Keeradoth finally. Usha sagged in her chair.

Sjolander took a deep breath. "And this one?" A new picture appeared on the screen.

"Joseph Stalin, ruler of the Soviet Union from 1924 to 1953."

"And these men?" a half-dozen smaller pictures flashed onto the screen.

"The military and political leaders of the Japanese Empire prior to and during the Second World War. I'm sorry, but I do not recall all the names."

"Well perhaps I can refresh your memory!" shouted Sjolander. Usha was vaguely shocked at the man's anger until she realized that he was Norwegian—a country occupied by the Nazis, if she recalled correctly.

"These men—all of these men—were your agents, weren't they? Perhaps not knowingly, perhaps not willingly, but they were carrying out your plans! You gave them aid: money and technology. You 'implanted' them to attempt world conquest and you 'implanted' their foes to sap their will to resist. It's all there in your own records!"

"We...we made a mistake," said Keeradoth. "We could see that a war was coming—and it would have come whether we interfered or not—and we thought we could guide it to ends that would benefit all of us. We did not intend..."

"Oh yes, you made a mistake! You even realized it after a while. You realized what monsters you had set loose. So you abandoned them and supported their enemies. And they were stopped—but only after a hundred million dead! And even then your meddling did not end. The Cold War was mostly your doing, too, isn't that true? You brought the whole world to the brink of destruction!"

"That was not our plan. We did not understand everything to begin with," said Keeradoth. "You are a difficult species to understand. But we have learned..."

"Yes, you've learned," interrupted Sjolander. "And your interference, your manipulation, continues to this day! Should we be happy that you are not making as many mistakes these days, Commander? Or should we be that much more afraid?"

"We meant no harm," said Keeradoth. "We feared the *Brak-Shar* and you should, too. We can aid you..." The alien's words came very quickly, the first sign that he might be as upset as Sjolander. Usha just sat in her chair shaking her head.

"Your aid comes at too high a price, Commander!" thundered Sjolander. "We will take our chances with the *Brak-Shar*. They cannot be here for another sixty years and if they do come we will be ready!"

The Secretary General paused and collected himself. "Commander, the General Assembly has already voted on this. We want you to leave."

Usha sucked in a hissing breath. She couldn't argue—not after what she had seen and heard. But it was still like a pronouncement of doom to her.

"But..." said the alien.

"There is no way we can force you to go, we know that," said Sjolander. "But we want you to leave. Pack up your ComBarrier. Pack up anything else of yours in this solar system. The crashed ship we will keep as payment for the harm you have done us. Pack up and leave us. Perhaps someday in the future we will be ready to invite you back. But if we do so it will be our decision—not yours!"

Silence filled the room. Every eye was on the alien. How would he react? He had the power to destroy the Earth if he chose. What would he do? The seconds dragged on and on...

"Very well," said Commander Keeradoth. "We shall do what you ask."

That was all. No apology. No excuses. Nothing. In that moment he seemed far more alien than ever. The screen went blank.

Usha Vasthare covered her face with her hands and wept.

Chapter Fifteen

Nisima could hear the voices again. She had memories of hearing them in her dreams. Over and over. But this time they were clearer. Closer. They were strange voices. Human voices, to be sure, but what were they saying? After a bit they faded away and she slept.

The next time the voices came, Nisima tried to pay more attention to them. It was hard. It was so hard to think. And she hurt. Pains she had never imagined before stabbed her everywhere. She forced herself to concentrate and the voices cleared momentarily.

English. American English. But I was supposed to be…where? Japan? What am I doing here?

It was too hard to think. The pain and the voices faded and she slept again.

The voices came and left many more times before she was able to focus on them again. It came almost as a surprise when she realized she could understand some of the words.

"…her condition, Doctor?"

"Better…much…in the last…days."

"…will…make it?"

"No doubt…was badly injured…but her stamina…remarkable."

It was too much work to try and follow the conversation. But she was in a medical facility, she knew that much now. And she did not hurt so much. Still pain in her head and her hips. For the first time in…how long…? She could see light beyond her closed eyelids. She made a huge effort and her eyes opened slightly. There was a fuzzy glare and she shut them again. It hurt. She could still hear the voices, but they soon faded and the light with them.

The next time the voices came they were much clearer and it was not nearly so much effort to listen to them.

"You have to remember that she was severely injured. Both legs broken in multiple places, pelvis broken, along with several vertebrae and numerous ribs and a very bad skull fracture. Frankly, I'm still amazed that she survived at all."

"But how long until she regains consciousness, Doctor? We have a lot of questions we want to ask her."

"She's out of the worst of the coma and she actually does regain partial consciousness from time to time. She's said a few words—nothing recognizable—and she responds to the light."

I have? I wonder what I said?

"When will we be able to talk to her?'

"That I cannot answer, General. She is still very weak and we have no idea the extent of any brain damage she may have suffered. I'm sorry, but she might not be able to answer any of your questions even when she comes to."

"What about that device you removed from her skull? Is there anything else inside her?"

"The device was crushed by the blow that broke her skull. We removed it during surgery. Your people have the remains now, General, so don't ask me about what it was for! As for anything else, there is another device inside her skull. We have no clue what it does and there is no way we can risk removing it at this point. She is far too weak for any further surgery of that nature."

"I see. Well, thank you, Doctor. Please keep me informed of her progress."

"Certainly, sir."

The voices ceased, but Nisima knew that she was still awake. Very carefully she tried to open her eyes. One seemed to be stuck shut, but the other opened slightly. Again, it was too bright and too fuzzy, but she forced herself to try and look. She blinked several times and the image began to clear. Tears formed and that blurred things again, but her other eye finally opened. With more blinking it was better than before.

Eventually she could see that she was in a bed, in a room, with all manner of equipment around her. She was propped up slightly in the bed and she could look down at herself. Her legs were encased in a bulky wrapping that seemed to extend up to her waist. She recalled the one voice saying she had broken legs and a broken pelvis. A gown covered most of her upper body. She could see her arms lying limply on the bed linen. Dozens of tubes seemed to be attached to her.

At the moment nothing was hurting too much, but she tried to remember what the voices had said about her other injuries. *Legs...pelvis...vertebrae... ribs...skull...He said something else, too. A device being removed?*

The communicator and her computer. One had been removed. She closed her eyes and concentrated on contacting the ship.

Nothing. No response at all. What about the computer? She concentrated again: *Access computer.*

[Ready]

The letters seemed to form on the inside of her eyelids. Nisima gave a tiny sigh of relief. At least she still had the computer. *Where am I?*

[Communications disabled. Global positioning unit offline. Unable to determine location.]

Not good. *Where is Nightpiercer?*

[Communications disabled. Unable to locate *Nightpiercer*.]

Where are the other Tadath-Belind?

[Communications disabled. Unable to locate other agents.]

This was bad. She was cut off. But how had she even gotten here? That question popped into her head and she guiltily realized it should have been the first one she asked. Her injuries had muddled her thinking. She tried to remember...

The *Brak-Shar* had attacked... she and the others had remained in their quarters...the ship was shaking... a sudden impact... Then blackness. She could not remember any more. She queried the computer for more information, but it had not been tied into the ship's tactical net so it could not tell her anything. In frustration she deactivated the device.

They must have crashed on Earth. The humans found her and brought her here for medical attention. Were the others here, too? She opened her eyes again and tried to turn her head. Almost immediately there was another voice.

"I think she's awake. Look, her eyes are open!"

A white blur appeared in front of her. It was hard to change her focus to the person looming over her, but eventually she was seeing a human female a short distance away. The woman was staring at her with great interest.

"Can you hear me, Honey?" she asked.

'Honey'? Is she referring to me? But who else? Following the English was not too easy. She certainly knew English, but she had been trained to think in Japanese, not English.

"Can you hear me?"

Nisima nodded her head a tiny bit.

"She heard me! Get the doctor!"

More people came into the room and they asked her a lot of silly questions. She was becoming exhausted nodding and shaking her head. But she had a question of her own: where were the others? The need to ask it became unbearable. She thought hard how to phrase it in English. Then she tried to speak.

A horrible rasping sound came from inside her and her throat burned like fire. The humans looking at her froze in surprise.

"W...w...w..." was all she could get out.

"What is she saying?

"I don't know."

"W...w...w...w..." she tried again.

"Water? Is she asking for water?"

"Get her some."

She wasn't asking for water! She was asking where her comrades were! Nisima was momentarily frustrated, but then she realized that she was, in fact, desperately thirsty. A small container with a tube was held in front of her and she felt the tube enter her mouth. A moment later a few drops of water trickled down her throat. It hurt, but it was wonderful. She tried to suck on the tube and she got some more. Nothing had ever tasted so good. A few more drops and the tube was withdrawn.

The humans were saying more things, but Nisima was worn out. She felt her eyelid drooping and without realizing it, she was asleep again.

*　*　*　*　*

"How are you doing today, Honey?"

Nisima opened her eyes and saw the nurse named Carol standing next to her bed. She wished she would stop calling her 'honey', it seemed so silly. She carefully phrased her reply.

"I...am...better...today." Her English was improving fast. She had set her computer to drill her on it and that was helping. She still was not thinking in English, but that would come in time.

"That's wonderful!" exclaimed the nurse happily. Nisima wished she had the strength to punch the woman. Her endless cheerfulness was becoming very irritating. But then she chastised herself for the thought. This nurse, and all the others, had treated her with great kindness.

The nurse bustled about, checking various medical equipment and after a few minutes one of the doctors came in and did so as well. Nisima took the opportunity to ask the question that had been burning in her.

"P...please. Where are the others?" Both the doctor and the nurse looked up in surprise. The doctor stopped what he was doing.

"Others?" he said.

"I...was with...other people. The last I remember. Where are they?"

"Nisima, what is the last thing you remember?" asked the doctor.

They knew her name. How? Did she tell it to them while she was delirious...or? What was happening? The ship crashed and the humans found it. How much did they know? What about the other ship? What did she dare tell these people?

"I was in a...room...with other people. There was a...heavy blow...and then I was here."

"This room was in the spaceship?"

There seemed to be little point in denying it. Clearly the humans knew about the ship. "Yes."

"The Someran ship?"

Someran? Oh yes, that is what the Race was going to call itself when contact was made! Have they made contact? They must have. Why hadn't they tried to communicate with her? The human was waiting for an answer. "Yes."

The doctor looked uncomfortable and a sudden shudder of fear went through Nisima.

"Nisima...I'm sorry, but you were the only one we found alive in the wreck."

No.

She felt dizzy and the room seemed to be spinning. It was hard to breath and tears were blurring her vision. The others...*gone*. It hardly seemed possible. She had worked with them for so long. And Danar...gone, too. They had loved each other, even though they knew they would be parted once they reached Earth. It was too much...

The light was fading. There was a sudden babble of voices, but they made no sense. Then the light was gone.

* * * * *

"...stupid of me to tell her like that. She is still very weak and the shock must have been pretty bad for her."

"But she's out of danger?"

"Yes, General. Her vital signs are stable."

The voices were back again. Nisima struggled to remember what was going on and then she was sorry when she did. The others were all dead. She still couldn't really believe it. They had been together for years training for this mission. Then the long voyage here. All for nothing. The others were dead and she was—what?—a prisoner? And what of the mission? What had happened to the other ship? And the *Brak-Shar*? Who had won the battle and what was going to happen next? The questions would not stop. She opened her eyes and looked around. The humans were immediately aware.

"How are you feeling, Nisima?" asked the same doctor as before. There were more people in the room now.

"I…I am all right."

"I'm terribly sorry about your friends. There was nothing we could do for them. We were afraid we were going to lose you, too."

"Thank you for helping me," said Nisima hesitantly. "W…where am I?"

"You are in a military hospital in Bethesda, Maryland. Your ship crashed about two hundred kilometers north of here."

"What…is going to happen to me?"

"You are safe here, Nisima. You don't have to worry about anything."

Safe. He says that I am safe. My comrades are all dead and I am cut off from my other friends. I'm here among these primitives. Safe?

"Nisima? There is someone here who would like to ask you a few questions," said the doctor. "Do you feel up to it?" She was briefly puzzled by the question. *'Up to it?'* What did he mean? She consulted with her computer and quickly deciphered the question.

"I will try." She glanced at the man next to the doctor. He was not wearing a uniform like the human military people did, but there was something about him, something hard. And she had heard the doctor say 'general' to someone earlier. Nisima felt a shudder of anxiety go through her. The man stepped up to the bed and looked down at her.

"Nisima," he began, "we found you on the Someran spaceship. What were you doing there?"

"I had come here from the S…Someran homeworld to help make contact with the people of Earth."

"You were born on the Someran home planet?"

"Yes."

"Are there a lot of humans there?"

"Several thousand, I think."

"Are they well treated by the Somerans?"

Nisima started. What sort of question was that? Of course they were well treated. What did this human think the Race had done to them?

"We…we are friends with the Somerans," she said, unable to think of any other reply.

"They told us that you and the other humans were volunteers. Is that true?"

"Yes." It was true. Nisima had eagerly volunteered to come to Earth. She had studied the horrible conditions the humans lived and died under and she wanted to help the Race help them. She had a mission here, but she was struggling to understand just what the mission now was under these totally unforeseen circumstances.

"And what were you going to do when you got here, Nisima?"

She hesitated. She knew the humans would not like what she had been trained to do. She didn't know what to say. All the training she had received did not cover this situation. The humans knew about the Race and they knew who she was. She had been trained to deny everything if she came under suspicion. But the denials would do no good now. What should she say? The silence dragged on and on.

"Nisima," said the man at last, "we have been able to translate the records we found on the Someran ship. I'm afraid your friends are not very good with computer security."

Nisima was startled again. If they had the Race's records, then they might know everything. Was this human telling her the truth or was it a trick to get her to say something she shouldn't?

"We know that you were supposed to infiltrate human society, Nisima. But there is a huge volume of records to work through. We still aren't entirely certain what your ultimate objective was. Could you tell me about that?"

Nisima sucked in her breath. She was getting very tired again. This questioning was exhausting. Too much responsibility...she couldn't concentrate.

"I...I think you should talk to the Somerans," she said. "I can't...I can't answer your questions. I would like to be able to talk to them, too, please."

The human stared at her and frowned. What was he thinking? Did he consider her some sort of traitor to her species? It was possible. She had been warned that they would think that way if she was somehow found out.

"I'm sorry, Nisima," he said. "We can't do that."

"But why?"

"Because they are gone."

Gone? Fear clutched at her chest. "Please, I don't understand. Gone where?"

"We discovered some very damning things in their records, Nisima. Your friends have proven themselves no friend of humanity. We sent them away."

The room seemed to be shifting around her. Gone? The Race was gone? It wasn't possible. They wouldn't leave her! She was having trouble catching her breath. She looked from face to face in the room. Everyone was staring at her. Sent them away? Suddenly anger flared in her. *Sent them away! Who did these savages think they were?* The Race had come hoping to help the humans rise up from their barbarism! What sort of madmen would refuse their help? She was furious, but the room was moving faster. She felt dizzy...

"I think that's enough for now, General," said a voice. "She's very weak and your questions are upsetting her."

"All right. I'll come again another time."

The doctor and the nurse were next to her now.

"Take it easy, Honey," said the nurse. "Just relax. Everything will be all right."

All right? How could anything be all right now? The truth slowly sank in and it was unlike anything she had ever felt before.

I'm alone.

She was alone as few people had ever been. Cut off from every single person she had ever known. Her family an impossible distance away. Her friends among the Tadath-Belind dead. Her friends among the Race banished. Alone. The anger drained out of her and was replaced by a numbing loneliness. Tears rolled down her cheeks and her breath came in ragged sobs. She wanted to cover her face with her hands, but her arms were stuck full of tubes and she could not move them.

The humans tried to console her, but Nisima wailed the cry of a child lost in the forest. She was alone and needed someone to come and find her.
But there was no one. No one at all.

Chapter Sixteen

"Captain Hancock, I'm certainly hoping you have some good news for us this week."

Bob Hancock rose to his feet and surveyed the sea of gold braid and ribbons that filled the conference room. The weekly briefing of the Joint Chiefs had almost become routine—almost. He glanced at Kay Youngs in the chair beside his. She cocked an eyebrow at him and gave a tiny smile. He cleared his throat.

"I have quite a bit of news, sir," he said to the Chairman. "I think that much of it is good, but I'll have to leave that to your judgment."

The general gave a faint chuckle. "Proceed, Captain, proceed."

"Yes, sir. Ladies and Gentlemen, if you will recall from last week's briefing, we were starting to make significant progress on the fabricators. Since then, we have made even more. It is becoming apparent that the Somerans considered fabricator technology to be the key in our technological development. Our current generation of fabricators, which I'll refer to as 'level one', were just the first step in a series of progressively more sophisticated devices that were intended to allow us to build many items used by the Somerans. This week we came across detailed instructions for using each generation of fabricator to construct the next. In other words, it is possible to use the level one fabricators to create the components for a level two fabricator. Once we have the level two, we can build the level three and so on. These later generations of fabricators are capable of some amazing things. Our current ones work strictly in metals and plastics. The more advanced ones are capable of crystalline and ceramic work, including finished computer chips."

"That's all very interesting, Captain," said the Chief of Naval Operations, "but when will we actually be able to build something useful with these? I don't have to remind you how tense the international situation has become. And we still have no proof that the Somerans are actually gone. We need some real, working, hardware and we need it quickly."

"Yes, sir," said Hancock. "I wish I could give you definite information on when you can expect something, sir, but we have a lot of learning to do. Unfortunately, it appears that the really sophisticated items like the anti-gravity generators, the aliens' space drive, defensive shields, and lasers are going to require at least a level four or five fabricator to construct. We are hoping to have a level two fabricator ready by next month. It will probably be another three or four months after that for a level three. We're shooting for level four by the middle of next year. After that, we aren't sure. For far too much of this we are just following the instructions without really understanding how the things work, sir."

"That doesn't sound like terribly good news to me, Captain. A year or more before we can expect anything concrete. A lot can happen in a year."

"Yes, sir, that's true. However, we are making some progress in other areas. Our chemists believe that they can start duplicating the solid propellant for the Somerans' missiles within a few months. They tell me that this fuel has about ten times the power of anything we have ever come up with. It should be possible to create near duplicates of their missiles in about six months, sir."

"'Near duplicates', Captain?"

"Yes, sir. The sticking point is going to be the guidance system and sensors. The Somerans have a gravity-detector that they use as a primary sensor. We are making some very good progress on building a gravity detector of our own based on the Someran designs, but unfortunately, the first models will be very large—far too large to fit into a small missile."

"Can't we just use radar or a thermal sensor, Captain?"

"Yes, sir, we could, and that would work well enough against any Earthly target," answered Hancock. "But I'm afraid it would be useless against any…extraterrestrial targets. The Someran shields appear to be able to damp out any sort of radar or thermal signatures. We're not certain why they were not using that capability during the battle, but they obviously switched it back on later. Our missiles might have the same range and acceleration as theirs, but we would have no way to hit them without a grav detector."

"And those will require the more advanced fabricators, I assume?" asked the Chairman.

"Yes, sir, I'm afraid so. However, the large gravity detector may be operational in less than two months. It will be crude, but it should be able to detect a ship like the Somerans' at some very impressive ranges. At least we should know if they have really gone."

"That would certainly be a good thing to know!" said the head of the Air Force. "Right now, they could still be hovering around our heads and we'd never realize it."

"Also," continued Hancock, "we have hopes of reducing the size of the grav detectors before too long. They will still be too large to fit into the small missiles the Somerans use, but we have hopes of retro-fitting them to our own ICBMs. At the same time, we think we can substitute the Somerans' solid propellant for those same missiles. It would increase their range dramatically and actually give us a chance to hit something."

"That sounds better, Captain! How long for that?'

"We estimate that we can have the first models ready for testing in about four months, sir."

"Well, that's better than nothing. At least we'd have something to use against them if we had to. Is there anything else, Captain?"

"Those were the primary points, sir. The rest of the details are in the written report."

"Very well. Thank you, Captain. Colonel Youngs, what do you have for us?"

Bob sat down and Kay stood up. He knew that she was nervous, but she concealed it well. As he watched her get her notes in order, he couldn't help but think about the fact that she really was an attractive woman. Tall, slender, and a pretty face. She cut her brown hair very short, as most women pilots did, but he could tell that if she let it grow it would be curly. He had really enjoyed working with her these last few months. She was smart and funny, too, which furthered his attraction. He had always had a personal rule about avoiding complications with co-workers, but he was becoming sorely tempted to break that rule now.

"So, Colonel," said the Chairman, breaking Bob's pleasant train of thought. "What progress are we making on the ship?"

"I'm afraid it is slow going, sir," answered Kay, "but we are making progress. The Somerans had given us a basic design for a simple vessel and we are constructing the hull now along with the power plant, life support, and controls. We have the plans for the drive system, but as Captain Hancock had mentioned earlier some of the critical components will require a later generation fabricator than we currently possess. In the meantime, we are attempting to salvage what we need from the wrecked ship. We have found a number of the items but we are still missing a few key pieces. We will continue to search, but if we cannot come up with them then we will have no choice but to wait for the fabricators to catch up with us. Naturally, we will proceed with those things that we can do. I'm sorry, sir, but that's how it is."

The Chairman frowned. Bob knew that the brass really wanted a functioning ship as soon as possible, but there were some things that took time no matter how many stars you were wearing!

"No need to apologize, Colonel. I realize that we are proceeding at a rather frantic pace here as it is. We'll just have to accept that the impossible takes a little longer."

"Yes sir, thank you, sir."

"That brings me to another item I wanted to discuss," continued the Chairman. "There is a Doctor Usha Vasthare on the ship construction team, Colonel. I've heard a few disturbing things about her. Apparently she got very chummy with the Somerans before we kicked them out. Since then she has made numerous protests about our policies concerning the distribution of the translated files, and most recently she has objected to modifying the ship design to incorporate weapons. I'm not sure she is someone we should have working on a maximum priority project like this. What's your opinion of her, Colonel?"

Bob saw Kay hesitate a moment before answering. She had talked to him about Vasthare a few times. It seemed as though she liked her...

"Doctor Vasthare is a person of dedication and principle, sir. In my dealings with her it has been obvious that she is very devoted to the pursuit of knowledge and not terribly sympathetic toward the military. The restrictions that have been placed on the data we have recovered would naturally upset her. That could be seen as a mark against her, sir. However, when it comes to compact fission plants for use aboard spacecraft, she's the best there is. We know that the Somerans use a very sophisticated fusion plant to power their vessels. Unfortunately, that technology is still out of our reach. Until we can get there, we will be dependent on fission power, and Doctor Vasthare will be a great asset. As an aside, sir, I should add that there is no one as eager as Doctor Vasthare to get this ship flying—and considering present company, that is saying quite a lot."

"So you trust her, Colonel?"

"Yes sir, I do. She may complain, but she'll get the job done—sooner and better than anyone else."

"Very well then, I think that wraps things up for today. Colonel, Captain, thank you for your reports."

Bob got to his feet. Neither he nor Kay were in uniform, so they did not salute, but they nodded their heads and quietly withdrew. A few minutes later they were in the basement garage, checking themselves and their vehicle through security.

"I think that went pretty well," said Hancock to Youngs.

"Yes, I think so," she agreed. "They're all so anxious to get the ship and the new technology working, but at least they are being reasonable about how long it is going to take."

"They don't like feeling helpless—can't say I like it much, myself," said Hancock as he steered the car up the ramp and out on to the street in downtown Alexandria. "Every one of them is accustomed to being the top dog with all the muscle on their side. To suddenly be put in a situation where none of their weapons are of any use at all is very difficult to swallow."

"Well, we're better off than ever against any terrestrial opponent," said Youngs. "Against the Somerans—or the *Brak-Shar*—we're still out of luck, but if neither of them is around…"

"Do you really believe the Somerans have left?"

"Hard to say and there's no way to tell for sure. At least they've taken down their ComBarrier."

"Yes, and isn't that driving the astronomers crazy?" said Hancock with a grin. "For decades they've been trying to detect signals from intelligent sources and they've been there all along. Now they're detecting dozens of new signals every day."

"Yeah," said Youngs, "pretty incredible. And the Somerans' attention to detail is frightening! They intercepted every one of our deep space probes and modified their communications systems so they could penetrate the ComBarrier but still not send any signals *out* that could be intercepted by other aliens. But all those new signals are stirring things up. As if we didn't have enough things upsetting our vision of the universe as it was."

"A lot of people are upset," said Bob, not quite so cheerily. "The world isn't what they thought it was and it's hard to cope."

The pair fell silent. Bob merged onto the main highway heading north. A few minutes brought them within sight of the Pentagon. Bob noticed Kay shaking her head.

"Never thought I'd see anything like that," she said in a low voice.

Hancock glanced out the side window. There were crowds of protesters outside the fences—new fences, Bob noted. Inside those fences were lines of soldiers, backed up by armored personnel carriers and tanks. Combat helicopters circled overhead. A frown creased his forehead. It had been like that for weeks. Many of the government buildings in Washington had been similarly fortified. The meeting they had just left had been held in an inconspicuous building in Alexandria rather than the Pentagon for this very reason.

"Which group is it today?" he asked.

"Looks like two different ones," said Kay. "I can see some "Share the Knowledge" banners in the one group. Not sure who the others are, but they don't look friendly."

"Let's get out of this neighborhood before the highway's blocked."

"Good idea."

They got past the Pentagon area, but it was impossible not to notice the sizable military presence all over the city.

"It's like wartime," said Youngs.

"Well, it is a war of sorts, I guess," replied Hancock. "We just haven't figured out all the sides yet."

"At least some of the sides have been especially stupid. I shudder to think what might have happened otherwise."

Bob nodded. Following the United States' revelation about deciphering the Somerans' files, the international situation had almost completely fallen apart. The initial unity in expelling the aliens had been followed by a demand that the US immediately give everyone equal access to the wreck and the records. The Americans had tried to stall, which immediately brought charges that they were trying to edit what they would give out and keep the most important information for themselves. Hancock somewhat guiltily acknowledged to himself that that was all too true.

Threats were made and even America's traditional allies were turning against her. It could have gotten extremely ugly.

Then, with exquisitely poor timing, several nations—and non-nations—made open broadcasts to the Somerans inviting them back. The thought that these other groups—international outcasts all—could end up with the aliens' technology and help, sent the world into a frenzy. American intransigence was forgotten—at least for the moment—and a cordon of military power was drawn around the offending nations and groups. Any attempt by the Somerans to land in those spots would be met with a massive response. Not that they could have harmed the Somerans, but there would have been very little left of any group trying to deal with them.

"Their stupidity certainly helped in the short term," admitted Hancock. "But the side effects have been pretty awful, too. Fifty years of arms control treaties undone in a matter of months."

"True."

Nations with nuclear capabilities were reassembling their warheads as fast as they could. Just a few months ago there were only a few thousand (acknowledged) warheads left in service. At the rate things were going, they would soon be back to levels not seen since the height of the Cold War—and everyone was on a hair-trigger.

But it *had* given them a breathing spell. More rational heads had prevailed in the United States and a system had been set up to share the alien technology—at least with those who could make the biggest stink about it. Fortunately, there were so many remarkable bits of technology of a non-military nature that it had further distracted most people from what the United States was *not* sharing. The medical community in particular was beside itself: apparently the Somerans, using their human specimens, had managed to cure a remarkable number of Earthly diseases. But the situation was still extremely uncertain. Hancock and Youngs had been run ragged over the past few weeks keeping their bosses informed.

Washington was eventually left behind and they headed north toward Aberdeen. This was not the first time they had made this trip. Bob and Kay chatted about their respective backgrounds and flying experiences. Bob found it very pleasant. *She really is very attractive…* He knew from her records that she was only a couple of years younger than him, but she could have passed for someone in their mid-thirties.

"Want to stop somewhere for dinner?" his mouth asked, suddenly.

"Sure," he heard her say. "It's kind of early, but I'm famished. Those meetings burn up a lot of calories."

Hancock got off the highway at the next exit and after a bit of searching found a small restaurant. Shortly, they were seated. Kay leaned back in her chair and sighed.

"I don't know about you, but I'm beat. If I'd known how much work this was going to be, I'm not sure I would have accepted your offer that first day back at Aberdeen."

Bob chuckled, but then his smile faded. "I'm glad you did accept, Kay. I...I've really enjoyed working with you."

He wasn't sure how she would react, but after a moment a small smile appeared on her face.

"I've enjoyed working with you, too, Bob."

Bob grinned—much too broadly, he realized, but he couldn't help it. He wasn't really sure what to say next. *I've been out of circulation too long!* After a moment, he decided that the direct approach was probably best.

"I've seen your security file, Kay. You've never married or had a serious love affair. Why not? You're certainly an attractive woman."

"Spying on my personal life, eh?" she said. For a second her face had a serious expression and Hancock was afraid he had blundered, but then she smiled. It only lasted for a few seconds and then she was looking very thoughtful.

"I'm not entirely sure," she said after a moment. "You know that I was in one of the first fighter squadrons to have women in it." It wasn't a question, it was a statement, but Hancock nodded. "The competition was incredibly fierce. Not just between the women, but with the men as well. We—the women, I mean—were extremely conscious that our every move was being watched. Somehow, it just didn't seem...proper...to have any sort of relationship with the male pilots."

Hancock nodded again. "But surely there have been other men around who weren't pilots—and you stopped flying jets after a while anyway."

"Well, the competition with the test pilots and in the astronaut corps was just as fierce," said Kay with a little laugh. "You didn't want to end up in bed with someone you might be up against for a plum flight assignment. As for other men...I tried dating some of them, but it was like they were from another planet."

"You've been dating Somerans?" asked Hancock in mock surprise. "That wasn't in your file."

"Silly! You know what I mean. Somehow non-flyers just didn't speak the same language. And all I've ever wanted to do was fly..."

"Yes, I do know what you mean," said Hancock. He looked away, nodding his head, and then took a gulp from his drink.

"It must have been hard being grounded when you smashed up your leg, Bob," said Youngs quietly. He looked up and she was staring at him. Her expression was exactly the right degree of sympathy without crossing over that terrible line into pity.

"Been looking at my file, too, have you?"

"Just a bit."

Bob was silent and stared at Kay across the table. She just stared back with that same expression.

"It was pretty hard," he said after a while. "I loved flying and to not be able to do that anymore...hell, I don't have to tell you about loving to fly!"

Kay smiled and nodded.

"But it was my own damn fault and I don't have anyone to blame for it but myself."

Kay cocked her head slightly and raised an eyebrow.

"I was so falling down drunk when I had the crash, I probably couldn't have walked even if I hadn't hurt my leg. Stupid. Really stupid."

Kay nodded her head slightly. Bob opened his mouth and shut it again. He was tempted to tell her exactly why he had been falling down drunk and driving like a madman, but he refrained. Maybe later, he thought. The idea that there could be a 'later' was actually rather pleasant. Later. It was like some destination that he—and hopefully she, too—was heading for.

"So I've been flying a desk ever since," he said instead.

Kay nodded again. "Well, when we get the Someran technology sorted out we won't have any problem making desks fly, Bob. Farther and higher and faster than anything you or I ever flew."

Bob laughed. "Interesting thought."

"All the rules have changed, Bob," said Kay earnestly. "A few years from now you may be flying again—and God knows what in or where to."

Bob Hancock sat there very thoughtfully for several minutes.

* * * * *

An hour later they arrived back at Aberdeen. Bob drove the car up to the temporary quarters Kay was staying in. He stopped and looked over at her.

"Long day," he said.

"But a good day."

"Yes, I guess it was."

"Thanks for the dinner. It was really nice."

"Yes."

She suddenly leaned over and kissed him lightly on the cheek.

"Good night, Bob. See you tomorrow."

And then she was gone.

He watched her go into the building.

He was smiling all the way back to his own quarters.

Chapter Seventeen

Ensign Melissa Hancock looked through the windshield of the car at the huge white dome in the distance. It was on higher ground than the road they were driving on and that made it seem even larger than it was. This was the first time she had come to King of Prussia by car and the different perspective was interesting…

The car braked sharply and that brought her attention back to the immediate vicinity. The traffic in front of them had slowed to a crawl.

"We should have taken a chopper, Melissa," said Lieutenant Steve Sokol, from behind the wheel. "Even with the wait to get it ready it still would have been faster than this."

"I didn't think it would be so bad with the mall shut down."

"It's always bad around here. And I think everyone is trying to make up for having the highways closed for two months."

"Do you think it was a good idea reopening them? I mean you have three major highways passing within a mile of the wreck. That's letting people get awfully close."

"No real choice, I'm afraid," replied Sokol. "The local politicians were demanding it and for once I can even see their point of view. Keeping the highways shut down was causing massive gridlock on the surrounding roads. Even with all the excitement going on, people still have to get to work."

"I suppose. And now that the danger from radiation has subsided, I guess they can't see any reason that they should keep their distance."

"Nope, and it is causing a security nightmare, I can tell you!"

"Anything really bad?" asked Melissa.

"Nothing they haven't been able to handle, but it is keeping them hopping. Demonstrators outside the fences night and day. News people, kooks, and the simply curious all trying for a closer look."

"Oh dear, I hadn't thought about that. Are we going to be able to get in without running some sort of gauntlet? I don't look forward to that." Melissa frowned. She didn't look forward to it at all! In fact, the idea frightened her considerably.

"Not to worry," said Sokol as they finally made it to the exit ramp. "I know a back way."

And so he did. After leaving the main highway he took them by some smaller roads that eventually led back underneath the highway they had just left and up to a gate. There were a few demonstrators there, but apparently the lack of any parking or assembly point within easy walking distance made this a less popular site. When she got closer, Melissa suddenly realized why this batch of demonstrators was here and not at the main gate.

A number of earnest looking people were carrying signs that read: 'Bring back the Somerans!'; 'The Somerans are our Friends!'; 'The Somerans can Save Us from Ourselves!'; and a few other slogans. When they caught sight of the car, they began shouting similar things.

"The minority voice is heard from," muttered Sokol.

Melissa nodded slightly. Steve was certainly correct about that. The vast majority of people distrusted or openly hated the aliens. It took quite a bit of courage to admit to a contrary viewpoint. Courage and, all too frequently, a lack of reason. While there were a few pro-Someran groups led by respected scientists, most were fanatics and cultists. There was even a 'Church of Somer' that claimed to have the aliens' religious doctrine. It was all nonsense.

Still, these groups were harmless, for the most part, and Melissa was glad that if she had to run a gauntlet, it was made up of these types. Some of the others—especially, the Somerans-and-all-their-tools-are-works-of-the-devil groups—had the potential for real unpleasantness.

Steve maneuvered the car up to the gate, rolled down the window and presented their passes. After a few moments, they were waved through into a fenced-in area that led to another gate. At this point they had to leave the car and submit to a much more thorough security check. IDs were scrutinized, fingerprints were taken, briefcases were opened, and they were required to take a different vehicle into the base.

"Whew! They certainly aren't taking any chances, are they?" said Melissa once they were on their way again.

"No, things have tightened up a lot since you were here last. Just too many people want to get in. You wouldn't believe some of the stunts they've tried to pull. Fortunately, most of them are just loonies and haven't made much trouble once they're caught. Where did you want to go first?"

"Right to the ship," replied Melissa, taking the change in subject in stride.

"Okay."

Melissa had not been to the crash site in nearly a month and was amazed at all the changes. She had seen the dome going up, of course, but now it was complete. It was not actually a dome, it was more of a barrel vault with rounded ends. Two hundred and fifty meters long, a hundred and fifty wide, and fifty high, it was as big as a football stadium. What really caught her eye, however, was what was not there: most of the mall buildings had been demolished and the dome stood by itself—making it look even larger.

"You folks have been busy."

"Not me," denied Sokol. "I still work at Willow Grove. I only get up here when important Navy-types like you come to visit."

"I'm not all that important," laughed Melissa.

"Well, you are pretty important to some folks," said Steve as he parked the vehicle. "Like me," he added, grinning at her.

Melissa did a double-take and then smiled back. "I've missed you, too, Steve."

"Oh, don't give me that!" he said, still grinning. "You're off hob-nobbing with the President and the Joint Chiefs and then going here, there, and everywhere on missions of national security. No wonder you don't have time for a lowly lieutenant."

"Hey, I didn't ask for any of this!" Melissa wasn't sure just how much Steve was joking. She had not had much time to stay in touch with him since she helicoptered off to the White House. And that seemed like a long time ago. Since then she had been her father's eyes and ears in the field, checking on the various operations involved in collecting and processing the data from the alien ship. Today was the first time she had seen Steve in a month. She was a little surprised at how nice it was.

She was also having a little trouble getting used to the changes that had happened in her life. The summer was over, but she had never gone back for her senior year at the Naval Academy. And yet she was a commissioned officer. She was not quite sure how that had happened. If things ever settled down, she would be going back to complete her degree and get her diploma, but for right now she was a serving officer in the United States Navy.

And she had a very exciting job.

"You may not have asked for it," said Steve, getting out of the car, "but you've got it. What's on the agenda for today?"

"Dad wants me to do a visual inspection of the ship and get an idea of how much more is left to do. Then I check in on the people doing the preliminary sorting of the Someran equipment. Tomorrow I'll head up to Indiantown Gap to look over the downloading operation there."

Sokol nodded as they walked toward one of the entrances to the dome. There was another security check there, although not as thorough as the one at the gate. Melissa caught her breath as the door was swung open.

Most of the debris had been removed from around the ship and this was the first time she had really been able to get a good look at the thing. It towered over her like a metal cliff. But it was a cliff in the process of being eroded away in fast motion. An enormous overhead crane was lifting off a hull plate that must have weighed thirty tons. Melissa could see where the ship's structural members had been exposed. To one side were piles of metal that had already been removed. The ship was being peeled like an onion. The whole operation reminded Melissa of an outing she had made in her sophomore year to the Newport News shipyard. She and her class had walked around an aircraft carrier that was in drydock. The alien ship was nearly as large, although much different in shape.

Melissa walked over to a small office that had been constructed inside the dome. A number of the engineers supervising the dismantling operation were there and Melissa talked to them about the progress they were making.

"Most of the work is pretty routine, miss," said one. "The alien metal is tougher to cut than most, but we're just working our way down, one deck at a time in most areas."

"Most areas?"

"We're going faster over the engineering spaces," he explained. "The bigwigs wanted a look there as soon as possible. In fact we just uncovered what we think is the fusion plant. Would you like to take a look at it?"

"Yes! That would be great," said Melissa.

The man, whose name was Dantzler, led them over to a small elevator attached to the scaffolding that encased the vessel. It took them up to near the top of the ship. From that height, she could see that all the dorsal hull plates had been removed along with several entire decks of the ship. In one area, even more of the ship was missing.

"There it is, over there," said Dantzler, pointing to that very area. "Come on, over this way."

He led them along a walkway that was much too narrow for Melissa's tastes and soon they were looking down into a large compartment. In it was a spherical structure about twenty meters in diameter. Numerous pipes and tubes and cables sprouted from all sides.

"Wow," said Melissa. "I've seen drawings of the reactor. The Somerans use their gravity technology to create the conditions for fusion. The power output is pretty amazing. Those smaller tubes bring in the fuel and the larger ones take the plasma out to the MHD units."

"It's not still functional, is it?" asked Sokol.

"No," said Dantzler. "Come over here and you can see why."

On the far side of the compartment, the bulkhead had a large hole in it. A number of the projecting pipes had been blasted away. There was a sizable gouge in the spherical housing.

"You can see that the hull on this side had been badly melted. We think that was from a nuclear explosion. Then a laser must have blown through to the reactor compartment."

"Lucky it did not punch all the way through the shell of the reactor," commented Melissa. "If it had, there probably wouldn't have been anything left of the ship to crash."

"Probably not," agreed Dantzler. "Ensign, we've submitted a recommendation that the reactor should not be dismantled completely. The actual damage to it is not that severe. We believe that it might be possible to repair it and get it operational. We haven't gotten any reply yet from the people upstairs and we need to know one way or another how to proceed. Can you get some action from you end?"

Melissa made a note on her computer and nodded. "I'll see what I can do. Is there anything else you want to show us, Mr. Dantzler?"

"That was the main thing from my department. I know the other salvage teams are still coming up with a lot of stuff and you'll want to talk to them, too."

"Yes. Can we get inside from up here?"

"Take that ladder down. You can get into the main part of the ship from there."

They followed his direction and were soon inside the alien vessel. Melissa had been through it a number of times in the past, but there always seemed to be something new to see. She and Steve spent several hours exploring and talking to the salvage people. Eventually they emerged from one of the airlocks back onto that narrow scaffolding and found their way down to the ground.

From there, they went into another office area inside the dome. This was where objects removed from the ship were collected. Melissa recognized one of the workers.

"Hi, Darren, how are you doing today?"

"Hey there, Ensign! We're still hauling stuff out of here by the bushel basket. Incredible how much stuff the aliens were carrying around with them."

"Well, from what we can figure out, they were planning on staying around for the next few decades. Guess they wanted to have everything they needed. Find anything unusual lately?"

"Nothing really out of the ordinary—I mean for artifacts from an alien civilization!" Everyone laughed at that.

"Getting a bit jaded, are we?" asked Melissa.

"Maybe a little," admitted the man. "Anyway, today's haul is over on those tables if you want to take a look."

"Thanks, we will."

Melissa and Steve walked over and looked around. Dozens of Someran devices were laid out. Melissa recognized a number of them, but others were new to her. Steve picked one up and laughed.

"Hey look! A plumber's helper!"

The object he was holding did look rather like that. A rod about forty centimeters long flared out into a shape similar to a suction cup, but the rod emerged from the cup and continued for a further twenty centimeters. It also looked a bit like a miniature version of the lance carried by a medieval knight—which was a better comparison, actually…

"Careful with that, Steve," said Melissa, very casually, "it's really a laser rifle, you know."

"What!" said Steve, nearly dropping it. "You're joking, aren't you?"

"Nope, I've seen a few others just like it. They've actually tested them on the firing range down at Aberdeen. Fairly powerful."

Sokol carefully put the item back on the table. Melissa was smiling at him. He noticed and smiled back.

"You were setting me up for that one, weren't you?"

"Hey, you put your own foot in it. I had nothing to do with it." They both laughed.

"Do you know what all these things are for?" asked Sokol.

"Not really. Some of them I can recognize, but not all." Melissa walked around the table and picked up one disk-shaped object and examined it for a moment. "This type I've seen before. Here, you might find this interesting." She set it down on a clear spot and used her little finger to touch several spots. "The Somerans sure have small fingers," she mumbled to herself.

"What's it do?"

"You'll see in a second…there!"

The air above the disk suddenly shimmered and a cloud of sparkles appeared. After a moment they cleared and the image of two Somerans, each about the size of a doll, could be seen. The image seemed as solid and real as if tiny aliens were actually floating there. They were wearing glittering robes, one gold, the other a metallic blue. A strange noise came from the disk. At first they were standing still, but then they began to move. The pair circled around each other in a swirling dance. Apparently they were in some sort of variable gravity because they could soar over each other's head and leap about in amazing bounds.

"It's an entertainment device," said Melissa. We've found a number of them before. Some of them have singing or musical instruments. This is the first I've seen with dancing. Sort of a ballet, I guess."

"That's music?" asked Steve, making a face.

"Kind of irritating, isn't it?" agreed Melissa. "I have a feeling the Somerans must deal with a different set of sound frequencies than we are used to. A few of the ones I listened to were enough to make you climb the walls after a few seconds."

"I'm about ready to do that now! Could you turn it off? Or at least turn the sound down?"

"Sure, I'll…"

"Hey, wait a second!" said Steve.

Melissa paused and then stepped back. The Somerans in the image were…what were they doing? They were taking their robes off and…and…

"Oh my," said Melissa.

"Wow," said Steve. "Do those gizmos come with parental advisories?"

Melissa found that she was blushing fiercely. "None of the others were like this," she said faintly. She glanced around quickly and saw that all the other workers had stopped to watch, too.

"Well, that answers one question I had about the Somerans," said Steve.

"The…the records we've translated so far indicate it's not quite as simple as that," said Melissa, unable to tear her eyes away. "Their gender can vary depending on…on…oh, hell." She reached out and switched the device off. There were a few faint cries of protest from the others in the room.

"I think we've…seen enough here." Melissa could feel her blush deepen and was furious with herself. The others were trying to stifle their laughter, but without much success. She tried to regain a few shreds of dignity by asking some inane technical questions of the unit supervisor. She could feel Steve's smirk even with her back turned.

"We're done here," she declared after a few minutes. "Let's go over to the main storage building."

"Right," said Steve, still smiling.

"Oh, Ensign," said the supervisor. "If you're heading over to storage would you mind taking this load with you? They're all catalogued and it would save us a trip."

"Certainly," said Melissa.

"I've got it," said Steve, grabbing up the sizable plastic tray.

They made their way out of the office and then out of the dome. Melissa noticed that the weather was clouding over and commented on the fact. Steve just walked alongside her, his smile growing larger.

"'Here, you might find this interesting,'" he said in a poor imitation of her voice which dissolved in laughter "Lis, if you could have seen your face!"

Her anger flared briefly, but she couldn't maintain it and in a moment she was laughing, too. For the next few minutes they just stood there laughing hysterically. Every time one of them would get their mirth under control, the other would do something to start them off again. Finally, they were out of breath.

"Are…are you going to be reporting this to your father?" asked Sokol between gasps.

"I…I may have to edit it a bit."

"Where are we going with this stuff—it's heavy," said Steve after another few seconds.

"This way," said Melissa, regaining her composure. She led the way around the side of the dome. "We have a temporary storage facility where we keep the items until they can be shipped out for analysis."

"Okay, lead on."

They walked a few hundred meters past the end of the dome and Melissa indicated a small building. As they got nearer, Melissa noticed a medium-sized truck standing outside the door.

"That's odd," she said.

"What?"

"That truck. It's what we use to transport the items. But there's no shipment scheduled today."

"Maybe there's been a change," suggested Sokol.

"I don't think so, I talked to the man in charge of the transport team just this morning, and he told me they would not be making a run until tomorrow."

By this time, they were about forty meters away and Melissa could see that the back doors of the truck were open and there were people moving around. A man was also standing by the cab. He was looking at them. Melissa's pace slowed.

"Steve, there's something not right here…"

"You and your hunches, again? I swear, you are the most suspicious…"

Melissa grabbed his arm and pulled him in a direction away from the truck. She fumbled in her pocket for her phone.

"What's the matter?" said Steve, not quite resisting her pull.

"I don't recognize that guy, and I've met the whole transport team."

"Maybe he's new. Maybe…holy shit! Look out!"

Melissa glanced back at the truck, now fifty or sixty meters away. The man had opened the cab door and he was taking something out…

"Run!"

There was a line of concrete traffic barriers only a few meters away and they dove behind them. An instant later there was the sharp crack of bullets ricocheting off the concrete. But there had been hardly any sound from the gun itself. *A silencer! These guys mean business!*

Melissa was on the ground with Steve next to her. She could hear a few urgent voices from the direction of the truck. Had anyone else heard or seen this? Where was her phone? She had dropped it out there! She peered around the edge of the barrier. Her phone was a half-dozen meters away, just beyond the tray that Steve had dropped. The man with the gun was headed this way…

"Steve! Use your phone to call for help! I dropped mine!" she hissed.

"Right!"

How long would it take him to make the call? How long for help to arrive? She looked around frantically. There was a chain link fence behind them—nowhere to run. Was that guy still coming? What would he do when he found them huddled here? Her heart was pounding as she realized that he would probably kill both of them. What could she do? They weren't armed…

The tray!

Without another thought, Melissa lunged out from behind the barrier and grabbed at the plastic tray. She caught a glimpse of the man with the gun about twenty meters away. When he saw her he stopped moving and brought up the gun. Melissa scrambled back to the barrier, dragging the tray behind her. Bullets tore up the dirt in her wake, but nothing touched her. Steve was staring at her wide-eyed, his phone to his ear.

"S…security alert!" he blurted. "We have armed intruders outside the storage building! We need help, *now!*"

Melissa scarcely heard him. Her ears were focused on the sound of approaching footsteps. The footsteps of a man with a gun. She dumped out the plastic tray and grabbed an object. It looked like a plumber's helper.

She had watched how it was done on the Aberdeen firing range. She slid open a panel on the side of the grip. She stabbed at a touch pad with her pinky and several lights started to glow. She drew her fingernail along a slider and a lighted bar went halfway up the scale. The footsteps were very close now...

She rolled on her back and put her hand around the grip. The Somerans used both their thumbs on the two triggers. She had to make her little finger do the job of the second thumb—fortunately, she had small hands or she wouldn't have been able to do it.

The man was *here*. His head and shoulders appeared above the barrier. He was raising the gun...

Melissa shifted her aim a fraction and pressed both triggers.

A bolt of light speared out from the muzzle, catching the man just below his chin. There was a flash and a crack like thunder and the man tumbled away, his gun flying into the air. The afterimage of the bolt fluttered before her.

"God!" exclaimed Steve.

Melissa turned on her side and crawled to the edge of the barrier. She could hear excited shouts and then the rumble of an engine starting. She peered out and saw a number of men piling into the truck. Just then a siren started to wail.

There seemed little chance that the truck or its occupants could get away now that the alarm was sounded. The truck was armored, it was true, but with all the gates and barriers and vehicles and helicopters around...

Melissa didn't have to do anything now, but a sudden anger surged up to replace the terror of a few moments before. Those men! They hadn't just asked the transport team if they could borrow their truck! They had probably killed them! And the other people who had been in the storage building...

She looked down at her weapon and used her fingernail to slide the power setting all the way to the top.

She popped up from behind the barriers.

"Melissa!" exclaimed Sokol. "Stay down!"

She ignored him. The truck was just starting to move. She sighted down the barrel of the laser and squeezed the triggers. There was another, brighter, bolt and a satisfying crack as the fender of the truck went flying away in pieces. She squeezed again and the left front tire exploded. Again, and the radiator grill disintegrated. Again, and there was a gout of smoke and the engine ground to a noisy halt. Again. And again.

The truck had stopped and the cab was a mass of flames by the time she realized the weapon wasn't firing. *Batteries exhausted.*

She stared as the back doors of the truck banged open and four men spilled out. They were all armed—and she wasn't anymore. They looked around in confusion and then one caught sight of her.

"Melissa! Get down!" Steve tackled her. There was a loud *rat-tat-tat* and bullets were bouncing off the barrier again. Small bits of concrete pattered around her. She was trying to decide what to do next when there was more firing. Some sounded like the first gun, but they were suddenly drowned out by the familiar snarl of a military assault rifle. Soon there was far more firing than the four men she had seen could possibly account for. She tried to twist around so she could see, but Steve was on top of her.

"Will you stay still?!" he shouted in her ear.

The gunfire grew even greater, but then she could hear the roar of a diesel engine and the clanking squeal of caterpillar tracks. Then there was the authoritative *wump-wump-wump* of an autocannon. After a moment there was a deafening silence. Melissa tried to look again, but there was suddenly a loud voice, from very nearby.

"All right you two, freeze!"

"I thought we were," muttered Sokol.

Melissa looked past Steve's shoulder and saw a soldier looming over them with his weapon pointing right at her. She held out her empty hands to either side and smiled. After a few moments an officer appeared. She thought she recognized him from security briefings. He looked at her closely. Steve twisted around a bit, too.

"It's all right, Private," he said. "These are friendlies—even if they are squids."

"Yes, sir." Both men withdrew, disappearing behind the concrete barrier. She and Steve lay there for a few more moments, and then Melissa stirred.

"You can get off of me now, Lieutenant." His eyes met hers and he smiled. So did she. "If you want to..."

"I don't think I do..."

"But we better get up and see what's happened."

A long sigh. "I suppose so."

He hoisted himself up and she dragged herself to a sitting position. Then with a groan, she was standing up...

...and looking at the face of a dead man.

The man she had shot was lying face up a few meters away. The bolt had blown through his neck, severing the spine completely. His head was only being held on by a few pieces of flesh. The expression on his face was one of extreme surprise. And there was a lot of blood...

"Are you okay, Melissa?" Steve was right next to her.

"No."

The adrenaline was draining out of her and her legs felt shaky. Her eyes drifted up to the burning truck—was anyone still in the cab? Other bodies were sprawled nearby...

"Maybe you should sit down for a bit."

"No."

She turned around and staggered a few steps to the fence behind her. Locking her fingers into the links, she deposited her breakfast into the weeds.

Chapter Eighteen

Expedition Leader Keeradoth stared out the viewport at the blue and white ball slowly spinning in the distance.

So long I have watched this world and now I shall see it no more. Very soon they would go home. But they went in failure. So much time, so much effort, so many hopes—all come to naught. What would the Council say when they return thus? What transpired was not their fault, and technically Keeradoth was not even in command at the time... *Bah! I have been here too long! Such paranoia. I am even starting to think like these Terrans!*

Keeradoth's shoulders twitched. Things may have changed at home, but the Council was not shooting people for being involved in failures! They would be disappointed, dismayed even, when they learned the news, but no wrath would be turned toward *Seeker of Truth's* crew or commander. That was not how it was done among the Race.

The com terminal chirped and Keeradoth answered it.

"Aye?"

"Honored One, the last of the ComBarrier satellites have been brought aboard and stowed."

"Very good. Has Tandalin lifted off from the fourth planet yet?"

"Aye, Honored One. The shuttle should reach us in two twelfthdays."

"Inform me when they arrive."

"Aye, Honored One."

Keeradoth closed the connection and returned to the interrupted musings. When Tandalin returned, the last of the Race's equipment would be recovered and there would be no more excuse to delay departure. Collecting the barrier satellites had been a lengthy process, and Keeradoth had been tempted to simply deactivate them and leave them behind. But the satellites, purchased from the *Kalnatradrenis*, were very expensive and the extra time would be well spent.

But that was not the real reason to salvage them was it? Truth to thyself always!

No, the real reason was to give an excuse to delay the departure. In hopes that something—anything—might change the Terrans' minds. But they had not. They were squabbling amongst themselves over the spoils from *Nightpiercer,* but aside from a shunned few, none wished their return.

And in a few twelfthdays *Seeker of Truth* would depart. The long journey ahead did not daunt Keeradoth in the slightest. Nine twelvedays under the ship's drive would boost them to near lightspeed and the relativistic effects would compress the long cycles of the trip into what seemed less than one. Then they would decelerate to the colony at Pardanor with its star portal. A few transits would bring them home at last.

But will it be home?

Keeradoth knew that much would change during this long mission. It was accepted that friends and clanmates would pass on before *Seeker of Truth* could return. But to accept the knowledge was not the same as to know the truth of the thing. Would they be strangers on their own world?

No, not entirely. Customs might change slowly and people pass on, but the world would still be there. Keeradoth thought fondly of the forests of Peridal and the great meadows in Girvaden. The sparkling shores along the Sea of Noofalanal. Those would still be there. It would be enough.

Keeradoth's thoughts of home could not prevent the musings on the mission from returning.

What will happen here? What will the Council decide? For that matter, what will the next ship do?

Seeker of Truth's mission had been long and lonely, but the pace was to have been accelerated greatly once the Terrans reached the point of usefulness. More ships were following *Nightpiercer*; the next would come in only ten cycles, and another in only five. Indeed, both those vessels were already on their way. Keeradoth had learned that these vessels carried many twelves of Tadath-Belind. They were to continue the program begun by the first group. Would the commanders of those vessels turn back when they received the report that Keeradoth had transmitted? What if they did not? The Terrans would be able to detect them by the time their ships arrived. Would they be sufficiently enraged to try and attack? So many questions.

And what of the Brak-Shar?

The destroyed vessel had broadcast a warning before it died. In about three-dozen cycles the signal would reach the nearest *Brak-Shar* colony—and then what? Past experience showed that the enemy would assemble an attack fleet by using their own star portals and come here to stamp out what they would no doubt believe was a colony of the Race.

The distance to Pardanor is less. We could return with a fleet sooner. Would the Council agree to that?

Doubtful. The entire point of this mission was to do it with a minimum expenditure of resources. When the natives on this planet were discovered, the scheme was hatched to outflank the *Brak-Shar* by surprise. Thrusts were made in other regions of the frontier to distract and deceive the enemy. All the while, the Terrans were guided toward the goal of technological sufficiency. A fully armed and industrialized world would spring into being before the *Brak-Shar* were even aware the Race was in this part of space. The strategic benefits would have been significant, to say nothing of the added strength brought by the Terrans.

But now the *Brak-Shar* would know of this world. Keeradoth did not know what information the destroyed enemy ship had broadcasted, but it would, no doubt, mention that an industrialized world existed here. They might not know the true nature of it, but they would surely react—just as they always have. A massive fleet would be assembled at their nearest colony and then they would come.

And the Terrans would probably die.

Their destruction was highly likely, but not an absolute certainty. The *Brak-Shar* were hard to predict in their large scale actions. They existed peacefully with some of their neighbors, but not with others. Surely not with the Race. If the Terrans could somehow convince them that they were not allies of the Race, perhaps the *Brak-Shar* would not destroy them.

Unlikely. The *Brak-Shar* would be suspicious and the loss of their ship would likely enrage them. They surely would not allow the Terrans to remain independent. The Terrans would resist an occupation and then extermination would likely result.

Still, the *Brak-Shar* would certainly send a large fleet here. It would be a major expenditure of resources. *Can we perhaps take advantage of that else-where on the frontier?* mused Keeradoth. *Turn our diversions into actual offen-sives? It is an interesting idea.*

It *was* an interesting idea. Perhaps a message should be sent ahead to propose it. Keeradoth's shoulders twitched again. *I am out of my depth. Strategies must be planned so far in advance and I am but a simple ship commander. The Council must decide what to do.*

While Keeradoth felt relief that the decision would be in the hands of others, there was also a vague uneasiness about the fate of the Terrans. It was strange: they were not of the Race, so were of no consequence once their use-fulness was at an end. The history of the universe was filled with species that had not survived. Why worry about one more?

And they will not all die. The community at home will continue to exist, and who know? Perhaps they will prove useful again. The Brak-Shar may also keep some alive, although I do not envy the ones they choose.

And perhaps the Terrans might even survive the first *Brak-Shar* attack.

That also seemed unlikely, but Keeradoth knew the Terrans were capa-ble of great ingenuity and prodigious efforts when properly motivated. With over five-dozen of their years to prepare, they might be strong enough when the *Brak-Shar* arrived to fight them off. They had the technology now. A few cycles would be enough to start building real warships. If they built enough of them…

Small chance of that! thought Keeradoth in disgust. While the Terrans were able to focus their energies to an amazing degree, observation showed that they could not maintain the focus for long. Without an immediate threat, they would waver. Five-dozen years was nearly the length of one of their minuscule lifetimes and they were not capable of such prolonged sacrifice.

So they would debate and procrastinate and only make real preparations when the Brak-Shar attack fleet appeared on their detectors—and it would be far too late then.

And that assumes they don't do the job of the Brak-Shar themselves!

That was the other distinct possibility: that the Terrans would destroy themselves. A great deal of the Race's task had been to curb the Terrans' war-like instincts. Accelerating their technology without allowing that power to turn to self-destruction had been a delicate balancing act. Keeradoth doubted that the Terrans would have sufficient restraint now that they were on their own.

And it was already beginning. The nations stood poised to strike each other lest one of them gain too great an advantage. Only a few twelfthdays ago a battle was fought near the crash site over a vehicle load of salvaged equipment! Like as not, when the *Brak-Shar* arrive they would only find a blackened world with a few helpless survivors huddling in the ashes. Madness!

Still, nothing was certain. Perhaps the Terrans would not destroy them-selves and perhaps they would take the *Brak-Shar* threat seriously. And perhaps, when the enemy attack fleet arrived, it would find an even bigger and more powerful fleet waiting for it. The chances were small, but Keeradoth knew that many stranger things had happened.

But, oh how much greater their chances would be if they would only accept the help of the Race! If only...

The communicator chirped again.

"Aye?"

"Honored One, would you please come to the Control Chamber?"

"What do you require?" asked Keeradoth in puzzlement.

"Honored One we have picked up a transmission. We believe it is *Brak-Shar* in origin."

Keeradoth started. A dozen questions presented themselves, but all could be answered more easily in the Control Chamber.

"I shall be there directly."

Keeradoth strode out of the cabin that had been home for so many cycles and walked down the familiar passageway to the Control Chamber.

"What is your status?"

"Signal detected, Honored One," said the sensor controller. "Definitely *Brak-Shar* code."

"What is its source?"

"There have been several repetitions of the signal, Honored One. Our own motion has allowed us to roughly triangulate. The approximate position of the transmitter is zero point six-twelve light cycles distant. The bearing is on the main screen."

Keeradoth looked at the indicated information. The transmission source was on a line with a nearby star system, but not the same one the first ship had approached from. *Another scouting ship? And so close!*

"What is its course?"

"The signal was highly violet-shifted, Honored One. We estimate the source's velocity to be near lightspeed. They appear to be headed in this direction."

"I see. And what is the nature of the transmission?"

"We cannot decode it, Honored One, but it appears to be a similar code to what we have found on the salvaged computers from the first enemy vessel. We have not put a great deal of effort into breaking that code because of other pressing matters."

"We shall expend the effort now, I think," said Keeradoth. "Put Naloram to work on it immediately."

"At once, Honored One."

What did this mean? Another enemy ship coming to this star system. Presumably just one, but there was no way to know for sure. They would not have to begin their deceleration and reveal themselves for many twelvedays yet. It was possible that the *Brak-Shar* were planning a rendezvous between scouting vessels in this system.

And in about nine of the local months they would be here. Another ship the size of the first one? Alone they have no chance of defeating it. They could leave, of course. But then the Terrans would be conquered or destroyed and it would happen now—not six-dozen cycles hence. The *Brak-Shar* would not be inconvenienced at all. Disaster upon disaster! *We should have left a heavier garrison here, but that is all hindsight now. What shall I do?*

"When Tandalin returns I shall wish a conference with all the senior officers," said Keeradoth.

"Aye, Honored One."

"We have much to discuss."

Chapter Nineteen

"My God!" exclaimed Kathryn Youngs into the telephone. "Is Melissa all right?"

"Yes, she wasn't hurt," answered Robert Hancock. "But she's pretty shaken up. She...she killed at least one of the bastards herself."

"Oh God," whispered Kay. *So young! Just a child and she has to deal with this.* "Where is she now?"

"Once her debriefing is done, she's going back to the house. Lieutenant Sokol will drive her down."

"What about the casualties? Were they bad?"

"We don't have the full picture yet," said Hancock. "Five of the six intruders are dead and the sixth isn't in good shape. Three of our security people were wounded in the firefight. The four people in the storage building were just tied up and stashed out of sight. But there's been no sign of the real transport team. I'm afraid it doesn't look too good for them."

"Damn," muttered Youngs. "And we have no clues about who these people are?"

"Not yet, but it was a frighteningly sophisticated operation. They obviously had a lot of inside information and quite possibly inside help. One of the security people has turned up missing, too."

"Damn," said Youngs again. "There's going to be hell to pay over this."

"You're not kidding. And the sad truth of it is that with the international situation as screwed up as it is, this could have been the responsibility of almost anyone. That team is as likely to be Brazilian, or French, or Israeli as it is Iranian or some terrorist group."

"Or a combination," said Kay. "There are loads of desperate people out there. So what do we do?"

"Right now, we sit tight. You and me and our people, I mean. Security really isn't our responsibility, thank God. For the moment, we are to proceed with downloading and translating what we've already got. It may be a while before we get anything new, but we've got plenty to work on as it is."

"That's for sure! Years worth!"

"But overall security is going to be tightened: more guards and more checkpoints on all our facilities. There will probably be increased security on all key personnel, too."

"That's us, isn't it? You mean if we go out to dinner again we'll have some watchdog following us?" Kay's statement was half in jest—but only half.

"Well, I hope not," said Bob. "Look, I have to run, now. I'll see you in the morning, okay?"

"Sure. See you tomorrow."

Kay hung up the phone and looked around the living room of her quarters. She walked over to a window and looked out, half expecting to see security guards marching back and forth. There were none, of course; in fact, the street outside was deserted. Lights shone in a number of windows, but everything was quiet.

Damn what a mess!

Kay was worried over the likely repercussions of this attack, and she was worried over Melissa Hancock. She liked Bob's daughter very much. She could not keep the thought out of her head that someday she might be her daughter, too.

Getting a little ahead of yourself, aren't you, girl?

Maybe. She was very attracted to Robert Hancock. More than to any other man in a long time. For once, the tension was not there; that subtle pressure that seemed to make any man a potential competitor. He seemed to have no problem with the fact that she had seniority over him (by only a few days, it was true), nor was he threatened by her greater flying accomplishments. Or if he was, he concealed it very well indeed. She had briefly had a lover or two in her life, but Bob was the first one who might also be a friend.

Meanwhile, the world comes apart around us. Am I really falling for this guy or is it just some ancient instinct to find a mate before one or both of us is lost to the gene pool?

Kay sighed and moved away from the window. She plopped down on the worn and dusty sofa and turned on the TV. It was an old, sit-on-a-table model rather than a wall screen and she leaned forward to see the tiny images. The attack on the crash site was being covered by all the news channels. She flipped through them trying to find some real information. Lots of fuzzy aerial photos and pictures of emergency vehicles coming or going through the crowds around the gates; lots of angry talking heads, but nothing of substance. The substance would come later—after the US had figured out who to bomb.

Eventually, she turned it off and got out her computer. Her rather shabby quarters did not even have a standard wireless hook-up, so she had to dig out a cable connection and plug into the wall socket. The Internet news sites were not doing much better with the story than the TV networks. She surfed around for a while until her screen suddenly filled with static.

The damn connection is probably...what?

Kay stared at her screen. The static cleared and there was the image of a Someran!

"Colonel Youngs?" said a voice on the speaker. She almost dropped the computer in surprise.

"Who...? What are...? Commander Keeradoth?" It was just a guess, all the aliens looked alike to her.

"Yes, it is I. It is good to see you again, Colonel." Kay glanced over her computer and saw that the minicam was now on. She had not turned it on...

"What... We thought you had left."

"We were in the process of recovering our equipment—as we were directed to—but a matter of great urgency has arisen. We need to talk to you, Colonel."

"I...I really shouldn't even be talking to you now..." Kay was half tempted to turn off her computer. The other half of her wanted to call up Bob on the phone.

"It is vital that we talk to you, Colonel. Please."

"What about?"

"We think it would be better if we met face to face, Colonel."

"What? You must be joking! I can't do that!"

"One of our small craft can meet you in a deserted spot. No one need know."

"I'm violating orders just to be talking with you now! If I meet with you, they'll throw away the key!"

"It is extremely important…"

"Then you are just going to have to tell me about it here! I'm not meeting with you just on your word—there's not much credit in that these days!"

The alien was silent for a few seconds. Ripples of color moved across its face in strange patterns.

"Very well. The *Brak-Shar* are returning. Another ship. It will be here in nine months."

"Oh my God…" A shudder of fear went through her. Images of the inside of her spaceplane skittered through her head.

"We must meet."

"I…yes. But, just me? Shouldn't you contact someone higher up?"

"I do not believe anyone 'higher up' would be willing to talk to me."

"No, I suppose not. Where shall we meet?"

* * * * *

Two hours later, Kay Youngs pulled her car off the road, turned off the engine, and got out. She wasn't really sure where she was. Somewhere on Maryland's Eastern Shore, she thought, although she could easily have crossed over into Delaware without knowing it. She had driven almost at random, trying to find some very out of the way place. Commander Keeradoth said they could track her if she kept her computer with her and they would land whenever she found a safe place to do so.

This place seemed deserted enough. Farm fields stretched out in all directions from the tree-lined country road. It was nearly midnight and the stars shone brightly in the crisp early autumn air. Somewhere out among those stars was an enemy. Someone else was out there, too. But were they really friends—or another enemy?

She paced in circles around her car, looking everywhere. She was nervous. She knew she was taking a number of very big chances. The Somerans might be lying to her and this could be some sort of trap. That seemed unlikely—they still had the ability to come and go unseen and they could easily kidnap her anyway, if that was their goal—but there was no way to know for sure. And even if they weren't lying, she was violating about a million different regulations as well as defying direct orders from the top to have no contact with the aliens. If she was found out, it would be the end of her career and possibly her freedom. That was the main reason she had gone without telling Bob—she didn't want to involve him in this.

So why had she come? She wasn't really sure. The risks were great, but the stakes were even greater. The thought of the *Brak-Shar* filled her with dread. She was still having the nightmares and knowing that her nightmares could soon become real again was driving her to action. But what could the Somerans want? What could she possibly…

A faint sound made her spin about. There was nothing to be seen. It was a hum and it was growing louder. She looked up and saw a coal-black shape overhead. It did not reflect any light at all and it seemed like a hole in the sky.

It was descending rapidly and a few seconds later it was resting on the ground twenty meters away. Kay let out the breath she had been holding. A hatch opened in the side of the thing and a faint blue light glowed from inside.

She took a deep breath and put on her best command face. She strode over to the alien craft and was proud that she hardly shook at all.

"Colonel Youngs?" came a voice.

"Yes, I'm here."

"Please, come aboard. We must be quick."

Kay ducked her head and scrambled into the Someran vessel. It was just like the other ones she had been on and the ceiling was still much too low. There were a half dozen aliens aboard that she could see—and someone else. She took a closer look and smiled.

"Well, Doctor Vasthare, I see they recruited you, too, for this insanity!"

* * * * *

"Nine months?" asked Kay Youngs.

"We believe so," said Commander Keeradoth. "That is assuming they do, in fact, decelerate to stop in this star system. We have managed to break into the Brak-Shar computers we salvaged from their wrecked ship and have found a set of their orders. The ship that we defeated was part of a squadron of eight that are exploring this region of space. The new ship is the squadron leader. It was scheduled to rendezvous with the first ship here. The message we intercepted was to inform the other ship that the squadron leader had been delayed, but the rendezvous was still to take place. At the moment, this new ship will still be unaware of the first ship's fate. When the messages sent by it reach them, we can only guess at how they will respond. There is a small chance that they might veer off and not come here at all."

"I see," said Youngs. She glanced around the compartment. It was the same arboretum they had been in before. She had not been terribly happy when the aliens had brought them back to their ship, but she supposed it did not really make any difference. Once they were higher than five meters it was too far to jump anyway.

"You'll pardon me for saying so, Commander, but you extraterrestrials are certainly sloppy with your computer security."

A pattern of blue and violet waves passed over the alien's face. Youngs had no clue what that indicated.

"The *Brak-Shar* computers are fairly primitive, Colonel. Given time, it was not that difficult to penetrate them. In the case of our own computers…we had not made sufficient allowance for your cleverness."

"But surely you must have safeguards and access codes normally?" said Doctor Vasthare.

"Actually, no, Doctor. At the risk of sounding insulting, our people are less prone to… mischief… than yours. They do not go where they do not belong. This phenomena of 'hacking' that you suffer with is unknown among us."

"There are no anti-social types?" asked Vasthare. She was clearly surprised. "No crime or deviant behavior?"

"It is not entirely unknown, but very rare. We can detect such individuals and..."

"Commander, Doctor," interrupted Youngs. "This is all very interesting, but we have a more urgent matter than the utopian Someran social system."

"Indeed, Colonel, you are correct. We must prepare for the arrival of the second enemy ship," said Keeradoth. "I propose that we must combine our forces if we are to survive."

"Why the concern for a batch of savages, Commander?" asked Youngs. "You could just pull out now and be done with us."

"We could," admitted the alien. "And we might still do so depending on what you Terrans decide. We cannot fight the enemy ship alone. If you do not agree to an alliance of forces, we will have no choice but to leave. As to why we wish to stay...I will be blunt: we wished to use you as allies in our war against the *Brak-Shar*. That has always been our interest in you species. If we leave now, the *Brak-Shar* will either destroy or conquer you and all our efforts will have been wasted."

"Mighty convenient for you that this second ship is approaching," said Youngs warily. "Assuming there really is one."

"Colonel!" gasped Vasthare.

"Why not, Doctor? They've already said how important this little 'project' of theirs is. They've lied to us and deceived us before, too. What's one more little lie if it gets us to do what they want?" Kay turned defiantly toward the alien commander.

Keeradoth was silent for nearly a minute, but there were no colored waves on his face this time.

"What you say is true, Colonel. We have used you. And we still wish to have you as allies. We have done what we have done to benefit our own species—that is the only rational behavior possible, is it not? You must now decide what is in the best interest of your own species. It is possible that we are trying to trick you, but the truth will be known in just nine months, will it not?"

Kay bit on her lip. *It could be a trick, a fake threat to drive us back into the Somerans' arms.* But some instinct told her it was not. As Keeradoth had said, they would know one way or the other in just nine months. What good would that do the aliens?

"I can also tell you that some of our claim can be verified," continued the alien commander. "The signal we intercepted was also received by at least a dozen of your radio astronomy facilities. Even now, this news is reaching your leaders. They have recognized that the signal is similar to those sent by the first *Brak-Shar* vessel during the battle. They also know that the source is nearby and closing."

"That does not prove a great deal, Commander. It could be one of you own ships just faking the signal."

"Perhaps, but that would have required us to have a ship in position to do it—a ship that could not even know of the original attack yet. That would be quite a coincidence. And again, you will know in nine months."

"Assuming it does not 'veer off' as you suggested earlier. It seems to me you could play this game again and again if you wanted."

"To what end, Colonel?" asked Usha Vasthare. "Clearly the Somerans are telling us this in hopes we will accept their aid in building ships and weapons to arm ourselves. If they were hoping to take control of us, they surely would not want us to have the strength to defy them, too."

"Unless they can control those ships and weapons or the people manning them," said Kay. It was an automatic response, but she knew the argument did not hold water. Right now the Somerans had complete military supremacy over Earth. They could conquer the planet if they chose. Once Earth had ships and weapons of their own, that would not be nearly as easy. Why arm the people you want to subjugate? She shook her head. This was all too much! She was just a spaceplane pilot, how did she get sucked into this?

"What…what are you asking me to do?" she said, finally.

"Colonel, we would like you to talk to your leaders and convince them that this new threat demands that our two peoples must work together to meet it," said Keeradoth.

"Oh! It that all? Why the hell didn't you say so to begin with? No problem! I thought you wanted me to do something difficult!"

The alien stared at her, or seemed to; those pupiless eyes were so strange. After a lengthy delay it spoke:

"You were joking again, were you not?"

"More sarcasm than a joke," said Kay. "Are you serious? Who do you think I am? They aren't going to take my word on something this big!"

"The logic of our proposal should be obvious to them, Colonel. You need only present it."

"The logic? Oh sure! They are really going to worry about the logic when I tell them I've been talking to you. Like I said earlier: they'll throw away the key!"

"Surely you are exaggerating, Colonel," said Vasthare. "This is so important that they will have to listen to reason!"

"No one ever 'has to listen to reason', Doctor! Our whole history is a succession of people who wouldn't listen to reason!"

"But we have to try!" insisted Vasthare.

Kay bit back an angry retort. There was no point in arguing about it. But what was she going to do? At a gut level she believed what the aliens were telling her. The *Brak-Shar* were on their way and they would be here all too soon. Earth had to prepare; somehow they had to prepare…

And only the Somerans could help them do it.

She had been at all those briefings with the President and the Joint Chiefs, and she knew the situation. They were expending every resource to develop the alien technology, but by the most optimistic estimate, it would be over a year before they even had their first small test ship ready to fly. A few weapons would be ready, but not the big ones and not the defensive shields.

Nine months. There was no way they could do it alone.

"Colonel! We have to try!" insisted Usha Vasthare again.

"Yes, Doctor, I suppose we do," she said reluctantly.

"I know they don't trust me," said the small woman with a scowl. "It will have to be you, Colonel."

Kay nodded, but then she looked over at the alien commander.

"Commander, I'm willing to try, but I'm going to need every scrap of information you can give me. Not just about the immediate threat, but about your whole program here. About your society and this war. You are going to have to convince me that this is the right move for us before I can hope to convince anyone else!"

"Very well, Colonel, what do you wish to know?"

"Everything! But we can start with this war: why are you fighting the *Brak-Shar*? What's the war about and why can't you stop it after so many years?"

"It has been going on for a very long time, nearly six hundred of your years," said the alien. "We did not start it, but then, the enemy probably believes the same thing. In its simplest terms, it started as a territorial dispute. We had known of the *Brak-Shar* for many years before the war began. Our dealings with them had been few, but we were at peace. Then we established colonies on five worlds that were near *Brak-Shar* territory. Worlds with habitable climates are relatively rare and to find five in such close proximity was very good fortune—or so it appeared. The *Brak-Shar* seemed to feel that this was an invasion of their space, even though the star systems in question were unoccupied. They attacked. We counterattacked. The disputed worlds changed hands several times and are now virtually uninhabitable. They are simply outposts on the frontier."

"Six hundred years!" exclaimed Usha Vasthare. "And over something that no longer exists! Why haven't you tried to make peace?"

"We have. Many times. Every effort has been rebuffed. The *Brak-Shar* are a difficult species to understand—even more so than yours. Obviously, they are intelligent, but they seem to act on a rather instinctual set of parameters. We theorize that our original entry into what they considered their territory has somehow branded us permanently as threats and enemies to be eradicated. We know that they share peaceful borders with several other races."

"So you have been fighting them ever since," said Kay.

"Yes, it has been a severe strain on our society. We are not natural warriors, Colonel. We would like to end this unproductive conflict, but we cannot see how, save by victory."

"And what are the chances of that? Are you winning your war?"

"We are not losing it, Colonel, but it is, indeed, a stalemate. With the restrictions of using sublight travel to launch an attack, the advantage lies overwhelmingly with the defense. Using the star portals, a defender can quickly shift their forces to meet an attack. Only an attack in overwhelming strength against several points at once can hope to succeed."

"I can see that. So how did we fit into all this?"

"Our strategy has been to try to englobe the *Brak-Shar* with a sphere of our colony worlds. To cut them off from the rest of the galaxy. In doing so, we will increase our own strength as our numbers increase and prevent them from expanding. Unfortunately, they seem to have the same strategy. For many years we and they have been sparring along the perimeters of our respective territories. We are both expanding in directions away from the frontier, but we are also attempting to spread outward and around the enemy. Establishing a new colony is difficult if the enemy is nearby. Until a star portal can be constructed the new colony is very vulnerable, and construction takes a great deal of time and enormous resources.

"When we discovered your world, we decided to try and trick the *Brak-Shar*. By acting aggressively in other areas we hoped to distract them from what we were doing here until you were fully ready to defend yourself and had a finished star portal. This would not have been a decisive move—I will not try to tell you that we stand or fall on the success of this mission—but it would have been a major victory. Your star system is positioned perfectly to allow us to turn their flank in this area of space. There are a number of other inhabitable systems in the region and with a functioning star portal, we—or you—would be in a position to colonize them and further our gains."

"You would allow us to colonize those other systems?" A giddy vision of interstellar exploration and colonization flickered in Kay's mind. It was tempting, so very tempting!

"Indeed, Colonel. If you were our allies, we would welcome it. Our own resources are stretched very thin as it is. You have tremendous potential strength and our people would rejoice at your help."

"And as allies, we would be independent?" asked Kay. "We have no desire to be a colony of yours, either, you know."

"That would be acceptable to us, Colonel."

"Really? What about this business with the human infiltrators—and Hitler and Stalin and all? It seemed like you had other ideas before we caught on!"

The alien was silent for a moment and those tell-tale ripples of color washed across its face. Kay wished she could interpret what they meant.

"As I tried to explain to your United Nations, we made many mistakes in dealing with you," Keeradoth said at last. "*Seeker of Truth* arrived here in the year 1899 by your calendar…"

"Wait a minute!" interrupted Youngs. "Are you telling me that you and your ship have been here for over a hundred and thirty years?"

"Yes, it has been a long time."

"How long do you people live, anyway?"

"Our average lifespan is about three hundred of your years, Colonel. I have spent nearly half of mine on this mission. I do not want to see it fail."

"Good grief," said Youngs, shaking her head. "But go on, you got here in 1899."

"Yes, and not a moment too soon. In the time since the first scout ship, you had advanced very quickly. We barely had time to deploy the ComBarrier before your radios became too noticeable. Then we began our study. We immediately noticed the problems caused by your multitudes of separate political units. War seemed endemic and soon after our arrival your first global war began. Such destruction! And what we could learn of your history told us that this was the norm! Our initial conclusion was that order could only result by reducing the number of separate nation-states. Sadly, the war had actually increased the number.

"It did not take long for us to realize that another war would soon break out. We hoped that if we could control its course we could bring about a reduction in the number of nation-states. In our ignorance, we thought that Germany could create a European super-state, while the Soviet Union would control central Asia. The Japanese would have their 'Greater East Asian Co-Prosperity Sphere' and that the United States would control the Western Hemisphere. By reducing the world to only four political entities, it would make things much more manageable."

"Good God!" exclaimed Youngs. "You actually expected that to work?"

"Our first great mistake," said Keeradoth, and Kay could almost hear a tone of sadness from his translator medallion. "We had not taken into account the great cultural and religious differences of your people. We looked at the problem strictly in political terms. We did not realize what the terrible…animosities…possessed by Terrans would mean. By the time we did…it was too late to avoid the catastrophe that ensued."

"But surely the people who were in charge should have tipped you off," protested Kay. "Hitler and Stalin were maniacs!"

"We, like most humans, did not take seriously the more extreme rhetoric of the National Socialists. As for the Soviet Union, we had great hopes for them. The system proposed by Marx and Engels is not so much different from our own. Sadly, it was badly corrupted by Stalin and his followers."

Great, thought Kay, *they're unreconstructed commies, too!* How the hell am I going to sell this to anyone?

"Ironically," continued Keeradoth, "the aftermath of the second global war polarized the world into two main camps—two fewer than we had hoped to achieve with our original plan. But once again, we erred. We had accelerated developments in nuclear energy because we feared it would be needed to stop the Nazi horror we had foolishly aided. The ensuing Cold War was also unforeseen by us. We had to expend every effort to prevent you from destroying yourselves. At least twice, *Seeker of Truth* was standing ready to destroy your missiles in flight had they been launched." The alien paused for a moment and when it resumed, Kay could swear she heard a tone of exasperation in the translated voice. "The end of the Cold War brought more unanticipated problems. The upsurge in religious conflict that followed was extremely troubling. Tamping it down has taken many years."

"And that brings us almost up to the present," said Kay sourly. "You were finally getting the hang of manipulating us. What was the next step? What were your trained humans going to do?"

"That part of the program was…controversial, even among ourselves, Colonel. The other ship, *Nightpiercer,* had come to relieve *Seeker of Truth*. I was no longer in command. The humans they brought were to be a test case to see if they could blend into your society. If they were successful then more would follow."

"And do what?"

"It is as you suspect, I am afraid. The ultimate aim was to take direct control of your political systems. With our access to your computers, our agents would have been given backgrounds and would have become very successful in your economic system. It was planned that their offspring would then become politically active. Again, with our ability to control your computer systems, success would be assured: news stories, polls, and even the vote counts could have been altered as necessary. Within a generation or two, most of your leaders would have been our agents. Our implantation techniques would have assured the cooperation of those who were not working directly for us."

"Generations," said Youngs. "You plan for the long term, Commander."

"Indeed yes, Colonel. None of this would have been possible without patience—a trait your people sadly lack. I know you will find this difficult to believe, but even our plans for taking control of your world was with your best interests in mind. Ultimately, when a unified political system was in place, we expected our agents to be re-assimilated into your society."

"Once we were ready to behave as you wanted us to," observed Youngs.

"Yes, we do not deny that we were doing this for our own advantage. But you have benefited, too. And I must point out that the *Brak-Shar* would have shown up here when they did even if we had left you alone. They have been exploring just as we have. What would you have done then? By our estimates your technology is approximately seventy years ahead of where it would have been without our help. You would have just been entering the nuclear age when the *Brak-Shar* ship appeared in your skies. What would have happened then?"

"I shudder to think," said Kay honestly. "But what are we going to do when they show up again in nine months? You needed two of your ships to beat the first one. Now you've only got one. Do you think we can build the equivalent of another one of your ships in just nine months?"

The alien commander twitched its shoulders and moved its head strangely. "I'm afraid that the problem is even more serious than that, Colonel."

"More serious? How so?"

"The ship that is approaching is much larger and more powerful than the first enemy vessel."

"Oh great. Wonderful. Commander, would you mind taking me back to my car? I've got some things I'd like to do before the end of the world."

"Colonel! You can't just give up!" exclaimed Doctor Vasthare.

"Larger?" said Kay, ignoring Vasthare. "How much larger?"

"From the *Brak-Shar* records we deciphered, we believe it is a *Naduratal* class Exploration Support Vessel. It is about five times as massive as *Seeker of Truth* with perhaps eight times the firepower."

"Do you honestly think we can build enough to match a monster like that?" asked Kay in dismay.

"I do not know, Colonel, but all we can do is try—and each minute that passes is one less we have to prepare."

Kay's mind was spinning. This really was too much. *One step at a time, girl!* First things first. And the first thing was to decide if she really trusted the Somerans. If she didn't then nothing else was going to happen. She thought she trusted them, but there were still things that bothered her. She needed to think. She needed time. But time was fast running out...

Chapter Twenty

"I wish you had called me, Kay," said Robert Hancock.

"I'm sorry, Bob, but I didn't want to get you mixed up in committing treason."

"Well, it's not technically treason since there is no declared war at the moment, but I see what you mean."

Kay paced back and forth in the small living room of her quarters. She knew she looked like hell. It was mid-morning and she had not slept at all the previous night. At least she had gotten back without anyone missing her—or so she hoped. She was more nervous than she could ever remember being and Bob's presence felt very good. Very good, indeed.

"So what are you going to do?"

"I don't know! You tell me that our astronomers have, in fact, picked up the *Brak-Shar* signal, so I guess I have to believe the substance of what Keeradoth said. But as for the rest, I just don't know."

"If they're coming, we have to prepare, Kay. There's no choice."

"There's no time to go through normal channels," she said, half to herself. "I suppose I could wait for the regular briefing for the President next week and just spring it on him then."

"That could work," said Bob. "At least you wouldn't be stopped by some underling who didn't agree with you."

"Or thought I was crazy—or a traitor. Let's be honest, Bob, some people are going to think exactly that."

"I know. What can I do to help you?"

She wanted to kiss him for that. Well, for a number of other reasons, too. *'How can I help?' Almost as good as: 'I love you'!*

"I'm not sure, Bob. In fact, that's the whole problem: I'm not sure about any of this! This is an incredibly important decision and I just don't have enough information to go on!"

"You think the Somerans may be lying to us again?"

"They could be. I think I believe them—I want to believe them, but what if I'm wrong? We have their records, but there are just too many of them. What if there is a whole file describing how they tricked and enslaved a dozen other races just like us that we haven't stumbled across yet?"

"It's a possibility," admitted Hancock.

"Damn! Keeradoth told the UN that there are thirty-eight other races out there that they've had contact with. If I could just talk with one of them! Find out what they know about the Somerans."

"You want a second opinion, eh?" said Hancock with a smile.

"Exactly!" said Kay in frustration. She sat down on the edge of the sofa beside him, put her elbows on her knees and rested her chin on her fists. Neither one said anything for several minutes.

Suddenly Kay straightened up. She looked at Bob with a small grin. "A second opinion," she whispered.

"What do you mean?"

"I need a second opinion, and I think I know who can give it to us!"

* * * * *

"Nisima? There are some people here to see you."

Nisima looked up from the strange paper book she had been trying to read and saw one of the nurses standing in the door of the solarium. She stood aside and two people entered, a man and a woman. They were not wearing uniforms, but something in the way they moved told Nisima that they were military.

More interrogations? Didn't they ever get tired of this?

They stopped a short distance away. The woman smiled and then spoke:

"Nisima? I am Kathryn Youngs. This is Robert Hancock. Can we talk with you for a while?"

"If you wish."

They sat down on chairs opposite her. Nisima wondered what it would be this time. The months since she had found herself here had seen a seemingly endless string of people coming to ask her questions. As her injuries healed, they came even more often. Lately, however, there had been fewer. She was almost glad to have someone to talk to. More than anything, however, she wanted to get out of this place. She was almost completely recovered from her injuries but she had yet to set foot outside of the hospital. The humans continued to insist she was not a prisoner, but they would not let her out.

"How are you feeling, Nisima?" asked the woman.

"I am doing well. My injuries do not bother me anymore."

"I'm glad to hear that; you were very badly hurt, I understand."

This was tedious. Every one of her questioners began by asking about her health. "What military branch or government agency are you two from?" asked Nisima. It wasn't polite, but she was tired of being polite. The woman glanced at her companion.

"I'm with the Air Force, Bob is with the Navy. We have some questions for you."

"So I surmised. I doubt if I can tell you anything I have not already told a dozen other people."

"Perhaps you know more than you realize," said the woman. She looked at the man with her and Nisima was surprised to see a small device in his hand. A red light was blinking on it and he shook his head.

"Do you feel up to taking a walk, Nisima? You must be tired of this place by now."

Nisima twitched in surprise. *Out? They could take her outside?* The thought sent a thrill through her. She was *so* sick of this place! For weeks she had been asking to go outside. There was a tiny courtyard where she could get some fresh air, but it was surrounded by the building and felt more cramped than the solarium.

"I…I would like that very much."

"All right, let's find you a coat and we can go."

Nisima was amazed. In only a few minutes, the hospital, which had seemed an inescapable prison, was left behind. She and the two humans strolled slowly down a paved area beside a busy highway. Despite the frightening vehicles that whizzed by it was exhilarating to be outside. The air was cool and keen, and it felt so good on her face. She did not know what these two people wanted with her, but she already felt incredibly grateful.

"What do you think now, Bob?" said the woman.

"It should be okay. No actual bugs planted and if they've got mics aimed at us, the traffic noise should take care of them."

Nisima was surprised again. She knew that she was being observed while in the hospital, but why were these two worried about listeners? They obviously had considerable authority if they could get her out of the hospital; why these precautions?

"Nisima, we have some very important things to talk to you about," said the woman. "We need to know about the Somerans."

"I have already told everything I know to other people, Ms. Youngs."

"Please, call me Kay. Yes, I've read a lot of the transcripts of your interviews. You've been very forthcoming, and given us a great deal of factual information. But I don't just need what's in here," the woman paused and pointed to Nisima's head. "I need to know what's in here, too." She pointed to Nisima's chest. To her heart.

"I'm not sure I understand what you want."

"I need to know how you feel about the Somerans. How you feel about Earth and its people. How you feel about your mission here. Not just the facts, but your feelings."

Nisima was surprised. No one had asked anything like this before. She wasn't sure what to say.

"The...the Somerans are a wonderful people," she said at last. "They are wise and kind. They mean only the best for your people. I have said this again and again."

"'Our people'?" said the woman called Kay. "They are your people, too, Nisima."

"My people are far away."

The woman frowned. "You may have grown up on another planet, but your roots are here. You are a human being, not a Someran. The Somerans might be wise, but they serve their own interests; they've told me that themselves. Those are not necessarily our interests."

Nisima started an angry reply, but then stopped and shook her head. "What difference does it make? They are gone. You sent them away. Fools."

"So you really believe that the Somerans should take control of us? Run our planet? Save us from ourselves?"

"Surely you can see that you need help!" exclaimed Nisima. Were they really so arrogant that they could not see it? "I've studied your planet and your history. You kill each other by the millions. Most of you live in ignorance and poverty, while a privileged few rule the rest for their own benefit. The Somerans offer a better way."

"I suppose there is no war or ignorance or poverty where you come from?"

"The only war is against the *Brak-Shar*. The Race live in peace with themselves. No one is poor. All work for the common good."

"'The Race'? Is that what you call the Somerans?"

"It's what they call themselves."

"And there is no strife at all?" asked the woman. "No dissension? Sounds like a race of insects to me. Drones."

Nisima was angry again but before she could say anything, a huge noisy vehicle roared by much too close to where she was standing. She cringed away in fright.

"Are you all right?" asked the man.

"I doubt that I will ever be all right again," she muttered. Then she looked up at the woman. "No, they are not insects, or drones. You simply don't understand about the Consensus."

"The Consensus? I don't recall reading anything about that in your statements or the aliens' records. What is that?"

"It is how the Race governs itself. It is a better way than yours, but sadly, it is not available to humans."

"But what is it? I don't understand."

"I don't entirely understand it myself," admitted Nisima. "In fact, I don't think the Race fully understands how it works."

"Sounds more like our government than you think," said the man. She looked at him and he was smiling. She decided it must have been a joke.

"The Somerans as a species seem to have a sort of mental link," she began.

"What? You mean they are telepaths?"

"No, not at all. They cannot transfer conscious thoughts between themselves any more than we can. It is more like an empathic ability: they can faintly detect each other's feelings. As I understand it, it is almost entirely subconscious, they are scarcely aware of it unless very strong emotions are present."

"If it is so faint, then what does it do?"

"It allows them to reach agreements. When decisions need to be made, they will debate, just as humans do. But when one idea for action is accepted by a majority, those that oppose are slowly brought around to full agreement by the empathic link. Finally, all agree on a course of action. They can act in unity, without dissent."

"Sounds like brainwashing to me," said the woman. "Like that 'implantation' process they were using on us."

"Oh! You humans! You always see the worst in everything! It has worked for the Race for thousands and thousands of years! Barbarians! You're all just a bunch of barbarians! You are predators that prey on your own kind! Every man for himself and the Devil take the hindmost—I've learned that much from studying you!" Nisima turned away and tried not to cry. The anger and frustration had been building in her for months and now it was bursting out. She could sense the two humans standing behind her, but they didn't say anything. Finally she turned to face them again. The woman was looking at her very thoughtfully.

"Perhaps we are just barbarians from the Somerans' viewpoint. I'm sorry you share their opinion of us, Nisima." The woman was silent for a few moments. She looked around. "But it is a lovely day, isn't it? Come on, let's go sight-seeing."

* * * * *

Bob Hancock watched the strange young woman as she slowly walked through the National Gallery. All the protesters in the city were keeping most of the tourists away and the place was not terribly crowded. Nisima seemed as interested in the people who were there as much as the artwork.

He found himself staring at her. She really was quite pretty in an exotic sort of way. She looked oriental, but not exactly. A strange mix of ethnicity. She also had a few faint scars on her face, the result of her crash injuries, no doubt. But it was her eyes that caught his attention. They were cold. Clinical eyes, studying what they were seeing. Judgmental eyes, too. What was going on behind them? Was there really a human woman there, or some terrible hybrid of human genes and alien values?

Bob was not entirely sure what Kay was hoping to accomplish here. Clearly, she was trying to expose Nisima to the better parts of human culture, but would it have any effect on her? She was certainly looking at what she was being shown, but she had been so eager to get out of the hospital, it might not have mattered what was on display.

"Are you enjoying this, Nisima?" asked Kay.

"It is...interesting. Some of the works are quite beautiful."

"Did you have places like this where you were born?"

"The Somerans are wonderful artists. They have many places devoted to art. I have visited some of them and seen images of more. You must have seen how they decorated their ship—everything is like that."

"But what about the humans? Don't they make art, too?"

"Some," said Nisima, but then she frowned. "Only a few, really. They try to copy the Someran work, but not very successfully."

"Just copies? Nothing original? Nothing of their own creation?"

"The Someran artwork encompasses all aspects of their world, anything we did would be a copy of something of theirs. But still...after seeing some of the things in this place, perhaps there is more than we thought."

"Didn't the first group of Earthlings brought to the Someran world try to preserve any of their original cultures?" asked Kay. "Something they could pass on to you?"

"There are a few old stories, but nothing else I'm aware of. The original people were from many different Earthly cultures. From the records, they were mostly concerned with adapting to their new home and establishing a stable society."

With a sudden shock, Bob realized just what Nisima was saying. He had pitied those humans because they had been torn away from their homes and loved ones and put into a strange and incomprehensible place. He had never even considered the aspect of culture! Plucked out of the sea with nothing but the clothes they were wearing; thrown in with strangers who spoke different languages; controlled by strange beings; how much effort could they have put into passing on their culture? A few stories, a few songs, verbal description of their homes, this is all they could have passed on to their children. And most of that would be lost with the next generations. The Somerans may have educated them, but nearly all of who they had been would have been lost. It was a terribly sad and numbing thought. The Somerans had not intended to be cruel, but this was perhaps the cruelest blow of all.

And Nisima seemed scarcely aware of what had been taken from her!

Bob exchanged looks with Kay. It seemed like she was thinking the same thing. He was tempted to say something, but when she did not, he restrained himself. They wandered for another hour and then ate lunch in the museum cafeteria. Nisima ate mechanically, but her eyes kept straying to the people around them. A noisy group of schoolchildren particularly interested her.

"They are so loud," she said. "Why don't the adults control them?"

"They're children." replied Kay. "They've probably been forced to be quiet for several hours. Now they're letting it out."

"Undisciplined."

"Children."

"Humans." And she made it sound like an epithet.

While the women were in the restroom, Bob checked in with his superiors. They wanted to know what the hell he and Kay were doing with Nisima. He spun them a yarn that seemed to satisfy them for the moment, but he wasn't sure how much longer it was going to last. He knew they were skating on some very thin ice, but he also knew that Kay had a decision such as few people had ever faced. If she felt that this might help her, then he would back her all the way. His admiration for her was growing by the hour.

After lunch, they strolled up the National Mall. They briefly went into some of the museums, but Nisima was more interested in being outside in the air. Bob's feet were getting sore, and he could see that Kay was exhausted after a night without sleep, but Nisima seemed tireless. They reached the Lincoln Memorial and went up the steps. Nisima read the inscriptions but seemed unaffected and soon went on.

"Gee, it worked on Michael Rennie," said Bob to Kay in a whisper. She elbowed him in the ribs.

Back down the Mall again. They briefly paused at the World War II Memorial, but Nisima just scowled.

"You glorify war. You will find nothing like this on the Race's planets."

"We remember and honor those who served and sacrificed," said Kay.

"Among the Race, all serve and all will sacrifice if necessary. They require no monuments."

Eventually they neared the Capitol Building. As usual, there were crowds of protesters. Kay tried to steer Nisima away, but she insisted on getting closer. As Bob feared, many of the people carried anti-Someran signs. But there were also 'share the knowledge' people and they were squaring off against the 'destroy the Devil's tools' groups. The police were moving in to break things up when Kay dragged Nisima away.

"You always fight yourselves," she said. "No cooperation, no unity."

"We believe in diversity. Each person is allowed his own opinion."

"It is self-destructive. You must learn to work together as the Race does."

Kay looked sharply at the woman and then glanced at Bob. "Perhaps we have learned to work together better than you realize. Come on, one more stop."

* * * * *

Nisima's feet were terribly sore and her legs ached. She could barely walk, but she forced herself to keep going. If she admitted how tired she was, they would take her back to the hospital. Any pain was worth this moment of freedom! And she had to admit, it had been a very interesting day! She was not entirely sure what these two humans were trying to accomplish, although she had her suspicions, but the things they had shown her had made a deep impression. The artwork, in particular, had been fascinating. It was so very different from what she had been used to. She wished she had received a fuller briefing on Earthly culture before she arrived, but the plan was for that to happen after *Nightpiercer* got here—to be sure the information was up to date.

Now they were taking her into another large building, although this one did not appear to be a museum. The man named Bob talked with someone for a while and then they were taken up in a lift. A short walk brought them to a small room that had a balcony overlooking a huge space filled with seats. Nisima was very grateful that the small room had seats, too. She sank into one with a sigh.

"What is this place, Kay?" she asked after they were settled.

"It is a concert hall. They play music here. I know the Somerans have music. Is your music a copy of theirs like your artwork?"

"We have a variation on it," she answered. "As you may have noticed, the Someran music is not well suited for human frequency ranges. Some of us have tried to adapt it, but I must admit I don't care for it a great deal."

"But no purely human music?"

"There are a few songs we sing. Some of them are very old, I understand. I have heard some of your music on the television and over the speakers in the hospital. Is that what we shall hear in this place?"

"Perhaps. What do you think of our music?"

"I have liked some of it. Some is rather grating on the nerves. I have trouble understanding the words to some of the songs."

"I have to agree with you there, Nisima," said Bob. "I find a lot of the current music pretty grating, too."

"The music they will play here tonight is called 'classical' music. Some of it is very old."

"Why such a large space? Is there a projection screen behind that curtain? You say the music is old, I did not know that you could make recordings from very long ago." Nisima found that she was getting excited at the prospect of this music. Some of the things she had heard she liked very much indeed. They stirred something inside her that she did not understand.

"The music isn't recorded," said Kay. "This will be a live performance. The musicians will be on a stage behind that curtain."

"We aren't supposed to see them? How strange!"

"No," laughed Kay, "they will open the curtain before they start to play."

"Oh."

Nisima watched as the concert hall slowly filled with people. The curtain opened up, but she was confused when there was no one behind it. Kay explained that the musicians would arrive shortly. And so they did. Men and women in black and white clothing appeared carrying strange objects and sat in the chairs on the raised platform.

"Those things they carry, they are what makes the music?"

"Yes. Those are the instruments," said Kay and she described some of them. Nisima was amazed to learn that they were not electronic, but functioned by physically manipulating them to produce vibrations in the air. And they seemed to be made mostly of wood!

"It must take great skill," she said.

"Yes, indeed. These people have spent many years—a large portion of their lives—to master their art."

"There are so many of them. Do they all play at once or each in turn?"

"Some of each, I imagine."

After a few minutes, they began to play. The sounds were strange and discordant. Nisima was disappointed. This is not what she had hoped for. Kay noticed her frown.

"What's wrong, Nisima?"

"I don't think I like this music very much, I'm sorry."

Kay laughed again. "No, *I'm* sorry, they are just tuning up! This is preparation for playing, not the actual concert."

"Oh, I see."

A few more minutes went by and all the players and the large audience became quiet. Then a man walked out onto the stage; all the musicians stood up and the audience clapped their hands together. Nisima recognized that as a way of signaling approval. She was slightly puzzled, because the man had not done anything yet.

The clapping stopped and the man turned to the musicians. He raised a small stick and the musicians raised their instruments.

And then they began to play.

At first the sound was so faint she could scarcely hear it, but then it grew louder. It had a strange tinkling sound like swirling water. Then a sweet melody filled the hall and Nisima was entranced. It seemed impossible that the sound was coming from those crude wooden devices. And all of those people working together in unison to produce it! Is this what Kay had meant earlier? It was wonderful! It flowed around her and through her. If seemed to fill an emptiness in her she had not even known existed. It made her think of her home and her family and her friends. It made her think of being in Danar's arms... Her eyes filled with tears.

All too soon, the music ended. The audience clapped their hands together. Nisima was tempted to do so as well, but she restrained herself.

"Did you like it?" asked Kay.

"Oh yes, very much! Is there more?"

"Yes, that first piece was a symphonic poem about a river in the composer's homeland. The next is what's called a violin concerto."

"Is the composer of the first piece here in the hall?"

"No, he lived many years ago, Nisima."

"Oh."

Soon they began to play again. The music was not quite so much to Nisima's tastes as the first piece, but she still enjoyed it. In particular, she was fascinated by the woman who played alone. She had such skill and seemed so involved in what she was doing. To Nisima it seemed as if the music was taking physical form inside the woman. Such passion! She had never imagined that these savage humans were capable of making such beauty. At the end of the music, she clapped her hands together a few times. Kay noticed and smiled.

The final piece was called a symphony. She was not entirely sure how it differed from the first piece except that it was longer. But it was beautiful, too. There were fast and lively parts as well as slow and calm parts. Each evoked different emotions. *How can mere sound make me feel sad or happy? This is so strange!* It *was* strange and as the music neared its climax, she found herself shaking with emotion and tears streaming down her cheeks. Kay reached over and lightly placed her hand on Nisima's arm.

When it ended, the people in the audience got to their feet and clapped their hands together vigorously and shouted. Nisima stood up and clapped her hands, too. Kay was smiling.

"Oh, that was wonderful! Thank you, for bringing me here."

"It was our pleasure, Nisima."

The hall slowly emptied and Kay and Bob led her out the way they had come.

"Where are we going now?"

"Well, that's a good question," answered Kay. "Are you tired?"

She was very tired, but she did not want to go back to the hospital! "A little, but not too much."

"Could we talk with you some more?"

"All right."

"Where would be a good place, Bob?" asked Kay, turning to her companion.

"Well, it's not that far to my house—at least we would have some privacy."

"All right, let's go."

They returned to the vehicle they had come in and then drove for quite a while. It seemed like they were going a long way from the city. Night had fallen while they were in the concert, but there were lights everywhere. Nisima sat in silence and thought about this amazing day.

* * * * *

Kay Youngs looked at the woman sitting next to her in the back seat of Bob's car and stifled a yawn. She had not slept in nearly forty-eight hours. If her plans were not foiled, she might not sleep for another twenty-four.

Plans? What plans? I'm flying this thing by the seat of my pants!

She shivered. Partly from fatigue, but mostly out of sheer terror. She was very, very aware that she was on the brink of the most important decision she would ever make. By tomorrow, at the latest, she would have to make that decision and act. This entire, so far totally fruitless, expedition had been one last attempt to convince herself she was doing the right thing.

I don't know what I was expecting from her. She does not even consider herself a human being—and maybe she's right.

No. Not entirely. Some of the things had gotten through to her, Kay was convinced of that. Her reaction in the concert hall had been honest and spontaneous. And that was what she was looking for: honesty and spontaneity. Statements from the heart, not calculated answers to expected questions. She had spent the day trying to coax this strange creature out of her shell, and she was close, so very close.

The car pulled into the driveway of Bob's house. She had visited here once before and she thought it was a very nice home. There were two cars already there.

"Well, Melissa's home," said Bob, "and it looks like she has some company."

They got out of the car and Kay escorted Nisima toward the front door. Suddenly, there was a loud barking from inside the house. *Oh dear, I'd forgotten about Cedric. I wonder what Nisima will think of him?*

Apparently she did not like what she had heard. She stopped short.

"What is that?"

"A dog. Bob's dog."

"It's all right," said Bob, "he's harmless."

"Really?" said Nisima. "I have seen a few small dogs today. This one sounds…much bigger."

"Well, he is pretty big, but he won't harm you."

Bob went to the door and unlocked and opened it. Immediately the Irish Wolfhound tried to push past him, but he grabbed his collar and hauled him back into the house. Kay followed with Nisima warily behind. *God, he really is big, isn't he?* She thought, staring at the shaggy gray beast whose shoulder came up to her waist.

"Lissa, I'm home and I have some company," shouted Bob.

"Coming, Dad!"

Kay looked at Nisima who was looking, wide-eyed, at Cedric. The dog was tugging at his collar to get closer to the newcomers. Kay put out her hand to let him sniff it.

"Hi, Cedric, remember me?" The dog gave her a friendly growl. Then he pulled toward Nisima who took a step backward. Bob let Cedric get a little closer, but after a few hesitant sniffs, he backed away. Bob looked up at Kay in surprise.

"He does not seem to like me," said Nisima.

"Oh, he just needs to get used to you," said Bob.

Just then, Melissa thundered down the steps. She was wearing sneakers and a sweat suit. Her face seemed flushed.

"Hi, Dad! Hi, Colonel!" she said and then stopped as she saw Nisima.

"Nisima, this is my daughter, Melissa," said Bob. "Melissa, this is Nisima. Say, your names sort of rhyme."

Melissa stepped forward and extended her hand. "Pleased to meet you, Nisima."

Nisima hesitated a moment and then took the proffered hand. "I'm pleased to meet you, too."

"There's another car outside, Squirt. Who's here?"

"Oh! St…Lieutenant Sokol stopped by to see how I was doing. He…he's in the bathroom right now. He'll be right down." Kay suppressed a grin as she watched Melissa's flush turn into a blush.

"I…see," said Bob, exchanging glances with Kay. She just raised an eyebrow.

A moment later, a young man came down the steps. He was blushing, too.

"Captain Hancock, good to see you, sir."

"Nice to see you, too, Lieutenant. I appreciate you keeping an eye on Melissa."

"No problem, sir." His gaze drifted over to Kay and Nisima. Introductions took a few minutes. Eventually, they were sitting down, waiting for the coffee to be ready. Cedric was curled up on the floor, watching everyone. Kay yawned. Nisima was looking back and forth between Kay and Bob and Melissa.

"Kay, are you and Bob ma…married?" she asked, at last. "Is Melissa your child?"

Kay started. Had she been about to say 'mated' instead of 'married'? Bob laughed a bit nervously.

"No, we aren't. Melissa is my daughter from an earlier marriage."

"I see."

"Do the people—the humans, I mean—back where you come from get married, Nisima?" asked Kay.

"Yes, they do. Monogamous relations seem to work best for humans we have found."

"Do the Somerans do that, too?"

"Uh, not exactly. Their sexual and family relationships are a bit more complicated."

"So you have not copied them in at least one thing."

Nisima scowled and said nothing.

"What about your family, Nisima? Your mother and father. Did you have any siblings? What did they think about you coming back to Earth?"

"I have a sister and two brothers. My family was very excited about me coming here. One of my brothers is training for this program, too…"

"With the time dilation of your journey, many years have passed. Your brother must be fully trained by now," observed Kay. "It must have been hard for you to leave them all behind."

"I…yes it was." Nisima paused and looked around. "I knew…I knew I would probably never see them again. But it was important. Helping the Somerans was so important…" She stopped. Kay looked closely and could see the tears in her eyes, hear the strain in her voice.

"I miss them." The strange young woman put her hand up to her face and let out a small sniffle. Kay moved over to sit next to her.

"Are you all right, Nisima?"

"No…no, I'm so confused. All those things you showed me today. I don't…I don't know who I am anymore."

Kay touched her shoulder gently. Nisima looked up at her in anguish.

"I don't know who I am!"

Nisima hid her face in her hands and sobbed.

Kay had been hoping for a spontaneous reaction out of Nisima all day. But now that she had gotten it, she was suddenly ashamed. She put one arm around her shoulder.

"It's all right, it's all right…"

"No it's not!" cried Nisima from behind her hands. "Nothing's all right! I'm all alone and I don't know who I am!"

"You're not alone," said Kay and she squeezed hard. "You are right here with us. And you are who you are: Nisima, a human being!"

Nisima continued to sob and Kay held her close. She didn't know what to say. Bob moved in on the other side of Nisima. Melissa knelt on the floor in front of her and Sokol stood behind. And then a gray furry snout was pushing its way into the huddle. Cedric had gotten up to see what was going on. Nisima reared back in surprise. The dog put his head in her lap and rolled his eyes up to look at her.

"I think you've been accepted," said Bob.

Nisima was still crying, but she hesitantly reached out her hand to the dog's head.

"Scratch his ears and he'll be your friend forever," suggested Melissa.

Slowly Nisima did so and Cedric turned his head to press against her hand.

"He likes it," said Nisima through her tears.

"He likes you," said Kay. "So do I."

The strange, sad woman got her tears under control and then looked at the people around her. "Thank you all for your kindness. Forgive me for acting this way."

"Nothing to forgive, Nisima," said Kay. "You've had a hard time and we want to help you if we can."

"How can anyone help me now?"

"Well, maybe by being your friend."

"It would be nice to have a friend." And she smiled.

* * * * *

Hours went by and they just talked. Mostly, Nisima about her people, the planet she grew up on, and the aliens she shared it with. Kay and the others asked questions or told stories and jokes to keep the conversation going. Cedric lost interest except when there was food around. Kay had cup after cup of coffee. Nisima had tea.

Finally, just as dawn was breaking, they ran out of steam. Nisima curled up on the couch and they put a blanket over her. The others withdrew to the kitchen.

"So what do you think?" Bob asked Kay.

"I'm convinced," she said. "The Somerans aren't saints, but I think we can trust them enough to do what has to be done."

"You look exhausted. You can have the spare bedroom, if you want."

Kay shook her head. "No time. I have to get going."

"Where? Back to Washington?"

"No. New York."

"Why? What's in New York?"

"The UN."

Bob looked startled. "You're not taking this to the President?"

"There's no time."

"All right, I can drive you there in my car. If we get going right now, we can beat the worst of the traffic."

"No, Bob," said Kay. "I better go alone. I don't want you mixed up in this."

Bob frowned. "Kay, we're in this together."

She reached over and squeezed his hand and smiled a tired smile. "I know you are, and I appreciate it—believe me! But if I screw this up, I will have burned just about all my bridges. Then it will be up to you to go see the President."

"But…"

"I need a back-up, Bob." She could see he was not happy, but eventually he nodded.

"All right. You can take my car. What are you going to do?"

Kay looked out into the living room where Nisima was asleep.

"She's convinced me. Now all I have to do is convince nine billion other people."

Chapter Twenty-One

Doctor Usha Vasthare looked nervously around the lobby of the United Nations Building. Where was Colonel Youngs? After that incredible night on the Someran ship, Youngs had made her promise to keep quiet until she heard from her. A day had passed and Usha had grown very nervous. They had to act! What if Youngs was just trying to stall until she made arrangements to cover it all up? Usha did not trust the American and had spent an entire day wondering if government agents would soon be arriving to take her away.

But then, a few hours ago, she had called and told Usha to get to the UN Building as quickly as possible and meet her there. She had taken the train and it was now almost ten o-clock. Where was Youngs? The security guards were starting to wonder why she was loitering here.

She slowly walked around the lobby, looking at the displays for the dozenth time and trying to look inconspicuous, when she felt a tap on her shoulder. She whipped around, expecting to see the guards, but it was Youngs, instead.

"Hello, Doctor," she said. "Sorry I'm late, but traffic was awful."

"Colonel, what is going on?" She looked at Youngs in surprise. The American looked exhausted. Eyes red with dark circles under them. "Are you all right?"

"Fine. Now let's go, we have an appointment with the Secretary General."

Youngs led her to the elevators and they went to an upper floor. The security guard and receptionist seemed to be expecting them and they were quickly ushered into the office of Lars Sjolander. He rose from behind his desk as they entered.

"Colonel Youngs, Doctor Vasthare, it is good to meet you." They shook hands. "I understand you have something of great importance to discuss with me, Colonel."

"Yes, Mister Secretary, I do. I need to address the General Assembly as soon as possible."

Sjolander looked surprised. Usha was a bit surprised herself.

"The General Assembly will be in session shortly, Colonel. I suppose we can change the agenda to give you a few minutes, but may I ask what you will be saying to them?"

"It is a matter of the greatest urgency, Mister Secretary, but I would prefer not to discuss it before I address the Assembly."

"I see. This is most unusual, you understand. Were it not for your reputation I doubt I could…" Sjolander stopped as the door to his office opened. His secretary was standing there looking rather agitated.

"Excuse me, sir, but the American Ambassador is here and he insists on seeing Colonel Youngs." Sjolander looked at Youngs. The woman just shrugged.

"May as well get this over with, Mister Secretary. I doubt the Ambassador is going to be happy with me."

"Very well, send him in."

A man walked into the office. The expression on his face was very serious. He glanced at Usha but then fixed his gaze on Youngs.

"Colonel Youngs, I was just informed that you were here. What, exactly, are you intending to do?"

"I have requested of the Secretary General that I be allowed to address the General Assembly and he has been so kind as to give me permission, sir," answered Youngs.

"Colonel, this is most irregular! What are you planning to say to them?"

"As I just told Mister Sjolander, I would prefer not to discuss that beforehand. I will only say that it is a matter of the highest urgency."

"I'm afraid that won't do, Colonel! I've gotten a call from your superiors and they tell me that you have been undertaking some very strange activities for the last day or so and now you have come here without authorization or prior warning. I'm going to have to insist you tell me what is going on before I can allow you to address the Assembly."

Youngs' eyebrows shot up. "I'm sorry, sir, I can't do that. I'm not here as an official representative of the United States. I am here as a concerned inhabitant of Planet Earth."

The ambassador's frown grew deeper. "Then I'm afraid you cannot be permitted to go ahead with this. Colonel, I have instructions to return you to Washington. Now if you'll come with me."

"No, sir, I'm afraid not."

"What?"

"Mister Secretary General, the United Nation's Building is neutral ground, is it not?"

"Yes, of course."

"Then the ambassador has no authority over me here, correct?"

"Technically, no…"

"Then, I repeat my request to speak to the General Assembly."

"Colonel!" sputtered the ambassador. "You're a serving member of the armed forces of the United States and you are obliged to follow orders!"

Youngs ignored the man. "Mister Secretary?" she said staring at Sjolander. The Norwegian hesitated for a few moments, his eyes flicking back and forth between Youngs and the Ambassador.

"Colonel, the Assembly session will be starting in just a few minutes. If you and Doctor Vasthare will accompany me, we can get down there."

"Mister Secretary, I must protest!" cried the ambassador.

"Sorry, sir," said Youngs with a wry grin. "But you can come watch them hang me after this is over."

"I have instructions from the President, Colonel!" he shouted as they walked toward the elevators.

"He can pull the lever on the scaffold, sir." said Youngs.

As they rode the elevator back down, Usha looked at the American in amazement. She had always been so perfectly military, disciplined, and by-the-book. Now, she seemed almost out of control. *What is she going to say?*

"What are you planning, Colonel?" whispered Usha.

"Why I'll just tell them the truth, Doctor. Surely they'll have to listen to reason."

Usha did a double-take and saw Youngs grinning at her. "Point taken, Colonel," she said nervously. "I just hope you are right."

"I just hope *you* were right, Doctor!"

* * * * *

The assembly hall was enormous. Usha uneasily scanned the rows of delegates. It was obvious that the rumor mill had been working and they knew that something unusual was going on. After a few minutes she saw the American ambassador stalk in and plop down in his seat. He did not look happy. Sjolander came over to where Usha and Youngs were sitting.

"Colonel, if this is as important as you say, perhaps it's a matter for the Security Council rather than the General Assembly."

"No, sir, too many potential vetoes in the Security Council. And this is something that concerns everyone. Every man, woman, and child on the planet."

"Hmm, I notice that you informed the news media before you arrived that something important was about to happen. You seem to have planned this carefully, Colonel. Very well then. I guess we better get started."

Sjolander went up to the podium and called the session to order. He then told the delegates what they already knew: the planned agenda was going to be changed slightly. After a brief introduction, he called Youngs up to stand beside him.

"Good luck, Colonel," said Usha.

"Thanks, Doctor. Better pray to those Hindu gods of yours, I'm going to need all the help I can get."

Youngs went to the podium, adjusted the microphone and cleared her throat. After a few seconds of hesitation, she began to speak:

"Ladies and gentlemen, thank you for allowing me to come before you today. Many of you know who I am, but I come before you not as an American astronaut, nor as an officer in the United States Air Force. I come to you as a member of the species *Homo Sapiens*, dominant life form of the planet Earth.

"I have information for you of the gravest nature. As some of you already know, three days ago a number of our radio astronomers picked up a radio signal of intelligent origin. In these amazing times, that in itself is not news. However, the source of this signal was from less than one light year away, much closer than even the nearest star system. The signal was clearly coming from a spaceship. Our scientists have also determined that the signal was similar in nature to transmissions detected from the *Brak-Shar* warship that was destroyed here some months ago."

Youngs paused as there was a nervous stir from the assembled delegates.

"I can now tell you," continued Youngs, "that these transmissions are indeed from another *Brak-Shar* vessel. Another ship is coming. It is coming here and it will be here in less than nine months."

There was another stir and someone shouted out: "How do you know this?" Usha didn't think it had been the American ambassador. Youngs seemed to draw herself up and take a deep breath.

"I have received this information from the Somerans—when I was on their ship, two days ago."

To say that pandemonium broke out would have been an exaggeration, but there was a great deal of talking and shouting and it took Lars Sjolander several minutes to restore order. All the while, Colonel Youngs stood there stony-faced, even when there was a cry of 'traitor' from the assembly.

"Yes, the Somerans are still here," she said when the delegates had quieted. "They were not defying your order to leave, but it took them longer than we had guessed to collect all of their equipment. They were preparing to go when this new signal arrived. They have been able to decipher the message and learn what is coming. The Somerans believe that we are in great danger and they offer us their help to prepare."

"It's a trick!" someone shouted.

"Yes, that was my first thought: it could be a trick. The aliens have tricked us before, so why not again? But, ladies and gentlemen, I do not believe it is a trick. We can verify much of this on our own, and we will know the truth—one way or another—in only nine months. The Somerans are offering to help us arm ourselves with weapons equal to their own. What possible benefit could they be hoping for if this is a trick?"

"We don't need their help!" came an angry cry. Others voiced similar views.

"Unfortunately, we do need their help," said Youngs. "Most of you know about my background and I can tell you that recently I have been involved in the United States' program to make use of the alien technology found on the crashed ship. The United States is expending enormous efforts to understand and duplicate what they have found. They have made more progress than most of you realize. However, it will not be enough. Even the most optimistic estimates say that it will be at least a year before the first small test ship will be ready. Even longer for the more important weapons and defensive systems. The *Brak-Shar* will be here in nine months. On our own, we cannot possibly be ready in time.

"And we must be ready," said Youngs, pushing on through a chorus of protests. "We must be ready. Commander Keeradoth has told me a great deal about the nature of the war between the Somerans and the *Brak-Shar*. While there is a faint possibility that we can convince the *Brak-Shar* that we are not allies of the Somerans, I believe this unlikely. And I have seen firsthand how the *Brak-Shar* treat their foes."

There was another outburst of shouting. Some of it was directed toward Youngs, but a considerable amount was also going at the American ambassador. Eventually it grew quiet again.

"I know that I am asking a lot of you to trust the Somerans," continued Youngs. "They have given us every reason not to trust them. They have abducted members of our species, they have manipulated us and tried to control us. They hoped, and still hope, to make us their allies in their war against the *Brak-Shar*. Their meddling has cost countless lives and done us great harm. We have every reason not to trust them."

Usha frowned. What was Youngs doing? It sounded more like she was trying to stir up anger against the Somerans than get people to accept their aid! For a moment Usha had the horrible fear that she had been betrayed once again.

Youngs had paused, but now she went on. "Ladies and gentlemen, I know you do not trust the Somerans and many of you probably have feelings of hatred toward them. But I ask you: what is the source of your distrust and your anger? Just what have they done that so outrages us?"

"Auschwitz!" cried one person. Other suggestions followed.

"Yes," said Youngs, "the Somerans have much to answer for. But let us be honest: we are more than capable of arranging our own atrocities without anyone's assistance. Our history was filled with blood long before the Somerans ever arrived. No, ladies and gentlemen, I believe that our primary grievance against the aliens can be summed up in two words: self-determination. The Somerans tried to steal our right to choose, to govern ourselves."

Youngs paused and there was silence in the great hall. "For the last two centuries, or thereabouts, humanity has been struggling to throw off the ancient bonds of autocratic rule. Bit by bit, democracy has taken hold across the world and people have learned what it means to be free. The twenty-first century dawned with the promise of freedom for everyone.

"But then, we discovered that we were not free at all. That we had never been free. We were being manipulated and controlled by outside forces we did not even suspect existed. Had it not been for the accidental arrival of the *Brak-Shar*, we might never have known until it was too late."

Usha was growing more agitated. What was Youngs up to?

"Yes, the Somerans have given us every reason not to trust them. And yet we must trust them now. But how can we do this? Self-determination is the answer to this puzzle and let that concept be our guide. We are faced with a number of choices. Our first option is to do nothing. Send the Somerans on their way and see what happens in nine months. There is a faint chance that there is no real threat. Shall we trust our fate to luck? It is more likely that a *Brak-Shar* ship will arrive—then what?

"Perhaps we can convince them that we had nothing to do with the destruction of their first ship. That we are not allies of the Somerans. Perhaps they will go away and leave us in peace. Perhaps. But even if they do, it will be their choice, not ours. More likely, they will either destroy us completely or smash us down to the point they can invade and conquer us. But again, it will be their choice, not ours.

"Our second option is to assume the threat is real, but reject the help of the Somerans. As I have already said, there is no hope that we can build a significant military force on our own, but we can try our best. Perhaps we can bluff the *Brak-Shar* and scare them off with the threat of force. It would be our only hope since we cannot fight them in fact. But in succeeding or failing, our fate will still be in the hands of the *Brak-Shar*. They would make the decision to attack or not.

"The last option is to accept the aid of the Somerans. With their help, we can build a force that could actually fight the *Brak-Shar*. We would still have the option to negotiate, but we could fight if necessary. The choice would be ours." Youngs paused and seemed to draw herself up. Usha just stared at her, wide-eyed.

"*Self-determination, ladies and gentlemen!* Only the last option gives us any hope for that! Any other course takes the decisions away from us. For too long we have been steered by others. It is time for us to take a path of our own choosing. I have presented you the facts and I thank you for allowing me to do so. Now it is up to you to decide. But decide well! Your decision here today will be the most important you ever make. And if you chose wrong, it will be the last important decision humanity is ever allowed."

Youngs stepped away from the podium and there was not a sound in the hall. An endless moment of uncertainty filled Usha. Then, Lars Sjolander rose to his feet and brought his hands together with a loud slap. Again and again. Then another person was applauding. And another. And more. Soon everyone was on their feet—well, almost everyone. Usha was clapping, too. As the roar washed over them, Youngs seemed to permit herself a tiny smile. Sjolander was shaking her hand and Usha came up beside her.

"That was brilliant, Colonel!" She shouted above the din.

"Just the start, Doctor. Lots to do yet."

* * * * *

And so there was. The debate went on all day and far into the night. Youngs was called to the podium time and again to answer questions. Usha was called up as well to provide technical information.

By mid-evening, a major decision was reached and Commander Keer-adoth was contacted and questioned. This led to more debate. Midnight came and went, but no one even suggested adjourning. Usha was nodding in her chair. Youngs was almost reeling with fatigue.

But in the end it was done. The Assembly voted to invite the Somerans back. The world would prepare for the *Brak-Shar*. They made their choice and Usha knew it was the right one.

"You did it, Colonel! You did it!" she said excitedly as she walked with Youngs out of the hall.

"We did it, Doctor," she answered, stifling a yawn. "We all did it. But this was the easy part.

"Now, we have to get ready."

Chapter Twenty-Two

"I guess I really put my foot in it this time, didn't I?" said Kay Youngs.

"I would have to say so, Kay," answered Robert Hancock. "But congratulations anyway." He stuck out his hand and she took it. She did not let go.

"I didn't ask for this, Bob. I didn't want it. I just hope that it doesn't..." she trailed off.

"Screw things up for us?" he finished.

"Yeah. Pretty damn awkward, though."

"Yes. So what are you going to do now?"

"Well, they say they have an office for me in New York, so I suppose I'll have to move up there. Today. In fact they are sending a car for me—should be here soon."

"Hopefully, they'll have some appropriate quarters to go along with the office. The most powerful person in the world rates more than a dump like this!"

"Oh, I don't know," replied Kay. "After being stuck in here for a week I've kind of gotten used to the place. And with nothing to do, I even caught up on my sleep."

"I'm sorry they treated you like they did, Kay. It was virtually house arrest! You deserved better than that considering what you did."

"I don't think they are too happy with what I did, Bob. Some of them even less so now."

Bob cocked an eyebrow and smiled. "I see you are not contradicting my statement about 'the most powerful person in the world'. What exactly is your title now?"

Kay sighed. "Officially, I'm the Supreme Commander, Earth Defense Forces. Pretty corny, huh? I don't have an official rank yet, although I imagine they will come up with something suitably embarrassing. I'm having this horrible image of a uniform with huge gold epaulets and flaming comets on the collar and a hat with a big feather. As far as how much power I really have, that remains to be seen."

"You've got a lot of people behind you, Kay."

"And some of them are probably holding daggers!"

"Maybe, but I'm not one of them. Sure you don't want me working with you in New York, Kay? I'd like that—for a number of reasons."

"I'd like that, too—for a number of reasons," replied Kay and she smiled. "But I need someone I can trust here, too. I did burn a lot of bridges doing what I did. I'm just afraid there will be people working behind the scenes to sabotage what we are trying to accomplish. I want you to be my eyes and ears in the US Military."

Now Bob frowned. "That's putting me in a hell of a position, Kay."

"I know. You're a serving officer and you swore an oath, too—just like I did. But I'm not asking you to betray your oath, Bob. The United States has formally signed into this alliance..."

"It hasn't been ratified by the Senate yet."

"Yes, but they are still abiding by it in the meantime. All I'm asking is they live up to their end of the bargain. At least you can try to let me know who's holding the daggers."

"That much I can do."

"Thanks."

The sound of a car door made Kay look out the window. She saw that a limousine had pulled up outside. A small United Nations flag flew from the aerial. Two other cars were also there, apparently as an escort.

"I have to go," said Kay. She looked into Bob's eyes and then suddenly embraced him. Their lips met, but the kiss was all too brief.

"We can pick things up from here when this is all over," she said.

"Sounds good to me. Take care of yourself, Kay."

"You, too. See you later."

* * * * *

The skyline of New York City was visible in the distance and Kay shook her head. *As soon as there's time I'm going to insist on a headquarters somewhere else. This place has always given me the creeps!*

She still couldn't believe this was happening. The immediate aftermath of the UN session had gone pretty much as she had expected, but nothing else had. As soon as she had left the neutral ground of the UN, she had been 'escorted' back to her temporary quarters at Aberdeen and instructed to stay there. If it wasn't house arrest, it was the next closest thing. They even took her phone and computer. Her only link with the outside world had been the television. Bob was allowed to visit her once, under supervision. She was quite certain that her career was over. She just hoped that it would all be worth it.

It was fortunate that there was very complete coverage of the following UN sessions on the television, or she probably would have gone nuts that next week. She followed the sessions until her eyes burned and then she watched some more. What she saw filled her with fear. After the first wave of enthusiasm the whole thing almost collapsed over the details. Voting to accept the Someran help and preparing to meet the *Brak-Shar* threat was one thing—actually doing it was something else.

How was it all to be organized? How would the technology be transferred? Who was going to build what? Who would pay for it? And most critically: who was going to be in charge? The arguments went on for days and Kay was embarrassed that the biggest obstruction was her own country.

The United States had been the top dog for so long, it was unprepared to become a member of an alliance of equals. For that was what was happening. The technological, industrial, and military dominance that the US had enjoyed for decades was about to be wiped away overnight. The influx of Someran technology would make everything else obsolete and everyone would have equal access to it. The playing field was suddenly level. The economic strength of the US was still to be reckoned with, but there were many other industrial powers, too: Europe, China, India, all had economies nearly as large as the United States. And perhaps hardest of all to accept was the fact that American military might simply didn't matter anymore.

A lot of people did not like it at all.

For days the United States had laid one unacceptable condition after another before the UN. Kay had truly feared that the alliance she had possibly sacrificed everything for was going to die aborning.

Fortunately, after a long recess, a major reality check set in. The other nations realized—with a shock—that they really did not need the United States in their alliance. With the Someran help, they could go it alone. It would be better if the Americans helped, but it wasn't absolutely essential. At that point, the Americans realized—with an even greater shock—that the rest of the world really did not need the United States in their alliance! With Someran help, they could go it alone!

And the US would be left out in the cold.

The Americans had all the records and equipment from the crashed ship, but it would be years before they could really make full use of it. Long before that, this new alliance would have the ships and the weapons and the new technology. The balance of power would shift completely and probably irrevocably.

Rather than have that happen, the Americans had finally come around. They withdrew their conditions and objections and agreed to become part of the team. Kay suspected that the President had a great deal to do with this decision. He had always seemed to be a reasonable sort to her.

Confined to her quarters, Kay had finally been able to relax—for almost a whole day.

She had expected almost everything that had happened so far, but suddenly, events took a completely unforeseen turn...

"Colonel Youngs?" A voice interrupted her musings. She turned her head to look at the young man sitting next to her in the limousine. Lieutenant Jonathan Cresswell-Jones of the Royal Canadian Navy was looking back at her.

"Yes, Lieutenant?"

"Ma'am, I want you to realize that even though I've been assigned as your aide, I completely understand that once you've gotten yourself settled, you will want to pick your own staff." The remark had been made in a neutral tone of voice, but Kay could sense a certain nervousness—or was it eagerness?—behind it. The young man did seem eager, but Kay was not entirely sure what she was going to do with him—or with any of this for that matter.

"I'll keep that in mind, Lieutenant. Thank you for being so flexible. Just how did you get stuck with this duty anyway?"

"Oh, I volunteered, ma'am."

"Really? Why?"

"I...it seemed like very exciting duty, ma'am." He paused and blushed slightly. "Canada has supplied a lot of peace-keeping forces for the UN in the past and this sounded like it would be interesting. At the very least, it will be great to have access to some up-to-date equipment for a change."

"I hope we can keep the peace this time, Lieutenant, but I'm afraid we may be in for a hell of a fight."

"We'll be ready if it comes, ma'am."

"I wish I had your confidence, Lieutenant."

"After the way you whipped the UN into action, ma'am, I'm sure you can get our forces ready the same way."

Kay stared at him with a slight frown. Was he serious? Just who did he think she was?

Supreme Commander of the Earth Defense Forces, that's who. At first she thought it was a joke, but to her horror they were deadly serious. The UN alliance needed a commander, but who? The United States was making trouble again by insisting on an American. The other nations were still annoyed by earlier US intransigence and were not in a mood to give in—until they thought of Kathryn L. Youngs.

The perfect choice, they said! An astronaut, combat veteran, a genuine hero, and the only human to ever kill a *Brak-Shar*. Amazing how the *Brak-Shar* were now the enemy—no one seemed to be thinking of negotiating with them when they arrived. Youngs would fit the bill! She was an American, but she had set her world and her species above national loyalties. The UN had put her name in nomination and the Americans couldn't do a thing to stop it. Behind the scenes they had fumed and sputtered, but Youngs was tremendously popular in some circles, so in public, they grinned and accepted it.

Of course, no one had even bothered to ask Kay if she wanted the job.

She had found out about it on the television. She could not believe it, but every channel was reporting the same thing. And then, suddenly, she had her phone and her computer back and she was talking with dozens of people she did not even know. She had tried to talk her way out of it. Tried to tell them she wasn't qualified. No one wanted to listen. She jerked her head around to look at her aide.

"Lieutenant, I'm sure you must realize as well as I do, that I was chosen because I was politically acceptable, not because of any military or organizational skills I might have. Before I transferred to test pilot school, I was only an assistant squadron commander. The biggest command I ever had was the fifty people up on the ship, up in space—and I lost three-quarters of them! I'm not sure what you—or anyone else is expecting from me."

Cresswell-Jones just stared at her nervously. "I'm sure you'll do fine, ma'am."

Kay laughed sourly. "Now that I think on it, I remember that my great-great-great-et cetera grandfather was an officer in the Civil War. He got an important command because of political connections. In his first battle his troops ran away and he got shot in the ass trying to rally them. Looks like I might be carrying on the family tradition."

The young Canadian chuckled politely. "What happened to him after that?"

Kay pondered for a moment. "He never really recovered from the wound," she answered slowly, "but he refused to quit. He ended up the war as a general. I guess maybe he's not such a bad role model at that."

"I'm sure you'll do fine, ma'am," said Cresswell-Jones again. Kay just shook her head. The whole thing seemed like some incredibly complicated nightmare. But she wasn't asleep.

And now, she was arriving at her headquarters in New York City. People—billions of people—were expecting her to save the day. Yeah, *I really stuck my foot in it this time!*

* * * * *

It was a nice office. Rather absurdly large in Kay's opinion, but it had a great view and very classy furniture. Her desk was big enough to play a game of ping-pong on and it had an ergonomically correct computer monitor below its glass top. There were several large wall monitors too, as well as very sophisticated communications equipment. There was a receptionist out in the waiting room and a conference room and another adjoining office, apparently for Lieutenant Cresswell-Jones. A half-dozen UN people were bustling about making sure she had everything she needed. The problem was that she did not know what she was likely to need.

Glancing at her computer monitor, she saw that she already had over fifty messages waiting for her and she suppressed a groan. *Looks like I'll be flying a desk for sure this time!* Eventually, she ushered everyone out except for the lieutenant and then flopped in her chair.

"Jonathan, do you have the slightest clue about just what I'm supposed to be doing here?" He looked startled.

"I assume you will be coordinating all the activities needed to organize a defense against any *Brak-Shar* aggression, ma'am."

"Of course. And just how do you suppose I should go about that? Have you ever worked on any high ranking officer's staff before?"

"Yes, ma'am, I was on Admiral Walker's staff for two years. That was one reason I was considered qualified for this duty."

"I see. Well, I have not done a great deal of staff work. I suppose what I did for the Joint Chiefs qualifies, but this is somewhat different." She paused and looked closely at him. "Jonathan? Can I trust you?"

The young man flinched slightly. "Of course, ma'am," he said, rather stiffly.

"I mean really trust you. I don't mean to be insulting, but I've just spent a week watching people on TV who were willing to put their personal or professional or national interests ahead of those of their species and their world. I have a feeling I'm going to be dealing with a lot of people like that in the near future. I can't fight front and rear. I need people I can trust around me."

Cresswell-Jones looked at her uneasily for a few seconds. "Ma'am, I would be honored to work with you. I believe in what we have to do here, and I want to help you in any way I can. If I ever give you reason to doubt me, I'd be obliged if you'd just toss me out the window, there."

Kay laughed. "I don't think that will be necessary, Jonathan. If it ever comes to that, you can take the elevator—but I don't think it will come to that. I'll be very happy to have you working for me."

"My pleasure, ma'am," and he smiled.

"Okay, enough chit-chat. What's task number one?"

"We need to assemble a staff, ma'am. I imagine the UN people have a few ideas, but we need to pick our own key people. There will be folks from various national militaries and agencies that want to grab the most important positions, and we'll have to watch out for that."

Kay grinned. Jonathan was already thinking in 'we' and she liked that.
"All right, I'm going to need a technical advisor; I want Doctor Usha Vasthare for that position."

"Very good, ma'am."

"Then, I'm going to want a liaison person with the Somerans. When we're done here, put a call through to Bethesda Naval Hospital. They have a patient there named Nisima, and I would like her brought here. They're going to fight you on this, but stay on it. Work your way up the chain of command, but get her here."

"Yes, ma'am!"

"Then, we are going to need a list of the various military officers we will be dealing with worldwide. Most of the ships we hope to construct are going to be built in naval shipyards, and I'll need to know who's in charge of all of them. I can give you the number for a Captain Robert Hancock. He used to be in naval intelligence and he can probably put you on the right track."

"Yes, ma'am."

"Next..."

* * * * *

"Colonel Youngs, that is completely unacceptable. We will be training our own crews at our own facilities."

Kay stared at the man in the wall monitor and tried to keep her expression neutral. It wasn't easy for a number of reasons. The primary one being that less than two weeks ago, Kay was working for him, instead of vice-versa. Not that the Chairman of the US Joint Chiefs seemed to believe he was working for Kay now...

"General O'Connell, I will remind you that the United States government has agreed to the conditions set down by the United Nations. The Earth Defense Forces will not be a 'multi-national' force composed of contingents contributed by different countries. It will be a true international force with completely integrated personnel and equipment. The primary training facility for the ship crews is being set up outside of Paris. The volunteers coming from America will train there along with everyone else."

The man on her screen frowned even more deeply than he had been. "I'm sorry, Colonel, that won't work. We will be providing our own crews for our own ships."

"They are not 'your' ships, General!" said Kay, trying hard not to lose her temper. "The ships that will be constructed in Norfolk, Charleston, and San Diego—along with any other equipment as part of this project—will be turned over to the EDF. That was also agreed, and we will be holding you to that. The crews for the ships will be completely international in nature and that includes the vessels coming out of American yards."

"My people are not going to accept that. Colonel! You won't get a single volunteer under those conditions!"

Kay gripped the edge of her desk and took measured breaths. Why was he being so damn unreasonable? She knew it was hard for him to accept the New Order of Things, but didn't he realize he wasn't holding a winning hand this time? Perhaps a gentle reminder...

"Then we can crew all the ships with non-American personnel, General. Do you want that? Please let me know, so I can inform the other countries that they will need to provide additional volunteers."

"The shipyard people won't build the ships for your damn EDF!" he exploded. "We'll build our own fleet to fight the *Brak-Shar!*"

The message wasn't getting through. Perhaps a stronger nudge…

"Then we will have to divert our resources elsewhere, General. You cannot build anything without components the Somerans will provide. Our supply of shipyards worldwide exceeds the supply of components the Somerans can manufacture in the time we have. Shall I alert the yards in Kobe, Hong Kong, and St. Petersburg that they can begin construction of additional ships?"

"Goddamnit, Colonel! You're a traitor!"

Oh dear, name calling. She had hoped it would not come to this. She had also been hoping that it would not hurt as much as it did. She closed her eyes and bowed her head slightly. Was she a traitor? A lot of people seemed to think so and it hurt. She loved America and she believed in American ideals. She hoped those ideals would eventually be embraced by the whole world. B*ut we have to save the world first!* And the United States simply could not do that on its own even with Someran help. The job was too big and the time was too short. They needed everyone. Maybe a multi-national force could have done the job, but that was not what the UN had agreed upon—and there was no more time to argue about it. And assuming they did beat the *Brak-Shar*, the thought of a dozen national fleets of the new ships suddenly scrambling for power afterward filled Kay with nearly as much dread as the *Brak-Shar* themselves. A new arms race with a dozen different players and with more *Brak-Shar* to deal with later… *No, this is the only way!*

She found that she was staring at O'Connell and to her surprise, he dropped his eyes first.

"I'm sorry, Colonel, that was uncalled for." He seemed embarrassed by his outburst. "This has been a very difficult time for everyone. I…I guess I'm having more trouble adapting than most."

"I know General, I know. I swore the same oath you did and this whole situation is pulling us all out of shape. But we need to work together on this. Our only chance is to hang together."

"Or we'll all hang separately?" asked the General with a small grin. "I suppose so, Colonel. All right, I'll pass on the instructions and arrange transport for our volunteers."

"Thank you, General," said Kay in relief. "I'll be talking to you again soon, I'm sure."

Kay disconnected and leaned back in her chair with a long sigh. After a moment she became aware that she was not alone. She turned slightly and saw Lieutenant Cresswell-Jones standing in the doorway with a slight grin on his face. How long had he been there?

"Yes, Lieutenant?"

"Ma'am? I must say, you are getting the hang of this pretty quickly."

Chapter Twenty-Three

Kathryn Youngs tugged her uniform jacket into place and regarded herself in the washroom mirror. It wasn't a bad looking uniform, really. A light, 'UN Blue' jacket with a few brass buttons, a pair of navy blue trousers, white shirt, black tie, and a light blue service cap. It was the 'undress uniform'. No one had come up with a dress uniform yet, and if Kay had her way no one ever would.

No, the uniform itself was not too bad, it was what was *on* the uniform that bothered her. Oh, the 'EDF' patch on the shoulder was all right, and even the crossed rockets on the breast and cap were tolerable. It was those six stars on the collar and the shoulder epaulets that were driving her crazy.

Six stars! Count 'em! Six! They must be out of their minds!

Granted, they were rather small stars—it was the only way they could fit six of them on the uniform. But they still seemed terribly ostentatious. And the rank that went with those stars: 'Space Marshal'. *It sounds like I'm some damn sheriff from Mars or something!*

She found herself quietly humming a song that had been taking shape in her head for the last few days: '*So stick close to your desk, and never go to space, and you too may be the savior of the human race...*' Gilbert and Sullivan were probably turning in their graves.

She knew why they had done it: it gave her a military rank that was higher than anyone else's. She outranked five star generals and field marshals the world over. In theory, that would give her the authority she needed to get the job done. *Only if everyone else takes this more seriously than I do!*

She let out a long sigh and shook her head. It had been three weeks since she had found herself here and she had to admit that this uniform was the least of her worries. She turned and walked out of the room. Jonathan Cresswell-Jones was waiting for her in her office. He was wearing his own EDF uniform and he had also been promoted a few notches above his old RCN rank.

"Looking sharp, ma'am, really sharp," he said appreciatively.

"Stuff it, Commander, and I don't need to tell you where," she growled. Jonathan smirked and that made Kay smile. The fact that she could say something like that to him and he knew it was a joke showed how good a team they were becoming.

" Everyone's waiting for you, ma'am."

"All right, let's go."

Kay braced herself and then opened the door to the conference room. A dozen faces, nine of them human, looked up as she entered.

"Good afternoon, everyone," she said. Most of the people in the room responded cordially. Kay found her place at the head of the table and sat down. There was a moment of silence as she looked over her staff and guests. Assembling this team had been a difficult but vital task, and the urgency of the situation had forced her to do it far more quickly than she would have liked. Still, she felt she had done about as well as possible. Of course, not everyone here was part of her staff...

"Commander Keeradoth, Sub-commander Tandalin, Chief Technician

Nalorom, thank you all for coming down here to meet with us."

"It is our pleasure, Marshal Youngs," replied the alien commander. The perfect, unaccented English coming from its translator medallion conveyed no emotion, but Kay could sense a certain tenseness in the creature. She was slowly learning to interpret those strange color changes and gestures. She wondered if there was something wrong.

"Well, let's get started," she said. "Captain Duvall, you can go first. How are things going with crew training?"

Captain Jacques Duvall, formerly of the French Marines, was in charge of personnel, her 'G-1' on the staff. He consulted his computer for a moment and then began:

"Madam, all of the volunteers have reported to the training facilities. The accommodations are rather Spartan, I fear, but the logistical infrastructure is in place to handle the meals, laundry, and the like. Some security features are still being installed, but I am satisfied with what is currently in place.

"We have started classroom instruction this week. The training videos provided by Commander Keeradoth are proving extremely useful, although there are a few language difficulties. So far the volunteers are responding as we have hoped. There is minimal friction between the nationalities, although they are tending to form cliques."

"That is to be expected, Captain," said Kay. "But we must work to prevent too much segregation. We want fully integrated teams."

"Yes, madam, I agree. Once the training simulators are completed and online, we should have an easier time of it. When we start selecting the actual ship crews, we can form teams with whatever mix of nationalities we choose."

"Have you given any more thought to the criteria for creating those crews? Particularly how we will set up the rank structure. That could be an especially delicate situation."

"Yes, madam, you are correct: we will have to move carefully. I have some of my people preparing a proposal for your review. I hope to have it to you by tomorrow."

"Very good. Thank you, Captain. Since the subject of security has been raised, why don't you go next, Piotr?" Kay turned to a heavyset man three placed down the table from her.

"Certainly, Marshal Youngs," he said and smiled. Kay had known Piotr Novakovic for years. They first met while she was studying life support systems with the Russians. He was a jolly sort, which effectively hid the competent security expert he really was.

"As Captain Duvall has reported, we are nearly complete with the security systems for the Paris training facilities. Actually, the exterior security is in place. We will continue to refine our interior security as the training routines are established. It is a pity, but we must admit that the recruits themselves pose the greatest threat."

Kay nodded her head. With several thousand people, coming from dozens of different countries, the potential for spies, saboteurs, and terrorists slipping in was a very real concern. She could not really understand why anyone would try to wreck what was the only real hope of survival for mankind, but she knew there were many people who did oppose the EDF.

"Worldwide, we are being more dependent on local security forces than I would like, Madam Marshal," Novakovic, continued. "But considering our own lack of personnel and the locations of the construction facilities, we really have no choice."

"Are the national security people giving your inspectors access to the facilities in question, Piotr?" asked Kay.

"So far, they are, but in many places our inspections have been very cursory since nothing is actually happening yet. Once construction begins, we will need more access and I fear that we may be denied that in some locations."

"Denied? I want to know immediately if that happens. Under the agreement, our people have absolute priority."

"Well, perhaps 'denied' was not the best word," said Novakovic. "It is just that we are going to be stretched very thin. It might not be a matter of being denied access, but of missing places we should be looking. Once the equipment starts arriving, it may be very difficult to keep track of it all."

"Yes, I see," said Kay. "And from what Doctor Vasthare told me just before the meeting, I'm afraid it will be even more difficult than that, correct, Doctor?"

"Yes, Col...er, Marshal," said Vasthare, "but I think the benefits of this new idea far outweigh the security issues. I'll let Nalorom explain."

Kay looked to where the Somerans were standing. She really wished they could sit down. She was starting to be able to tell the aliens apart, but she was glad they had agreed to wear name tags!

"Thank you, Doctor. You are all familiar with the fabricators we use. They are essential to creating the components we shall need to meet this crisis. As you had already discerned, there are different models of fabricators, with different capabilities. Using the terminology that you had already set up, the twenty-four fabricators on *Seeker of Truth* can be considered level six fabricators. These are at the cutting edge of our own technology—or at least they were when we left home—and they are extremely sophisticated. They are capable of creating the critical components for the ship drive, the defensive shields, and the core of the fusion reactors. Sadly, however, their ability to replicate themselves is very limited. While it is possible, there are certain components that still have to be painstakingly hand constructed. The amount of time this would take at first led us to believe that the vast majority of fabrication would have to take place aboard *Seeker of Truth* and that this would severely restrict the number of weapons and vessels that could be constructed."

"But you have a different idea now?" asked Kay.

"Yes, Madam Marshal. Upon further evaluation, we realized that ninety percent of the required items for the ships can be created using level five fabricators or below. And our level six units can create all the parts for a level five machine in only a week, although another week would be needed for final assembly. This would allow us to give you a set of level five fabricators which *are* capable of replicating themselves. I am sure you can see the possibilities."

"Yes! Our set of fabricators could make another set which could make another set and so on. It would multiply our capabilities many fold."

"Exactly. This will be particularly critical in the matter of constructing missiles."

Kay nodded. She thought back to that last meeting with the Joint Chiefs when Bob had told them that they could start cranking out missiles in about six months. Wrong! In the mad rush to get some working technology, the American chemists and engineers had overlooked a few important details. The exotic fuel used by the missiles was not just a mix of chemicals. Instead, they were finely crafted crystal lattices formed into rods that would undergo some amazingly complicated chemical-nuclear reaction when ignited. These fuel rods could only be made in the fabricators where they were built up literally molecule by molecule. If the Somerans had been forced to make all of them in addition to the vital components for the ships, it was going to stretch their capacity to the breaking point. But the rods could be made in level five fabricators, so the Earthlings could make them themselves.

"That's excellent news, Nalorom," said Kay, but then another thought struck her. "Tell me, you say that your level six fabricators cannot replicate themselves completely. Would it be possible to set just one of your fabricators to work making parts for level six units? Then finish them and turn them over to us as you can?"

"I suppose we could do that," answered the Someran. "It would cut down on production slightly, but not critically. May I ask why you would want us to do that?"

"Why, I would think that would be obvious, Nalorom," said Kay with a grin, "so we would have some of our own. I think this will be critical, not just for technical reasons, but for political. Part of this whole scheme was based on the idea that we would be given enough of your technology to build the ships and weapons on our own. If people were to learn that you still held the monopoly on certain key items, it could blow this whole thing up in our faces."

"Ah, yes, I see," said Keeradoth, breaking in. "Very well, it shall be done as you say."

"Thank you, Commander. So, once we start getting the level five units in operation, we should have no difficulty creating the components for the dozen ships we hope to build, plus enough missiles to arm them. On the other hand, we will be making Piotr's job more difficult. With all those extra fabricators and all the items they will be producing, we will have to keep a close eye on everything. Still, I'm feeling better than I have all day." She smiled and as she looked around the table, most of the people were smiling as well.

All except one.

"Mister Breyer, is there something wrong?" she asked.

Siegfried Breyer was a German who had emigrated to the United States about twenty years earlier and had become big in the ship building industry. On Bob Hancock's recommendation, Kay had selected him to oversee the construction of the new spaceships. He had been fidgeting all through the meeting and the look on his face now sent a chill down her spine.

"Ma'am…I…ma'am, I had hoped to talk to you before the meeting, but my people were working on the new estimates right up to the last minute…" Breyer spoke very good English except when he was excited or upset Kay had noticed. Now he was speaking faster and faster and his accent was becoming thicker and thicker. *What can be going on?*

"Is there a problem?" she asked, knowing full well that there must be.

"Yes…yes there is. I'm sorry, but our new projections are indicating that we can't get the ships ready in time!"

Kay was struck dumb. Everyone else followed her lead.

"What...what do you mean?" she said, finding her voice at last. "Your projections from last week indicated that we could do it!"

"I know, ma'am and I'm sorry. Those first projections were based on very sketchy data and with further study we've had to revise our estimates. Right now, we think there is a slim chance that the one ship that will be built in Norfolk might possibly be operational in time by using the salvaged reactor from the crashed ship, but the others will take several additional months. I've run our figures by Commander Keeradoth's people, and they have confirmed them."

Kay looked to the alien commander and it nodded. "I'm afraid Mister Breyer is correct, Marshal Youngs. The design for the ships you are attempting to build is one we had devised some time ago. It is basically a modified version of *Seeker of Truth*. Enlarged in detail to accommodate your larger bodies, but smaller overall because we eliminated all elements not needed by a warship. The result is a vessel half the size of our own, but with similar fighting abilities. Unfortunately, we had anticipated that you would have progressed further before we reached the point of constructing these vessels. Our initial time estimates had assumed a whole generation of construction robots that you do not possess yet. Even then, our plans called for a year and a half to finish each vessel. We did not anticipate this situation."

"Well, there must be something we can do to speed things up," said Kay. "Perhaps we could reduce the size further or simplify the design..."

"I don't believe that we can make any significant changes that would speed construction," said Keeradoth. "The design as it stands is the minimum needed for a real warship. We need the drive, the shields, the weapons, a fusion plant to power them, and a hull to contain them. A smaller vessel is certainly possible, and we do plan to construct smaller vessels as you know, but their fighting value will be severely limited."

"Then we have to work harder! Put more people on the job! I don't have to remind everyone that the fate of our planet rests on this."

Breyer shook his head. "I'm sorry, ma'am, it just doesn't work like that. Our estimates assume working three shifts with a maximum crew. Simply throwing more people at it is not the answer. The ships are of a finite size. Only a given number of people can work on it before they start getting in each other's way. You can only operate so many cranes in the space around the ship. And construction has to be done in a specific sequence. You have to assemble the skeleton first and then add the decks and some of the skin before you can start adding equipment. The structural steel alone is going to take time to fabricate. We won't even be able to lay the keels for another month."

"Can't we work with modules?" asked Kay in growing alarm. "Make sub-assemblies elsewhere and then bring them in? For God's sake, people, they built cargo ships and destroyers that way in World War II in a matter of weeks!"

"Yes, ma'am, they did," said Breyer, "but if you look at the records, the first units in those projects all took a year or more. They had to get the system set up and running before they could produce at that rate. I have no doubt that future ships could be built much faster, but these first ones are going to take time. We will be working with modules, as you suggested, but our time estimates take that into account. And keep in mind that this is entirely new. The construction workers are going to be learning their jobs as they go along—and that takes time."

"We don't have the time," said Kay, slamming her fist down on the table. "We have to do something!"

"I know, ma'am, but I don't know what. You've seen one of your space-planes under construction, haven't you? These ships will be far more complex."

"But..." began Kay, but she shut her mouth. She did remember visiting the production facility for her spaceplane. There had been dozens of technicians swarming over it, fitting kilometers of wiring into the constricted framework. The complexity was awesome. And there had been no way to hurry it...

"Well what about these smaller ships?" asked Captain Azuma Kagami. The former Japanese officer was Kay's head of planning. "Can we not make better use of them than you indicate, Commander Keeradoth? I am working my way through your tactics manuals as quickly as I can and I know that I still have much to learn. But from studying the records of your recent battle against the *Brak-Shar*, it seems as though if we had a few dozen such vessels, each carrying a few dozen missiles, that we could launch a very large salvo that should overwhelm the enemy's defenses at a blow. I realize that the small ships have very weak shields and lasers, but in an attack such as this, they would need little staying power."

The alien commander shook its head. Kay knew that this was not a normal gesture of the Somerans, but Keeradoth obviously knew what it meant to the humans.

"I am sorry, Captain, but as you get further into the tactical instructions, you will learn why your idea will not work."

"Can you give us a brief idea why not, Commander?" asked Kay.

"Certainly, Marshal Youngs. First, you have to realize that vessels such as *Seeker of Truth* and the ships you hope to build are very small as warships go. To put things in more familiar terms, you can think of them as destroyers or perhaps even corvettes. The *Brak-Shar* vessel that is coming here might be compared to a cruiser, or perhaps slightly larger. Not a true battleship, but certainly very powerful. Also, a large battle in our war might involve hundreds of ships. With those factors in mind, you can see that if it were simply a matter of launching large numbers of missiles to overwhelm the enemy's defenses, then large warships would not be cost effective at all. They would simply be large, expensive targets, and navies would consist of only the very small, expendable ships."

"But why can't a large salvo of missiles be effective?" Kay was confused. From the briefings on the first battle, she had read, it took a sizable number of missiles to get past a target's defensive lasers.

"Missile tactics are very complicated," said Keeradoth. "In addition to our defensive lasers, ships can also launch defensive missiles. These missiles will accelerate and move away from the launching ship to a distance of several hundred kilometers and then explode, releasing a cloud of small metal particles. This creates a barrier that will disable incoming missiles that hit the cloud at high velocities."

"But if you can do that, missiles should be nearly useless," protested Kay.

"Not exactly. The collision with the particle cloud will not usually destroy a missile completely. It will just knock out the guidance or propulsion system. The wreckage will continue on. This means that a target must keep accelerating, or it will still be hit. This, in turn, means that the defensive particle barrier will be left behind. To continuously renew the barrier would soon deplete a ship's supply of missiles. Keep in mind that depending on the velocity of the incoming missiles, the barrier must be set up some distance away from the ship, or collisions will still occur. This means that perhaps as many as fifty missiles must be used each time the barrier is created.

"A missile duel thus becomes a guessing game. How many missiles do you fire? Enough to get some past the defense lasers, but not so many that the target deploys the particle cloud and destroys your entire salvo. Defensively, it is the same puzzle: can my lasers stop enough of the incoming missiles to prevent serious damage or should I set up a particle barrier? Since I cannot afford to waste my defensive missiles on a small salvo for fear of running out, it is a difficult decision. Of course, there are circumstances when there might not be time to deploy a particle barrier. We were quite fortunate to destroy the first *Brak-Shar* ship in the manner we did.

"Forgive my long explanation, but I think you can see why Captain Kagami's idea will not work: if we launched a massive salvo, the enemy would just deploy a particle barrier and destroy them all."

"Then we will have to send the small ships in waves and attack with smaller salvos," said Kagamai.

"That may be our only option," agreed Keeradoth. "In conjunction with *Seeker of Truth*, we may hope to inflict some damage on the enemy. But I fear not enough. The smaller ships have very weak shields, limited missile supplies, and limited endurance since they operate off batteries rather than a reactor. They have very little staying power."

Kay looked on as several other ideas were raised and discarded. One idea for mines seemed to have some merit and was slated for further investigation. Missiles launched from the ground or space platforms also seemed to have some promise. They even discussed the possibility of repairing the ship in orbit and arming it somehow. The small ships—which they were already referring to as 'fighters'—appeared to have the best potential. But overall, the situation did not look good. Apparently, you needed real warships to fight a real battle.

Kay glanced at the people in the room to judge their reactions. Most seemed as upset at this turn of events as she was. Her gazed lingered on Nisima for a few moments. She had been happy when the woman was turned over to her care and her reaction when she learned that the Somerans were still around had been priceless. Just at the moment, however, she seemed as upset as anyone. Nisima seemed to consider the *Brak-Shar* as the ultimate Bogey Men. Kay shook herself and returned her attention to the discussion. The ideas had run out and now they were just rehashing the old ones. A feeling of dread was growing in her. Everything that she—and they—had done could turn out to be for naught. She had sold the whole world on the idea of preparing, how could she tell them that it could not be done?

For that matter, *should* she tell them? The truth could cause panic if it became widely known.

"All right, people," she said at last. "We've gone about as far as we can right now. I want you to go back to your own groups and get to work. Explore these ideas and try to come up with some new ones. Siegfried, keep working on the estimates and see if there is any way to speed things up. Also, I don't need to tell you how sensitive this all is, but make sure your people know! If this gets out prematurely there will be hell to pay! We will reconvene at 0600 tomorrow. Thank you."

Kay watched her staff file out of the conference room.

It was going to be a late night for all of them.

Chapter Twenty-Four

"So how have you been doing, Ed?" asked Captain Robert Hancock.

"Not too bad," answered Captain Edward Osborne. "*Tennessee* is in to take on the rest of her missiles. I heard you were here in Norfolk, so I borrowed a car to come up and chat for a bit. After being at sea for three months with no news, it would be great to know what is really happening. I know that you've got an inside track to all the good scuttlebutt, Bob."

"Well, I did, and I guess I still do have a few tracks. But you might not want to be seen in my company anymore, Ed. I'm not too popular in some circles these days." Bob looked pointedly around the small coffee shop they were in where numerous uniforms were present.

"What? Because you had the incredibly poor taste to become friends with Youngs? I've heard some of that shit, Bob! To hell with all of them, I say! You've been my friend for close to twenty years and it will take a lot more than this nonsense to affect that!"

Bob smiled at his friend. The words were not unexpected, but they were no less welcome because of it. "Thanks, Ed. I knew I could count on you to understand. So how's the family?"

"Joannie and the kids are fine. But I don't get home enough. I can't believe the kids are in high school already. They'll be off to college before I know it."

"Yeah, they sure grow up fast. It seems like yesterday that Melissa was just a baby."

"How's she doing?" asked Osborne with a concerned look on his face.

"I think she's all right. But I know what happened bothers her and I don't really know what to say. I guess some of those bombs I dropped on North Korea must have killed some people, but I've never killed anyone like she had to—face to face like that—so I can only guess what she's feeling." Osborne nodded. Bob was worried about his daughter, but she really did seem to be okay. And he had to admit that the attention of Steve Sokol seemed to be helping her. Bob felt a twinge of jealousy that someone else was taking care of her now, but it had to happen sooner or later...

"Is she back on duty?"

"More or less. With the way things have been shaken up lately, the crash investigation and processing has a lot lower priority than it had. I don't really have much for her to do."

"And what are you doing? I heard you were involved with constructing the new ships. That's why you're in Norfolk, right?"

"Again, more or less. Sometimes it seems less rather than more. My association with Kay has put me on a number of important peoples' blacklists. They don't trust me it seems."

"Damn fools. I know what Youngs did rubbed a lot of people the wrong way, but it had to be done. Without somebody taking the lead, we'll still be arguing and arguing when the *Brak-Shar* show up we won't be ready."

Bob nodded. He was glad that his friend saw things that way, but his comment about being ready sent a chill through him. He had talked to Kay two days ago and what she had to tell him was not good. He looked up and Ed was staring at him.

"We are going to be ready, aren't we?"

Bob bit his lip. He owed Ed Osborne in a lot of different ways. Just as Ed owed him. What should he tell him? But even no answer was an answer... He leaned forward and said quietly: "Ed, if I were you I'd get Joannie and the kids as far away from any city as I could. And I'd do it soon."

"My God," he whispered. "Is it that bad?"

"Bad enough. But even if everything was going according to plan, they are going to announce voluntary evacuations starting next month and then mandatory ones later on. Even if we win, we can't assume nothing's going to hit us down here, and the cities are the obvious targets. The evacuations are going to be pure chaos, so don't wait."

Osborne stared at him for nearly a minute before nodding. "All right, I'll make the arrangements. I assume this is all top secret?"

"Yes, please don't spread it around, Ed."

Osborne nodded again but then looked sharply at him. "You said, 'even if everything was going according to plan'. I assume it's not?"

"No."

"Technical problems with the new ships?"

Bob glanced around. No one else seemed to be paying attention to them. "Not so much technical problems, as a lack of time. Our current estimates indicate the new big ships just aren't going to be ready."

Osborne nodded. "I thought the whole thing was awfully ambitious when I first heard about it. A completely new class of vessel being built from the keel up in just nine months. And they're not small vessels either! They're what? About forty thousand tons each?"

"About that. Thirty-eight to be exact."

"Can't they downsize them to something more realistic?"

"They've thought about it, but there are problems with that, too. The Somerans' fusion reactor is very large. By the time you include that, the drive, the shields, life support, and the weapons, you just can't get it much smaller and still have it be an effective warship."

"What about an alternate power plant?"

"You mean like a standard fission plant? Well, there are some technical problems with that, too. And whatever time savings in construction that might result would probably be eaten up by the design changes that would be needed. I know they are looking at all sorts of ideas. It's driving Kay out of her mind."

"Hell," muttered Osborne. "There has to be an answer."

Bob nodded. He'd been trying to think of something—anything—since he had talked with Kay. It looked as though they could produce a lot more of the small ships—the 'fighters'—than they had originally planned, but they could not win on their own. And once the *Brak-Shar* had control of the space around Earth, they would be nearly helpless. While it was possible to build effective ground-based weapons, they could hardly do so with the enemy staring right down on them. They could smash anything that was remotely suspicious—or just smash *everything* and be done with it.

The image had been growing in his head and he could not shake it. Nuclear fire raining down on Earth's cities from space. Factories and transportation lines smashed. Mobs of refugees fleeing into the countryside trying to find food and shelter. Order collapsing. Isolated pockets trying to build weapons to fight back, but each one being stamped out as soon as it revealed itself. Would they just kill everyone, or try to spare enough of the ecosystem to colonize the planet themselves? What would happen to the human survivors?

What would happen to his daughter? He shook his head.

Bob looked up at Osborne and saw that his friend was staring out the window toward the docks. He was surprised to see a grin growing on his face.

"What is it?"

Osborne's head jerked around and he was staring right at him. His grin was even bigger.

"Mind letting me in on what's so funny?" asked Bob.

"I think I've got the answer."

"What? What do you mean?"

"The answer to the problem! Come on, let's get out of here and I'll tell you about it."

In a daze, Bob was led out of the coffee shop. Osborne had him by the arm.

"Ed! What answer? Tell me what it is!" he demanded after a moment.

His friend stopped and he still had that grin.

"First I'll tell you what it isn't: it's *not* an aircraft carrier!"

* * * * *

"*Submarines?*" asked Space Marshal Kathryn Youngs of the Earth Defense Forces.

"Yes, ma'am," said Bob Hancock. "It was Captain Osborne's idea and we think it may be the answer."

Youngs paused and rubbed the bridge of her nose. Bob and his friend, Osborne, had just showed up at her office unannounced. And while she was always glad to see Bob, what he was telling her was... *crazy*. "Let me get this straight: you are suggesting that we take the world's fleets of nuclear submarines and turn them into *spaceships*?"

"I know it sounds outrageous, ma'am," said Osborne. "But think about it for a moment; your ships need a number of characteristics, and the subs already have a lot of them. They have a strongly constructed, air-tight hull, they have a nuclear reactor to provide power, they have their own life support systems, they already have trained—well, at least partially trained—crews..."

"And they're already built," finished Youngs.

"Exactly! You would save months of time on the basic construction."

"But can we make the necessary conversions? Most of them are a lot smaller than the ships we had hoped to build. Can we fit the drive and the shields and the weaponry—and the controls to run them—into hulls that size?"

"I don't know, ma'am. I think we can empty out a lot of space on them if we have to, but I don't know enough about the size or shape of the alien gizmos. Just as a guess, I would expect the individual units to be a lot weaker than what you were trying to build—but we could probably make a lot more of them!"

"Captain Hancock," said Youngs. She made eye contact with him from across her desk and there was the flicker of a smile. "How many nuclear boats are currently in service worldwide?"

"Nearly two hundred, ma'am. And that number has been increasing as a lot of mothballed units are being reactivated."

"That's a lot of submarines." Youngs pondered for a few moments and Bob stared at her face. She looked incredibly tired. Dark circles under her eyes. Lines that had not been there even a few weeks before...

"All right," she said suddenly. "It's too crazy an idea not to consider." She touched a button on her desk. "Jonathan, get Doctor Vasthare and Mister Breyer up here right away."

"Mister Breyer is on an inspection tour today, ma'am," came back a voice over the intercom.

"All right, then get the senior person from his department who's available. Are any of the Someran tech people in the building?"

"I believe one of them is with Doctor Vasthare, ma'am."

"Excellent. Send them up, too. When they get here, you come, with them."

"Right away, ma'am."

Youngs closed the intercom and then leaned back in her chair. "Do you really think this can work?"

"I think there is a chance, ma'am," answered Osborne. "However, there will be at least one major technical problem we need to solve: the issue of waste heat."

"Heat?" asked Youngs.

"Yes, ma'am. The reactors on a submarine work by running water through them. The water is heated to high temperatures under pressure. This is then allowed to turn to steam to run turbines which produce electricity. The electricity powers the ship systems as well as the electric motors that actually propel the boat. The steam has to be condensed back into water to be sent back through the reactor to begin the cycle again. To cool the steam, we take cold sea water and run it through a condenser unit. The sea water gets heated and we just dump it out—that's the waste heat I was talking about. The problem is..."

"Cold sea water is going to be hard to come by in outer space," interjected Youngs.

"Exactly, ma'am. We have to figure out some other way to get rid of the excess heat. I'm hoping your engineers—or the aliens—may have some good ideas."

After a few minutes people began arriving. Hancock was a little startled when two of them were not human. He had seen their bodies, but he had never met one of the Somerans face to face. It felt very odd being in the same room with them, but it was even odder the way no one else seemed to think it was odd—not even the aliens themselves. Everyone acted like it was a perfectly normal thing.

Introductions took a few minutes and then Kay had Osborne briefly outline his proposal. The reactions on faces varied from extreme surprise, to hope, to excitement to skepticism.

"You are correct, Captain Osborne," said Doctor Usha Vasthare. "The heat transfer problem will be the main stumbling block with the reactors."

"We were going to use a nuclear reactor on the ship we were constructing in orbit, weren't we, Doctor?" asked Youngs.

"Yes, but there were significant design differences from what exist aboard these submarines. The reactor aboard the ship would have been operating at lower power levels and we were using that heat to provide the propulsion. The design allowed us to have relatively little 'waste' heat. In the case of the submarines, we must somehow cool down the water that circulates through the reactors—and then somehow dispose of that heat."

"Naloram, is there anything your people can do for us here?" Youngs directed the question to the Someran technician.

"Perhaps, Madam Marshal," said the alien. The perfect English coming from its translator medallion was in strange contrast to the sounds coming from its mouth. "We have not used fission reactors very much for some time, but we do have applications where waste heat must be dealt with. It is possible that we can devise a heat exchanger connected to a set of external radiators. We shall have to study this closely."

"What about this proposal as a whole? Do you believe it has merit?"

The alien was silent for a few seconds before answering. "Madam, I would be lying if I said this proposal had not taken me completely by surprise. The capacity of your species to do the unexpected is remarkable. None of our scenarios had even considered the possibility of combining our technology with yours. This is an extremely imaginative and creative idea and I believe it should be pursued. It will require some study to determine its feasibility and considering the shortage of time, we should begin immediately."

"Very well, then," said Youngs. "We will need to get detailed drawings of all the different sub types to the Somerans as quickly as possible. They can tell us if they can fit their equipment inside our hulls. We'll need to contact the various navies to see about getting use of their boats. I don't know how much they will fight us on this, but I have a feeling that after they give it some thought, they won't fight us at all."

A number of surprised looks appeared on faces around the room.

"Unlike the new ships we are building," she explained, "there is no way we can hope to staff these ships with international crews. I'm afraid we are looking at the creation of a number of national space navies—in spite of all I have done prevent that."

"We'll have to insist on EDF control of all those ships, ma'am!" said Youngs' assistant, a young Canadian named Cresswell-Jones. Bob wasn't sure he liked him. He seemed very eager, and he was working very closely with Kay, and he was darn good looking…

"Yes, we'll have to have overall command, Jonathan, and I imagine they will agree to that. But there is no doubt that we'll end up with an American contingent and a Russian contingent and a British contingent and God knows how many other contingents. I suppose we'll have to live with it, because I doubt we can live without it.

"But first we need to know if this can work at all. All right, people, get together with your staffs and hammer this out! I want a go/no-go answer by this time tomorrow. I know it will take a lot longer to work out the details, but we have to know if it is possible immediately. Let's get to it."

* * * * *

"That's quite a friend you've got, Bob," said Ed Osborne. "She's really something."

"Yes she is. Something very special." Bob looked around the lobby of the New York high-rise where the EDF had its headquarters. "I guess we better hit the road. It's a long way back to Norfolk. I just hope you don't get in too much trouble for coming here with me, Ed."

"Don't much care if I do or not. But you do owe me a favor now and I know what I'm going to want in payment."

"Oh really?"

"Yup."

"And just what might that be?"

"Seems to me they are going to need a boat to use as a test bed for this. You know, to actually see if the stuff is going to work. I was kind of thinking that *Tennessee* would be just perfect for that, don't you?"

Chapter Twenty-Five

Doctor Usha Vasthare sat in the construction office at the Groton, Connecticut shipyard and looked at the list on her computer screen. After a moment she smiled.

"You can scratch these two items off the list, Henry," she said shaking her head.

"Which two?" asked the engineer.

"Item seven, the diving planes, and item eighteen, the propellers. We haven't got the time to waste to remove them."

"But we can't just leave them on, Doctor!"

"Why not?"

'Well think of the *drag* they'll create when the ship is...is..." he trailed off.

"Yes?" She smiled.

"Okay, scratch seven and eighteen," said the engineer who was blushing furiously. "Damn it's hard to keep in mind what we're doing here!"

"That it is," said Usha. She turned her head as the door opened and her assistant hurried in.

"Marshal Youngs is here, Doctor," he said.

"Thank you, I'll be right there." She got up from her chair and followed her assistant out the door. The office was part of a building—more of a shed actually—sitting next to a dry dock. In the dry dock was the *USS Tennessee*, the submarine they would try to turn into a spaceship. No, not *try*, they *would* turn it into a spaceship! Failure would be simply unthinkable. Failure might well doom the human race to slavery or extinction.

She walked toward one of the boarding ramps, but stopped and looked back at her assistant in confusion. "Where is she? You said she was here."

"She had been right here a moment ago, Doctor. She must have gone aboard."

Usha frowned. She had wanted to talk to Youngs before Captain Osborne had a chance to get to her first. She sent her assistant to get a pair of hardhats and then waited and watched the stream of workers entering and leaving the vessel. Leaning over the railing she could see a party cutting into the side of the ship about fifty meters in from the stern. The radiators she and the Somerans had designed would be attached there. She was rather proud of those radiators...

"Here we are, Doctor," said her assistant, offering her a hardhat. She took it and fit it on her head before walking across the gangway. She reached the sub, but then had to wait while three workers manhandled an acetylene torch down the hatch she wanted to use. Once inside, her ears were assaulted by the sound of power saws, portable exhaust fans, banging hammers, and people yelling to be overheard amid the other din. She thought fondly of her work aboard the ship in orbit. Orderly and *quiet*.

"Hey, watch it, lady!"

She stopped as a man held out a gloved hand in front of her. A moment later a shower of sparks from a cutting torch rained down on where she had been about to walk. She looked around to try and find someone in charge. She finally picked a man at random.

"Have you seen Marshal Youngs or Captain Osborne?" she shouted.

"I saw some brass headed forward a little while ago," he shouted back.

Usha had to walk aft to find a companionway down to get past the area where the cutting was going on. At least it was a little quieter down here. She went forward again, through the crew's galley, and after asking a few more people was directed down again to the ship's torpedo room. There she found Youngs talking with Osborne.

"Ah, there you are, Doctor," said Youngs when she spotted her. "Captain Osborne was just showing me how they are going to be modifying the torpedo tubes to use the new missiles."

"Yes," said Osborne, "they are going to construct the missiles so they will fit in our existing tubes. We'll have to modify the compressed air system to actually shove the missiles out the tubes, but it will still work pretty much as it did with the torpedoes. With the zero-G situation, we'll actually be able to store a lot more missiles aboard and reloading will be much faster. As you can see we are removing some of the crew facilities to increase missile storage space."

"How many will you be able to carry, Captain?" asked Youngs.

"Probably around a hundred, ma'am."

"Twenty-five salvoes," said Youngs. "I hope that will be enough."

"Plus our big birds."

Usha frowned; that was a sore subject with her. "Marshal Youngs, are we really going to retain the nuclear missiles on these vessels?"

"Why not, Doctor?" asked Youngs in apparent surprise. "There's not much else we can do with the space unless we wanted to rip out the missiles and try to install more of the conventional missile tubes. That would be a hell of a lot of work. And some people on the staff think the nukes might come as a nasty surprise to the *Brak-Shar* since the Somerans don't use them."

Usha's frown deepened. She was afraid Youngs was going to say that and she did not have any real counter to it.

"Perhaps if we refrain from using nuclear weapons, the *Brak-Shar* might refrain from using them against the planet." It was all she could think to say.

"An interesting notion, Doctor," replied Youngs. "From what the Somerans have told us, it does not seem too likely, but we can discuss it at our next staff meeting." She turned back to Osborne. "Captain, what about the back-blast from the missiles after they're launched? From what I understand they have a hellacious amount of thrust, could they damage the ship?"

"We're aware of the potential problem, ma'am. Apparently the Somerans use their drive field to yank their missiles sideways a bit before they ignite so the exhaust doesn't hit the launching ship. I believe Doctor Vasthare is looking into that. If that doesn't pan out, we're planning to weld some armor plates over the parts of the hull that might be affected."

Osborne continued to point out features of the torpedo tubes and loading system while Youngs nodded her head. Usha was simultaneously fuming about the nuclear missiles and chastising herself for doing so. *They could be right about the missiles, but why am I so afraid?* Usha shuddered. She had spent most of her adult life working for the peaceful use and exploration of space. And now she was helping to build space warships, something she vowed she would never do.

But what choice was there? The *Brak-Shar* didn't care about her personal principles! They had to fight and they had to win and she had to help however she could.

Even so, she was still afraid. It made no sense; those missiles could destroy the world just as easily launched from the surface of the planet as from above it. So why did the thought of having them on spaceships frighten her so? She looked over at Osborne; he was smiling and patting one of the torpedo tubes lovingly. Youngs was smiling and nodding.

Maybe that was it. Osborne obviously loved his boat and Youngs knew how he felt. Usha supposed it must be like how she had felt about the ship up in orbit, but the idea chilled her. How could you love something designed to kill millions of people without warning? The idea of men and women like those two, wielding the sort of power the submarines—and the subs converted to space-ships—represented, terrified her.

Can I trust Youngs? Right now I have to, but what will happen afterward?

That was the scariest part. Fighting the *Brak-Shar* was necessary, but what about when the battle was over—assuming humanity won? There could be dozens of these vessels left flying around. The ones without the nuclear missiles could still do frightful damage, but the ships with the nukes… Would Youngs be able to hold the EDF together or would the fleet fragment into a dozen rival navies? Even if she did hold it together, then what? What would Kathryn Youngs do with her fleet? A fleet that would get stronger and stronger as new ships got built. Because this was only the beginning; there were more *Brak-Shar* out there and Earth would need a huge fleet to survive. What would Youngs do with her enormous power? Usha did not know.

Usha looked up as Youngs and Osborne approached. Osborne was no longer smiling.

"Doctor, Captain Osborne tells me there is some disagreement over the installation of the shield generator," said Youngs.

"Yes, Marshal," said Usha, wishing again that she could have gotten to Youngs first. "I am of the opinion that we should not attempt to test the shields on the same vessel we are using to test the drive. The shield installation is more complicated and involves far more work than the drive. Not only would the two installations interfere with each other, but it would delay our ability to test the drive. It makes far more sense to use two separate vessels."

"We've already discussed that, Doctor, and I have no arguments with it," said Osborne, "but you have indicated that even after testing is complete *Tennessee* should not receive the shields. I have to object to that."

"Why would we not install shields on *Tennessee*, Doctor?" asked Youngs.

"Not just *Tennessee*, Marshal," said Usha, "none of the missile submarines. Or more precisely: the missile submarines should receive them last. We should do the attack submarines first and then, if there is time, do the others."

"Why is that?"

"I was discussing this with Nalorom yesterday. It has to do with how the Someran shields function. They believe that the smaller attack submarines will work better with the shields."

"Oh? Why is that?" asked Youngs. "I would have thought the larger vessels would give you more room to install the equipment."

"Well, yes and no. The main problem is the length of the larger submarines. It will take a substantially larger number of capacitor and deflector units to provide the same level of protection."

"I'm not sure I understand, Doctor—but then I'm finding the whole principle behind the shield system rather confusing to begin with."

"I can understand your difficulty," replied Usha, "It took a great deal of explanation for me to understand. The shield is perhaps the most complex technology the Somerans possess. I will try to explain."

"I would appreciate that," said Youngs with a grin. Osborne said nothing, but continued to frown.

"The shield system consists of two main components. There is a central generator, and then there are numerous deflector/capacitor units that must be mounted on the skin of the vessel to be protected. The main generator creates a spherical field around the ship. This field provides no real protection, although it is possible to have it absorb radar signals and other forms of low level radiation."

"So that is how they can avoid detection on our radar," said Youngs.

"Yes. It does take a considerable amount of power, however, which is why they had to shut down that aspect of it during the battle. The field created by the main generator does not provide any significant protection from weapons attack, as I said, however, it provides a carrier wave for the deflector units."

"I'm not sure I understand," said Youngs.

"It is rather complicated. The field provides a sort of early warning system for incoming attacks. When an attack enters the field, it triggers the capacitors and deflector units nearest the point of attack. These release a burst of energy that will attempt to negate the attack."

"Sort of like the reactive armor on tanks?" asked Osborne.

"Yes, that was the exact analogy Nalorom used, although I don't know much about armored vehicles."

"Okay, I think I can understand that," said Youngs, "but I still don't see why the smaller subs would be better."

"Unfortunately, all the submarines are rather poorly shaped to take advantage of the shields, but the missile submarines are generally the worst. You see, the main generator's field is spherical in shape. Someran ships are nearly spherical as well so the field does not have to be that much larger than the ship. Our submarines tend to be long and thin. This will force us to have a rather large field to enclose the whole submarine, which takes more power. Also, the actual strength of the defense comes down to the number and size of the deflector units. The more units for a given surface area the better. Unfortunately, on the subs there is relatively little surface area to mount the deflector units and capacitors. The bottom line, ma'am, is that we will need nearly twice as many deflectors to get the same amount of protection for the missile subs as we would for the attack subs. Since both types of subs will have nearly equal combat power it will make more sense to install shields on the attack subs first and only do the missile subs if we have the time."

"I think I understand," said Youngs.

"I understand that," said Osborne, "but I don't agree that the attack subs have equal firepower with the missile boats. The nukes could make a big difference."

"We don't know how effective they will be, Captain," said Usha. "And you will still be able to use them in any case."

"With no protection! I don't like the idea of taking my boat into combat naked, Doctor!"

Youngs looked back and forth between Osborne and Usha. It was obvious she was pondering the problem. Usha had already tangled with Osborne over the question, and she had hoped to convince Youngs to her views without an open debate like this.

"Well," said Youngs at last, "I believe Doctor Vasthare is correct as far as the initial tests go. We'll get another sub to try out the shield on. As to how we'll go about the other issue, I'll want to do some additional thinking about that. I'll add it to the agenda of our next staff meeting. Can you live with that, Captain?"

"I can live with it, ma'am, but I'm not sure I'll be able to live without it."

"Understood, Captain. None of our ships are going to be much compared to what the *Brak-Shar* are coming with, but I don't intend to treat them like cannon fodder, either. Now, what else do you have to show me?"

Osborne led them up a ladder into a compartment where work was going on. It was quite noisy there and conversation was impossible. Usha was relieved that Youngs had sided with her on the question of the shields. Despite her early distrust of Youngs, she had to admit that the woman could make good decisions. She just hoped that Youngs would continue to do so.

"We're ripping out a lot of the crew quarters, dining, and recreation spaces, ma'am," shouted Osborne. "Since we won't be doing any months-long patrols anymore, we can cut the crew by nearly half and do away with a lot of the 'luxuries' us sub jockies are used to. This space will be for more missile storage. If you'll follow me, I'll show you the control center."

They followed him up again. This compartment was also being worked on, but the activity was quieter and appeared more orderly.

"We are going to have to rework most of the control stations, but we are going to keep the same general layout. Helm, navigation, sensors, engineering, weapons, we still need all that stuff. Obviously, we'll have all new computers and displays. Just forward is the main sensor control. Main navigation is just aft. Above us will be the new laser installation."

"That goes in the conning tower?" asked Youngs.

"Yes. As I understand it, the main mechanism will fit into the volume taken up by the periscopes and radar boom. The emitter will be mounted on top. In that position it will give us a pretty good field of fire, but there will also be a pretty substantial blind spot."

"I'm afraid so, Marshal," agreed Usha. "We've looked at the possibility of mounting other lasers to give better coverage, but we would need at least three and the modifications would be difficult."

"Understood," said Youngs. "Actually, Captain Kagami has been working on the problem with the Somerans. We intend to group our vessels into squadrons and we believe that a coordinated defense system can be set up. All the vessels in the squadron would coordinate their fire. Doing that, we would have a better defense than a much larger vessel."

"Sounds good, ma'am," said Osborne.

From there they went down again to an area called the 'auxiliary machine room one'. This contained a lot of the environmental systems including air recycling for the forward part of the vessel. Usha was a bit surprised when it turned out Youngs knew more about the equipment than either Osborne or herself. She had forgotten Youngs had been studying the subject. Youngs had several important suggestions on modifications that would be needed to make the equipment function properly in zero-G. Unfortunately, there would be no time to install an artificial gravity system in the vessel.

Then it was back up again and aft. Usha shuddered when they entered the next compartment. A long space stretched away from them. Huge cylinders grew out of the deck and went up to penetrate the overhead. Two dozen of them.

"This is the missile compartment and main crew berthing," explained Osborne. "Most of the enlisted men berthed here. Since we're ripping out almost all the quarters in the forward section, we'll be subdividing this space for the whole remaining crew."

Usha scarcely heard him. She could not tear her eyes away from those cylinders. They were like enormous sarcophagi. *Containers of death. Except death comes out of these instead of going into them.* Twenty-four missiles. Each with ten warheads. Each warhead capable of destroying a large city. With careful targeting one submarine was capable of destroying half the earth.

And I am helping to put this into space. What am I becoming? Am I becoming a servant of Kali?

Usha shook her head to try to get rid of that thought and then hurried to catch up with Osborne and Youngs. Immediately aft of the missile compartment was 'auxiliary machine room two'. Workers were there, dismantling several large pieces of equipment.

"These are the pumps for the ballast tanks," said Osborne. "Obviously we don't need them anymore. We will be using this compartment for the main drive. I'll let Doctor Vasthare tell you about that, ma'am."

"Uh, yes," said Usha, still trying to rid herself of visions of Armageddon. "The drive needs to be as close to the ship's center as possible. This is not a perfect location, but it will do. The reactor is just on the other side of that bulkhead. There are also several subsidiary pieces of equipment that must be located elsewhere in the ship. All of them, acting in concert, can create the gravity fields that will move the ship."

"I see," said Youngs. "And how long do you estimate for the installation of the equipment?"

"We believe it will take about three months before we can begin testing."

"Three months? We have about eight months left, Doctor. I don't think we can wait that long just to see if this is going to work."

"No, I have to agree with you. Unfortunately, I believe we will have to proceed on the assumption that this *will* work. It will probably take some time to arrange the construction facilities for the other subs around the world, and to begin fabrication of the needed components. That will allow us to make significant progress here. We can discover all of the problems and pitfalls and then pass on our findings to the other work crews, so they don't have the same difficulties."

"That makes sense to me, Doctor," said Youngs, nodding her head. "Hopefully we won't end up following some false trail and screw everything up, but you seem to have thought out most of the problems already."

"I hope so, Marshal."

They headed aft through the reactor compartment. They used the shielded passageway, but they did not linger. Beyond that was the engine room.

"In spite of the name, the drive won't be in here," said Usha. "You can see the turbines, there, that take the steam from the reactor to make electricity. The old condenser units will be removed and the new heat exchangers will go in their place."

"You and the Somerans have gotten that sorted out?" asked Youngs.

"Yes, we believe so. The Somerans can supply us with a compound that will soak up the heat from the steam very nicely. Then we pump it outside the ship to a set of radiators. The heat is given off there and then the compound is pumped back in to begin the cycle again."

"Doctor, you said a few disturbing things about that compound," said Osborne. "Is it going to be safe?"

"Unfortunately, the compound is rather volatile at high temperatures," conceded Usha. "We will have to be careful with it."

"Damn right!" exclaimed Osborne.

"Just how dangerous is it, Doctor?" asked Youngs. "Perhaps we should try another approach."

"Unfortunately, we really have no option, Marshal. No system we can devise on our own will do the job and this was the only idea the Somerans had. As far as the danger, I don't believe it is too extreme. The primary danger would be if the system took battle damage. The radiators are the most vulnerable and we will build them so that very little of the compound is in any one place on the radiators. Naturally, there will be emergency seal-offs in the case of punctures. The main reservoir, which will be located here, could be a bigger danger, but if an enemy weapon punches through into here, the ship is probably doomed anyway."

"Thanks a lot, Doctor," said Osborne, grumpily.

"I'm sorry, Captain, but there are going to be risks no matter what we do!"

"Yes, I'm afraid that's true," said Youngs hastily. "We'll just have to do whatever we can to minimize the danger. As long as the system is safe under normal usage, I think we'll have to be satisfied."

"All right, Marshal, if that's your judgment," said Osborne. Then he laughed. "I guess I'm just slipping back into my boomer mentality. We were never supposed to take any risks with the missile boats. It's hard to remember that in this coming fight, any and all of us are expendable if it allows us to win."

A chill went through Usha. The warrior mentality—would she ever get used to it? Youngs seemed a little startled, too, but she nodded.

"I don't want to think of any of my people as expendable, Captain. We'll do what we can to lessen the risk and keep casualties down. But I'm also afraid you're right—we have to win. We won't get a second chance."

The conversation came to a halt and then they made their way up a ladder and out on to the deck of the submarine. A minute later, they were across the gangway.

"What's that going on there?" asked Youngs, pointing to the cutting Usha had seen earlier.

"That is where the coolant will be piped out to the radiators. We are going to kill two birds with one stone with the radiators. We are going to build a sturdy framework to hold the radiators. The frame will also act as a pair of braces to keep the sub from rolling when it is sitting on the ground. You can see how they have it braced with wood blocks right now. Once we complete all the modifications, I don't think we will be able to put the submarines back in the water, so this becomes a concern."

"Good idea, Doctor, well done," said Youngs with a smile. She turned back to Osborne. "Well, Captain, thank you for the tour. I have to get back to my office, but I plan to be back from time to time to check on progress. And I certainly intend to be here for the first test flight!"

"Very good, Marshal Youngs. You are welcome aboard *Tennessee* any time."

Osborne escorted Youngs to her vehicle, but Usha remained behind. Her gaze was drawn back to the deck of the submarine. They were not that noticeable, but she had no trouble seeing the outlines of the twenty-four hatches that were the reason for the vessel's existence.

Chapter Twenty-Six

"How many casualties, Piotr?" asked Kathryn Youngs in dismay. The man on her communications screen shook his head.

"We are not sure yet, Marshal," replied Piotr Novakovic. "With the explosions and fire, it may take some time to know for sure."

"What about damage to the facility?"

"Unfortunately, it is quite extensive. Apparently the attackers wanted to put it out of commission in addition to whatever they could steal."

"And did they get away with much?"

"I do not believe so," said her chief of security. "The Italian police and military responded with gratifying quickness. Several ground vehicles were stopped at roadblocks and one helicopter was shot down. A number of the attackers escaped on foot, but it seems unlikely they could have been carrying anything very large. Certainly not one of the fabricators."

"Well, that's one bit of good news, anyway. Do we know who they were, Piotr?"

"I have my suspicions and we did take several prisoners. I will let you know when we get any definite information."

"This is the third attack like this that we have had, Piotr, and the worst by far. We have to put a stop to them. In addition to the loss of life and material, it is costing us time and that's the one thing we simply can't waste!"

"I know, madam, I know. We will do what we can, but there are so many facilities now and they are so scattered, it is difficult."

"I know you will. Thank you for all your efforts, Piotr. Please keep me informed." Kay closed the connection and she let out a long sigh. Another terrorist attack, this time on a fabricator facility in Italy. They were becoming too frequent—and too deadly. There was a certain amount of slack built into their construction schedules to allow for disruptions like this, but only so much.

Why are these madmen doing this? Don't they realize this is our only chance? She had asked herself that question before, but unfortunately, she knew the answer. *They don't trust the UN or this alliance...or me.* And she could almost see their point. The extremists, the disenfranchised, and the desperate had always distrusted the established order. The new technologies of the Somerans had been promised to all, but in the emergency, Youngs had no choice but to operate through the existing governments and agencies. There was no time yet for humanitarian work. To outsiders, it would look like the wealth and the power was going to stay in the hands of the same people as before.

And they might even be right.

Youngs' job was to get ready to fight the *Brak-Shar*, she had no say on what happened with the technology in the civilian sector. Already private corporations were trying to get hold of it for their own profit. People were angry and she could not blame them.

But no matter how other people felt, Youngs had a job to do and she was not going to let anyone or anything stop her. Which reminded her...

One more call to make today and I better get it over with, thought Kay. She typed in a code on her communications terminal and then sat back and waited. After a moment a woman appeared on the screen.

"Chairman's office, may I help you?"

"Yes, this is Marshal Youngs, I'd like to speak to General O'Connell, please."

"Of course, Marshal, please hold and I'll tell the general you are on the line."

"Thank you." The screen blanked and Kay straightened up in her chair. While she waited, her eyes drifted over to a small desk calendar. It was specially made and nearly everyone in her headquarters had one. It gave the actual date, but in big red letters it also announced how many days were left until the *Brak-Shar* arrived. Today's number was '150'.

Five months. They had five months left. They'd accomplished a lot in the last four, but would it be enough? They were all working themselves to death, but would it be enough? She asked herself that question at least ten times a day. *God, I'm tired!*

The screen came to life and she was facing General O'Connell, Chairman of the US Joint Chiefs.

"Good morning, Marshal," he said. "I guess this is the big day, isn't it? Are you going to be attending the test?"

"Yes, General, I'll be leaving shortly. Are you going to be there?"

"No, I'm afraid not. Too much to do here. I'll try to watch it on TV, if I can."

"I see. General, I need to talk to you, and not about the test."

"Yes?"

"General, I don't want an unpleasant scene, but I need to talk to you about the diversion of certain components from your fabricator facility. Specifically, the lasers."

The general's expression darkened and Kay could see that he was blushing. She and the general had gotten along amazingly well in the last few months, and she hoped that was not about to end.

"You seem to have a very efficient spy network, Marshal."

Kay frowned, but inside she was suppressing a grin. She was glad to know that the general's people had not caught on to the fact that all the fabricator units kept exact records of everything they produced—and that those records could be accessed remotely if you had the right codes.

"General, you have been constructing the parts for laser weapons beyond what will be needed for the vessels you have under construction. I'd like to know what you are doing with them."

O'Connell looked at her warily. "If your intelligence is so good, I'm surprised you don't know that, too."

"I have my suspicions, General, but I'd like to find out from you if I'm correct."

The general stared at her for a moment and then sighed. "Marshal, we have a pretty good working relationship. I know we got off to a rocky start, but we got past that. Each of us is aware of the duties and responsibilities of the other. I think you can understand that I have certain responsibilities toward the United States of America."

"Yes, I can, General. I understand them. Once upon a time I shared them. In my heart, I still do. But I have other responsibilities, too. What are you doing with the lasers, General?"

"I'm trying to protect my country, Marshal! When the *Brak-Shar* arrive, there is going to be a hell of a fight. The first ship did not drop any nukes on the planet. I don't think we are going to be so lucky this time. We have been producing extra laser weapons to set up defenses for our major cities."

"Thank you, General," said Kay. "That is what we thought. Orbital observation has shown new installations going up in a number of American cities. We assumed that is what you are doing, but I wanted to confirm it."

"Marshal, we are not going to back down on this!" said O'Connell sternly. "We have a responsibility to protect our people. The lasers we have diverted will not be needed for any of the ships and will not weaken your fleet at all."

"I know that, General. Could you possibly supply us with the plans for your defense installations?"

"Now don't try and talk me out of-... I beg your pardon?" The general stopped suddenly and looked at Kay in surprise.

"I said: can we get a copy of the plans? It sounds like a very sensible precaution, General. I think other countries would be interested in doing the same thing."

"You...you mean you don't object?"

"I would have preferred that you had discussed this with me rather than doing it the way you did, General, but no, I don't object. How many of these defense lasers are you planning for?"

"Right now we have plans for about thirty sites. If we have enough time we hope to do more. We won't be able to put one in every big city, but we are hoping to have enough coverage to stop some attacks. I suppose we could supply you with copies of our plans."

"That would be excellent, General. I'd like to run them by the Somerans, with your permission. They might be able to suggest some improvements."

"Very well, Marshal, I'll do that. And thank you."

"Thank you, General. I'll be talking to you later." Kay cut the connection, leaned back in her chair and sighed. *Whew! That went better than I'd hoped. I just wish everyone was as honest as O'Connell!* Sadly, there were many other places where fabricator production was disappearing and Kay was having far more trouble tracking it down. Still, the sub conversion was proceeding satisfactorily and she supposed she could live with it.

Her com terminal beeped. "Yes?"

"About time to be going, ma'am," came the voice of her aide.

"All right, Jonathan, I'll be right there." Kay got up from her chair and grabbed her cap. She met Cresswell-Jones in the outer office and smiled.

"Is everything set, Commander?" she asked.

"Yes, ma'am. The shuttle is waiting on the roof."

"Great." She led the way out of the office and to the elevators. Shortly, they were heading up to the rooftop landing platform.

"Any problems with the schedule, Jonathan?"

"Not really, ma'am. A few people are a little put out at having to wait. If you don't mind my asking, ma'am, can you really afford not to have *any* meetings for the next four days?"

"I think the world will survive, Jonathan. And I need the break."

"No argument there, ma'am. You really do need to pace yourself better. You've been working yourself to a frazzle."

"I'm not working any harder than a lot of other people—like you, for instance."

The elevator stopped and the doors opened. They were in a small lobby. The glass doors looked out on the helicopter pad.

However, the vehicle sitting on the pad was no helicopter.

A silvery disk, twenty meters in diameter, rested there. A hatch was open in one side and several people were standing next to it. Kay strode out through the doors, happy to be outside. Happy to be out of her office. Doctor Vasthare was waiting for her with several of her staff.

"Good morning, Doctor," said Kay cheerily. "Ready to go have a look?"

"Yes, Marshal, I'm looking forward to it." Kay noticed Vasthare shivering in the cold wind; she probably wasn't used to this sort of weather. Kay reflected that she had never carried through with her promise to relocate her headquarters from New York. She really should find someplace else—someplace warm. She wondered if the British would be willing to lease out Bermuda?

"Okay, let's go." Kay walked through the hatch of the vehicle. She instinctively ducked her head, but then grinned sheepishly. The ceiling was more than high enough. This was not a Someran shuttle, it was her shuttle. One perk of her position she did not mind at all. She went into the control room and sat down in the copilot's seat. She wanted to fly the thing herself, but she had not had the time to train on it, so she reluctantly left it to the normal pilot—who could not have a great deal of practice time either, she reflected. She looked over her shoulder and saw that everyone else had found seats in the passenger compartment and the hatch was shut.

"I think we're ready to go, Mister Seaton," she said to her pilot.

"Very good, ma'am. Lifting off now."

Kay felt a tiny twinge in the pit of her stomach as the anti-gravity unit came on. A moment later, the rooftop was falling away along with the New York skyline. A few more seconds and they were leaping forward under three gravities of acceleration—even though there was no sensation of movement at all.

She stared out the window and sighed. She really did need a break. This was the first time she had been able to get away since Christmas. She always tried to spend Christmas with her family back in Ohio. Sometimes her duties prevented her, but whenever she could, she did. She had not been sure she could spare the time this year, but her public relations officer had assured her it would be a good thing to do for public morale.

So she had gone home. She took Nisima with her, partly out of pity for this most orphaned of orphans and partly because she was coming to like the woman quite a lot. She had been a little amused when Jonathan had hinted that he would like to come along. She was starting to suspect that Jonathan liked Nisima quite a lot, too. Kay wondered if Nisima even knew what a 'knight in shining armor' was.

Coming home had been nice, but not as nice as it should have been. Too much had changed. Not with her family or her home, but with her. She had a horde of nieces and nephews who idolized their crazy aunt who flew spaceships and she enjoyed playing with them. Her sisters and brothers-in-law and her mother always enjoyed seeing her, too. But this time... This time it was different. The kids still mobbed her and they insisted she put on her uniform and tell stories about fighting the *Brak-Shar*. That she had expected. It was her sisters and her mother that made it so awkward. They welcomed her, of course, but the way they looked at her, especially when she was playing with the kids. Their expressions seemed to be saying: 'Are you going to save my children?' 'Why are you here playing when you should be working to save my children?' Friends and neighbors came to visit, but their expressions seemed to ask the same questions. Or was she just imagining it? Was it her own fears that seemed to put those questions on other peoples' faces? It was so strange. At least Nisima and Jonathan appeared to have a good time.

Going to church was the worst. The people there looked at her the same way her sisters had. There was a crowd of news people and curious onlookers and security forces ringing the place. The Christmas Eve service was always packed, but this year it was a circus. Nisima was curious about the proceedings. Somehow she made it seem like she thought it was superstitious nonsense while admitting that the Somerans did have an ancestor-based religion at the same time. But she loved the music. The service itself was nice, but Kay nearly lost it when the pastor asked God to 'grant wisdom to Space Marshal Youngs' and the entire congregation stood up and applauded. She *did* lose it when they sang 'A Mighty Fortress is our God'. Her PR officer insisted it made wonderful press.

Wonderful press—and a week later they blew up her apartment.

An old model, wire-guided anti-tank missile flew through her window one night. If she had not been next door, talking with Nisima, she would have been killed. The perpetrators declared loudly that they would not accept a *Christian* defender of the world. Most nations and groups had denounced the action, but not all. And there were plenty more crazies out there waiting to take their own shots.

Yes, I need a break.

She turned away from the sights out the window to watch what the pilot was doing. Not because she did not trust him, but just to see how it was done. Someday she intended to fly this thing herself! Soon they had passed through Mach One and were screaming down Long Island Sound. The sonic boom was probably disturbing some people, but that was another little privilege of being the Supreme Commander of the Earth Defense Forces.

And there were not as many people to disturb as there used to be.

The voluntary evacuations had begun last month. Several hundred thousand people—mostly children—had left the New York area for the camps that had been built upstate. Next month another wave of them would go. Another month after that, the mandatory evacuations would begin. Kay shook her head. America had never seen anything like this. She wondered how well it would work.

The shuttle reached a speed of three kilometers per second and then ceased accelerating. Less than a minute later, the pilot cut in the drive to slow them down and start the descent toward Groton, Connecticut. Kay had him circle the shipyard several times before landing. She could see the familiar dry dock where *Tennessee* was situated. Several other submarines were being worked on in nearby docks. An improvised landing pad had been set up nearby and the shuttle descended to a smooth landing. Another minute and Kay and her party were outside in the late winter sunshine.

There were crowds of people waiting, but Kay was looking for one person in particular. After a moment she spotted him. He spotted her at the same moment and they walked toward each other.

"Hi, Bob," she said.

"Hi, Kay. Good to see you," said Captain Robert Hancock. She almost reached out to him, but no, there were too many people watching. Watching her every move.

Bob was not alone and Kay greeted his daughter Melissa, Lieutenant Steven Sokol, and Captain Edward Osborne, skipper of *Tennessee*.

"Well, is everyone ready for the big show?" she asked.

"I think so," said Hancock. "Thanks for inviting all of us, Marshal."

"Yes!" said Melissa enthusiastically. "Thank you, so much! This is going to be great!"

Kay looked at the young woman and smiled. She had not seen her in four months and she was glad to see that she seemed to have recovered from her ordeal during the terrorist attack.

"Marshal Youngs," said Osborne. "We are ready to proceed at your word."

"Very well then! Let's get this show on the road."

"If you'll follow me, ma'am."

Osborne led them to the edge of the dry dock. The twenty thousand ton submarine did not look all that different from when the work started. The main difference was a large assembly that jutted out from the hull about forty meters in from the stern. That was the heat radiator that Doctor Vasthare had designed. There was another, smaller assembly near the bow, but this was simply a brace to further stabilize the ship against rolling. A long walkway extended from the side of the dry dock to the deck of the vessel. Osborne led the party across this and then through a hatch in the conning tower. Then it was down a ladder into the main control room.

Kay remembered what the inside of *Tennessee* had looked like before, but there had been some changes made. Dozens of new control consoles lined the bulkheads, the periscope was gone, and several large video monitors had been mounted at the front of the compartment. These were showing views of the ship taken by some cameras mounted around the dock. There were also a number of chairs bolted to the deck that she knew were not standard equipment for a submarine.

"Welcome back, Marshal," said Osborne. "We have completed the final systems check and we are ready to raise ship whenever you are ready."

"'Raise ship', that's a new one. I guess we need a whole new set of terminology," said Youngs with a grin.

"Actually, ma'am, it's rather old terminology. The Navy was using that expression back in the days of the airships—the old dirigibles."

"I stand corrected, Captain. But you may raise the ship, by all means."

"Aye aye, ma'am! Commander Lakner, all hands to stations, prepare to raise ship!"

"Aye aye, sir!" said Osborne's executive officer, a woman Kay had met only once before. She bustled about, snapping out orders. Crew members at the various stations began reading off information from their consoles.

"Reactor at fifty percent power."

"Radiator fin temperature is nominal."

"Gangway has been removed."

"All mooring lines cast off."

"Groton Control has cleared us to raise ship."

"Drive unit standing by."

Kay knew the crew had been spending weeks in the simulators and going through dry runs, but she was still impressed with the efficiency she was seeing.

"All stations report ready, sir," said Commander Lakner.

"Very well. Sound the zero gravity warning. Marshal Youngs, if you and your people would be seated and strap yourselves in, we can get underway."

Kay and the other observers found chairs and fastened their seat belts. Osborne took a quick look around and seemed satisfied that all was ready.

"Engineering, anti-gravity to full nullification."

"Aye aye, sir. Full null...now."

Kay's stomach dropped out from under her and she was weightless. She swallowed the saliva pouring into her mouth. *I will not be dropsick!* She was more than a little sorry there had been no time for luxuries like artificial gravity. She forced herself to concentrate on the image in the monitor. Against all reason, it was showing a submarine slowly drifting upward out of its dry dock.

It was also drifting sideways toward the side of the dock.

"The wind's pushing us to port, sir," said the helmsman.

"Upward thrust at point one gravity," ordered Osborne.

"Aye sir, upward thrust at one meter per second squared."

The images in the monitors showed the sub moving upward. Faster and faster. In a dozen heartbeats it was clear of the dry dock. A few more seconds and it was above the surrounding cranes. One of the monitors switched to a camera mounted on *Tennessee* herself, and it showed the shipyard dropping away below them.

"We are clear to maneuver, sir," said Commander Lakner.

"Very good, increase thrust to point two gravities."

"Aye aye, sir."

The images in the monitors continued to recede.

"Marshal Youngs," said Osborne. "I'm afraid we'll have to be satisfied with this slow rate of acceleration until we are clear of the lower atmosphere. We're not really streamlined properly for transonic flight. The old girl can do twenty-five knots under water, but she wasn't designed for this."

"I understand, Captain," said Kay.

As the ship gained speed and altitude, Kay could sense a slight vibration coming through her chair. The air was thinning rapidly, but it was still thick enough to buffet the submarine... ship... whatever it was now.

"Speed five hundred meters per second, altitude sixty thousand meters," reported the navigation officer after a few minutes. The shipyard was hardly a speck in the monitor now. The other monitor was looking ahead and Kay saw the familiar—and beautiful—sight of the sky turning to black and the stars coming out. She glanced to her side where Bob and Melissa Hancock were staring wide-eyed. She reached over and gave Bob's hand a quick squeeze. He squeezed back, but his eyes never left the monitor.

"Wow," gasped Melissa. "That's incredible."

"Can't argue with that," said Kay.

"Atmospheric friction near zero, sir," reported Commander Lakner. "We can open her up if you want, sir."

"Very good. Helm, forward thrust at one gravity. Course one-eight-zero by oh-five. Put us in orbit, Mister Burrell."

"Aye aye, sir."

At the increased acceleration, it only took fifteen minutes to reach orbital velocity. Then Captain Osborne cut the thrust and the anti-gravity. They were now in free fall. It felt exactly the same as the earlier weightlessness. Kay took deep breaths and her nausea remained at bay.

"Course is nominal, sir," reported the navigator. "We're in orbit."

"Very good. Engineering, reactor status?"

"Purring like a kitten, sir. The heat exchanger and radiators are operating perfectly. Fin temperature is one hundred eighty degrees centigrade, exactly per spec."

"Good. Environmental, any leaks?"

"No, sir. Internal pressure is holding steady."

"Doctor, any problems with the drive?"

"No, Captain," said Doctor Vasthare from her position at an engineering console. "The drive is functioning exactly as planned."

"Well, Captain," said Kay. "Your ship seems to be functioning perfectly."

"Thank you, Marshal Youngs. We had some good people working on her. With your permission, I'll begin our test routine."

"By all means. Carry on, Captain."

For the next hour Captain Osborne put his ship through a series of tests and maneuvers. Everything was working perfectly including the full power test with the reactor. The radiator fins did their job and Kay could see the look of satisfaction on Doctor Vasthare's face. After a bit, Osborne allowed them to unstrap and the observers floated around the cabin. Melissa loved the zero-gravity, but her friend, Lieutenant Sokol, had that greenish look that Kay knew so well. He quickly strapped himself back into his seat. Eventually, Captain Osborne floated over to Kay.

"We've completed all the tests on our schedule, ma'am. We can return to Groton now—unless you have something else in mind."

Kay smiled at Osborne.

"Actually, Captain, I was thinking of a somewhat more extensive shakedown cruise."

"Really, ma'am? *Tennessee* is at your disposal. Where would you like to go?"

Kay's grin grew wider.

"How about…Mars?"

* * * * *

Melissa Hancock stared at the orange ball growing in the monitor and shook her head in amazement.

"Mars at last!" said Kay Youngs, who was floating beside her.

"Incredible, isn't it, ma'am?" said Melissa.

"Yes. I've spent most of my life dreaming of this. I always hoped I'd make it here, but I never could have guessed I'd come by submarine!"

Melissa laughed. "Ma'am, thank you so much for inviting us along."

"My pleasure, Melissa. And please, call me 'Kay'."

"Somehow that doesn't seem quite proper...Kay," said Melissa uncertainly.

"Nonsense! We're friends, aren't we?"

A warm feeling spread through Melissa and she smiled at the older woman. "I'd like that. A lot." She was tempted to say more. Or ask some question about Kay and her dad. But she wasn't certain what. She liked Kay Youngs a great deal. She admired her, too. She knew her father liked her very much as well. Melissa approved. She was saved from not knowing what to say when Captain Osborne drifted over to them.

"We're in orbit, ma'am. Do you have any new orders?"

Kay grinned. "Well, Captain, I didn't drag us all the way out here just to go home again! Let's go down and have a closer look!"

"Aye aye, ma'am," said Osborne, grinning in turn. He pushed himself toward the helm position to give the orders.

"We're going to land?" asked Melissa excitedly.

"Why not? We have all those new vacuum suits to test out."

"Oh wow," gasped Melissa. They were going to land on *Mars*! She would have a chance to walk on the surface! It was just too much. She was surprised when she saw that Kay was no longer smiling.

"Selfish of me, really," she said in a near whisper. "Pure ego. I really should be back at work. But I may never get another chance."

"What do you mean? There will be plenty of opportunity later. And not just Mars. The other planets and maybe the stars, too."

"If there is a later, Melissa," said Kay. Melissa started and a shudder went through her. "Even if we win, there will be a lot of casualties."

"Are...are you going to be with the Fleet when the battle comes?"

"Of course. I couldn't sit it out, Melissa. Victory or death, you know—maybe both."

"My God. I never even thought... Does...does my dad know what you're planning?

"I'm sure he knows. I'm a bit interested in what his plans are though."

A chill went through Melissa's heart as the meaning of Kay's words sunk in. She had not thought about that either. Her father had been deskbound for so long it never even occurred to her that he might be thinking of... She turned away to hide the look of shock on her face. A hand gently touched her shoulder.

"We're military, Melissa. This is what we were trained for. And if we don't do our jobs Earth could look like that in a few months." She gestured at the dead planet in the monitor. "I'm sorry, I shouldn't have said anything. I've spoiled your Mars-walk."

"It...it's all right. I was just surprised, that's all. And I'm military, too, don't forget." She forced herself to smile and look back at Kay. Youngs' hand was still on her shoulder and she gave a squeeze.

"I know you are, Melissa." Then she let go and turned to the monitors.

"Let's enjoy this while we can."

Melissa forced her fears to the back of her mind and concentrated on the wonder of the moment. A whole different planet! The ship lost altitude quickly and the red-brown orb soon completely filled the monitors, but Kay had them do some sight-seeing before they landed. Olympus Mons was the first attraction and Melissa found it rather disappointing. It might be the largest volcano in the solar system, but it just looked like a nearly featureless lump. There was nothing to give it any sense of scale.

The famous 'Face of Mars' was a little more interesting. From certain angles it really did look like a face. Still, there was no doubt that it was a natural formation.

"Where would you like to land, ma'am?" asked Osborne after a while.

"Let's set down on the edge of Valles Marineris, Captain. That should be worth seeing."

"Very good, Marshal."

Melissa looked on in fascination as the ship slowly descended to the Martian surface. The helmsman seemed a little nervous, but he eventually brought the ship down to a soft landing. It sank into the sand a trifle and the ship took on a tiny list. Captain Osborne had the drive kept ready for several minutes, but there was no additional settling and he declared the ship secure. When the anti-gravity was switched completely off, Melissa found herself under gravity for the first time in a day and a half. She knew it was only about a third of a G but it felt almost like she was back on Earth. She looked over at Steve and saw that he had a relieved expression. The weightlessness had been hard on him.

"Marshal Youngs," said Osborne, "I assume you intend to debark?"

"With your permission, Captain. I imagine some of the others would like to go, too. But it is your ship, if you would like to be first, I won't object."

"Not a chance, Marshal!" laughed Osborne. "None of us would be here except for you. You should certainly go first."

"Thank you, Captain. Not that it really matters, I suppose. The Somerans have already been here and those humans they collected have all been a lot farther from Earth than this. It's not really anything for the history books."

"That's a matter of opinion, ma'am."

Kay smiled and then headed for the space suit lockers. Melissa tagged along as did her father, Doctor Vasthare, and several others.

"You had this planned all along, didn't you, ma'am?" said Youngs' aide. "I should have guessed when you had me clear your calendar of all those meetings."

"Yes, I guess I did, Jonathan. I trust you'll forgive me this indulgence."

"I suppose, ma'am. But I'm a little concerned about all the important people on this ship. What if something went wrong? We can't afford to lose you."

"Well, I'll admit that I did take a few precautions," said Youngs with a grin. "*Seeker of Truth* has been shadowing us this whole time. I had a little talk with Commander Keeradoth before we left and he's making sure we stay out of trouble."

Melissa's father laughed. "The marshal is famous for having a good backup, Commander. I'm surprised you haven't noticed that yet."

"I'm learning, Captain, I'm learning."

Youngs started handing out the vacuum suits. Melissa took hers and looked it over. It seemed very…insubstantial…for something she would trust her life with. It was just a jumpsuit of some silvery material with a helmet that attached at the collar. A small backpack completed the outfit.

"This is a Someran design," explained Youngs. "I know it does not look like much, but it will keep you alive for hours. Warm enough or cool enough, too." Melissa shrugged and pulled the suit on. It only weighed a few kilos in the low gravity. There was a zipper-like device on the front that sealed the outfit. She carried her helmet under one arm and followed the others.

The airlock had originally been an escape chamber when *Tennessee* had still been a submarine, but it worked perfectly well in its new function. Youngs, Melissa, and her father put on their helmets, tested the seals, and then crowded in. After a moment she could feel the pressure die away and her suit puffed out like a balloon. Youngs opened the hatch over their heads and easily climbed up on to the deck. Her father followed and then it was Melissa's turn. She pulled herself out of the lock. Her father closed the hatch after her. Melissa stood up.

She looked out on the surface of Mars.

"My God…" she whispered.

The sky was pink straight ahead and faded to black as she looked higher. The distant sun was bright enough to obscure the stars. The whole landscape was a pinkish orange. Boulders and smaller rocks were scattered everywhere and reached off to the strangely close horizon.

Except to the left.

To the left was an enormous canyon that stretched out of sight in both directions. She had seen the Grand Canyon on Earth, but that paled beside what she was seeing now. It seemed to just go on—and down—forever. She grabbed the handrail that encircled the narrow deck to steady herself.

"Now there's something you don't see every day," said Youngs. Her voice came clearly through the speakers in Melissa's helmet.

Melissa started slightly when the hatch opened beside her and more people began climbing out. Doctor Vasthare led the way, followed by Youngs' aide and one of Uncle Eddie's officers. They goggled at the view just as she had. The low gravity allowed the land to have slopes and overhangs and outcropping of the rocks which would have collapsed under Earth's gravity. Here they just… were. Unreal… *unworldly*. Yes, that was the word! After a moment, Youngs walked over to the ladder that had been welded down the side of the ship. She turned herself around and then began to descend. Melissa's father was right behind. She would have followed, but Doctor Vasthare got there first.

"Should we be worrying about possible contamination, Marshal?" asked the doctor as they slowly went down the rungs.

"I don't think so, Doctor. The Somerans have already been here. They told me that there are some microscopic life forms in some areas, but they are all a few meters down. The surface is completely sterile and they doubt any bugs we may have brought along will survive for long on the surface."

"So there is life on Mars, eh?" said her father. "Do you suppose there might be life elsewhere in the universe?" That brought a laugh from everyone.

Melissa slowly went down the ladder. The low gravity made it easy, but there was still a substantial fall, so she was very careful. Eventually, she reached the bottom of the ladder and hopped down on to the sandy surface. She looked around. First at the sub-ship towering over her, then at the landscape. It was incredible. *Mars!* She looked down at the ground and while part of her said that all she was seeing were rocks and dust and pebbles which could have come from the driveway of her home in Maryland, the rest of her wasn't listening. They were *Martian* pebbles, by golly! She bent down and scooped up a handful and put them in a pocket of her spacesuit.

She wandered for a bit and then noticed her father and Kay standing together beside a large boulder. She walked over to them. As she got closer, she saw Kay take something out of the pocket of her suit. It was very small and she carefully placed it on top of the boulder. Then she stepped back and saluted. "Sorry, Gerry, but this is the best I can do right now," she heard her whisper over the com.

Kay and her father moved away and Melissa slowly came up to the boulder in curiosity. She looked closely and saw a small gold oak leaf, the rank insignia from a military uniform, sitting on the rock. *What was that all about?*

More people were coming down the ladder and Melissa spotted Steve among them. There was a growing babble of voices in her earphones until she figured out the channel selector. She managed to get a private circuit to Steve.

"So what do you think of all this?" she asked.

"It's great! This place has gravity and that's all I care about right now!"

"I'm sorry you're having a hard time with zero-G, Steve," said Melissa with a grin.

"Oh yeah! I saw you bouncing off the bulkheads up there! You love it, you rat-fink!"

"Well, it is a lot of fun. I'm sure you'll get used to it eventually. You've got the whole trip back after all."

"Don't remind me! I might just set up housekeeping here and stay."

"I'm not sure the Marshal would approve. But maybe you could hitch a ride back with the Somerans—they have artificial gravity in their ship."

"Say, that's an idea! Do you think they would let me?"

Melissa wasn't sure if he was serious or not, but she smiled at him and he smiled back. They walked around for a bit and they both picked up interesting rocks to take back as souvenirs. After a while, Melissa noticed Kay and her father standing near the edge of the canyon. They were holding hands. She stopped and watched them for a while. Steve was next to her and her hand found his. They stood there until the older pair turned and came back toward them.

"Well, this has been fun," said Kay Youngs, "but it's time to get back to work."

The party headed for the ladder. Melissa looked back. The wind was already starting to erode their footprints.

Chapter Twenty-Seven

"You're really going to try and move this all in one piece?" asked Melissa Hancock in astonishment.

"We're certainly going to try, Squirt," said her father.

"But it must weigh thousands of tons!"

"About eight thousand, we estimate," agreed her father. "But apparently that doesn't matter to the antigrav lifter unit."

Melissa shook her head and continued to stare at the enormous metal sphere below her. It was the fusion plant on the crashed alien ship. It looked much as it did when she last saw it, except that all the pipes and conduits that had been hooked to it were now disconnected. Most of the surrounding hull and bulkheads had also been stripped away. The spring sunshine was streaming in through the large gap that had been opened up in the protective dome. Smoke from a dozen cutting torches drifted lazily upward.

"Really? The mass doesn't matter?"

"No, apparently it is the volume that is critical. Don't ask me to explain the math of it—that's more in your line! But if you accept that gravity is just an effect of space that has been curved by matter, then the antigravity unit works by 'un-curving' space in a sharply defined volume. Inside that volume there is no gravity. The lifter will latch on to the reactor and then negate the gravity holding it down. Once that's done, all we have to do is fly it down to Norfolk."

"Oh, is that all? Piece of cake, eh, Dad?"

"Let's hope."

"When's this lifter-thing going to get here?"

"Right about...now," said her father pointing skyward.

Melissa followed his finger and gasped. A huge shape had appeared in the sky overhead. It looked uncomfortably like some colossal spider descending on an invisible thread. As it got closer, she could see what looked like three of the aliens' shuttles joined together in a unit with large grasping claws sprouting out from the bottom.

"I understand the Somerans had to put this lifter together. It's not a standard piece of equipment on their ship," said her father. "Good thing they were willing to help out."

"Are you really going to be able to get that ship completed in time, Dad? I know there's no chance without doing this, but even with it, will you make it?"

"There are no guarantees, but by using this salvaged reactor, we should save at least a month, maybe more. We're hoping it will be enough. The sub conversions are coming along well, but there's no denying that they are just jury-rigged stopgaps. We need real ships."

Melissa nodded, but she kept her eyes on the descending lifter. It was now just above the opening in the dome and its speed slowed to a crawl. She and her father were on some scaffolding that was not directly under the opening, but the huge object seemed to be right overhead.

Very, very slowly the lifter drifted downward through the opening. Melissa's eyes flicked down to a group of men who were guiding it in. They were speaking through their headsets and making motions with their hands.

"I'm surprised Kay isn't here to watch this," said Melissa.

"She wanted to be, but she's on an inspection tour in Asia. I'm sure she's having reports sent to her."

"Good grief, does she ever rest?"

"I don't think she even slows down."

Melissa looked at her father and smiled. "You're pretty fond of her, aren't you, Dad?"

"Yes, I guess I am," he replied, glancing at her and blushing ever so slightly.

"I like her a lot, too. I'm really glad you two are... friends."

"She's...really something. I've never met anyone quite like her. I'm glad you like her, Squirt. She likes you, too."

"After this is all over, do you think you might..."

"We're not making any plans. Just too many unknowns right now."

"Well, when the time comes to make some plans, I just want you to know that I approve—not that you need my approval."

"Maybe I don't need it, but I would certainly want it. Thanks, Squirt."

Melissa smiled and turned her attention back to the lifter. It was now hovering directly over the reactor. Its legs...claws...whatever, were moving to clamp themselves tightly around the housing. The workers scurried about checking clearances and passing along instructions. After about ten minutes, the claws were in place and tightly clamped to the reactor. Some more checking and double-checking went on and then a new crew of workers moved in. They removed the last fasteners holding the reactor to the ship. Finally, the signal was given to start the lift.

Watching closely, Melissa could see when the anti-gravity field was extended to include the reactor. A multitude of small objects and dust, which had been lying unnoticed on the deck, suddenly began floating about. With the sunlight streaming in, it was like a snow globe that someone had shaken. Except this snow globe was not solid. When objects reached the boundaries of the field, they suddenly dropped to the deck.

More orders were shouted and then the reactor began to move. So slowly at first that Melissa had to stare hard to convince herself it really was moving, but then fast enough to see. Workers were on all sides making reports and checking distances. She discovered that she had been holding her breath and let it out in a gasp.

It was a meter above the deck. And then two. More. As it cleared the surrounding obstructions, the rate of movement increased. After a few more minutes, it was moving up through the opening in the dome. Slowly, the lifter and its burden began to move laterally and it was eventually lost to view because of the remaining dome.

"Come on, let's go," said her father, startling her into action.

She followed her father down from the scaffolding and out through a door in the dome. There was quite a crowd of people with them. Outside, she could see the lifter, still gaining altitude and heading south. They worked their way through the crowd toward the landing pad where their helicopter was waiting.

"How long will it take to get the reactor to Norfolk?" she asked as she buckled herself into her seat.

"They are going to keep the speed at under a hundred KPH, so it will take nearly six hours."

"Are we going to follow?"

"Well, we don't have the fuel to stay airborne that long. I figure we'll pace the lifter for a while and then go on ahead to Norfolk."

The helicopter took off and headed in pursuit of the lifter, which was now several kilometers away. Melissa soon noticed that they were not the only escorts. In addition to a half dozen helicopters there were a number of the small 'fighters' and at least three of the converted submarines. All were cruising around in a protective perimeter.

"Wow, they're not taking any chances with this, are they?" exclaimed Melissa.

"Nope. With all the crazy stuff that's been going on, we are taking every precaution. What you see here is only the inner defense. We have a lot more stuff further out. There are ground patrols, too. We can't get another one of these reactors at the local hardware, so we're darn well not going to lose this one."

"I can't understand why anyone would want to sabotage this," said Melissa, shaking her head. "I mean I can sort of understand why those guys tried to raid the storage building here. Things were different then. But now everyone should be working together."

"I can't answer you, Squirt. It makes no sense to me either. I guess some people are just so tied up in their own ambitions that they're willing to destroy everything to get their way."

"I still can't believe they tried to kill Kay," she said in a whisper.

"She's a symbol of everything we are trying to do." Melissa looked at her father and saw his grim expression. "Symbols can be powerful things."

The helicopter was now alongside the lifter and about three hundred meters away. The northern outskirts of Philadelphia were drifting by a thousand meters below them. Their course would take them directly across the city and then down the Delaware River. Looking down, Melissa could see long lines of traffic snaking out of the city. Cars and buses and trucks piled high with baggage.

"Another evacuation convoy," observed her father.

"I sure hope they can keep order. Both in the relocation camps in the cities themselves," said Melissa.

"I hope so, too. But we have more manpower to do it all the time."

Melissa nodded. The United States had its first peacetime draft in almost sixty years. There were nearly a million new troops being trained and more on the way. All the reserves and National Guard had been called up, too. The official justification was the threat of invasion, but she knew it was primarily for keeping order. She could see military vehicles all over the city below her. Martial law had been declared throughout the country.

"I guess conditions in some of the camps are pretty bad."

"So I've heard," said her father. "They've done their best on them and while there is food, shelter, and sanitation provided, it's got to be pretty boring, especially for those who have already been there a few months. No wonder there have been disturbances."

"Do you think the evacuation was a good idea, Dad?"

"It will only turn out to be a 'good idea' if the worst happens. If the cities get nuked it will have been a great idea—small comfort though it will be. If we get off lucky, then it will have been 'a colossal waste of money and effort'. We can't really win on that score no matter what happens. But I suppose we'll know for sure in another two months."

"I wonder what will happen to our house?" she said in a low voice.

"Well, it's far enough from both Washington and Baltimore that it should survive direct hits on those cities. Of course if they hit Frederick we're out of luck. And there's no telling how much looting or vandalism will happen. But houses can be replaced, we have to save the people."

"I worry about Cedric. He's a people, too."

"Yes. Well, Mrs. Gabriel said she'd keep him with her no matter where they end up going. He should be okay."

"I hope so."

The conversation came to a stop. They paced the lifter until it was well south of Philadelphia and then the helicopter picked up speed and headed for Norfolk.

* * * * *

The security around the shipyard was just as tight as it had been around the crash site and the lifter. It was odd though; it was not like normal security where you were trying to keep people from knowing what was going on inside. Here, everyone *knew* what was going on. No, it was more like wartime security near the front lines where you were afraid of an actual attack. The security was very obvious, with lots of fences and guards and armored vehicles and missile launchers. They were challenged several times on their way in.

Melissa's father wanted to circle the construction slip, but was not permitted to. They had to go straight to the helipad and land. They were met there by more security. Once down and checked, things were not as bad. Certainly no worse than they had been at the crash site. They were not accosted as they walked from the landing pad to the construction slip.

"Wow, they've really made a lot of progress, haven't they?" said Melissa when they got near.

"Well, it looks more impressive than it really is. Most of the hull is in place, except for the part we left open to get the reactor in. But there is still a huge amount of work to do inside."

"It still looks pretty impressive to me," insisted Melissa. "And when you consider that six months ago there was nothing here at all, it's doubly so."

"Maybe, but unless we get it finished in time it doesn't matter a damn. A ninety-nine percent finished ship that can't fight is no more use than one that's only reached the blueprint stage. The *Brak-Shar* aren't going to give us any points for effort."

"My, aren't you cheery today!" said Melissa, with a smile.

"Sorry, Squirt. Guess I'm just a little worried."

There were swarms of workers and vehicles around the construction site and they eventually climbed some nearby scaffolding to get out of the way. From that height, Melissa could see the ship much better. It looked like a slightly smaller version of the wreck—except this one was brand new. No battle or crash damage, just lots of bare metal. The opening where the salvaged reactor would go was the only part that looked unfinished—at least from the outside.

"That really is something. I understand that Kay is planning to make this her flagship if it's done in time," said Melissa.

"Yes, that is her plan—if it's ready. She'll be the pride of the fleet."

"Who? Kay or the ship?" asked Melissa with a grin.

"Both, I guess," said her father, chuckling slightly.

"Does the ship have a name?"

"Not yet, but I think Kay is favoring 'Terra'."

"What about the crew, have they been picked yet? And who's the captain going to be?"

Her father did not answer right away. Then she saw that he had taken something out of his pocket and was holding it out in his hand. She looked down and saw that it was an EDF shoulder patch. Her head jerked up in surprise.

"You're looking at him, kiddo," he said, smiling broadly.

"Oh, Dad, that's great!" exclaimed Melissa. "How did you arrange that?"

"Wasn't easy, I can tell you! Kay had to twist more arms than a professional wrestler, and I think I called in every favor anyone ever owed me."

"I'm so proud of you, Dad! Captain of the flagship! So what about your crew? Do I volunteer to you or someone else?"

"No."

Her father had answered so quickly and in such a determined voice, Melissa did a double-take.

"What do you mean?"

"I mean you can't come, Squirt. Sorry, but there's just no way. I've thought about it a lot and you can't come. I'm sorry."

"But why?" She could not quite believe she was hearing this! For the last year they had been a team. She had gotten to know him better than any time before. And now he was telling her to stay home? Like she was a little girl again!

"Because…because there will be a good chance we won't be coming back."

"I know it will be dangerous, Dad!" she exclaimed. Anger flared up inside her. Did he think she didn't have what it takes? "I'm Navy just like you are! I can do a job just like anyone else!"

"I know that, Squirt. That's not the point."

"Then what is the point?" She was angry, but she was blinking back tears, too. Her father's words were hurting her. Hurting worse than anything in a long time. "Why can't I come?" She cursed the squeak that had crept into her voice, it made her sound like a whiney little kid.

Her father turned from her and didn't say anything. She could see he was struggling with something. Her anger melted away. She had never been able to stay angry with him…

"Dad?"

"Melissa…Melissa, this battle isn't going to be like any other. We have to win. We have to. There can be no halfway measures. No 'run away to fight another day'. No negotiated settlements. We win or we perish."

"I know that! Why do you think I want to be there?"

"I know, Squirt, I know. And I'm very proud of you. But you can't come along this time—just listen for a minute, will you? We have to win. We have to do whatever it takes to win. If that means sacrificing my ship, I have to be able to do that..." He paused and then reached out to take her hands. "If you're on board, I might not be able to do what has to be done."

Melissa stepped back, her eyes wide. She pulled her hands from his and put them up to her face and turned away. The tears came in spite of all her efforts. Her father moved up behind her and put his hands on her shoulders.

"Lis..."

"Oh, Dad!" She turned around again and buried her face against his shoulder.

"It's all right, it's all right..."

"No it's not all right!" she cried. "You're going off to get yourself killed—you and Kay! And you tell me I have to stay behind! Nothing's all right!"

"Lissa, please," he said, stroking her head. "It has to be this way. We're fighting for the whole Earth, for humanity's future. *You're* my future. How can I put that at risk if I'm going to help save everyone else's future? If I hesitate because you are there, it could kill us all—kill our future. Please try to understand."

She nodded and sniffed. "I guess I do." She pulled away slightly and looked at her father.

"I love you, Dad."

He pulled her close again. "I love you, too, Squirt."

They stayed like that for a long time.

"So where are you going to pack me off to? Nome?" she asked at last.

"Not quite. Close, though."

She clung to him, not sure if he was joking. But she didn't care. If she could not be with him, it didn't matter where he sent her.

She looked over his shoulder at the huge shape in the building slip. A moment ago it looked like a spaceship.

Now it looked like an enormous metal tomb.

Chapter Twenty-Eight

Expedition Leader Keeradoth watched the tactical display in the control chamber aboard *Seeker of Truth*. Dozens of purple icons moved slowly across the holographic projection. One larger yellow icon moved amidst the others. From time to time one of the purple ones would flare brightly and then vanish. The Someran's shoulders shook in disappointment.

"We have lost again, Honored One," said Tandalin.

"Yes, the Terrans are having difficulty grasping the proper tactics, I'm afraid."

"We must do better before the enemy arrives—and there is so little time left."

"Truth, but the Terrans improve each time. They are working hard and I feel that our simulator is perhaps more clever than the *Brak-Shar* will actually be."

"We can hope for that, Honored One, but we must not count upon it."

"Truth again. If they can complete the one ship they build at Norfolk, it will increase our chances a great deal. How does the construction proceed?"

"They may complete it in time," replied Tandalin. "By using our anti-gravity lifters to move the entire reactor assembly from *Nightpiercer* in a single piece, they have saved perhaps four twelvedays in construction time. It may be enough. But even if they succeed in that…"

Tandalin looked at Keeradoth, shoulders twitching apologetically. "Forgive my asking, Honored One, but if the battle goes against us, what do you intend? Shall we fight to the death to aid the Terrans?"

"It is proper for you to ask, Tandalin. You are my second and it is right that you should know my intentions should I fall. Sadly, I am not sure in my own mind what the proper course of action should be. If we could assure victory and save the Terrans, then I believe our sacrifice would be for the good of the Race. But if the fight becomes hopeless and a clear route of retreat presents itself…then, I do not know. Does honor demand that we stand by our allies to the end?"

"A fair question, Honored One. Much of the Terrans' danger results from our own actions. Do we owe them this? But they are not of the Race. A puzzle indeed."

"And even if we are victorious and survive the battle, what then?" asked Keeradoth. "What will the Terrans do then? They have much reason to distrust us. Will they send us on our way when the danger is past?"

"I believe much will depend on Marshal Youngs. She has much honor for a Terran."

"Truth, and if it were only she that had to be dealt with, I would not fear. But she does not control the Terrans. They follow her lead now because they must. Once the immediate threat is gone, they may turn against her—and there will be little we can do in her aid."

Keeradoth's attention returned to the tactical display. The simulation had come to an end and the *Brak-Shar* were victorious yet again.

"We should do this again, Honored One."

"We shall, but not today. The Terrans' ceremony will begin in a few twelfth-days and we must attend."

"I do not see the purpose, Honored One."

"It eludes me as well, Tandalin. Perhaps our 'liaison' can explain. Is she still aboard?"

"I believe so, Honored One. Shall I send for her?"

"Please do."

Keeradoth's second sent for the sole surviving Tadath-Belind. While waiting, the expedition leader regarded the tactical display which was replaying the last exercise. *The coming battle will be unlike any I have ever heard of. Many twelves of small ships against a single large one. Our combined force outmasses the enemy by a considerable margin, but our actual combat strength is uncertain. We can but hope that the enemy will be as confused as we!*

"What do you think of this Terran, the one called Nisima?" asked Keeradoth suddenly.

"I am uncertain, Honored One. But I have had little direct contact with the Terrans. We left home when their community was still new. Perhaps you should ask one of the survivors of *Nightpiercer*."

"I have. I find their attitude…disturbing."

"Indeed?"

"Yes, they think of them almost as trained animals. Not of the Race, certainly, but not as equals, not worthy of great respect."

"Perhaps if they saw the Terrans in their natural habitat…"

"Perhaps," said Keeradoth. "But perhaps they are right—about the Tadath-Belind. The more I ponder, the more I am uncertain. The Terrans down on the planet, we think of them as savages, barbarians. But they have built a civilization. It was in existence before we discovered them. Primitive, perhaps, but on the road to enlightenment. Many species never survived to make it so far. The Terrans have much to be proud of, Tandalin. But those who we took? We tried to shape them in our own image. What is the result? Just what are the Tadath-Belind?"

"I…am not sure what you are saying, Honored One. Are you suggesting that we were wrong to take the Terrans? That our actions were…immoral?" Keeradoth could sense the shock and bewilderment in Tandalin.

"Immoral? Nay, you know as well as I that true morality, by definition, cannot extend beyond our own species. Were it necessary to exterminate the Terrans—or any other species—that ours might survive, it would be entirely moral to do so. But I begin to think that our actions were…arrogant. Yes, that is the word: arrogant. That we could somehow 'domesticate' another intelligent species to do our will. Clearly it is possible to do so—we have done so! But the results? Are the results truly Terrans that we have 'civilized' somehow, or have we just created some terrible hybrid that is neither of the Race nor Terran any longer?"

"Such things are beyond my wisdom, Honored One."

"And mine, my friend."

Keeradoth turned as the Terran named Nisima entered the chamber. She was small for her kind, but still much too tall. Keeradoth was interested to see that even though the fur on her head was brushing the ceiling, she did not crouch down the way the other Terrans did. Clearly she was used to the low ceilings of the Race. *Domesticated indeed.* She stopped a few paces away and bowed slightly, her hands together in front of her.

"You asked to see me, Honored One?" she said. She spoke the language of the Race amazingly well considering her very different vocal apparatus.

"Yes, I have several questions for you before you return to the planet."

"I will attempt to answer, Honored One."

"This ceremony we will be attending in a few twelfthdays, what is the purpose of it?"

"I believe it has several purposes," answered the Terran. "First, there is the stated purpose of inspecting the forces who shall do battle against the enemy."

"Inspect?" interrupted Tandalin. "From the description of the proceedings we have received, I do not see how any useful inspection can result. Each vessel will only be under the eyes of their commander for a few moments."

"Truth, Respected One. But each crew, knowing their commander will see them—no matter how briefly—will make extra efforts to ensure their vessel is in the best condition possible. However, I believe that the stated purpose is the least important reason for the ceremony."

"Indeed?" said Keeradoth. "What is your evaluation?"

"Another important function is for the fleet to pay honor to their commander and for the commander to do likewise to the fleet."

"For what purpose? Surely it need not be said that commander and subordinate respect each other."

"Among the Race, perhaps, Honored One. The humans lack your... our unity. They must continually reassure themselves of their loyalty. You must remember that this fleet is composed of people from many nations, some of which are rivals. This ceremony is a statement saying: we will fight for the good of all."

The slight slip the woman had made caught Keeradoth's attention. *Interesting. How has her time among the Terrans affected her? Her actions have been strange at times. She has even refused to have her communicator implant replaced.*

"I begin to understand. You imply that there is yet another purpose?"

"Yes, Honored One. The ceremony will be shown on their television. The display of military might will serve to calm the fears of the people. The evacuations and the coming battle have filled many humans with dread. It is hoped that the sight of the massed fleet will give them confidence."

"Yes, I see. There have been incidents of panic and disorder."

"It seems a waste of effort," said Tandalin. "Surely these Terrans know that their fleet will fight to protect them. What else was it constructed for? I see no need to state the obvious."

"Perhaps, Respected One, but the people are afraid. This crisis has caused many changes in their lives. The humans cling to routine and when those routines are disrupted it frightens them. Nothing like this has ever happened before. They have the need to feel safe."

"Well, if it will help to keep order among them, I suppose it is worthwhile," said Tandalin. "The lack of discipline with these creatures is almost beyond belief. It is amazing that they have survived at all."

"But they are capable of great bravery and sacrifice as well, Respected One," said the woman. "Given the chance, we will go far."

Keeradoth studied the female Tadath-Belind carefully. Her use of the word *we* sparked a thought within the expedition leader.

"One last question, Nisima."

"Yes, Honored One?"

"Who do *you* serve now?"

Keeradoth was slowly learning to interpret the expressions of these humans, but there was no doubt the woman was startled by the question. She stepped back slightly and the color of her face changed. She did not answer for several moments.

"I...I have served the Race and the Tadath-Belind..."

"But now?"

"I...forgive me, Honored One. For some time I was not sure myself. But now..."

"Now?"

"Now I serve Space Marshal Kathryn Youngs. I am sorry, Honored One."

Keeradoth's shoulders twitched slightly. *Yes, we were arrogant, indeed.*

"There is no need for regret, Nisima. You have chosen well."

* * * * *

"Whose idea was this anyway?" asked Kathryn Youngs, unbuckling her seat belt and standing up.

"I'm not sure, ma'am," answered Commander Cresswell-Jones. "The first I heard of it was in a memo from the Secretary General's office, so I suspect it may have been his idea. However, I think this may be one of those things that 'just grew' of its own accord."

"Damn waste of time! We've only got a few weeks left and there's still a lot of work to do."

"No argument about the work, ma'am, but I'm not so sure this is a waste of time."

Kay led the way out of the shuttle and looked around.

"Hmph! Well, at least we have a nice day for it." The sky was blue with fluffy clouds and a mild June breeze was blowing across New York Harbor. *June. Almost a year since this whole...nightmare began. Hard to believe.*

Kay was not sure that 'nightmare' was the proper word, but she could not think of anything else that even came close. She supposed that some good might come from all of this in the end, but for the moment it seemed like a bad dream.

She turned around to regard the enormous statue behind her and in spite of herself felt a tiny thrill go down her spine. Liberty Island. Whoever had planned this certainly wasn't sparing the symbolism.

She turned again and almost bumped into one of the hulking security guards who surrounded her. "No room to swing a cat around here," she muttered as she maneuvered past the man.

"Ma'am, I don't have to remind you that they have already tried to kill you once—twice if you count the group we arrested before they could act," said Cresswell-Jones.

"If you don't have to remind me, why did you just do so?"

"Someone has to, ma'am. We can't afford to lose you. You're the only thing holding the alliance together."

"No one's indispensable, Commander, not even me."

Cresswell-Jones said nothing, but raised an eyebrow. Kay glared at him.

She and her escort walked toward the waterfront. There were crowds of people, mostly dignitaries, news people, and security all around. A band was playing somewhere in the distance. Kay scarcely noticed. Her mind was focused on her aide's words.

Was she indispensable? But if she were killed, who would take her place? The people she trusted didn't have the political pull to get the job. And the people who did have the pull... did she trust any of them? Maybe. That was the most honest answer she could come up with. There were a few that she thought she could trust, but not many.

And there was the distinct possibility that no one would take her place. Right now, with the *Brak-Shar* threat only weeks away, she did not fear that any-one in the EDF or any of the national militaries would turn against her, but what about afterward? Assuming they won and beat the approaching enemy, assuming she survived, what then? Would the EDF be seen as necessary? Would those twelve ships under construction be seized by the countries building them? Would the submarine fleets go back to their home services? Would Kathryn Youngs have a job—or even a life expectancy?

She knew it was foolish to be worrying about such things when the main threat had not even been dealt with, but she could not help it. The thoughts had been intruding more and more of late.

What happens afterward?

If the immediate crisis was dealt with, they would have breathing space. The other ships of the *Brak-Shar* squadron were far away. The nearest could not possibly get here in less than ten years. Plenty of time to build ships capable of dealing with the smaller scouts.

But what about later?

Keeradoth had provided some frightening figures on just what a *Brak-Shar* attack fleet might consist of. Several *hundred* battleships, each massing over a million tons. Thousands of smaller ships. Millions of troops. A force larger than all the ships ever built by man combined. The Somerans' projections showed that Earth could build a fleet big enough to resist such an assault given sixty years, but there would be very little time to spare. *Certainly no time to spare on wars among ourselves!*

She could see it happening. What could she do to prevent it? For that matter, how could she stay alive if she tried? She had visions of just taking her flagship and heading out—away from all the problems.

She reached the steps of a reviewing stand that had been constructed at the water's edge. She mounted the steps to join a crowd of dignitaries. She spent several minutes shaking hands and exchanging pleasantries, but her mind was not paying attention as she continued to wrestle with her problems.

She turned as a new group of people came on to the reviewing stand.

"Commander Keeradoth, Sub-commander Tandalin, it is good to see you, again. Nisima, welcome home. Thank you for attending."

"It is our pleasure, Marshal Youngs," replied Keeradoth. "Nisima has ex-plained the importance of this event and we are pleased to participate."

"Really? Perhaps she can explain its importance to me."

Keeradoth's shoulders twitched and Kay saw the Someran's head swivel quickly back and forth. "Marshal, I don't know if this is the proper time to discuss this, but I think you should know that our detectors have picked up the primary drive of the *Brak-Shar* vessel. It is definitely decelerating to stop in this star system."

Kay frowned. They had been expecting this and the Somerans had kept their detectors focused on the patch of space they expected the enemy to materialize from for the last week. But it was still a shock. Like an expected, but still dreaded, pronouncement by the doctor that surgery would be needed after all.

"So how long do we have, Commander?"

"About two weeks, Marshal. The gravity waves have taken that long to reach us. The enemy began decelerating two weeks ago and in another two weeks they will be here."

"So much for them veering off."

"In truth there was probably little chance of that. The information the first ship sent out would leave them to believe that only our two small ships were here to defend this place, both of them damaged to some degree. There would be little chance for reinforcements to arrive in the meantime. The enemy has no way of knowing what you have accomplished in these past months."

"Perhaps when they see what we have waiting for them they'll write us off as a bad deal and get out of here."

"There is that hope, I suppose. I would not count on it, however."

"No. Two weeks. We should have a half-dozen more subs converted by then, and a few more fighters."

"What about the ship being built in Norfolk?"

"I'm hoping it will be ready. As you know, I'm planning to make it my flagship. I have another ship picked out if it is not ready, but we are keeping our fingers crossed."

"Why would you...?" asked Keeradoth in obvious bewilderment. "Oh! Yes of course. We too shall cross our fingers on your behalf."

Kay smiled, but she was definitely crossing her fingers about the ship at Norfolk. She was hoping desperately that it would be completed in time. Not just because it would be her flagship. Not just because it would be the single most powerful ship in the Earth Defense Fleet. But because the captain of that ship was a certain Robert Hancock, United States Navy. And Kay knew that he would take his ship out to fight if it could move at all, never mind if the weapons—or the shields!—were operational. He would go. She wished he was here with her today, but he was with his ship, pushing and pushing to get it ready.

"Here they come, Marshal," said Cresswell-Jones from beside her.

Kay looked out across the harbor and then turned her gaze southward toward the harbor mouth. There was a line of specks on the horizon that were growing larger very quickly. She was tempted to borrow the binoculars her aide was carrying, but she knew the specks would be closer—a lot closer—very soon.

She glanced around the reviewing stand. There were dignitaries and VIPs from all over the world. There were also the flag officers who would command the various squadrons the fleet had been divided into. Uniforms from a dozen different nations were evident, but each and every one of them had an EDF patch on the shoulder. She did not know these men nearly as well as she would have liked, and far too many of them had gotten their jobs because of political connections, but she was going to have to depend on them. *Of course none of them got their jobs because of prior experience—not even me! No one's got any prior experience in anything like this!*

The specks were much bigger now. The first one could now be recognized for what it was, although what it was made no sense at all. It was a submarine, speeding along about a hundred meters above the waters of New York Harbor. There was another behind the first, and another and another, in a long line leading back to the horizon. It really was a very strange sight. The former subs almost looked like blimps, which the mind could accept a lot more easily... almost. The strange radiator assemblies sticking out from the sides ruined that image, however. In truth, they looked like nothing anyone had ever seen before.

As the leading sub neared Liberty Island, it slowed to a more sedate pace, perhaps twenty kilometers an hour. Kay could see a hatch on the conning tower open and then crew members began scrambling out. They were in their dress uniforms and they quickly lined up along the deck, between the safety handrails. By the time the vessel was abreast of the reviewing stand, several dozen people were standing at attention.

"*Baton Rouge*, Captain Charles Duffy, flagship, First Battle Squadron," whispered Cresswell-Jones in her ear.

She nodded and then saluted. The crewman on the ship, only a hundred meters away now, were saluting back. Three flags flew from the conning tower, the United Nations flag, the Stars and Stripes, and a flag bearing a single star— the flag of Rear Admiral John Lindsay who was standing a few meters away.

"Smart looking flagship, Admiral," said Kay.

"She's a fine boat...er...ship, Marshal, thank you."

Baton Rouge drifted past and the next vessel was only a few hundred meters behind.

"*Memphis*, Captain Diane Ortlieb," said Cresswell-Jones.

She saluted again, reflecting that her arm was going to be tired before this day was over. One by one, the other eighteen vessels of the First Battle Squadron cruised by. After they passed, they went another kilometer or so north and then swung around to take up a position across the harbor near Governor's Island.

"*Poltava*, Captain Demitri Varkonyi, flagship, Second Battle Squadron," whispered Jonathan as the lead ship of the next group approached. This vessel had the UN flag, the flag of the Russian Republic, and another admiral's flag flying from it.

"Admiral Oleszak, your squadron performed very well during the last exercise, my compliments."

"Thank you, Marshal Youngs," replied the lanky Russian. "But we must do better if we are to win the battle."

"We all must."

And so it went. Ship after ship, squadron after squadron passed in review. Kay was not particularly happy that the squadrons were mostly homogeneous by nationality, but there had been little choice. Language difficulties alone would have made it necessary even if there had not been political concerns. The first squadron was American, the second Russian. The third was European—primarily British and French, then two more American, and another Russian. Flights of the small fighters were interspersed with the larger squadrons. These looked like slightly larger versions of the shuttles. Kay knew that they carried a dozen missiles, a small laser, and virtually no shields. If she was forced to commit them, they were going to pay a high price. *As if any of us will get off cheaply!*

After the Sixth Battle Squadron came the First and Second Reserve Squadrons. These were composed of smaller diesel boats from a variety of countries. By including tanks of liquid oxygen, the diesels could run for about six hours in the vacuum of space and they did not need the new heat exchangers that the nuclear subs had needed. Even so, there had been no time to install shield generators on these vessels. They would only be used in the last emergency. They had been included in the Fleet primarily to broaden the international nature of the force. Kay glanced over at Admiral Juan Hernandez, the first squadron's commander. He was actually from the Brazilian Air Force, but she reflected that at least half the commanders had not been Navy men before they got their current commands. Admiral Xiyu Zhang, from China, commanding the second squadron was standing next to Hernandez. Kay hoped she would not have to commit these squadrons either.

Or the other two. Bringing up the rear of the parade were the two squadrons of missile boats. The ballistic missile subs were half again as long, on average, as the attack subs and it had made more sense to put their limited resources into refitting the smaller boats with shields. The drive units were simpler to install than the shields and it had been possible to refit the missile boats with them. They were also carrying a full load of nuclear missiles. They had been refitted with new sensors, but they still had their original propellants. Even so, launched in space they would have fairly impressive ranges and the nukes might just take the enemy by surprise. But without shields they could not hope to mix it up with the *Brak-Shar* and survive for long.

She found herself wishing she did not have to commit any of these ships. In the long months of construction and training, she had managed to meet almost every one of the crews. She felt it was very important that she do so. Soon she would be sending them out to a desperate fight. She wanted to know the men and women she was sending.

Kay spotted *Tennessee* among the boats of the Fourth Reserve Squadron. Captain Osborne was not on deck, naturally, but Kay felt a warm memory of her time aboard his ship. Osborne had not been happy when he learned that his boat would not get a shield generator and was to be assigned to a reserve squadron. He had complained—briefly. Kay was certain that Bob had talked with him about it.

Finally, the last ship had passed by and taken its place near Governor's Island. The massed fleet, hovering above the waters, was an incredible and impressive sight. Kay felt pride in what they had accomplished and the power it displayed dispelled a few of her nagging doubts. Every television network on the planet was covering the event and she hoped the people watching were feeling a bit more confident, too. But then her eyes were drawn to the waterfronts of the harbor. There were people there, to be sure, but not as many as you would expect. Almost half the city's population had been evacuated. She turned her head and looked at the defense laser installation atop the Liberty Tower. In her mind's eye, she could see it—and the city—dissolving in a nuclear fireball. *If we fail. What will happen to them if we fail?*

"Marshal Youngs?"

She turned to find Lars Sjolander standing next to her. He was smiling.

"You've done an incredible job, Marshal. Allow me to congratulate you."

"Thank you, Mister Secretary, but they were the ones who did the work," she said, gesturing to the Fleet. "Them and a lot of other people."

"Well, I suppose there is enough credit to go around. But the job has been done. We are nearly ready."

"Yes, we are nearly ready, sir." Kay's eyes drifted upward…toward space. The enemy was there. And very close…

"We're ready. Now all we have to do… is win."

Chapter Twenty-Nine

Shipmaster Rradak'nuar, commander of the exploration support vessel, *Vardunal*, swiveled his head to allow each of his eyes to study the image on the sensor display. The solar system it showed was utterly ordinary in its physical make-up; a main-sequence yellow sun surrounded by the usual swarm of gas giants and small rocky planets, asteroids, and comets. Only the third planet was of any real interest. Spectrographic analysis indicated the presence of liquid water and oxygen. Life could exist there.

But Rradak'nuar already knew that.

The messages from his brothers aboard *Darnaruadool* had said there was life, intelligent life, on the planet.

But the Enemy was there, too.

Two ships of the thrice-cursed Enemy had been waiting in ambush and the brothers had died. Now Rradak'nuar brought his own ship to avenge them.

He reached out his hand and a claw touched the switch that would replay the last message that had come. He had experienced the message several times, but now that they were nearing the objective, he needed to do so again. The speakers in his command chair played the voices of his brethren as they realized death was upon them. The scent synthesizers duplicated the fear they had exuded—and the hate. As the smells touched his receptors, Rradak'nuar felt the same anger and shame they had felt when they knew death and defeat would be their fate. It kindled his own hatred and the scent glands along his neck spontaneously spewed pheromones about the command deck. He watched his subordinates stir in agitation at their control nodes, tails whipping about excitedly. Good. He would renew the message—for the entire crew—when battle was near, but a small reminder now was good.

Anger and determination filled him, but Rradak'nuar was filled with doubts as well. He ruthlessly clamped down on his feelings to keep even the tiniest scent of those uncertainties from escaping, but the doubts remained. What would they face in that solar system ahead? Only two more turnings would bring them there and then what? His ship could easily crush the two Enemy vessels that *Darnaruadool* had reported but would that be all that he faced?

The reports were confusing. A world surrounded by a very sophisticated communications barrier, a world screaming with electromagnetic radiation, obviously highly industrialized and heavily populated. The scans proved that. But only two small ships defending it. Why? An Enemy world should be much better protected. And how had the Enemy built a colony here without being detected? The Nestlords had paid the outrageous fees of the *Tarlangians* to know what traffic went through the Enemy star portals and there was no indication of a colonization force passing through the Enemy's nearest systems.

And the communications barrier had been removed for some reason several hundred turnings ago. It had obviously been in place for many cycles, but now it was gone. The signals that had been intercepted were very strange. Like and yet unlike the signals of the Enemy. What did they mean? Was this a world of the Enemy or not? Very strange.

Still, his duty was clear, despite his doubts. Discover what lay ahead and destroy anything that smelled of the Enemy. The cries of his dead brothers demanded no less.

* * * * *

"They are continuing to decelerate, Marshal Youngs," said the alien on the com screen. "Their course has not deviated. If nothing changes they will come to rest approximately ten million kilometers from Earth, about twelve hours from now."

"I guess they want to give us a looking over before they come barging in, Tandalin," said Youngs. "Cautious. I'm not sure if that is good or bad. We might be able to take advantage of a reckless charge. Still, this will give us a chance to negotiate before the shooting starts."

"Do you still intend to try negotiating?"

"We may as well. They know we are here and as soon as our ships activate their drives or bring up their shields, they'll know about the Fleet. I don't see that we have anything to lose by trying."

"I suppose not, Marshal," conceded the Someran. "*Seeker of Truth* will have to remain in hiding while you make your attempt. If the Enemy detects us, there will be no hope for negotiations."

"Yes, that's true. And even if the *Brak-Shar* do not attack, they may hang around for a while. I suppose you'll have to stay grounded on the Moon's backside until they're gone. There's too much risk that they'll spot you otherwise."

"That will put us somewhat out of position in the defense plans, Marshal."

"I know, but if the *Brak-Shar* stop at ten million klicks and then reject our proposal, you'll have plenty of time to come back."

"Very well, Marshal. I will pass on your instructions to Commander Keeradoth."

The com screen went blank and Kay Youngs leaned back in her chair and sighed. *Twelve hours. Twelve hours and then we'll know.* It seemed impossible. She had been scrambling around without a pause for nine months. The days had gone far too fast, but it had still become a routine. Even though the big red numbers on her desk calendar had gotten smaller and smaller, the routine seemed like it would go on forever. And now, suddenly, the routine was going to end. The months had turned into weeks and the weeks into days. And now there were only hours left.

And not enough hours!

She looked around at the orderly bedlam that filled the bridge of her flagship. Technicians were scurrying here and there and the ship's exec, Commander Josip Nadj, was hounding them to work faster. Twelve hours left and the ship was still not operational. There were lots of little things to do, but the main problem was the reactor. Either battle damage or crash damage or damage from the move had jarred something loose inside. Someran techs and human techs were crawling around in it to try and find the problem. Bob was down there urging them on.

Kay was drumming her fingers nervously on the arm of her command chair. She noticed what she was doing and forced herself to stop. They had to get finished. She suddenly thought guiltily of the time she took off at Christmas, the joyride to Mars. It would not have made any difference here, but she begrudged every hour, every second, she had not been working.

She pressed a button on the chair arm. "Captain Hancock, come in please."

"Hancock here, go ahead," came Bob's voice after a moment.

"Bob, Kay here. What's the situation down there?" She congratulated herself that she had waited a whole thirty minutes since the last time she asked him.

"Hard to say, ma'am. We think the problem is in the grav generators. Some of them may be mis-aligned. They had all checked out okay earlier, but there's something wrong now. We're going to have to open up the main reaction chamber to get at them."

"How long is that going to take?"

"Not sure. Hours certainly. Sorry I can't give you a better answer, Marshal."

Kay sighed. "I see. Tell me, Captain, you have auxiliary power lines bringing in electricity from outside, don't you?"

"Yes, ma'am, that's what we're running the ship on right now."

"All right, it occurs to me that the shield capacitors have not been charged up. We might not get the reactor up and running until the last minute. We might not have time to charge those capacitors. Can we divert power from the auxiliaries and start charging now?"

"I think so, ma'am, I'll get some people right on it."

"Good, keep me informed."

She closed the circuit and stood up. The ship was far roomier than the converted submarines, but it did not have a flag bridge. She and her staff would be sharing this space with Bob and his crew, although she imagined she would be spending a lot of her time in CIC, the Combat Information Center. She headed there now.

Several of her staff, including Commander Cresswell-Jones and Captain Kagami were already there, studying a large holographic display. Kay thought that this bit of Someran technology was just the greatest thing since sliced bread, but most of her staff treated it like any other tool. Right now it was showing a three-dimensional image of Earth and the immediate space around it, out to the Moon's orbit. Dozens of small blue specks gleamed in orderly formations both in space and on the two planets. Kay knew that the Somerans' color perception was shifted toward the violet and it had taken some tinkering to get the display to make the icons blue and red instead of purple and yellow.

She stepped up next to her two officers and they stopped their discussion and looked at her expectantly.

"They're coming on in," she said without preamble. "In twelve hours they'll be stopped about ten million klicks out. I guess we better activate our little messenger and then power down the fleet. The Brak-Shar will be able to spot our drives sometime in the next five hours."

"Very good, ma'am," said Kagami, "I'll pass on the orders."

Kay nodded and Kagami moved off to a com station. Kay studied the holographic display. The six battle squadrons were in a very high orbit around Earth. Several of the fighter groups were out there, too. The four reserve squadrons were still grounded. The two squadrons of diesel boats had to remain down until just before going into action; their endurance was so limited, there was no choice. One was sitting in Sicily, the other was in eastern China. The two squadrons of missile boats were also in reserve. The Russian boats were down near Moscow, and the American ones were at her old stomping grounds of Edwards Air Force base.

A single blue icon that represented the Someran ship was heading toward the Moon. Jonathan touched a control on the display and the scale changed. It now showed a much larger volume of space. Earth and the Moon were reduced to small marbles, and the icons for the ships were clustered too closely to see individuals. Far off to one side a single light was blinking. This was their messenger to the *Brak-Shar*: a communications satellite made with no Someran technology—or at least they hoped nothing *revealingly* Someran. It had been taken out to the rendezvous point days earlier. It would be waiting for the *Brak-Shar* near where they would come to rest.

"I don't like having the Fleet shut down its drive and shields, ma'am," said Cresswell-Jones. "I wish it was not necessary."

"I know how you feel, but we need to keep things under cover until we've made our pitch to the *Brak-Shar*."

Her aide nodded. Kay did agree with him, but unlike the sort of aerial warfare she had trained for, there was very little stealth capabilities in the spaceships. Apparently none of these alien races had ever figured out a way of blocking or masking the gravity waves created by a ship's drive, or by a shield generator. Either one was like a beacon that could be spotted millions of kilometers away. The only way to remain unseen was to turn off the shield and not use the drive.

"How do you think the *Brak-Shar* will react to our messenger, ma'am?"

"I don't know, Jonathan, I just don't know."

* * * * *

Shipmaster Rradak'nuar stared at the display in puzzlement. *Vardunal* had nearly ended its deceleration. The target world was not far off now. But he still did not know what he faced. The storm of electromagnetic radiation continued to come from the planet itself, unabated, and there were a few faint grav readings as well. But no ships. No sign of the Enemy.

Except for that tiny vessel waiting directly ahead.

They obviously knew he was coming: the craft was waiting a short distance from where his deceleration would end. It was also broadcasting a request for parley in the trade language of the *Looranar* people. That surprised him. While the *Looranar* ranged widely, trading with many races, he did not know they ever came this far. Still, their trade language was used by many people as an intermediary tongue, so it meant little that this ship should be using it, too.

But a parley? What did that mean? It seemed unlikely that it was the Enemy who wished to talk. Long ago, they had often tried to talk. Often tried to make amends for their transgressions and end the Great War. But they had given up. Why would they ask to talk now? And if it was not the Enemy, then who?

Rradak'nuar twitched his tail once, but then forced himself to immobility. His subordinates must not know of his indecision. What should be done? His orders were plain enough: scout this region of space and report his findings back home. Destroy the Enemy wherever he might find him, if possible. Flee and report back if the Enemy's strength was too great. Should intelligent beings not of the Enemy be found, his orders were less clear. As the commander of a scouting squadron, far from any base, he had more initiative permitted him than most. He had taken pride in the confidence his masters had in him, but now he almost wished they had not so honored him.

As he pondered, *Vardunal's* velocity fell to zero. Some time was taken while the main drive was secured. But still the strange vessel hung there, broadcasting its request for a parley. Finally, Rradak'nuar stirred.

"Communications, acknowledge the signal of that vessel," he rasped. "Identify ourselves and demand that they do likewise."

"At once, Lord." He looked on as his underling crafted the message, translated it into the *Looranar* language, and transmitted it. Shortly, the message the small ship had been repeating ended. Then there was a considerable delay. The Shipmaster was starting to lose patience when a reply finally arrived. It was a lengthy message that raised as many questions as it answered. The senders claimed to be a race known as 'Terrans'. They admitted that they had been in contact with the Enemy and had been trading with them. But they claimed not to be allies. They also confirmed that a battle had been fought here and that the brothers' ship had been destroyed by the Enemy. But the Enemy was now gone. The Terrans wanted no part of the war that was going on and only asked to be left in peace.

He read the words twice, hating this form of communications. How could you send a message using only words? The lack of an olfactory attachment proved that whatever these creatures were, they were very different indeed!

Now Rradak'nuar's tail did twitch and he made no effort to stop it. This was completely unexpected. What should be done? The Nestlords would not want him to start a war against a neutral planet. The one war they already had was more than enough. But at the same time it was vital that the Enemy gain no clawhold in this region of space. That they were here at all had come as a rude shock to Rradak'nuar. If the hated foe had been in contact with these new beings, there was no telling what lies they had spread. He had to be sure of what was really happening here.

* * * * *

"Incoming message, Marshal," said the communications officer aboard *EDS Terra*. Kay Youngs looked up at the main monitor. A text message appeared on it an instant later. She was very glad that there was no need for direct visual communications with the *Brak-Shar*. Even this mode seemed…wrong somehow, but to have actually seen the aliens on the screen would have been just too much.

She quickly scanned the message. It was short and to the point: the *Brak-Shar* demanded to assume a close orbit around Earth and make a thorough inspection to assure themselves that there was no Someran presence.

"Well, at least they are willing to talk, ma'am," said Commander Cresswell-Jones.

"Yes, Commander Keeradoth was skeptical that they would even do that. Unfortunately, they aren't cutting us much slack here, are they?"

"So now what do we do, ma'am?"

"We've discussed this possibility," replied Kay. "We can't let them do it. There's too much of a chance they would find something they didn't like or we would slip up somehow. And we wouldn't know it had happened until they started shooting. Hell, there could even be some lunatic who would deliberately tell them the Somerans are here. And if they get a close look at us, they'll see how unprepared we are for a real fight. No, we'll have to do what we've agreed on."

Kay took a deep breath. Her next action would almost assure a battle. But there was no choice. "Communications, send out message Alpha-six." She turned to her Operations Officer.

"Captain Kagami, tell the Fleet that it's show time."

"Aye aye, ma'am!"

* * * * *

Rradak'nuar hissed as the new message appeared on the monitor. These 'Terrans' were refusing his demand! And they warned him that they would defend themselves if necessary. A series of other hisses from his command crew drew his attention back to the tactical display.

A large number of unknown contacts were appearing on the screen. At least six score of them. Every one of them read as having an active drive and shields! Long cycles of training allowed him to clamp shut the scales covering his scent glands before the tiniest whiff of the shock—and even fear—he was feeling could escape. Some of his command crew did not have the same discipline, however, and their dismay could be plainly smelt. Rradak'nuar snarled an angry rebuke and then turned to the sensor technician.

"Report! What are these new contacts?"

"Analyzing now, Lord." A few moments went by and Rradak'nuar's impatience and unease continued to grow. If this was a major force, he would have to retreat at once...

"Drive and shield signatures match those of the Enemy, Lord," said the tech finally. "Absolute confidence: the match is exact." Anger welled in Rradak'nuar, in spite of his fear. He hissed and readied himself to give the retreat order.

"Lord! I cannot identify any of these ship types," continued the technician. "The masses are all too small! The largest is only a few percent of our own mass. These are much smaller than any warship of the Enemy we have record of."

The shipmaster's tail twitched in unconcealed agitation. What did this mean? Enemy drives and shields on ships that were not the Enemy's? Was it possible these new creatures were telling the truth and they had obtained the equipment through trade? He watched the display as new data was added to the icons. The combined Terran fleet massed several times what his own ship did, but the individual units were tiny. He could not imagine them having much combat power. *I can crush them, but should I?* Once again, he regretted the initiative his masters had granted him. It was his decision and his alone.

He pondered the problem while his crew waited for instructions. Let them wait. It was unlike any problem he had faced before. But as he weighed his options and his duty it soon became clear what he had to do. There were only two choices: crush the enemy or leave. If he left, it would mean trusting that these creatures were indeed neutral and would give no aid to the Enemy. That would be a great risk. If they were lying, then the Enemy might soon have a base here. That was unacceptable. To crush them, however, what was the risk there? Defeat was the only risk. Victory would solve the problem. These Terrans would only be a threat as an ally of the Enemy if there *were* any Terrans! If there were no Terrans, there was no threat. Simple. Rradak'nuar appreciated simplicity.

His decision brought inner calm. But calm was not what was needed now! He reached out and again played the death-message of his brothers. The anger, the hate, welled up inside him. This time he spewed out his pheromones without restraint. He pressed another switch and the chemical analyzer in his command station recorded their pattern. Throughout the ship synthesizers went to work spreading the message to all aboard.

He watched his command crew begin to twitch and thrash their tails. The pheromones were whipping them into a fighting frenzy as he intended. He felt it himself, of course, but much training allowed him to think clearly at the same time. His subordinates could think well enough to do their jobs, but the only job they would want to do now was fight.

The amount of hissing and spitting going on made him wonder if he had, perhaps, overdone it. He had not brought his crew to full battle readiness in a long time and they might be having difficulty controlling it. He snapped a few commands demanding steadiness and attention to duty and that seemed to have the desired effect. Sometimes a crew could enter into an uncontrollable killing rage if not properly supervised. He would not allow that to happen here!

"Helm!" he commanded, "full ahead! Set course for high orbit about that planet. Engineer! Shield at full readiness! Weapons! All systems to full alert! When ready, destroy that communications relay." A chorus of acknowledgments came from his crew.

Rradak'nuar hissed and spat for the pure pleasure of it. The Enemy was there. The Enemy or the Enemy's pawns, it did not matter which. He took a deep breath and savored the anger and hate that filled his lungs.

Battle and destruction and victory. It had been too long since he had tasted those!

Chapter Thirty

Captain Robert Hancock pushed the intercom button next to the door and waited.

"Come," said a voice.

The door slid open and he stepped into the compartment and closed the door behind him. Kay Youngs was sitting at the small desk in her small cabin. She looked up at him.

"Hi," she said.

"Hi."

"How's it going?"

"We're sealing the reactor up again. We think we've got it sorted out. We'll know in a couple of hours."

"Good."

"I haven't been up to the bridge yet, what are our friends up to?"

"After they destroyed the com satellite they just set course for Earth and are coming right at us. They're doing about three Gs and it will be another five hours or so before they get close enough to engage."

"Three Gs? Is that their maximum acceleration?"

"Keeradoth thinks so, but there's no way to know for sure."

"Most of our ships can do nearly four. That means we can outmaneuver them. One bit of luck anyway."

"And we are going to need every bit we can get."

Bob looked at her and frowned slightly. She looked terribly tired. Dark circles under her red rimmed eyes, creases that months of worry had put on her face. As he looked more closely he almost suspected she'd been crying—if that was possible.

"Are you all right, Kay?" He had asked that question on other occasions and he expected her to say 'sure' the way she always did. When she didn't say it he was startled.

"Bob...have you ever been afraid?"

Now he really was startled. "I...I suppose I have. Once or twice, maybe." He grinned halfheartedly. She didn't grin back.

"I'm afraid, Bob. I've never been so afraid."

He didn't know what to say so he just held out his arms. She rose from her chair and almost threw herself against him. She clutched at him with surprising strength. He put his arms around her and hugged back—although not quite so hard.

"Kay...I...going into battle is always scary..."

"Not like this. Never like this! Korea wasn't like this. Even up on my shuttle, fighting them face to face it wasn't like this. Those times, the worst that could happen was me and a few buddies getting killed. This time...this time I'm responsible for everyone. God, Bob, I'm so scared!"

He fumbled for something—for anything—to say that might reassure her. But what could he say? Didn't she have every right to be afraid? She was carrying a heavier responsibility than anyone since Noah; small wonder that she was a little spooked.

"You've done everything you could, Kay. Far more than anyone had a right to ask of you. Now we have to fight—all of us, together. We fight and we win." He could feel her trembling in his arms, but she nodded her head. After a moment she stepped away.

"Yes. Now we fight. Let's get up to CIC." She headed out the door like nothing had just happened. Bob shook his head and followed.

* * * * *

"Could you explain again just what the hell we're doing here, Lis?" asked Lieutenant Steve Sokol.

"Well, my dad did say that Nome was a pretty close guess. I suppose I should have believed him," said Ensign Melissa Hancock in reply. She looked out through the pine trees to the distant Yukon River. They were standing on a hillside in a deserted region about halfway between Fairbanks and Dawson. It was high summer in this part of Alaska and the meadows beyond the trees were a carpet of wildflowers. The setting sun tinted all the flowers pink no matter what their true color. Unfortunately, flowers and pine trees were not the only life forms in abundance…

"Damn!" said Steve as he slapped another mosquito. "I'm getting eaten alive!"

"I told you to put on more repellent," said Melissa. "But come on, let's get inside and grab some chow. It's going to be a long night—well, not so long this time of year, but you know what I mean." She turned and headed into the woods.

"You really plan on trying to watch the battle?" asked Steve following along.

"Yes, it should get started sometime after midnight if the reports are true. I don't know what we'll be able to see from here, but I damn well intend to be watching!"

"They'll be nothing to see except specks of light and some very bright flashes, Melissa."

"One of those specks will be my dad's ship. I have to watch, Steve. You don't have to if you don't want to."

"What? And miss the chance of spending a night under the stars with the prettiest girl in a hundred miles? I'll be there, don't worry. But that still doesn't answer the question of what I'm doing here." Steve gestured toward which 'here' he was referring to. Ahead of them were a number of buildings set against a steep hillside. They were new and carefully camouflaged to be invisible from above. The only building that was not new or camouflaged was a tumbled-down mining structure off to one side.

Melissa shrugged. "As I recall, you're here because you volunteered—which is more choice than I had."

"I volunteered to keep an eye on you for your dad! I wasn't told we'd be shipped off to the back of the beyond!"

Melissa glanced over at him as they entered the building that was the mess hall. Steve had been complaining like this for the last two days. By this point, she wasn't sure if he was kidding anymore.

"Sorry if you are finding this such a burden, Mister Sokol," she said. "It's not too late to un-volunteer, you know."

"C'mon, Lis, you know I want to be here with you, but at least you have a real job. I'm starting to feel like I was included as...well, as breeding stock."

"I don't know if that's really true, Steve, but in the long run that might be a more important job than mine." Sokol just grunted as they filled their trays with food and then found a table. There were dozens of other people there, eating. Some of them were military, but many had a decidedly un-military look to them: tchnicians and scientists and others that were deemed important enough to try and save from Armageddon.

Melissa had not really been surprised when her father told her about this place. It was one of several dozen sites that had been created as a hedge against disaster. If the *Brak-Shar* won the battle and smashed the cities, but did not reduce the whole planet to a ball of radioactive glass, then this installation—and the others—would be the key to rebuilding and carrying on the fight.

The abandoned mine was now packed with tools and equipment—including a level six fabricator—and enough supplies to last for many years. It would also be their fallout shelter and a refuge in case of a nuclear winter. They had weapons, too, of course, but the primary mission for this installation was to preserve itself and help rebuild. There were other, strictly military, installations that were tasked with fighting any *Brak-Shar* occupation force.

Melissa was here—at least officially—because of her computer skills and her familiarity with the Someran technology. Steve was here—at least officially—as part of the base security force. Of course, the truth was that Kay Youngs and her father had pulled the strings to get her here—and they had sent Steve along to keep her company.

Well, maybe 'company' wasn't really the word. There was no doubt about what was going to happen if they stayed here long. She wasn't sharing a bed with him yet, but if the battle went against them tonight...

But if we do win, I'm damn well going to insist on a wedding first!

She checked her watch. Just a few more hours and they would know.

* * * * *

Nisima sat and chewed the bland military rations and watched Melissa and Steve at the table across the room. She envied them. They had each other. Nisima was alone again.

Kay had sent her off to this place to try and keep her alive during the coming battle—just as Bob Hancock had sent off his daughter. She had not wanted to go. She was terrified of the *Brak-Shar*, but she had wanted to stay with Kay and help in the fight. Kay would not allow it. She said Nisima had a unique perspective on the Somerans and she must survive.

It made sense, she supposed, but it also hurt very much. In the months since she and Bob Hancock had walked into the hospital solarium, Kay had become like family—the only family she had now.

Well...there was also Jonathan—but he was gone, too. She wasn't quite sure what to make of Jonathan. It was obvious he was attracted to her. He kept finding excuses to share her company. At first she had been startled, then amused. Now she wished he was here with her. But he was off with Kay, fighting the *Brak-Shar.*

She finished her meal and returned her tray and utensils, and then stood there uncertain what she should do next. She had no official duty beyond staying alive. Having nourished herself, that duty was satisfied for a while. She looked again at Melissa and Steve. She hesitated for another moment and then walked over to them. Melissa looked up as she approached.

"Hi, Nisima. How are you doing?"

"I am doing as well as can be expected, I suppose, considering the circumstances."

"Yeah! I know what you mean. Steve and I were going to go up on the hill a little later with some of the others and see if we can see anything. Would you like to come?"

"Yes, it would be nice to have someone to go with. Thank you."

"And we really ought to have a chaperone," said Steve with an odd sort of smile. Melissa grimaced and kicked him under the table.

"Would you like to sit down?" asked Melissa, gesturing to an empty chair.

"Thank you."

Nisima sat and regarded the two young people opposite her. She was glad they were here, they were the only people she knew at this facility.

"I have a question to ask," said Nisima after a moment. "Forgive me if it is a foolish question, I am still learning about you people."

"That's all right," said Melissa, "what is it?"

"You are going out tonight to try and watch the battle. Melissa, your father will be fighting in the battle. Are you afraid for him?"

The woman looked startled and leaned back slightly. She glanced at Steve and then nodded. "Yes, I'm afraid. Very afraid. Who wouldn't be?"

"I…I wasn't sure," said Nisima, both embarrassed and curious. "I know that you are both military—warriors. I am still learning just what that means. I know in some societies you would be proud and happy he was going into battle and would not admit you were worried."

"I am proud of him," said Melissa with a glint of defiance in her eyes, "but I'm also very worried about him."

"Yes, I can see that. Thank you. Those feelings make a great deal of sense to me. I…feel the same way about Marshal Youngs."

Melissa tilted her head and now she looked curious. "You're pretty fond of Kay, aren't you?"

"Yes, she has been very kind to me. I like her quite a lot. She…she has become like a new family. Not exactly like a mother," Nisima paused and laughed slightly. "With the time dilation of my journey, I'm actually older chronologically than she is. But she is almost like an older sister. I am very worried that she may be killed in the coming battle. Sometimes it seemed like she was expecting to die."

"I know," whispered Melissa, shaking her head, "my dad, too. They're both so driven to win this fight I'm afraid…I'm just afraid." She trailed off to silence.

Nisima looked at her for a moment. For months people had been trying to comfort her and make her feel like she belonged. Now she could see that perhaps other people needed some comforting, too. She reached out her hand to touch

Melissa's.

"Then we will be afraid together."

Melissa looked at her, then smiled and nodded.

* * * * *

Doctor Usha Vasthare realized she was cursing in her native tongue and forced herself to stop. *Damn! What the hell is the matter with this thing?* Cursing in English did not seem to help any either. She stared at the readout on her display and drummed her fingers nervously. The gravity generators for the fusion reactor of *EDS Terra* were still out of whack.

And time was quickly running out to fix them.

"Do you have any ideas, Nalorom?" she asked the Someran standing next to her.

"It is possible that we are having a telemetry problem, Doctor. We have checked and rechecked all the systems…"

"Including the telemetry systems," she interrupted to remind him.

"Yes, and there are no obvious faults that we can find in any of them."

She pointed to the display that showed a three dimension representation of the reactor core. "According to this, these two gravity generators are not functioning properly, but we can't find anything wrong with them. What would happen if we tried to go ahead and start the reactor?"

"You would have to override certain safety features to even try," said the alien. "The readout indicates that these two generators, while functional, are not properly creating this portion of the containment field. If we were to try to operate the reactor, one of three things could happen. If our readings are false and the generators are operating within the safety limits, then we would have ignition and everything would be well."

"And otherwise?" asked Usha.

"If the containment should fail before fusion ignition takes place then there would be an escape of extremely hot gas that would probably cause serious damage to the reactor. If the failure takes place after fusion has begun…well, we could be looking at an explosion large enough to seriously damage, if not destroy, the entire ship."

"Captain Hancock and Marshal Youngs are depending on this ship in their battle plans, Nalorom. In the last extremity, they will order the reactor started. You know that to be true."

"Yes, you are surely correct, Doctor. That being the case, I suggest we redouble our efforts to ensure the reactor will work."

"Easier said than done." Usha sighed. She had been at this for almost a full day. But there was no time for rest now.

"What should we try next?"

* * * * *

Captain Edward Osborne looked up at the darkening sky. The desert sunset was just a band of color on the western horizon. The brightest stars were already visible. As the night deepened, more bright specks could be seen. Some of them were moving.

"Looks like things will be heating up shortly, sir," said Commander Donna Lakner. Osborne turned and saw that his exec had joined him on deck. He was standing aft of the conning tower, leaning against the rail. He wished he could be up on the conning tower, but with the installation of the laser, there was no room up there for anything but the emitter.

"Yup, and we're still stuck down here. Damn! I wish we could have gotten the shields installed!"

"No argument there, Skipper. But I've got to admit that this is still a sight worth seeing. Damndest thing, isn't it?"

"Sure is," agreed Osborne, turning his attention to the griddle-flat plain *Tennessee* was sitting on. Scattered about were the twenty-two other ships of the Fourth Reserve Squadron. A few months ago these had all been submarines. Perpetually in water, usually deep beneath the surface. Now they were sitting on the desert flats of Edwards Air Force Base, hundreds of miles from any water deep enough to even float them, let alone to submerge.

"Where's Admiral Jameson?" asked Lackner.

"He's over visiting one of the British subs, strengthening Anglo-American unity, I guess. Don't worry, he'll be back aboard his flagship before anything happens."

"Wasn't worried," denied Lackner. "Just wondering why it wasn't so crowded down below. Well, I hope he likes tea or cocoa. Those Limeys don't drink coffee from what I've heard."

"I think that's a myth," said Osborne. "Most of the Brits I've met have drunk coffee. How is the crew taking things?"

"About like you'd expect," said Lakner, taking the change of subject in stride. "Eager for something to happen, nervous about what it'll be like when something does."

Osborne looked skyward again. The desert night was crystal clear. There were dozens of bright specks moving slowly across the sky.

"About another hour until they engage. Damn I wish we were up there!"

"We may get our chance, sir. We may get our chance."

* * * * *

Expedition Leader Keeradoth studied the tactical display in hopes of finding some inspiration. The *Brak-Shar* were still coming on. With the vectors the various forces had taken on, there was no way to avoid an engagement now even if they wanted to. Still, there was hope for victory...

The Terran fleet was divided into six squadrons, each with about twenty ships. Two of the squadrons were now beginning their attack runs, accelerating toward the enemy to launch salvoes of missiles. The relative velocities of the missiles and the target would be fairly high. The potential for damage to the foe was good. Unlike the earlier battle, there were sufficient forces to launch an attack like this and still have reserves available to protect the planet.

But the attacking squadrons would have to be careful. Keeradoth hoped that the massed defensive lasers of the squadrons would be sufficient to deal with the enemy missiles, but they must be wary of the *Brak-Shar* lasers. This vessel carried eight main lasers, all much more powerful than what the first ship carried. At close range they could punch through the Terrans' shields and do heavy damage without even a preliminary missile attack to weaken them.

"So it begins," said Tandalin from the adjacent command station. "The long expected battle is here at last."

"Yes."

"Honored One, you never answered my question about your intentions if the battle should go against us."

"No, you are correct, I never did. I find it no easier to give you an answer now than I did earlier. But I feel that our fate is now tied to this world. It would be difficult to abandon it now."

"Yes. I do not wish to die here, but perhaps honor does demand that of us. The Terrans move forward boldly."

"Let us do our best and pray to the ancestors that we need not die here at all. Victory is not impossible."

"It would be a great deal more likely if the new Terran ship was with us. They still struggle to activate the reactor?"

"Yes. Nalorom is there with them. They hope to be operational shortly."

"They have been saying that for nearly a full day now. If they do not succeed soon, it will be too late."

"With or without it, the battle starts now. Observe." Keeradoth pointed to the tactical display. The first missiles were streaking away from the leading Terran squadron.

Battle had been joined.

Chapter Thirty-One

Shipmaster Rradak'nuar hissed in anger and delight as the enemy neared firing range. He would enjoy crushing these faithless creatures. For they were liars indeed! In spite of their claims to the contrary, they were allies of the hated Enemy! *Vardunal* had barely started forward when one of the Enemy's ships had revealed itself near the large moon of this planet. Now it had joined these Terrans' fleet. His anger at their deception was mixed with relief, for this at least removed the last of his doubts. His decision had been the right one. These creatures must be destroyed or subdued.

But doing so might not be easy. Their ships were small, but they appeared to be well organized and trained. Two groups of them were approaching in orderly formations. Each group was angling to launch missiles from a different direction and each was on a course that would allow it to avoid a close range encounter. Groups of smaller fighter craft were also out there, although none were currently on attack vectors. The rest of their forces were keeping a reserve position close to the planet along with the one ship of the Enemy.

Rradak'nuar was not sure of the proper tactics in a battle like this. The enemy vessels seemed to have an edge in acceleration so if they were careful he would have difficulties closing to short range. That was unfortunate. His ship mounted eight heavy lasers, which could do considerable damage to ships that must be as lightly shielded as those he faced. Still, his missiles should be able to do the job. Even near misses with the nuclear warheads might well be all that was needed to smash those tiny ships.

"Lord, the enemy has opened fire," said the sensor operator.

He observed the tactical display and saw that the twenty ships in the first group had each launched a single missile. Radar and spectrographic analysis told him that these were identical to the ones used by the Enemy. Small, fast, difficult targets and equipped with kinetic warheads. A moment later the second group also launched. Rradak'nuar hissed. These were classic tactics of the Enemy. Too few missiles in a given salvo to make it worth deploying defense missiles to erect a particle barrier, yet enough that they might penetrate his defenses to strike his shields.

Rradak'nuar was an old, experienced shipmaster, but he had never commanded in battle before. He had fought several actions as an apprentice shipmaster and he had learned much from those. Many cycles of training had honed his skills. But now he was discovering the weighty responsibility of commanding an action himself. Still, his training had taught him what to do.

"Defense controller, lasers on automatic. You may employ the main battery in our defense as well at this time. Weapons controller, target the first group of enemy ships and commence fire with missiles."

"Yes, Lord!" said both in unison. It would be a short while before the lasers could fire upon the enemy missiles, but it was only a moment before *Vardunal* shuddered as the first salvo of its own missiles leapt away.

"We shall burn these creatures in the fires of justice!" hissed Rradak'nuar. He released another small burst of pheromones to keep his command crew at the proper level of alertness. Then he returned his attention to the incoming missiles.

The first wave was destroyed by the defense lasers before they could get very close. The next wave got much closer and a single missile eluded all the fire and impacted on the shield. Rradak-nuar spat as his ship lurched.

"Report!" he hissed.

"Capacitor thirty-eight drained to eighteen percent, Lord. No other damage," replied the damage controller.

Rradak'nuar twitched his tail in irritation. His ship had not been harmed, but the defensive capacitors took considerable time and energy to recharge. Another hit in the same spot was unlikely, but as more and more of the capacitors became drained, that eventuality became far more probable. And more enemy salvos were on their way.

He could not afford to remain under fire like this for long. He stared in furious anticipation as his own first salvo neared its target.

* * * * *

Space Marshal Kathryn Youngs looked at the display in CIC and clenched her fists. The ships of the Earth Defense Fleet were engaging the enemy. The ships and the crews she had helped to build and train were out there fighting.

While she was stuck here.

She resisted the tremendous urge to inquire about the reactor again. If there was any change they would inform her immediately. Doctor Vasthare and Nalorom had said they thought there was a good chance they would have it running soon. Were it not for their reassurances, she would have transferred her flag and headed out there long ago. The *Cincinnati* was standing by for just that purpose and she was becoming very tempted to make the move.

"Things seem to be going well, ma'am," said Commander Cresswell-Jones. "We've scored several hits and taken no damage in return. The combined missile defense system is working very well."

Kay nodded. She had sent two of her six battle squadrons out on attack runs against the *Brak-Shar* vessel. Keeping Commander Keeradoth's lessons in mind, she had arranged it so that there were no massive salvos that could be destroyed with a particle barrier. That had worked well so far. A few missiles had slipped through to score against the enemy shields. There had probably been no damage, but it was encouraging. Equally hopeful was the fact that they had managed to destroy the enemy missiles with their massed defense lasers.

In a few more minutes, the first two squadrons would be past the enemy ship and begin their deceleration. They would turn around to attack again. Meanwhile two more squadrons would begin their attack. By shuttling the squadrons in and out of action like this she hoped to keep the enemy under constant attack.

"There's another hit, ma'am," said Jonathan.

"Good. If we can just keep this up…"

One of the CIC people suddenly cried out. "An enemy missile has gotten through to the Second Squadron! Detonation very close to *Borodino*! I'm still getting radar returns, but the drive and shield readings are gone!"

"Damn," muttered Youngs. The battle was still nearly a hundred thousand kilometers away, but she knew that a third of a second ago, one of her ships had just died.

"They're still in one piece, ma'am," said Jonathan as if reading her thoughts. "There could be survivors."

She just shook her head. If the nuke had exploded close enough to knock down the shields in one blow, it had probably ruptured the hull, too. She hoped it had. Anyone who might have survived the blast would have surely taken a fatal dose of radiation in any case. She clasped her hands together behind her back to keep from fidgeting. Her people were dying out there and she was still grounded!

"First and Second Squadrons have completed their attacks, ma'am," said Captain Kagami. "Third and Fourth Squadrons are beginning their runs."

"Very well."

The loss of *Borodino* hurt, but she knew this was only the beginning. They had been lucky so far. The *Brak-Shar* were not doing anything unexpected or clever. They were coming straight in—or as straight as their modest evasive actions would allow—and just giving and taking fire. Her first attack had scored four or possibly five hits for the loss of one ship. It took nearly an hour to recharge a drained capacitor and a ship that size would have over a hundred of the capacitor/deflector units. The EDF attacks were going in about every thirty minutes. If they could keep it up, they would be draining capacitors faster than they could be recharged. With luck, sooner or later, they would start hitting the shield in places where the capacitors were still drained. Then they could expect to do some real damage.

Speaking of capacitors...

"Commander Nadj, how are we coming with charging our capacitors?

"They are currently about twenty-five percent charged, ma'am," he answered. He was from Croatia, but his perfect English sounded like he had attended Oxford. "The power lines we have coming into the ship don't have all that much capacity, so it is slow going."

"We probably should have started sooner. I should have thought of that."

"*We* should have thought of that, ma'am," insisted Nadj. "You have enough on your mind."

She smiled a grim smile and turned back to the tactical display. Her next two squadrons were going into action. The first two were decelerating. The last two—along with *Seeker of Truth*—were still in reserve. The timing was set up so that by the time those last two squadrons went out, the first two would be coming back in. Hopefully, that would allow them to always keep a couple of squadrons near Earth in case the *Brak-Shar* made a move for it. Of course, there were still the four reserve squadrons dirtside and the fighter groups. She was very reluctant to commit any of those, although she fully expected that at least the fighters would become engaged. She had half the fighters out with the Fleet to fill in if any gaps developed in their attack plans. The rest were on Earth where she could use them as an emergency reserve, or to help back up the ground defenses in the event the enemy launched missiles against the planet.

Had she done everything she could? Was there anything she was overlooking?

She clenched her hands and watched her people fight.

* * * * *

Rradak'nuar snarled as his ship lurched slightly. Hit again! He snapped at his defense controller, who cowered beside his console and offered apologies. That he did not also offer excuses mollified Rradak'nuar slightly, but only slightly. The enemy was scoring far too many hits. There was still no damage, but an eighth of the capacitors were drained to some extent. The second enemy attack had passed and they had been even more accurate than the first. The fact that he destroyed a second enemy ship and possibly damaged a third was heartening, but the enemy ships were so tiny, it hardly seemed significant. It was also much harder to kill the cursed things than he had expected. They were combining their defensive fire against his missiles with remarkable effectiveness. In larger battles you tried to keep all the opposing ships under fire so they could not do this, but here, there were just too many targets and they were so close together they were almost like a single, much larger, vessel.

And now the first two groups were returning and another wave of two groups was also approaching. The enemy tactics were both effective and extremely annoying. Their superior acceleration was the problem. He had tried to close on one of the groups in the second attack, but they had managed to stay beyond laser range.

"Lord, the Enemy vessel is in the approaching group of ships," said his sensor controller. Rradak'nuar looked and saw that it was true. The Enemy of enemies was no longer cowering in the rear. Was this an opportunity to crush them? Oh how he wanted to crush them! They were, no doubt, commanding this fleet and to destroy them would be doubly satisfying. He called up the navigation display to see how he could bring about an interception. Yes, it was possible! They had grown careless and he could... He was just about to give the command to change course when he saw it.

Curse the filth!

A trap. A clever trap. If he went after the Enemy, he would be attacked by all four enemy groups at once! The two returning groups and these other two would hit him from four directions simultaneously. Still too dispersed for a particle barrier to be effective, yet concentrated enough that his defenses would be stretched beyond the breaking point. *Vardunal* could well suffer dozens of hits in such a crossfire. No, as satisfying as it would be to smash the Enemy, the risk was too great. No, he would have to wait. The shipmaster gave the command to change course in a different direction. He would still have to endure the attacks, but at least not all four groups at once. And the planet was drawing nearer and nearer. He was starting to believe that perhaps the planet was the key to this situation...

* * * * *

"They have seen through the ploy, Honored One," said Tandalin.

"Yes. They have not acted in a clever manner so far, but they have been clever enough to avoid this stratagem. A pity. But the battle goes well."

"We cannot expect them to continue these passive tactics. I am surprised that they have not even launched fighters."

"They may be conserving them for later—if they even carry any."

"Our data indicates a ship of this type may carry three-twelves or even more, Honored One," said Tandalin.

"True, but our information may be out of date. There is no telling what this vessel may be carrying. For now, all we can do is proceed with our own battle plan and try to respond to any developments that arise."

The pair fell silent and Keeradoth observed the activities of the command crew. They were all working with cool efficiency. The last battle had blooded them and given them confidence. Keeradoth was proud. They were proud, too. They could all feel it. Keeradoth turned back to the tactical display.

Seeker of Truth was currently with the Terrans' Fifth Battle Squadron, twenty-one ships from the United States. 'Battle Squadron' was a rather grandiose term for a formation that would not have even made a patrol flotilla in a proper fleet, but it was as good as these Terrans had—at least at the moment. Along with the Sixth Battle Squadron, composed primarily of Russian ships, they were nearing missile range with the enemy. The First and Second Squadrons were also approaching from nearly the opposite direction, but they could not engage until later.

"We have entered missile range, Honored One," said the weapons controller.

"Fire on the squadron commander's orders," said Keeradoth. There were a few startled reactions from around the command deck. It was understood that *Seeker of Truth* would cooperate with the Terrans, but this was the first indication Keeradoth had made that they would accept the Terrans' *orders*.

"Aye, Honored One."

A moment later the command came and Keeradoth felt his ship shudder as the salvo leapt away. *Seeker of Truth* was using all twelve tubes, while the Terran ships, with their much smaller magazine capacity, were only firing single missiles. The total from the squadron was probably still small enough that the *Brak-Shar* would not erect a particle barrier, but they would soon find out for sure.

"The enemy vessel is launching missiles," said the sensor controller. "They appear to be targeted on Squadron Six."

Yes, the enemy had not taken the bait to come after *Seeker of Truth* and leave themselves open to a four-way attack. The Sixth Squadron was closer and that was who they were firing at.

Time passed and fire was exchanged. Half a twelve of hits were scored on the *Brak-Shar* ship. That was good, but two of the ships in Squadron Six were destroyed in reply. Then the range grew too long and the two squadrons began their deceleration to turn back and attack again. Shortly after, the first two squadrons attacked and more hits were scored.

"The enemy is foolish to continue these tactics," said Tandalin. "Simple mathematics should show them that we will beat down their shields before they can deplete our ranks. Even with the lost ships we can maintain our volume of fire by having the Terrans launch more than one missile per vessel. At the least they should expend some of their defensive missiles to blunt one of our attacks so that they may recharge their shield capacitors."

"It is fortunate that you are not directing the *Brak-Shar*, Tandalin." The expedition leader had worked with Tandalin for so long there was no doubt the humor in the remark would be interpreted properly.

Yet, Tandalin was correct: it did seem strange, and Keeradoth was becoming concerned about how close they were coming to the planet.

What are they planning? They cannot be as foolish as they appear.

* * * * *

Melissa Hancock sat on the blanket next to Steve and watched the skies. The short northern night had finally fallen. Steve and Nisima and a small crowd of other people had climbed the hill behind their base to a high meadow, which had a good field of view. They had brought blankets and food and drink, but it was the most somber picnic Melissa had ever been to.

"Have you got your glasses?" asked Steve.

"Yes I've got them. That's about the third time you've asked me that!"

"Sorry, but you could really mess up your eyes when the nukes start popping. And I am supposed to be looking out for you." Steve's tone seemed a little defensive and Melissa realized she had just snapped at him without even noticing.

"I'm sorry, Steve. I…I guess I'm just a little tense."

"Understandable. Don't worry about it." Melissa smiled and scooted a little closer and put her arm around him. He responded in kind.

"Look! There's something!" said a voice in the darkness.

Melissa scanned the skies and caught a glimpse of a flash fading away to the northwest. Almost immediately several more appeared. They were no bigger or brighter than a firefly on a summer evening. There was a cloud of fainter specks climbing up the sky.

"Not all that bright, are they?" said Steve. "I guess they're still pretty far…"

He broke off as a much bigger and brighter flash lit up the sky. A half dozen more followed immediately and Melissa turned her head away quickly.

"Whoa!" cried several people.

Melissa hastily put on the dark glasses Steve had been nagging her about. "Those first flashes must have just been the kinetic missiles—*these* were the nukes!"

"Damn right! Hell, I can still see spots!"

She just nodded and thought back to another summer evening, just about a year ago. There had been bright flashes of light in the sky then, too. She had called her father and Uncle Eddie out to look. Now they were going up there to make flashes of their own.

God protect them! she prayed silently.

She shuddered. The last word they had gotten over the military radio led her to believe that both her father and Captain Osborne's ships were still on the ground, but that was several hours old. There was no telling where they were now.

The dark glasses dimmed out most of the other specks of light, but the flashes were coming more and more rapidly now. A veritable fireworks display.

She looked down and took off her glasses for a moment. The flashes lit up the meadow. They were bright enough to read by.

She started as Nisima sat down beside her on the blanket. The woman had been standing alone. Now she was next to her. She was staring at the sky and shivering. It was a pleasantly warm evening and Melissa suddenly realized that Nisima was not shivering because she was cold. After a moment Melissa shifted over slightly and put her other arm around Nisima. She looked over and then smiled. Her arm came up to go around Melissa's waist.

Melissa Hancock hugged the two people next to her and then tilted her head back to watch the lights in the sky.

*   *   *   *   *

Kathryn Youngs paced nervously back and forth as much as the confined space in CIC would allow.

"Marshal, that deck is brand new and you're going to wear a hole in it."

Kay turned as Bob Hancock came into the compartment.

"Well, at least you've got something to do, Captain, all I can do is stand here and watch!" said Kay grumpily. Bob smiled a tired smile.

"How's it going?" they both asked simultaneously.

Kay laughed. "You first."

Bob's smile faded and he shook his head. "They're still working on it. I have the urge to grab a monkey wrench and start banging on things, but I guess that won't really help."

"Hell, we have got to get moving," said Kay. "Isn't there anything we can do?"

"Well, by threatening her with a rubber hose, I got Doctor Vasthare to admit that we could try to fire that sucker up if we were willing to risk blowing up the ship and half the shipyard with us."

"That doesn't sound too appealing, but it's good to know we do have at least one option if we need it."

"Are we likely to need it? How's the fight going? You may be wearing a hole in my deck, but you haven't started chewing the bulkheads yet—that must be a good sign."

"Actually, it is going far better than I had any reason to expect," said Kay, gesturing to the display. "The *Brak-Shar* aren't doing much except sitting there and getting pounded. We've hit them with seven separate attacks and the eighth is going in now. You can see Third and Fourth Squadrons just starting their attack run. Fifth and Sixth and *Seeker of Truth* are back near Earth again, waiting their turn. We've scored a lot of hits on them."

"Are we hurting them?"

"I sure hope so," said Kay, earnestly. "There's no evidence of true damage to their ship, but we must be draining their shield capacitors badly. Keeradoth certainly thinks we are. If he's wrong about that, then we are seriously out of luck."

"What about our losses?"

"Eight ships lost and four more out of the fight with serious damage."

"Not too bad, really."

Kay nodded grimly. "Not as bad as I had feared, but that's still ten percent of our total force. We need to do some real damage soon."

"Well, it looks like you've got the right plan to do it, ma'am. The enemy seems bamboozled."

"Maybe. But things aren't going perfectly—not by a long shot! We've got a bit of a mess developing right now."

"What?"

Kay gestured to the display again. "First and Second Squadrons are badly out of position. The *Brak-Shar* have gone into a high orbit around Earth. Well, it's not really an orbit, they are traveling about four times the orbital velocity for that far out, but they are using their drive to curve around the planet. They've done almost one complete circuit. Anyway, when First and Second Squadron made their last run, the *Brak-Shar* lunged out at them and they had to evade sharply to stay out of laser range. As a result, they are way over there and still heading outbound. It will be nearly two hours before they can get back in and attack again. "We've been trying to keep them under constant attack and keep draining their capacitors. If we let a big gap appear in our attacks, they'll be able to recharge and all our efforts will have been wasted."

"You've got Fifth and Sixth Squadrons in position to attack," pointed out Bob.

"Yes, but if I send them out now, there will be nothing but the reserve squadrons guarding Earth, and we still end up with at least an hour with no attacks going in."

"There is a solution, ma'am," said Captain Kagami who was standing to one side. "I know you don't want to commit them, ma'am, but it may be our only choice."

Kay sighed and nodded. "Yes, Group Commander Hazelton's fighters," she said indicating another blue icon on the display. "Damn! Sending them in would be as good as murder. Their shields are so weak even a burst ten klicks away would probably fry them. Hell, the *Brak-Shar* lasers could probably kill them at twice the normal range."

"Marshal Youngs," said Kagami, very formally, "if we do not keep up the attack then all of those who have already died will have done so for nothing."

"I can't damn you for being right, Captain—no matter how much I might want to. All right. Send out the order."

"Aye aye, ma'am." Kagami headed for the com station.

"I hate this," whispered Kay. "Sending other people out to die. I hate it."

"I'd be worried if you felt any other way. After this is all over you can relax," said Bob. "The next *Brak-Shar* attack won't be coming for seventy years. You'll be safely retired by then."

"Safely in my grave, you mean. But that would be just fine, too."

Bob looked at her closely. "You're doing fine, Kay," he said quietly. "Just hang in a little longer, okay?"

She smiled at him. "Okay, Captain, if you say so." She realized she had her fists clenched again and she forced herself to relax. This was so hard. Harder than anything she...

"Marshal!" exclaimed one of the CIC operators, suddenly. "Commander Keeradoth is reporting debris, air, and water vapor from one of the last hits on the target! We've gotten through their shields!"

A small cheer went up around the compartment. Bob was suddenly wearing a big grin.

"Thank God for that," he said.

"Yes. But it's not over yet. Not yet."

* * * * *

Shipmaster Rradak'nuar snarled as his ship lurched from the impact of an enemy missile. The feel instantly told him his ship had been hurt; not just a capacitor drained.

"Report!" he snapped at the damage controller.

"Shield penetrated in section forty-nine, Lord! The deflector and capacitor have been destroyed. Additional damage to sensors. Defense laser nineteen is damaged. There is a substantial hull breach. I am dispatching repair parties." Rradak'nuar hissed and spat, but the prompt and efficient report of his subordinate restrained any further chastisement.

Curse these vermin! These damnable Terrans had hurt his ship! He thrashed his tail in barely contained fury. He raked his claws along the edge of the station and willed himself to remain calm. *Patience! Our time is nearly at hand!*

Yes. He had endured attack after attack. Watched his shields being drained bit by bit. Accepted the puny losses they had been able to inflict on the foe. Even let the Enemy pass unattacked, let alone unharmed.

Waiting for this chance.

The enemy ships would soon be where he wanted them to be. The enemy planet was nearby. As soon as this last attack was over…

The ship shook again but this time it was just a shield impact. Quick revenge was gotten when one of the enemy ships vanished from the display. A short while later the enemy ships drew out of range.

It was time.

"Flight control! Launch all fighters. Engage the enemy force that just attacked us. Any losses are acceptable, but keep that force engaged!"

"Yes, Lord!"

"Helm! Come to course one-four-eight, by negative three-nine. Ahead at maximum!"

"At once, Lord!"

"Weapons! Bring all tubes to bear on the planet. Target radio and heat sources. Open fire immediately!"

Unlike his other subordinates, this one hesitated. "Lord, we are out of powered missile range of the planet. Our missiles will be easy targets for any defenses."

"I am aware of that," said Rradak'nuar.

"And, Lord, we do not carry bombardment warheads. The speed at which our missiles will enter the atmosphere of the planet will certainly destroy them before they can reach detonation altitude. They will burn up first."

"I am also aware of that. Carry out your orders."

"Yes, Lord!"

Rradak'nuar waved his tail in mild amusement. His weapons controller had clearly been terrified, but he had acted properly. That one had potential. After this battle it might be worthwhile to take him on as an apprentice. There was always a need for more shipmasters. But he also had much to learn besides the technical capabilities of his weapons. The missiles he was firing could truly do no harm to the planet fired from this distance.

But the planet was not the real target—not yet.

* * * * *

"Honored One, the enemy is launching fighters!" exclaimed *Seeker of Truth's* Sensor Controller. Keeradoth looked to the tactical display and saw that it was true. Over three-twelves of small fighters had been disgorged by the *Brak-Shar* vessel.

"Estimated course?"

"They appear to be in pursuit of the Third and Fourth Squadrons, Honored One."

"At last they make a move," said Tandalin.

"Stand ready," said Keeradoth, "I expect another move very shortly."

"Course change! The enemy ship is now accelerating toward the planet. They are launching missiles! Honored One, the enemy is launching missiles against the planet!"

"Yes," said Keeradoth. "They have divined our weak point. I feared this."

"I do not understand, Honored One," said Tandalin. "They are far out of range of the planet. Those missiles are no threat. We can destroy them easily."

"How shall we do that?"

"They will pass close by us to reach the planet. A small repositioning on the part of our squadrons and we can destroy them with our lasers as they pass."

"Truth. And the next salvo?"

"The same, of course."

"And the next? And the next? As the enemy draws ever nearer?"

"We can...ah, I think I see. They seek to pin us here while they close."

"Yes, and it will work, I fear."

"But if we see through this ploy, we can avoid it, can we not?" asked Tandalin in confusion.

"Can we? If we do, what will happen to the planet? And do you really think the Terrans would agree in any case?"

Tandalin was silent.

"Honored One, a communication from Admiral Mercader: 'All ships take up position to interdict incoming missiles. Prepare to attack the enemy on his command'," said the communications controller.

"Yes, they cannot abandon their planet. The enemy has deduced that they will stand and fight rather than allow them to attack their home."

"This will allow them to close with their lasers," said Tandalin.

"Yes, I fear heavy losses."

"Do we stand with them, Honored One?"

Keeradoth said nothing.

"I believe you have answered my earlier question, Honored One," said Tandalin after a moment.

"I suppose I have. Stand ready to engage. At the least, we should be able to harm the enemy badly as he makes this charge."

The first wave of missiles coasted past and were easily destroyed by the mass lasers of the waiting squadrons. The next salvo was dealt with in the same fashion. Then the order came and the two squadrons, and *Seeker of Truth*, accelerated toward the enemy.

Another wave of missiles was destroyed and then the enemy was in range. Missiles leapt from the tubes of the squadrons. Suddenly the sensor controller exclaimed:

"Honored One! The enemy is launching defensive missiles! A particle barrier is being deployed."

"They will have to renew the barrier constantly," said Tandalin in surprise. "It will use many of their missiles to do this!"

"Apparently they think it worthwhile," said Keeradoth. The expedition leader's voice was calm, but that was a mask. This move had come as a surprise. If the enemy had enough defensive missiles to expend they might slip past with minimum damage. The only good was that the enemy had to severely reduce their offensive fire to do this.

Keeradoth watched as the squadrons' first salvo was wiped out by the particle barrier. The missiles collided with the cloud of small metal grains at high velocity and were torn apart in an instant.

"Message from Admiral Mercader: 'All ships begin maximum fire using plan Zeta-four. Stand by on lasers for concentrated fire at effective range'," said the communications controller.

Keeradoth's shoulders twitched in approval. Neither side could vary its course significantly. Massed missile fire could well score hits even with the particle barrier. The particles could not totally destroy the missiles and the wreckage would do as much damage as an intact missile. The combined laser fire of three-twelves of ships was not insignificant either.

"Set our lasers for continuous fire," commander Keeradoth. "Focus all five together in concentration."

"Honored One, that may burn them out," said Tandalin.

"That it may, but I doubt we shall have much further need for them after this."

"As you command, Honored One."

The range shortened rapidly as the enemy bore down on the planet. Salvo after salvo went out, but almost all were destroyed to no effect. A few got through, but it was not enough.

Then they were in range of the enemy's main lasers. They lashed out in pairs and in an instant four of the human ships were blown apart.

Again, and four more died.

Now the range was even less and the squadrons could return the fire. A volley of lasers and a final salvo of missiles blasted into the face of the enemy. Hit and hit again. Were they doing any damage? More enemy fire and more human ships died. *Seeker of Truth's* lasers continued to flay the foe and at last debris ex-ploded away from the target. The opposing forces flashed by at impossibly close ranges, lasers clawing at each other.

Keeradoth was looking with satisfaction at the damage estimates on the enemy when the side of the control chamber exploded inward. Smoke and flame filled the compartment. A mighty blow slammed Keeradoth against the command station's restraints and consciousness fled.

Chapter Thirty-Two

"What the hell happened?" asked Captain Robert Hancock. He had just entered CIC after hearing a chorus of shouts and exclamations from Kay's staff. One look at Kay's face told him it wasn't good, whatever it was. She looked up at him and then just shook her head.

"I screwed up," she said simply.

"What do you mean?" he demanded. She turned away and said nothing. Hancock scanned the faces of her staff looking for an answer.

"The *Brak-Shar*, have broken through Five and Six Squadrons," said her aide, Cresswell-Jones. "They're headed right for Earth."

"Not just broken through," added Captain Kagami. "Virtually wiped them out. *Seeker of Truth* along with them."

"My God! How?"

"They changed course unexpectedly and started launching missiles against the Earth. Admiral Mercader moved to intercept. There was a short-range fight with lasers. We've got about five ships left out of the two squadrons."

"Holy shit. And the enemy is still headed this way?"

"Yes, they are about two thousand klicks out," said Cresswell-Jones. "Coming down toward the north pole—it looks like they are going into a polar orbit, but it is too early to tell about that. In any case, they are braking hard and their current course is going to take them right down the east coast of North America."

"A bombardment run," said Bob, grimly.

"It looks like that."

"What about the other squadrons? Can they intercept?"

"Not for some time," said Kagami. "First and Second Squadrons are just starting back this way now. It will be two hours before they can attack. Third and Fourth are still braking and the enemy has launched about forty fighters that are on an attack vector to intercept them. We are going to be on our own for a while, I'm afraid."

"I ordered Mercader to stand off and let the ground defenses deal with the missiles, but he wouldn't listen," said Kay in a whisper that could barely be heard. Bob turned to look at her and she was slumped in a chair staring at nothing. He walked over to her and put a hand on her shoulder.

"Kay, what's done is done," he said very quietly. "We still have a battle to fight. You have to think about what we are going to do *now*." She was trembling slightly and when she looked up at him there were tears glistening in her eyes. He stepped back.

"What are your orders, Marshal?" he said in a much louder voice. Kay stared at him for an instant longer, then shook herself and stood up.

"Alert the reserve squadrons, have the diesel boats fire up their engines," she said. Her voice quivered slightly but grew stronger each moment. "We will concentrate all forces over North America."

"Ma'am, we can't hope to get them all in position, before the enemy passes over us," said Captain Kagami. "In fact, none of them can get here in time."

"Yes, I know. But if they go into an orbit, they'll be back again before long. We can hit them on their second orbit. We must concentrate our forces for this."

"Very well, ma'am, I'll give the orders."

"And tell Group Commander Hazelton to abort his attack on the *Brak-Shar* vessel and assist Three and Four Squadrons against those fighters. He can get there much sooner and his people will be a lot more effective."

"Aye, ma'am."

"Jonathan, alert all the local defense forces. Laser weapons to full readiness; get the fighters in position for missile defense. Order all the aircraft up, ground and sea units, civil defense, the whole ball of wax, you know the drill."

"Aye aye, ma'am, right away."

"Captain Hancock," she said turning to Bob, "I am going to require my flagship to move. Please have your engineer and Doctor Vasthare start the reactor."

He hesitated for a fraction of a second and then saluted. "Aye aye, ma'am."

Bob walked to a com panel and called the reactor room. "Doctor, we need to start the reactor now. There's no option. Begin the procedure."

"Are you sure, Captain?" came back Vasthare's voice. "I've explained the risks…"

"There's no choice, Doctor, the *Brak-Shar* are attacking the planet and we have to get into the fight."

There was a pause. "All right, Captain, but we have to disable a number of safety features. That is going to take at least twenty minutes. I'd suggest you use the time to clear the dock area of all the construction people…just in case."

"Very well, Doctor, but please hurry." He closed the connection and headed for the bridge.

"Commander Nadj, we are going to start the reactor. Clear anyone not part of the crew from the area. Seal all the hatches and have the crew stand by to raise ship."

"Aye aye, sir! Uh, sir, there's still some scaffolding on the hull and other equipment nearby. And what about the auxiliary power lines?"

"We need the power, the rest of it is expendable."

"Yes, sir!"

Nadj quickly carried out his orders. Bob wished he knew the man better. The last two months he had been shuttling between the construction site and the training school near Paris to take a cram course on how to command a ship like this. He was far more dependent on his better-trained subordinates than he would like, but they seemed to know how to do their jobs.

The bridge crew was scurrying about to carry out these new orders when Doctor Vasthare and Nalorom came on the bridge.

"Status, Doctor?" he asked.

"It will be at least a half-hour, Captain," she answered without pausing as she threw herself into a seat at the engineering station. He was tempted to remind her that time was of the essence, but as he watched her fingers flying over keyboards, he realized that would be non-productive. After assuring himself that everything was proceeding satisfactorily, he went back to CIC.

Kay was talking with her staff. She seemed to have come out of the momentary funk she had been in.

"They are definitely going into an orbit, ma'am," Cresswell-Jones was saying. "You can see here on the display: They are currently just southwest of Iceland. Their course will bring them over Quebec and Nova Scotia and then down the eastern seaboard. They are at about twice orbital velocity, but still decelerating."

Kay looked up as he approached. "What's the story on the reactor?"

"The Doctor thinks we can try in about thirty minutes."

"Not good enough! They'll be right overhead in less than twenty!"

"I don't think we can hurry it, ma'am, but I'll check."

"Ma'am," said Captain Kagami, "I would strongly urge that we wait. None of the reserve squadrons can be here until the enemy has gone by. If we try to engage on our own we will end up like *Seeker of Truth*."

"But if we stay here we'll be a sitting duck!" protested Kay. Bob could see that she was still on the ragged edge. The loss of those two squadrons had been devastating. Not just to the battle as a whole, but to her personally. He knew she desperately wanted to get up there with her people and fight.

"If we don't try to start the reactor, there will be nothing to draw the enemy's attention to us," persisted Kagami. "With all the other targets they are going to have, they will probably leave us alone."

"Other targets! Like the cities, you mean!"

"All the other defenses are on alert. We won't make that big a difference, ma'am."

Bob could see that she was going to argue. He stepped up next to her. "Marshal, Captain Kagami is correct. Our shield capacitors are still only at forty percent. If they catch us as we are trying to power up we're dead. I don't want to take that risk." He stepped even closer and whispered: "Please, Kay."

She stared at him with wide eyes. He stared back and grasped her arm. "We'll get our shot—I promise you."

She looked away and took a deep breath.

"Very well, we'll wait. But tell Vasthare that as soon as they have gone past we are powering up! And order *Cincinnati* to clear the area. Rendezvous with the Fourth Reserve Squadron. I'll be keeping my flag right here."

"Yes, ma'am."

"Ma'am, they are just crossing the coast of Quebec now," said Cresswell-Jones. "If they are going to bombard, they should start any second."

They all turned their attention to the display. It had zoomed in on the northeast quadrant of North America. Hundreds of blue icons crawled across the surface. A few of them were fighters and Bob could see the pair that represented *Terra* and *Cincinnati*. But most of those icons were not officially part of the EDF. The vast majority of the world's military forces may have been completely obsolete against something like the *Brak-Shar* cruiser, but that did not mean they were completely useless. Officers like General O'Connell had been determined to do everything in their power to help defend their countries. Now it was fortunate that they had.

In addition to the ground laser installations, they had pressed anything that could possibly shoot down an incoming bomb or missile into service. Before he was given command of *Terra*, Bob had learned quite a bit about those activities. Right now those forces were going into action. Hundreds of F-35 fighters were lifting off from airfields and carriers. They were armed with specially modified Phoenix IV missiles which were, in theory, capable of intercepting a missile at ranges up to two hundred kilometers. Area Theater Defense Systems were also coming online. Even some of the obsolete Patriot batteries were there, waiting.

Bob's eyes were drawn to a cluster of icons off the east coast. For the first time in almost eighty years the United States Navy was all in home waters. All fourteen carrier battle groups were poised to defend their homeland. One was near Hawaii, one in the Gulf of Alaska, four off either coast, and four more in the Gulf of Mexico. One of those icons represented the *USS Ronald Reagan*. Bob said a silent prayer for the young aviators who were preparing to do battle with this threat from the stars.

But then his eyes came back to a glaring red icon that was moving across the map. As he watched, smaller red dots appeared.

"The enemy is launching missiles, ma'am," said Cresswell-Jones.

* * * * *

Die! Die, you vermin! thought Rradak'nuar to himself. He looked on in satisfaction as his subordinates launched death against the enemy world. The one circuit they had made around this planet before striking had given him the needed data to plan this attack. The planet was heavily populated and industrialized, but the habitations and industry was clustered together in relatively few locations. A half-dozen orbits would all that would be needed to smash the majority of it.

And smash it he would. Payment for what these creatures had done! He glanced at the damage display and hissed. His ship had been hurt. Hurt badly. The Enemy and their allies had fought bravely, he had to admit. They had stood claw to claw and barred his way to the planet. They had died, but not before inflicting heavy damage on his ship. One of the main lasers, three defense lasers, four missile tubes, and a number of sensors had been lost. Five ragged holes now pierced the hull of *Vardunal*. Three more deflector units were also gone and that created several dangerous weak spots in the shield coverage. And he had expended nearly half his defensive missiles. Perhaps worst of all, one of the secondary drive nodes had been damaged and his ship's acceleration was reduced by over ten percent.

But the enemy and the Enemy had paid a far stiffer price. Over thirty of the small ships destroyed and the one larger Enemy ship crippled completely. And now very little prevented him from devastating this planet. A few small drive sources were evident. No doubt more of these fighter craft he had observed. But no other grav readings at all. The way appeared clear...

"Lord, I am picking up numerous small craft on radar ahead of us," said the sensor operator suddenly. "They appear to be air vehicles of some kind... Lord! They are launching small missiles!"

Rradak'nuar looked on in surprise. He could see the icons for his own missiles speeding ahead of his ship toward their targets. But now other icons were headed in the opposite direction. They were ridiculously slow compared to his own, but they were directly in their path. Anger coursed through him when those icons merged with his and both vanished! They were destroying his missiles before they could reach their targets! What were those things?

"Continue launching!" snapped Rradak'nuar. "Direct laser fire against those air vehicles!"

"At once, Lord!"

More missiles leapt from *Vardunal,* but even more countering missiles came to meet them! Some came from those vehicles, and some from the ground. They were nearing a heavy concentration of habitations, but still not a single one of his missiles had reached their target!

"Laser fire from the surface, Lord! At least two laser installations in those cities just ahead. They are destroying our missiles in flight."

Curse these creatures!

"Concentrate main lasers on the ground installations! Maintain fire!"

"Yes, Lord!"

Rradaknuar thrashed his tail in frustration. He had already passed beyond several habitations he had wished destroyed. These next ones might escape destruction as well! His lasers were smashing the small craft by the score. The ground lasers seemed to be tougher targets but they were eventually knocked out as well. But too late! The habitations they were defending disappeared around the curve of the planet. It would require another pass to smash them.

Destroying these creatures was going to be far more difficult than he had thought.

* * * * *

"They're stopping them, ma'am! They're stopping them!" exclaimed Commander Cresswell-Jones. Kay nodded her head and let out the breath she had been holding. The local defense forces had been able to knock down the enemy missiles. They had paid a high price, but they were doing it!

"It looks as though everything south to Boston is out of immediate danger, ma'am," said Captain Kagami.

"Any major damage?"

"Several of the missiles did explode. Their warheads are very large with considerable shockwaves in the atmosphere. We are getting reports of some damage from a burst near Boston and another near Hartford. The Boston laser site has been destroyed along with one of the two at New York."

"What's headed at us?"

"The enemy is just passing near Philadelphia now. A number of missiles are heading for Baltimore and Washington, but nothing directly at Norfolk."

"Good. What other losses?"

"The enemy is using his lasers against us. About a hundred aircraft have been destroyed so far. Aside from the laser installations, they are ignoring the ground based defenses. But our defensive missiles have been more effective than we expected."

Kay nodded and returned her attention to the tactical display. The big red icon for the *Brak-Shar* ship was moving across the map of the US very quickly, nearly eight hundred kilometers every minute. Smaller icons denoting their missiles sped away from the big one at intervals. But so far, all of those missiles were being destroyed before they could hit their targets. Some were destroyed by ground fire, but most were stopped by the missiles launched from aircraft. A web of orbiting satellites was providing the data those missiles needed to do the job. Kay clenched her fists when she saw how many of those aircraft were being destroyed in response. She probably knew some of those pilots...

But their sacrifice was not in vain. The red icon continued to move and Philadelphia was still there. Baltimore was still there. The defenses of Washington opened fire. General O'Connell had taken no chances with the nation's capital. Six lasers lashed out, not only destroying the missiles headed their way, but scoring several hits on the enemy ship itself. Three of those lasers were still in operation when the enemy moved over the horizon.

Richmond survived. Kay was starting to hope they might just get through this...

"We've got a leaker!" exclaimed one of the sensor operators. Everyone turned. "Impact near Raleigh, North Carolina!" A pulsing orange dot appeared on the display.

"Oh damn," hissed Kay.

She knew it had been bound to happen. She knew they had been lucky it wasn't a bigger city. She knew that many of the cities had been at least partially evacuated...

But she also knew that at least a hundred thousand people had just died. People she was supposed to defend. She wanted to scream. She wanted to run shrieking out of the room. Instead, she swallowed hard and forced herself to keep looking.

Atlanta survived, Columbia and Charleston survived, Mobile and Biloxi...

"Impact, Pensacola, Florida!"

Damn.

"I was stationed in Pensacola for a while," said Bob from beside her. "Nice city."

Kay nodded and bit on her tongue hard. At least the *Brak-Shar* ship was heading out over the Gulf of Mexico. No more cities—for a while.

"Where are they headed now?" she asked.

Cresswell-Jones punched a button on the display and it shifted to a view of the whole Earth. The track of the enemy ship was superimposed. It crossed almost through the center of the Gulf, well west of Cuba, but then...

"Oh my God," whispered Kay.

* * * * *

Rradak'nuar hissed in frustration. The large land mass was being left behind—almost untouched! He had picked it for his first attack because it had one of the highest concentrations of industry on the planet. He should have realized it would be heavily defended, too. He had expended almost three hundred missiles and scored only two—two!—hits. And those were on small habitations. He had destroyed hundreds of those strange air vehicles and a number of ground laser sites, but it was still maddening that he had not burned all those habitations to ashes!

He calmed himself and forced his tail to be still. He looked at the display and saw that another land mass lay ahead. It was not large and his readings did not show a great deal of energy output. But there was one very large habitation just to the right of his flight path. Only a few of those miserable aircraft were in evidence. Yes…

"Weapons! Target that habitation—maximum firepower!"

* * * * *

"What…what was the population of Mexico City?" asked Kay Youngs in a voice like a small child's.

"I think it's about…" began Captain Kagami, but Bob Hancock grabbed his arm and shook his head.

"Never mind, Captain. What do we do now?"

"The enemy is heading out over the Pacific. Unless they change course, they will not come near any land mass for quite some time. This will give us a chance to get our forces into position. The First Reserve Squadron is almost here from Sicily. The Fourth Reserve is also nearly here from California. The Second and Third have further to go."

"Where will we hit them?"

"Well, Captain, as you can see, the enemy's course takes them past Antarctica and then up through the Indian Ocean. They pass over the subcontinent and…"

A choking sound made Bob turn and look behind him. Doctor Usha Vasthare was standing there; her dark complexion had turned to a sickly gray color. She was staring at the line showing the enemy ship's course.

"We…we are ready to begin, Captain," she gasped.

"Uh, yes, of course, Doctor, let's…"

"Marshal Youngs!" said one of the sensor operators. "Second and Third Reserve Squadrons are changing course!"

Bob turned back to the display. It was true, the Second Reserve Squadron, which had been crossing the North Pacific to join the concentration over North America, was reversing course. The Third Reserves, the Russian missile boats, had been over England heading west, and they were turning back, too.

"What are they doing?" asked Kagami.

Bob looked at Kay. She seemed to be shaking off the effects of the destruction of Mexico City. "Communications, get me Admirals Zhang and Gornikov, at once!"

"Yes, ma'am." A few moments passed, and then the admirals of the two errant squadrons were on the com.

"Gentlemen, where are you taking your squadrons?" demanded Kay.

"Marshal Youngs," came a voice with a heavy Russian accent, "the enemy's course will soon bring them directly across central Russia. Very near to Moscow. I cannot leave the Motherland undefended."

"Admiral, we need to concentrate our forces…"

"There is no choice, Marshal Youngs," interrupted the Russian, "I could not hold my people back even if I wished it. I am sorry."

"But Admiral," said Captain Kagami, breaking in, "you are too far out of position! You won't even be able to set up a proper launch for your nuclear missiles!"

"Then we will use the conventional missiles and our lasers."

"And end up just like Five and Six Squadrons!" exclaimed Kagami.

"We do what we have to."

"But our plans! You can't..." Kagami subsided when Kay put out her hand.

"We should have expected this when we made our plans," she said quietly. "Very well, Admiral Gornikov, God go with you. Admiral Zhang, what are your intentions?"

"I was intending to support Admiral Gornikov...and protect our homeland. We do not have the same level of local defenses as America and Russia, Marshal Youngs."

"You can't possibly get back there in time to help Gornikov, Admiral Zhang."

"Not on this orbit of the enemy, perhaps, but we will be there for the next pass."

Bob watched Kay's shoulders slump and she sighed. "Very well, Admiral, good luck to you all." She had the communications officer cut the connection.

"Marshal! We can't let them do it!" protested Kagami. He was Kay's chief operations and planning officer and Bob could see he was not happy.

"There's no way we can stop them, Captain. Just be thankful that Admirals Hernandez and Jameson are obeying orders—and probably only because they are both from the Western Hemisphere. This is why I feared national contingents in the Fleet."

She turned away from Kagami. "Doctor Vasthare, you were saying you are ready to start the reactor?"

"Yes." The woman was still staring at the holographic display. The red icon was now over the South Pacific, heading for Antarctica. In a few minutes, it would be heading north again—toward India.

"Let's do it, Usha," said Kay gently. The woman tore her eyes away and nodded.

They headed to the bridge. Bob took his spot in the captain's chair, Vasthare and Nalorom were at the main engineering console. Kay and some of her staff stood wherever they chose.

"Proceed, Doctor," said Bob.

"Very well. Activating main fuel injector." Bob stared at the woman. He could see the intense concentration and strain on her face. Was it because of what she was doing, or what was about to happen over her native country?

"Grav generators online. Beginning phase one compression."

"Doctor, the two generators are fluctuating," warned Nalorom.

"I see it. Proceeding with compression."

Bob found that he was gripping the arms of his chair. The strain and tension of watching the battle had distracted him, but he was now suddenly very aware that his ship might explode in the next few seconds!

"Fuel temperature seven hundred and fifty thousand degrees centigrade, containment holding."

Deep in the heart of the ship, hydrogen isotopes were being compressed in an artificial gravitational field. Just like in the heart of a star, they were being squeezed and squeezed and squeezed some more. As the pressure increased, so did the temperature. Hotter and hotter, but still not quite hot enough.

"Fuel temperature at one point two million degrees centigrade and holding," said Doctor Vasthare. "We can proceed with phase two compression on your order, Captain."

Bob Hancock looked at the woman's face. It was like a block of carven stone. All through the initial phases of the start-up, reports had been streaming in from CIC. India was being hit—hit heavily—but she had not faltered. He looked over to Kay. Her face could have been a mirror of Vasthare's. She saw him looking her way and she nodded.

"Doctor, proceed," he said.

"Aye aye, sir," she said in a voice like iron. Bob started. So did Kay. Vasthare had never—ever—slipped into military-speak before.

"Beginning phase two compression. Fuel temperature at one point five million degrees and rising."

The gravity generators were increasing their power and squeezing the fuel even more. The pressure and forces involved were beyond human comprehension—if the containment field were to fail now...

"Temperature three point eight million degrees and rising. Three point nine...four million degrees."

Everyone on the bridge seemed to be holding their breaths.

"Temperature still rising...containment holding...beginning final compression...now!"

In the core of the fusion reactor, the conditions reached the proper point. Temperature and pressure were now so high that the hydrogen could not remain hydrogen anymore. The atoms slammed into each other and...

"Ignition! We have ignition! Fusion is underway!" exclaimed Vasthare. A cheer went up around the bridge. Bob gave a small whoop of his own.

"The reactor is online and operating within acceptable parameters, Captain," said Vasthare. "We can proceed with power-up at your command."

"Doctor," said Nalorom, "you—we—have been extremely fortunate so far. Perhaps a little more caution is in order before we go to full power." Bob could not be sure, but the alien did not seem terribly happy.

"There is no time for that, Nalorom," said Vasthare. "We have to get this ship into the fight. Waiting for your order to proceed, Captain."

Bob smiled and nodded at the woman. "Proceed with power-up, Doctor. Let's get our ship into the fight."

"Aye aye, sir. Increasing to full power. MHD units operating normally, drive and shield units standing by."

"Very good," said Hancock. "Activate the drive. All excess power to the capacitors. Give the forward units priority. Stand by to raise ship!"

"All stations reporting ready, Captain," said Commander Nadj. Bob grinned—all stations had been standing ready for twenty minutes.

"Uh, sir, the outside power conduits are still connected," said one of the engineering techs.

"Are they fitted with standard disconnects?" asked Bob.

"Yes, sir."

"Then screw 'em. Helm! Anti-gravs at full nullification!"

"Aye aye, anti-gravs at full null."

Unlike the first trip on *Tennessee*, there was no noticeable change: *Terra* had artificial gravity.

He turned to look at the helmswoman. "Upward thrust at point five gravities. Raise ship, Ms. Paine."

"Aye aye, sir! Raising ship!"

The huge metal ovoid sitting in the Newport News Shipyard began to move. There was no one there to watch it—the watchers were all under cover in case the ship decided to explode instead of move. But move she did. Scaffolding and equipment that there had been no time to remove came crashing off her. Electrical cables tore loose in an explosion of sparks. A crane that had not been fully retracted was brushed aside.

With a roar of crashing metal *EDS Terra* leapt skyward.

Chapter Thirty-Three

"Honored One! Honored One! Can you hear me?"

Someone was talking far too loudly in Expedition Leader Keeradoth's ear. It hurt. Indeed, pain was the sum total of Keeradoth's existence. There was a tiny prick of new pain—a mere nothing compared to the others—but shortly those other pains began to fade and Keeradoth could spare some attention for the insistent noise in the vac helmet's communicator.

"Honored One, can you hear me?"

"Yes. What...?"

"You have been seriously injured, Honored One," said the voice. "But you are out of danger now."

Out of danger? But the ship, the battle...

"What...what is our situation?"

"Honored One, I am Medtech Baztal. You should not try to move."

Baztal. Yes, there was one named Baztal in the ship's medical department. After so many cycles Keeradoth knew each and every crew member.

"What is the status of my ship?" said Keeradoth in growing agitation. A mighty effort—and intense pain—and the expedition leader twisted around to look at the control chamber.

Or what was left of it.

There was a massive hole in one side of it. Blackness filled the hole. Wreckage was floating everywhere. Keeradoth dimly realized the artificial gravity was out. There were bodies floating too. Some of them were medical personnel, but many had been part of the control crew. A short distance away was another body, still strapped into its control station.

"T...Tandalin..."

"The Respected One is dead, Honored One," said Baztal sadly.

My friend. My old friend. I will take your ashes home again and make the ritual offerings. I promise you this—if any of us ever see home again.

"The ship. What is our situation? I must know."

"Honored One, I am not an engineer. But from what I have heard, the drive and the shield and the reactor are all not working. We have emergency power, but that is all."

Keeradoth pondered this. *Seeker of Truth* had been heading away from the planet at far more than escape velocity when the damage occurred. At the least they would not have to worry about suffering *Nightpiercer's* fate. And the fact that they yet lived proved that the enemy had not returned.

"What...what of the battle?"

"I have no information, Honored One, but I believe that it still goes on."

But what is happening?

* * * * *

Captain Edward Osborne looked around the control room of *Tennessee*. The mixture of excitement and anxiety among the crew could be felt as well as seen. The squadron was up and moving at last! But this was not what they had been hoping for. Instead of meeting the enemy out in space, they were meeting him on their very doorstep. Earth was under attack.

And Earth had been hurt.

Osborne could still scarcely believe the reports. This whole situation had always had a slightly surreal edge to it. Somehow, in spite of all the preparations and worries, it did not seem possible that anything would actually happen *down here.*

But it had.

Raleigh and Pensacola had been nuked. There were hundreds of thousands of casualties. Mexico City, Osborne didn't even want to think about Mexico City. He had vacationed there once. A dozen nukes, a dozen big nukes—twenty megatons or more—had obliterated the entire city and the surrounding area. Casualties…God only knew.

And that probably wasn't even the worst of it. The *Brak-Shar* ship had just passed over India. India had better defenses than Mexico, but there were just so many people there. The first reports were indicating that New Dehli had survived, but there was an impact near Bombay and several smaller cities. To the north, Karachi, in neighboring Pakistan, had also been destroyed. The two countries had been threatening to nuke each other for so long. Now it had happened, but not by their own hands.

Osborne turned his head as Admiral Jameson floated into the control room and pulled himself down into a chair.

"We're on station, Admiral," said Osborne. "*Terra* is off our starboard side, about ten kilometers. The rest of our squadron is in formation. The First Reserves will be with us in about five minutes."

"Good. I'm assigning *Cincinnati* to the second division. Since she's the only one in the squadron with shields, I want her in the lead, adjust our formation accordingly."

"Yes, sir. Any word from the Third Squadron?"

"They are scrambling to get back to Moscow before the *Brak-Shar* get there. Russian air defenses are going into action now. It's going to be a hell of a mess, I'm afraid."

Osborne nodded. The Third Reserve Squadron contained all the Russian boomers. They didn't have shields either. Of course, from the reports they had gotten about Five and Six Squadrons, it probably didn't make any difference at close range. *We'll find out for sure soon enough!*

Tennessee and the others ships were gathering just north of Washington. Marshal Youngs believed that the enemy would come back along the same path as it had before—to finish the job they started. It was their job to prevent them from doing so. There were still plenty of aircraft and ground missiles, and a few of the laser installations left, but it was up to the reserve squadrons to try and hurt the enemy ship itself. In just a few minutes the order would come and they would start forward. The plan was to meet the enemy head-on over the Arctic. Maybe if they hurt the bastards enough, there would be no need for the other defenses.

"Captain Osborne," said Jameson, "please unlock your missile controls. We need to be ready to launch your big birds. Communications, pass the order to the rest of the squadron."

"Aye aye, sir." He relayed the order to Commander Lakner and she quickly took care of all the preliminary operations. The launch procedures had been dramatically streamlined from the old ones, which required thirty minutes of meticulous check and counter-check, into a process taking only a few minutes. Finally, it was all ready except for turning the keys and pressing the big red button. In the current mood he was in, Osborne couldn't wait to push that button and fry those alien sons-of-bitches! In spite of the skepticism of some of Marshal Youngs' staff and the Somerans, Osborne had great hopes for his big birds.

"First reports coming in from Russia, Admiral," said the com officer.

"What have we got?"

"I...it's not good, Admiral," the man looked shaken. "Third Reserves has been almost wiped out, sir. Only one boat left answering signals."

"Damn. What about other damage?"

'They seem to have done their job, sir. Moscow, Kiev, and St. Petersburg are okay. There have been impacts near Smolensk and Minsk, though. The enemy is passing over the Gulf of Finland now. The Swedes are engaging with their aircraft."

"Did the Third hurt the bastards at all? What about their nukes?"

"They...they never had the chance to launch the nukes, sir. It took them too long to get in position. The survivor thinks they hurt the enemy ship, but has no details."

Osborne shook his head. The one drawback of the big missiles was that they were so slow compared to the smaller kinetic missiles. The only way they had a chance to get a hit was to launch them from right in the target's path. If the Russian subs were out of position, they would not have had the opportunity.

"What about Second Reserves? Admiral Zhang's squadron?"

"They didn't engage, sir. They could not get there in time. Marshal Youngs is having them hold position... Hold on sir, message from flag: 'Stand by to get under way. Course oh-one-five by oh-oh'—global coordinates, sir."

"All right! Let's go get those miserable so-and-so's!"

Osborne gave a few orders, but little needed to be done. He and his ship were ready for action. All they needed now was the word to go. He sat and waited, idly drumming his fingers on the chair arm.

"Message from flag," said the com officer. Osborne readied himself to give the order. "Admiral, Marshal Youngs wants to speak to you directly."

Osborne started. What was up? A moment later, Youngs appeared on a monitor. It was the first time Osborne had seen her today and he was shocked at her haggard appearance.

"Admiral, change in plans," she said. "The enemy has altered course. He's coming in further west than we had expected. I'm going to go ahead with the First Reserves and hit him over Canada. I want you to stay here and then get in position for when he comes around again."

"But Marshal," protested Jameson, "we can't stay behind!"

"God *damn* it, Admiral!" snarled Youngs. "I've already lost three squadrons today because they wouldn't follow orders! You are not going to be the fourth! You can't get into position to launch your nukes on this pass. Now follow the orders I've given you!"

Osborne looked on in stunned amazement. Youngs was almost always polite. He'd never seen her like this before. Admiral Jameson seemed nearly as surprised. He hesitated and for a moment Osborne thought he was going to continue to argue, but then he nodded.

"All right, Marshal, we'll wait. And good luck to you, ma'am."

"Thank you, Admiral," said Youngs, regaining her composure. "We're going to need it."

* * * * *

Shipmaster Rradak'nuar was not happy. The smell of his anger and frustration filled the control chamber. When he had smashed the ships barring his way to the planet he thought the battle was all but won. Now, now he was not sure what he had put his tail into. Each time he thought he had beaten down the enemy defenses, they threw another force against him. The first attack run on that one continent had been sobering. Hundreds of small air vehicles and ground launched missiles and lasers had blunted his attacks. But then, he had smashed several large habitations with much less resistance. Perhaps that first continent had been the most heavily defended. The rest would be easier.

But no. The much larger continent had been even more heavily defended. Most of his missiles had been stopped, and then, unexpectedly, he had run into another large group of those small warships. They had appeared with almost no warning at all. He had smashed them, it was even easier than before since these ships did not have shields, but they had hurt him in return. He had taken a number of missile hits and their massed lasers had done more damage. Three new holes pierced the hull of his ship. Another main laser and several other weapons gone. And his capacitors were nearly drained again. The gains on recharging them he had made while passing over the long stretch of empty ocean had been lost.

And these Terrans continued to fight back! Even over the cold, rocky, sparsely inhabited regions, there were defenders. It was daunting, but Rradak'nuar was more sure than ever that these creatures had to be destroyed. Their determination and numbers would be truly frightening if they had modern equipment.

But could he smash them? He had less than fifteen hundred missiles left in his magazines. Considering how few of them were reaching their targets, he was no longer sure of success. And the main enemy fleet was returning. His fighters were still harassing part of their force, but enemy fighters were moving in. Soon the whole lot of them would be coming back.

Now *Vardunal* was hurtling back over the polar region where his attack had first begun. He had been tempted to follow the same path as the first time and finish the job, but he was sure the enemy would be expecting that and have all their defenses massed along that path. Rradak'nuar cursed the fact that he did not know what lay ahead of him. He had been launching reconnaissance drones continuously, but those miserable fighters of the enemy had been trailing behind him and destroying them almost as fast as they were launched. The curve of the planet blocked his view. He was flying into the unknown.

So he had ordered a course change. They would pass well to the right of their previous course. His scans from high orbit had shown plenty of targets in that area, too. And maybe the enemy would be taken by surprise this time, instead of him.

*   *   *   *   *

"Capacitors are still only at sixty-three percent, ma'am," said Captain Robert Hancock.

"I understand, Captain," said Space Marshal Kathryn Youngs. "Communications, signal the squadron to prepare to engage."

"Aye aye, ma'am!"

Kay gripped the arms of her chair. At last she was going into combat. The long, agonizing wait was over. Sitting grounded while others were fighting and dying was harder than anything she had ever had to do.

Now I can go out and die with them!

She jerked in surprise as the thought formed in her head. Did she really mean that? Sometimes she had thoughts—really terrible thoughts—that formed for no reason. Things she didn't really mean. She guessed that everyone had them—the subconscious encroaching on the conscious? But this time, this time did she mean it? Was she hoping to die in some sort of payment for all the people who had already died today? She had never had suicidal thoughts before. Never. She looked over at Bob. *I do have things to live for. So did all those other people. Stop it. This is not helping anything. Do your job and what happens, happens.*

"Can you take us any lower, Captain?"

"We can go a lot lower, ma'am, but the other ships can't. There's appreciable atmospheric drag even at this altitude. If we go any lower, it will tear the heat radiators right off those unshielded ships."

"Understood. Captain Kagami, how close can we get without them spotting us?"

"They are at approximately two hundred kilometers altitude, Marshal. If we can stay here at fifty, they'll see us at around two thousand kilometers distance."

"Damn, too far, but it's the best we can do. It should take them at least a few seconds to respond. Hopefully they'll only get one shot off with their big lasers before we're in range."

"Yes, ma'am."

"Marshal, the enemy is currently over the Davis Straight between Greenland and Ontario," said Commander Cresswell-Jones. "I estimate a zero-range intercept somewhere near Fort George."

Fort George? Where the hell is Fort George? Somewhere in Canada, I guess…

Kay suddenly looked at her aide. *He's Canadian! Where's his home town? Toronto, isn't it?*

She looked at the estimated course of the *Brak-Shar* ship. It went nearly over the city of Toronto. Before she could even look back at Cresswell-Jones, her eyes followed the track a little farther. It went right across western Ohio. Right across *her* home.

Now she did look at her aide. He was staring right back at her.

"They'll be all right, ma'am," he said quietly.

She nodded with a jerk of her head, but she could see her sisters' faces asking that question again: *are you going to save my children?*

I'll try. I'll do everything I can—but I'm not God!

"Estimated contact in sixty seconds," said Kagami. Kay shook herself and gripped her chair again.

"Very well. All ships stand by to fire!"

"All ships report ready, ma'am."

The distance to the enemy shrank rapidly. The twenty diesel powered subs of Admiral Henandez's squadron had been joined by four survivors from Five and Six Squadrons. And, of course, there was the *Terra.* The only real warship in the lot—and she was outmassed twenty to one by the ship she was hoping to destroy. Missiles would fire the instant the enemy came into view. The lasers would have to wait a little longer. It was almost time…

"Contact! Solid fix on the target!"

"Fire!"

One hundred and eight missiles streaked away.

Five heartbeats went by and there was no response from the enemy. Then his lasers began picking off missiles. They were forty seconds from impact.

"Enemy is launching missiles and taking evasive action," reported the sensor officer. "No fire on the fleet, ma'am! Their main lasers are firing at the missiles, too!"

"Caught the bastards by surprise!" said Bob.

Thirty seconds away and there were still ninety missiles left. Maybe…just maybe…

"Enemy missiles detonating! Particle barrier being deployed!"

Damn!

The missiles were converging on their target and the cloud of metal particles was right in their path. They could not avoid them and the tiny metal grains tore through the missiles at over forty kilometers per second. Guidance systems were shredded, engines disabled, and fuel rods exploded. Almost every missile was hit. But in their place was an expanding cloud of debris that was still closing on the enemy. Closing very rapidly. The enemy twisted to avoid this cloud, but it could not do so—at least not completely.

"Multiple impacts! We hit them!"

"Entering extreme laser range, ma'am."

"All ships, commence firing!"

The twenty-nine lasers of the squadron lashed out. The range was under a thousand kilometers, and against a target the size of the *Brak-Shar* ship, they could not miss. Almost immediately air and debris began puffing away from the target. The missiles had bought down some of the shields and the enemy was naked.

Naked, but not helpless.

"Enemy returning fire! Hits on *Tonelero* and *Riachuelo*! *Daphne* and *Galatee* also hit!"

"Maintain fire!" commanded Bob Hancock. Kay scanned the readouts, trying to take in everything at once.

The opposing sides flashed by each other only a few kilometers apart. *EDS Terra's* five lasers focused on a single point and tore a hundred-meter gash down the side of the *Brak-Shar* vessel. Sensors, weapons, and deflectors were blown apart in an instant.

Unfortunately, the enemy could do it, too.

The ship lurched sharply and Kay was thrown against the restraints on her chair. Another blow and she was thrown the other direction.

"We've been hit!" shouted someone. Kay thought it was the most unnecessary statement she had ever heard.

"Shields are down!" cried someone else. Now that was useful information. Not good, but useful.

"Take evasive action!" commanded Bob.

The ship lurched several more times, but not as violently. Then the pounding stopped.

"That's it, they're beyond the horizon," said Captain Kagami.

"Report," said Kay, still slightly shaken.

"We've lost eight ships out of the squadron, ma'am. Not too bad considering what happened to Admiral Gornikov's squadron. We must be hurting them ma'am, their firepower is greatly reduced."

"But they're still in the game. What about the damage to *Terra*, Captain? I mean the ship, not the planet."

"Now that *could* be confusing, ma'am," said Hancock. "We took a solid hit. Burned into us pretty deep. The main shield generator is out, I'm not sure if it can be repaired. But that's the worst of it. Drive and weapons are mostly intact. We lost two missile tubes." Bob took on an annoyed expression. "Y'know, I was hoping to take her around the block at least *once* before getting that first ding."

Kay laughed slightly. It felt good. "Sorry, Captain, we'll have to get her into the body shop when this is all over."

"Okay, but other than a few dents, she's still fit for combat, ma'am."

"Good," said Kay, "because we're going to have to do this again in thirty minutes. Captain Kagami, alert Admiral Zhang that we will be rendezvousing with his squadron in about fifteen minutes. We will then proceed to intercept the enemy over the Indian Ocean.

"Oh, and Captain Hancock, I'd see if I could get the shield fixed if I were you—we'll probably need it."

* * * * *

Again! They had done it again! *Another* new force of ships—including a real warship! Where were they all coming from? Rradak'nuar raked his claws on the station once again in his fury.

"Lord? Lord, we are nearing some heavily populated regions. Should I resume the bombardment?" The weapons controller indeed had courage to address his lord when he was in a rage like this!

"Yes! At once! Blast these vile creatures! Blast them to atoms!"

"Yes, Lord! Commencing fire!"

Missiles streaked forward, but Rradak'nuar could see that there were more defenses waiting for them. More of those ridiculous air vehicles. More ground launched missiles. More lasers batteries. Maybe a few less than on the first attack, but still far too many. His missiles were destroyed again and again.

In addition to this frustration, the shipmaster was still fuming about the damage the last engagement had inflicted on his vessel. More weapons lost, more capacitors, more sensors. The damage was reaching critical levels. The enemy seemed to have inexhaustible forces, but how much more could his ship take? And why had the enemy held all these new forces back? Was it some trap to draw him in? Surely they did not think he had failed to send a signal to the nearest base before starting in! It made no sense that he could smell.

And this enemy refused to die!

* * * * *

"Marshal Youngs reports that the enemy vessel has taken heavy damage, Admiral," said the com officer aboard *Tennessee*. "She says First and Second Reserves will take one more crack at them and then it's our turn, sir."

"Good. Any reports from the local defenses?"

"We're getting some feeds from the tactical network, sir. I'm switching it to the main display."

Ed Osborne watched the visual display along with everyone else in the control room. It was showing the central United States and the red icon of the enemy ship was just crossing Lake Huron into Michigan. Swarms of blue icons were trying to place themselves across the enemy's path.

"No hits so far, sir. The Marshal's attack must have distracted them from launching against any Canadian targets, they have just started firing now."

Osborne bit on his lip. There were a hell of a lot of cities along the projected track. Detroit was nearly right underneath it, so was Cincinnati and Louisville. Chicago was pretty far to the west, but still in range. So were a dozen other major cities. And then there were all those relocation camps all over the place. A hit on one of them would as bad as a hit on a city.

But the minutes passed and there were no hits. Dozens of enemy missiles were destroyed; none got through. Scores of aircraft paid for this success however and as Osborne's eyes tracked south, he was dismayed to see very few blue icons remaining.

"Where the hell's the air cover south of Memphis?" asked Admiral Jameson, suddenly.

"It's all off to the east, sir," said the sensor operator. "The air wings from the carriers were responsible for the lower Mississippi, but they thought the enemy would be coming along the same track as before. They're trying to get back…"

"They're not going to make it in time. Hell's bells, we're naked down there."

"Not quite, sir, look at those icons along the river itself," said Osborne. Jameson did so and swore.

"Well I'll be damned. I sure hope those swab-jockeys are keeping their eyes open!"

"Amen to that, sir."

The carriers were the glory hounds. They got all the press and all the praise. But this time they weren't around. This was the time for the little guys to shine.

All along the Mississippi, the Aegis cruisers and destroyers of the Navy went into action. Their missiles had been given the new software and guidance systems just like the ones carried by the fighters. With fiery roars and towering pillars of smoke they streaked upward to intercept the death falling on them from space.

Bomb after bomb was blasted apart before they could reach their target. The enemy reacted quickly and fired on the launching ships, but through the thick atmosphere, they had to wait until nearly overhead to do so.

Ships with proud names like *Gettysburg* and *Antietam* went to the bottom as lasers sliced them in two, but they had already done their jobs. They had saved the people they were sworn to. Little Rock was safe, Jackson, Baton Rouge, and New Orleans, all survived because of the little ships.

Osborne let out the breath he had been holding as the red blip moved off the coast. He clenched his fists when he saw the glowing orange blob near Shreveport. *Not all, they couldn't stop them all.*

And once again, Mexico lay ahead.

"All right," said Admiral Jameson, suddenly. "Let's get ourselves into position to stop these bastards before they come round again!"

* * * * *

"The break is in through there, ma'am, but we are going to have to do some cutting before we can get at it."

"We don't have time for that," said Usha Vasthare. "Show me."

The damage control officer led Usha and Nalorom through a hatch into a compartment that had one bulkhead crumpled in by the enemy fire. Several large hunks of wreckage had been cleared away and pushed to one side. The officer knelt down by an open access panel and shone his flashlight inside. Usha squatted beside him, mindful of her bulky vacuum suit and peered in.

"The break in the power feed to the shield generator is about five meters that way, ma'am, but you can see that there has been damage here, too. We'll have to cut to clear a path."

Usha took out her own light and stuck her head through the hatch. She stared for a few moments. The side of the passage was buckled inward and several pipes were twisted into strange shapes. But the way wasn't completely blocked...

"Nalorom," she said, pulling her head back out. "Take a look. Do you think the two of us could fit through there?"

She made way for the Someran and it made its own inspection. "Perhaps, Doctor. Perhaps you and I could do it. I doubt anyone else aboard would fit."

"It is certainly worth a try. Vasthare to Captain Hancock," she said into her suit com.

"Hancock, here, go ahead."

"We have located the break. We think we can repair it."

"Good! But you'll have to hurry. We'll be engaged in less than twenty minutes."

"Understood. We shall hurry. Vasthare out." She turned to the damage control officer. "Lieutenant, if you'd be so kind as to let us have those tools and the replacement conduit, we'll get at it."

"You sure about that, ma'am? It's awful tight in there. You could tear your suit on all that sharp metal."

"We will be careful." She took the tools and went through the hatch. The first two meters was not bad. The artificial gravity was off and that made it easier. Then she got to the more constricted area and she had to slowly maneuver herself past some obstructions.

"Are you all right, Doctor?" asked Nalorom.

"Yes, I'm fine. But we need to get this done in a hurry. We need to get back to minding that balky, water buffalo of a fusion plant before it decides to act up on us."

"Not to mention getting the shield back up before we fight the *Brak-Shar* again," said Nalorom. Usha paused for an instant. She was often uncertain when the Somerans were trying to use humor—this time she had no doubt.

But she was in no mood for humor right now. She had a job to do and she had to do it before she started thinking about the battle or how scared she was… or about India.

She squirmed her way past a large pipe and then through the small opening left when the side of the chamber was pushed in. Getting her helmet through was the toughest. All the rest of her was flexible to some degree, but not that. She had to pause and drag the tool kit behind her. Nalorom was burdened with the conduit, but helped as much as he could.

All this time and I still don't really know if he really is a 'he', she thought incongruously. Her brain was spinning madly. There were too many places it did not dare to go right now. Her thoughts scrambled for a safe refuge, like a mouse on a bare tabletop.

She pulled herself past one more obstruction and came to the location of the break. It was a slightly larger chamber, but one side had been blasted to bits and she could see through to an adjoining space that was even more badly damaged.

"Okay, I'm here."

"Can you locate the end of the conduit?"

"I'm looking now. All right, there is the end that leads to the generator. It's fully exposed. There should be no problem attaching the patch to that. Now where's the other end?" She shone her light around trying to spot what she was looking for, No luck.

"Doctor, how's it coming?" said a voice in her helmet. It was Captain Hancock.

"I've reached the break. I'm working to patch it now."

"Good. We have about ten minutes left."

"Understood."

Where was the other end? It had to be over there. She started pulling pieces of wreckage loose, mindful of the zero-gravity.

"Lieutenant, you are sure the power is turned off? I don't want to grab a live wire."

"Yes, it's safe, Doctor, go ahead," came the voice of the DC officer.

She stuck her hand into the debris and felt for the conduit.

Like rooting in a rice paddy for a missing trowel…

Usha came up short with the image that stray thought brought to mind: her as a small girl helping her family plant a crop. Her brothers and sisters and mother all working together. She could feel tears forming in her eyes…

No! I can't afford to think about it. I don't even know where all the bombs fell! They are all right! Vishnu protect them, they have to be all right!

"Are you all right, Doctor?" asked Nalorom.

"Yes, fine," she blurted, resuming her search. She pulled a large plate away and found the conduit.

"Here it is. Let me have the replacement cable, please."

The Someran pushed the end of the thick cable through to her and she pulled it into her little metal cave. Each end had a large clip to make the connection with. She got the one end on with no trouble, but the other end gave her a fight. There was some sort of plastic, or maybe it was insulation, melted all over it. She needed to scrape it off if she was to get a good circuit.

"How's it coming, Doctor? Five minutes," said Hancock.

"Almost there…get ready to turn on the power."

"Right, standing by."

She had a knife from the tool kit and was scraping away frantically. The damn stuff didn't want to come off! She scraped harder and the knife slipped and she almost cut through her suit. She forced herself to slow down. Scrape, scrape, brush, scrape. Bit by bit it was coming off.

She thought she had enough cleaned off. Quickly she clipped the cable on. She made one last inspection to make sure no bare conduit or cable was touching anything. The last thing she needed now was a short circuit. She pushed herself clear.

"All right, turn it on!"

"Power on. The shield's coming up! Great job, Doctor, just in time!"

Usha gave a sigh of relief. She started gathering up the tools and clipping them back in the kit. She shut the lid and started to turn toward the narrow exit.

"Okay, Nalorom, let's get back to…"

The ship lurched and Usha was thrown against the bulkhead. Before she could even recover, there was a blinding flash and then a shower of white fire washed over her.

* * * * *

The stench of fear and anger and defeat filled Shipmaster Rradak'nuar's receptors. He could taste it.

How could this have happened?

His fine, proud ship battered to a wreck by these miserable creatures! He scanned the damage reports and hissed and spat. Only three of the main lasers still operational. Eight of the secondaries. Over half his missile tubes gone. Dozens of deflectors destroyed. And another drive node; acceleration was down by a third. It was impossible. Those little ships, those tiny, insignificant ships had done this to him!

He had been shocked when that new warship had appeared. It was of an unknown class, but it was unmistakably an Enemy design. But he had hurt it badly, its shield was definitely down when it passed out of sight. There were only a few of the small ships escorting it. Yet half an orbit later, there it was again, shield up and working, and reinforced by another twenty ships! Was there no end to them?

He had smashed a dozen of those ships and seriously damaged the new warship again, but they had hurt him badly in reply. His shields had been too weak. Too many capacitors drained, too many deflectors missing. Missiles and lasers had torn great holes in *Vardunal*.

But his ship was still alive.

They were speeding toward the pole again. Another continent lay just ahead. It was a great desert land with only a few habitations. He smashed several against weak resistance, but then his sensors showed another swarm of those air vehicles in his path, across a narrow sea. It was a heavily populated—and heavily defended region.

"Cease firing," he commanded.

"Lord?" said the weapons controller in surprise.

"I said: cease fire! How many missiles remain in the magazine?"

"One thousand thirty-two, Lord."

"We shall not waste them in this futile manner. Cease fire."

"Yes, Lord."

Too few. He could expend hundreds and make no impression. Rradak'nu-ar checked the long range sensor read-out and saw that the other enemy ships were returning. They had destroyed the last of his fighters and at least sixty enemy ships were heading his way. His fighters had died bravely, but to no avail. Sixty ships. Not that long ago, he would have sneered at such a force. But not now. His crippled ship could not fight sixty and live.

What should he do? His duty was to smash this world so it could not be used by the Enemy as an advanced base. But was there now any way to carry out that duty? The thought of returning home in failure was almost too much to bear.

Some of his missiles had gotten through. Perhaps forty, all told. Millions of the enemy had died, but billions more remained. A few hundred more warheads had detonated high in the atmosphere, but they would have little effect. Perhaps some small environmental damage, but nothing catastrophic...

Rradak'nuar's tail stiffened suddenly.

Environmental damage...

The warheads that had reached targets and exploded would have raised huge clouds of dust and smoke into the atmosphere. There would be some effects from the radiation, but if these creatures had the medical techniques of the Enemy, they would be minor. The dust and smoke would block off some sunlight and lower temperatures a small amount. A few cycles of below average temperatures, but nothing more.

That from forty warheads...how much more from a thousand?

Yes, it could work.

"Helm! Come five degrees right!"

"Yes, Lord!"

"Weapons! Set up a bombardment pattern for the next continent. You will not target cities or anything else that might be heavily defended. Bare ground will do! Set detonation for zero altitude. You will fire five hundred missiles against this continent."

"At once, Lord!"

Rradak'nuar could smell the puzzlement of his weapons controller, but he twitched his tail in approval that he did not question his orders.

Yes. He had altered course so that *Vardunal* would pass over desolate and sparsely populated territory on this next orbit. There would be few defenses to stop his missiles. Five hundred warheads would blanket this continent—this entire hemisphere—in a shroud of smoke and dust. There was a large island in the other hemisphere that was similarly bleak. Another four hundred warheads there.

In a short time this entire world would be wrapped in darkness. Temperatures would fall dramatically. Plant life would die off. Famine would follow. Yes! Fire and ice and death! He had no hope that this would kill all of them, but it would be a major disaster. Hopefully, order would break down as the food grew scarce. All their resources would have to go toward survival. Little would be left for building ships or weapons. It could take many cycles to recover. When the attack fleet arrived from home, there would be little to oppose it.

Rradak'nuar twitched his tail and sprayed pheromones of contentment about the control chamber. The confused reactions of his subordinates were most amusing. They could not imagine what their lord could possibly be content about!

As the polar icecaps approached, the shipmaster expanded his plans. Once the bombardment was complete, then what? Fight to the death against the approaching enemy force? No, that wasn't necessary. When the last missile was away, full acceleration outbound. The enemy could catch up to him, of course, but in open space, he should be able to fend them off. He still had defensive missiles. Those tiny ships of the enemy could not possibly have much endurance or ammunition. With a little luck, *Vardunal* could escape.

Then what? Flee to the nearest base? No! *Vardunal* was a support ship as well as a warship. It carried supplies and repair and manufacturing facilities to support a squadron of scout ships. Some of those supplies and equipment had been damaged, but not all. Once the enemy had been eluded, a temporary base could be set up in the outer part of this solar system. Asteroids could be mined. His ship could be at least partially repaired. More missiles could be manufactured.

And he could come back.

Yes! It might take a cycle or more to get ready, but he could come back! The enemy, locked in perpetual winter might be taken unawares. Victory might yet belong to Rradak'nuar! At the very least, he would harry these creatures again and again until the fleet arrived.

The shipmaster snarled in delight. The ice cap was rushing past. Very shortly it would be time.

Chapter Thirty-Four

Bob Hancock groaned and shook his head to clear away the whirling stars. It did not help at all. The second attack against the enemy ship had been much worse than the first one. Even though they had gotten the shields back up just in time, the *Brak-Shar* had concentrated a lot more firepower against *Terra*. Bob knew, just from his own aching body, that his ship had been hurt. But how bad?

"Report," he groaned.

"Heavy damage, sir," said Commander Nadj.

"I figured that. Can you get me some specifics?"

"I'll try, sir."

Bob looked over to where Kay was strapped into her chair. She looked a little dazed, but otherwise okay. Several other moans and groans attracted his attention to people who were not okay.

"Medical team to the bridge," he said into the com. He unstrapped and gingerly walked over to where a chair had broken loose from the deck and been thrown against a control console. He saw that the chair's occupant was Kay's aide, Commander Cresswell-Jones. The visor on his helmet had cracked and he had a nasty cut on his head with blood running down. But his eyes were open and moving.

"Are you all right, Commander?" Bob pulled the chair away from the console, slightly and started unbuckling the straps.

"I think so, I...aahh!"

"What's wrong?"

"My back, sir. I think it's my back." Bob stopped what he was doing. If it was a spinal injury he had better not risk moving him. He looked up as Kay knelt down beside him.

"Can you feel your legs, Jonathan?"

"Yes, ma'am. It's not a problem of *not* being able to feel things! Ow!"

A moment later the medics arrived and Bob stepped away.

"Commander Nadj, damage report, please."

"Yes, sir. We've been hit pretty bad. The shield is out again and we've lost all the lasers except for one of the secondaries. Only two missile tubes left. The drive is still okay, but we haven't got much left to fight with."

"Casualties?"

"Not sure yet, sir. There are some, though, no doubt about that."

"All right. Damage control on all the major systems." It was an unnecessary order. He was sure Nadj had already set them to work.

"What's the situation, Bob?" said Kay coming up beside him. She was looking far more animated than she had all day. Fighting the enemy toe to toe seemed to suit her. He could hardly believe it.

"We can still move, but we don't have much to fight with, ma'am."

"Are any repairs possible?"

"I don't know yet. I doubt that anything significant can be done before our next pass."

"I see. Captain Kagami, what's the status on the rest of the fleet?"

"We have eighteen ships left from the First and Second Reserves with us, ma'am, but one of the diesel boats has developed a serious leak in their oxygen feed. They are going to have to make an emergency landing before they asphyxiate themselves. First through Fourth Battle Squadrons have regrouped and are heading back along with the survivors of Hazelton's fighters. They should be in attack range in less than an hour. Admiral Jameson's squadron is trying to position itself for a missile launch. I think he's put himself a little too far west, but I suppose his guess is as good as anyone's."

"What's the enemy doing?"

"They are heading across Europe, ma'am. For some reason they're not firing."

"Not firing? Are they withdrawing?"

"No, ma'am, they are maintaining the same altitude. Still well above orbital velocity—just as we are—but no sign that they are leaving."

"I don't think I like this," said Kay, frowning. "If they've got ammunition, why not use it? If they don't, why stick around?"

"I don't know, ma'am."

"I've got a bad feeling about this, Captain," she said, turning to Bob. "I don't think we can afford to wait for the rest of the fleet. We need to kill this bastard on the next pass—before he does something we won't like."

Bob wasn't sure if her 'animated' state was verging into a berserkergang, but the gleam in Kay's eye was a little frightening. On the other hand, she could very well be right...

"Well, there's Jameson's boomers. If he gets lucky..."

"Yes, we can hope for that, but we shouldn't plan on it. If he can't kill them, then we have to."

"Marshal, I'm not sure what we have left here is enough for the job," said Kagami. "With only eighteen ships and us being almost weaponless..."

"Captain Hancock, you said the drive is undamaged?" asked Kay, interrupting Kagami.

"Yes, ma'am," said Bob.

"Then we do have a weapon...a big one."

A chill went through Bob Hancock. Kay's eyes were fixed on him. Unblinking. "Uh, yes, I suppose we do—if I'm reading you correctly."

"I think you are."

"Right. You sure about this, Kay?"

"I think it's the only option."

She continued to stare at him. Finally, he nodded.

"Very well, ma'am, if that's what you want."

"It's not what I want, Captain..."

"Yes, ma'am. Captain Kagami, how much time do we have?"

"Less than thirty minutes until our next intercept."

Hancock took a deep breath. "All right. With your permission, ma'am, I'd like to evacuate our wounded. We still have a shuttle and some escape pods."

"Certainly, Captain. Carry on."

Bob turned away. "Commander Nadj. Inform Sick Bay to get all the wounded and all but a skeleton medical crew to the shuttle."

"Aye aye, sir."

Bob looked over to where the medics had Cresswell-Jones strapped to a backboard. He seemed like he was in a lot of pain, but he was arguing with Kay. Bob stepped over to him.

"Please, ma'am, let me stay."

"I can't let you do that, Jonathan. You're hurt."

"Just strap me into a chair! I can still do my job!"

"I appreciate the offer, Jonathan, but I'll need you back at headquarters after this. If…if I don't make it back I'm counting on you to break in the next EDF commander. I couldn't run things without you and the next guy will need your help."

"Ma'am, please!"

Bob stepped up beside the stretcher. "Sorry, Commander, I'm kicking you off my ship. But if you could, please tell my daughter that I love her."

Cresswell-Jones looked stricken. "I…I'll do that, sir."

"And give Nisima a hug for me, Jonathan," said Kay, gently.

The young man turned his head away, but he nodded. The medics picked him up and he was gone.

Bob blew out a long breath. Kay reached over and gave his hand a squeeze and smiled. She let go and went through the hatch leading to CIC. Bob went back to his chair. He watched the tactical display update itself. *Terra* was heading north from Antarctica. The enemy was heading south from the North Pole. The opposing forces had been spiraling around the planet in opposite directions, taking shots at each other, for over two hours. In about twenty minutes they would meet again—for the last time.

Bob found himself thinking about Melissa and about Kay. There were a lot of things he wanted to say to them. Things he wanted to do with them. No time now. His eyes came to rest on the ship's helmsman.

"Lieutenant Paine," he said.

"Yes, sir?" The young woman turned to face him. She was one of the international volunteers who made up *Terra's* crew. He thought she was from Ireland or Scotland or some such place. She had a noticeable accent. She didn't look much older than his daughter.

"Lieutenant, were you following my conversation with Marshal Youngs a little while ago?"

"Yes, sir, I was."

"Do you understand what she has planned?"

"Yes, sir, I believe I do."

"You are the one who will have to carry out her plan, Lieutenant. Things will happen too fast for me to give you any real orders. You'll have to act on your own judgment. Do you have any problems with that? If you do, I'm sure we can find another person for the helm…"

"With all due respect, sir, I'm the best damn pilot on this ship. I'd take it as a personal insult if you decided to replace me, sir. You can count on me to do what has to be done."

Hancock smiled. "All right, Lieutenant. It's 'Annie', isn't it? I'll be counting on you."

"My pleasure, sir."

He leaned back in his chair and sighed. He really did not want to have to do this. But he feared that Kay was right. The *Brak-Shar* must have some plan or they would not be sticking around. It would be better to make sure they never had a chance to carry it out. He looked at the main display. The red blip of the enemy was heading south. Directly in its path was the icon for Jameson's Fourth Reserve Squadron. There was still a chance that they could do the job.

Bob said a silent prayer for them.

* * * * *

Usha was in pain. That was all she knew. Her hands and her arms and her chest were on fire…

Fire!

Her eyes snapped open and she tried to sit up. Something was holding her down! But there was a fire!

"Easy, Doctor! Take it easy!" said a voice. She didn't recognize it.

"Yes, Doctor, lie still. You will be all right." This was from another voice. She did recognize this one.

"N…Nalorom…?"

"I'm here. You are out of danger. You have suffered some serious burns, but you will be all right."

She turned her head and saw the Someran standing next to her. She was on a stretcher, her suit had been cut away and her hands and arms were wrapped in bandages. But where was she? She looked again. It was the ship's small boat bay.

"How…how did I get here? I was in that access tunnel…"

"The little guy, here, pulled you out from what I understand," said the man standing on the other side of the stretcher. A medic.

"Thank you," she said, turning back to the Someran. He made a small gesture with his hand that she knew to mean: 'it was nothing'.

There seemed to be a lot of activity going on around her. More people on stretchers…

"What is happening?"

"The captain ordered all the wounded evacuated, Doctor," said Nalorom. "Rumor has it that they will attempt to ram the enemy on the next attack. Knowing Marshal Youngs, I tend to believe it."

"Ram? But…but that's insane!"

"No, simply necessary. We do what we have to do. You Terrans are more like us than we often think."

"I…are they taking me?"

"Yes, you need proper care. You will be loaded into the shuttle shortly."

"You are coming, too, aren't you?"

"No."

"But you must!" said Usha in sudden panic. "You have to come along!"

"If I were to go, who would watch over that 'balky, water-buffalo-of-a-reactor', Doctor?"

"No…" She had lost so much today—maybe everything. Not this, too.

The Someran reached out a hand and lightly touched Usha on the knee.

"Goodbye, my friend."

Usha held back her tears until she was on the shuttle and the hatch was closed.

* * * * *

"The target is coming right at us. You guessed right, Admiral," said Captain Ed Osborne with a shark-like smile.

"Time until launch?" asked Admiral Jameson.

"Six minutes, thirty seconds, sir."

"All right. Signal to squadron: cease acceleration and take launch positions."

"Aye aye, sir!"

While the com officer relayed the admiral's order, Osborne started giving his own. The squadron had been accelerating directly at the enemy. Now they ceased. The launch plan for their nuclear missiles was rather complex.

"Helm, ninety degree yaw to port; ninety degree roll to starboard."

"Aye sir, coming around."

Tennessee and the other ships of the Fourth Reserve Squadron positioned themselves so that the top of each ship was pointing in the same direction that they were moving.

Pointing toward the enemy.

"Have *Cincinnati* fall back," commanded, Jameson. "Get the hell out of the way and let the boomers do their job!"

"Yes, sir!"

It took another minute of jostling and adjusting, but finally the squadron was where their commander wanted it.

"Four minutes, sir."

"Open hatches and prepare to fire."

Buttons were pressed and the twenty-four heavy hatches along the top of *Tennessee* slowly swung open. The same thing was happening on the twenty-two other ships of the squadron.

"Hatches open, awaiting final firing order," reported Commander Lakner. On Osborne's signal, he and his exec unstrapped from their seats and floated over to the firing panel. He positioned himself by one of the keys. She was by the other. He glanced over at the admiral.

"Two minutes," said the sensor officer.

"Admiral to squadron," said Jameson, "unlock your birds."

Osborne looked at Lakner. She nodded back.

"Three...two...one...turn," said Osborne. He turned his key and so did she. Twenty-four lights on the panel went from red to green.

"Fire control is free. We can launch on your command," said Osborne.

"All ships reporting ready to launch, Admiral," said the com officer after a few moments.

"One minute, sir."

"Stand by."

Osborne positioned himself by a large red button. In the old days, each missile had its own button and own firing procedure. That had all changed. The missile launch now was a closely orchestrated operation involving the whole squadron. The button would simply give the computer the go-ahead. After that, it would all be automatic.

"Thirty seconds."

"Jameson to squadron: fire on the mark according to Plan Omega-One. And may God bless us all."

Osborne swallowed as the seconds reeled down. He had trained for years for this one moment. But now that it had come, the situation had altered almost beyond belief. Instead of destroying the world, his big birds were going to save it—he hoped.

"...five...four...three...two...one...*Launch!*"

Osborne pushed the big red button.

The ship shuddered as the first missile was pushed out of its tube by a blast of compressed steam. Three seconds later it ignited its engine and the ship shuddered again as the exhaust hit it. The second missile was leaving its tube at the same moment. The helmsman had to apply a tiny bit of power to keep the ship from being pushed out of position.

One by one the missiles streaked away from *Tennessee*. All through the squadron the same thing was happening. Salvo after salvo, each twenty-three missiles strong, pulled ahead of the ships that launched them and curved away toward an enemy that was still invisible beyond the horizon.

With each jolt of a launching missile, Ed Osborne thumped his fist on the console. He held tight with his other hand to keep from floating away. The lights on his board changed from green to amber as the missiles left their tubes.

He became aware that someone was chanting: "Go...go...go..." quietly. More and more voices joined this strange chorus.

As the last few birds took flight, he found himself hammering the panel and shouting along with everyone else.

Go, you little beauties, go!

* * * * *

Rradak'nuar twitched his tail in anticipation. Soon, very soon. His ship was speeding over the polar ice caps. The target continent was fast approaching. His missiles were poised to rain fire down on the landscape...

"Weapons, commence firing."

"Yes, Lord," said the weapons controller. A moment later the first salvo launched. Just the first of many. Rradak'nuar's tail twitched again. Suddenly, the sensor controller cried out:

"Lord! Enemy missiles detected! Directly ahead, closing fast!"

What? There are no enemy ships on the screen!

"Where did they come from?"

"Unknown, Lord, but these are not standard Enemy missiles. They are much larger and much slower. Ninety-two in four waves—correction! One hundred-fifteen in five waves!"

Rradak-nuar stared at the display. A swarm—several swarms—of missiles were coming around the curve of the planet toward him.

"Cease offensive fire! Launch defensive missiles! Lasers on automatic!"

"At once, Lord!"

His own missiles streaked away. A moment later the remaining primary lasers reached out and destroyed three of the enemy missiles. Suddenly, the targets on the screen multiplied.

"Lord! The first wave has stopped accelerating and broken into multiple targets! The second wave, as well. Two new waves detected!"

What was happening? The twenty surviving missiles in the first wave had each split into a dozen new targets. The following waves were doing the same thing. And still more waves were appearing on the horizon!

These new targets were not under power it seemed. What *were* they? How could they hope to intercept him without power? But they were forming a curtain right in his path. His lasers killed a few more, but there were now hundreds of the things. His defensive missiles exploded and the particle barrier formed in front of *Vardunal*. He should be safe from these strange weapons.

Unless...

"Sensors! Analysis of those objects! Quickly!"

"Yes, Lord!"

While he waited, Rradak'nuar became agitated. What he was seeing on the sensors was unlike any attack ever used by the Enemy. But it was all too similar to a form of attack sometimes used by his own people! *No! The Enemy has never used...*

"Lord! I am detecting radiation from those objects!" squawked the sensor operator.

"Helm! Hard right!" exclaimed Rradak'nuar. "Launch additional defensive missiles!"

Rradak'nuar hissed and sputtered in fear and anger. The leading enemy warheads were very close now. With the reduced acceleration of *Vardunal*, it was doubtful they could be avoided. But perhaps the particle barrier...

"Lord!"

The tactical display suddenly blossomed with light as the first wave detonated.

* * * * *

Nisima sat on the blanket and shivered. She could feel Melissa beside her; feel her arm around her. It was very comforting to have her here. Dozens of other people were nearby in the surrounding darkness. No one was saying much. A military radio was playing softly, with intermittent bursts of static. They had been sitting there for a long time. There were no more lights in the sky.

The radio reports had explained why: the battle was no longer far out in space. It was right here. On Earth. Cities were being destroyed. People were dying in enormous numbers. The *Brak-Shar* were killing them. All her life Nisima had lived in fear of the *Brak-Shar*. The Somerans missed no opportunity to reinforce that fear in the Tadath-Belind.

Now, here she was on a planet being bombarded by them. A nightmare come true. She was afraid, but she was surprised at how little of that fear was for herself. She was afraid for the people she cared about. For Kay Youngs and Bob Hancock—and for Jonathan. She was afraid for people she did not even know. The people in those cities.

Her people.

She wasn't quite sure when these barbarian, savage Terrans had become 'her people'. But they had. She had made her choice. Thrown her lot in with them. Willingly chosen to share their fate. It still amazed her.

When she volunteered to come here, it had been to help the Somerans first. Trying to 'civilize' these savage Terrans had been a distant second. She did not even consider herself the same species as the Terrans. She was better. Superior.

Now she knew differently.

She was one of these people. There was no use denying it. She felt more comfortable with them now than she ever had with the Somerans. And this world. It just felt...*right*. The sunlight was the right color. The gravity had just the right pull. She reached out and brushed the dew-covered grass. That was right, too. All those things back on the Somerans' home planet had not actually seemed wrong, but they had never felt this *right*. Melissa's arm felt right, too. That fleeting kiss that Jonathan had given her when they parted had felt very right. Somehow it was even more right than Danar's long-ago embraces.

And now she was probably going to lose all of it.

The enemy was smashing this world. The reports were very bad. Perhaps she would not actually die this night or the next day, but...

"What's that?" said a voice, suddenly.

Nisima looked up but did not see what the person was talking about.

"See that? Over there! On the horizon!"

Nisima scanned about and now she saw it: a red glow above the distant mountains.

"What is it, dawn?" asked someone else.

"Wrong direction. That's the northeast. And it's an hour too early. Look, it's fading...Yow!"

The man's exclamation was caused by a new burst of light. Much brighter than the first one. At first it was blindingly bright and Nisima fumbled for her dark glasses. As she put them on, the light became an orange ball, seething along the horizon. After a few seconds there was another dazzling flash. The shadows of the watchers stretched like spilled ink across the meadow.

"What it that?" asked another.

"I don't know, but I have a bad feeling about it."

A sense of dread seemed to wash over them. Nisima shivered. What new weapon was the enemy using now?

But then Melissa stirred beside her and stood up. Nisima could see her staring into this strange glow.

"Wait a minute..." she said, speaking almost to herself.

"What is it, Lis?" asked Steve Sokol.

"One of the briefings I was at with Dad. They were talking about how they could use the..." she trailed off.

"Use the what?"

"Yes!" she suddenly shouted. Everyone turned toward her. "Yes! Yes!"
"Melissa! What's going on?"

"That's not the enemy! Those are ours!" Melissa was shouting at the top of her lungs and jumping up and down. Nisima just stared at her open-mouthed.

"Those are ours! That's my Uncle Eddie! *That's the Boomers! Yes! Yes! Yes!*"

Melissa was dancing about like a madwoman and her madness seemed to be infecting the others. They started to shout and bounce around, too. Nisima was on her feet, not knowing what to do. She wondered what future this false dawn was heralding.

The glare continued to grow. It covered the whole horizon and reached up the sky blotting out the stars. Melissa was like some cheerleader at those bizarre sporting events. She shook her fist at the sky and screamed.

"Burn you bastards, burn!"

* * * * *

Two hundred kilometers above the ice, nuclear fire tore away the waning polar night. The local wildlife burrowed into snow banks or dove deep to escape this unnatural glow.

One hundred and ninety-seven thermonuclear warheads detonated simultaneously and created a wall of fire in front of the approaching *Brak-Shar* vessel. They were still too far away to do it any harm, but the particle barrier it had launched was much closer. The billions of tiny metal grains puffed to vapor under the searing radiation. The vapor still had its initial velocity, but it soon dispersed to harmlessness.

The next wave of missiles, safe from any defensive fire behind the first wave's explosions, came as close to it as it dared and then detonated in turn. The *Brak-Shar* ship was much closer now. Still too far for any real affect, but getting closer every second. It was trying to turn aside, to escape, but the missiles formed a curtain over a hundred kilometers across and a hundred high and there was just no way to avoid it.

Or the waves coming up behind.

Satellites high overhead were tracking both the missiles and their target. The missiles would detonate at closest approach, each wave exploding as the enemy ship tried to pass through it.

The *Brak-Shar* were not facing a curtain of fire, but a tunnel. *A gauntlet.*

The third wave was close enough to start gnawing at the enemy's shields. The much-abused capacitors had to discharge some of their energy to fend off the growing storm of radiation. The fourth wave was still worse. The nearest warhead was only six kilometers away when it burst. The *Brak-Shar* reactor was frantically pumping energy into the capacitors to replace what was being used, but it was rapidly losing the race.

The fifth wave exploded all around their target, draining capacitors on top, bottom, and sides. By the eighth salvo, the shield began to fail in spots. Heat and radiation blasted through to the hull plates. By the twelfth, most of the shield was down and parts of the ship were glowing red hot. A warhead in the fifteenth wave was only a kilometer away when it detonated. A thousand square meters of the ship's hull boiled away. And still the missiles came, smashing and clawing at the vessel. Sensors and weapons were destroyed. Laser emitters shattered and missile tubes were melted shut. Interior shielding spared most of the crew from the radiation effects, but the outer layers of the ship burned.

The humans had launched over five thousand warheads at their enemy. They had hoped for a direct hit that would end the battle at a blow. But space is vast and while some of the warheads came very close indeed, none of them actually hit the target. The *Brak-Shar* vessel was a glowing meteor when it emerged from the last of the inferno—but it was still there.

* * * * *

Shipmaster Rradak'nuar was thrown from side to side in his command station. The restraints kept him from serious injury while the enemy missiles battered his ship, but blow after blow hammered him as the warheads detonated. The smell of fear and panic filled the control chamber. His crew squawked in fright as the ship was buffeted with radiation and hot gas. It was impossible to know what was happening or take meaningful action. He just hung on and waited for it to end.

Finally it did end. He looked and saw that the damage display was almost a solid mass of blinking lights. Too much to take in at once. And the tactical display…was nearly blank.

"Report!" he snarled.

"Heavy damage, Lord! All sensors are out except for those pointing directly aft. All weapons except the stern lasers read as inoperable!"

"Rotate the ship! Bring the stern sensors around to look forward!"

"At once, Lord!"

It would take a few moments to carry out. He was blind forward, blind in almost every direction! He needed to know what was coming at him! Those missiles had to have come from somewhere! The ship was coming around, in a moment…

"Lord! Enemy vessels directly ahead!"

The tactical display updated and there was a swarm of ships on the screen. An instant later the ship twitched as lasers began to pound it. The shields on the stern were still in operation, but terribly weak; they would not last long. The range shortened very rapidly. Apparently *Vadunal's* survival must have surprised the enemy because none of the smaller missiles were in flight, only their lasers.

"Commence firing!" snapped Rradak'nuar.

"Yes, Lord!"

The shipmaster was still shaken by this turn of events. What to do? All the missile tubes were damaged. He could not carry out his planned bombardment. The only hope now was to escape. The drive still worked, he could still escape and carry out the other part of his plan! He just had to get past these last few ships. But…but they were moving right toward him! Did they actually intend to…?

"Weapons! Clear our path! Fire!"

"Yes, Lord!"

The range continued to fall. The lasers damaged two of the enemy ships, which tumbled aside. The others were sweeping past all around. Now there was just one more in the way...

* * * * *

The *Brak-Shar* lasers lashed out and hit *Tennessee* squarely, just aft of the reactor compartment. These were only the lighter, secondary lasers rather than the murderous main lasers, which had killed so many ships of the Fleet. They blasted through the heavy pressure hull of the submarine-turned-spaceship. This used up most of their energy, however, they still had enough to rupture a large storage tank in the main engine compartment.

At their touch, the tank burst and four thousand liters of the Someran cooling compound flashed to vapor, instantly filling the whole, large compartment. A microsecond later the vapor ignited with the explosive force of fifty tons of TNT. The rear half of the ship was blown to bits in a huge explosion.

* * * * *

Rradak'nuar hissed in satisfaction. The last enemy ship barring his path was destroyed. They were through! Now to escape!

"Helm! Full thrust away from the planet!"

"Yes, Lord!"

"Collision alert!" exclaimed the sensor operator suddenly. "Large object directly ahead!"

"Evasive action! Lasers!"

Rradak'nuar dug his claws into his station. Some bit of debris from that last ship! The lasers stabbed out and hit it. A missile would have been vaporized, but the lasers only succeeded in blowing a small piece off it! What was it? It was too close...it was here...

* * * * *

Two hundred kilometers above Victoria Island the *Brak-Shar* ship tried to dodge aside, but it was too late. The object was too close and closing too fast. Most of the debris cloud was small fragments of metal that could be handled by the ship's shield.

Most of it.

It could *not* handle the twenty-five ton, solid titanium propeller of *USS Tennessee* that now smashed into it at a relative velocity of almost thirty kilometers per second.

The shield did hold long enough to convert the propeller to a ball of super-dense plasma, but it made no difference. The expanding ball blew through the ship from stern to stem, annihilating everything it touched. Storage compartments, crew quarters, missile magazines were wiped away. The shield generator, drive compartment, and fusion reactor obliterated. The control chamber as well. Shipmaster Rradak'nuar died without knowing what it was that had killed him.

The remains of *Vardunal* shattered into three large pieces, each of which soared away from Earth on an escape trajectory. A few smaller pieces, their trajectory altered by the impact, fell in various spots across northern Canada.

* * * * *

"They did it! The boomers got the bastard!" shouted the sensor operator aboard *EDS Terra.*

Kay Youngs' head jerked up in astonishment. The red icon, which had been burning in her brain as well as on the display, blinked out. It was impossible. That blip had devoured everything she had sent at it. Ship after ship, squadron after squadron, had vanished from the tactical display, but that one red one had always remained. She had been preparing to throw herself at it and she had no real hope that the results would be any different.

But now it was gone. Impossible.

"Quite a lot of wreckage left, but it should pass well above us if we stay at this altitude," said the sensor officer, almost having to shout to be heard over the cheers.

"Very well, maintain the present course," said Bob Hancock. He turned toward her, but she deliberately turned away. She couldn't look at him. She had been prepared to sacrifice him, too. She wasn't sure she'd ever be able to forgive herself for that. She looked around the bridge at the people there. She'd been prepared to sacrifice all of them. And what about everyone else? What was left of the Fleet…of Earth?

"Damage to Admiral Jameson's squadron?" she asked.

The elation subsided a bit. "Two ships appear to have been destroyed, ma'am. The flagship's transponder is still active, but I'm not reading any drive signature."

"Try to raise them."

"Aye aye, ma'am."

Now she did look at Bob. He smiled at her, but she could see the worry on his face over his friend, Ed Osborne. After a few minutes the com officer spoke up:

"I've got them, ma'am. Captain Osborne is on audio only."

"Captain Osborne, what is your situation?"

"Well, ma'am, I seem to have misplaced about half my ship. The reactor's gone, the drive's gone, and we are going to need assistance."

"Is Admiral Jameson there?"

"He's here, but he's…indisposed at the moment."

"Injured?"

"Not exactly. When things blew it put a hell of a spin on the ship. It…it's kind of hard to get used to, ma'am."

"I see." In spite of all the strain and anxiety, Kay found herself grinning. Jameson was probably puking his guts out right now. She sympathized completely. "Very well, Captain, we'll try to get someone over to you ASAP. By the way, that was a hell of a good job you did. My compliments—and thanks."

"What? You mean we got him?" asked Osborne and Kay could hear the surprise in his voice.

"You sure as hell did, Captain!" exclaimed Bob Hancock. "Blew him to Smithereens and points south!"

"I'll be damned. Our sensors are out. The last thing we saw was the son-of-a-bitch coming out of the nukes straight at us. I figured we had blown our chance. How'd we happen to kill him?"

"I guess we'll have to figure that out later. For right now, hang tight and we'll get some help to you," said Kay.

"Right-o. We'll stand by. Osborne out."

Kay sagged in her chair. Some of the bridge crew was starting to cheer, slap each other on the back. Kay wanted to join them, but she found she didn't have the energy for it. But it was over. It was really over.

Well, not quite...

"Captain Kagami. Tell the Fleet to stand down. Are there any other ships in need of assistance?"

"Quite a few ma'am. About a dozen ships still have their transponder beacons functioning. A number of others have been in radio contact—including *Seeker of Truth*."

"Really? That's wonderful. Can you assign ships to assist all those vessels, Captain?" Could Keeradoth still be alive? She hoped so, she really did.

"Certainly, ma'am, right away."

Kay turned to the communications officer. "Get a message out to EDF headquarters that the enemy has been destroyed. The danger is passed."

"Yes, ma'am!"

"You did it, Kay." She looked up to see Bob standing next to her. She reached out and took his hand.

"We did it, Captain, we all did it. And it's not over yet."

"There's still a hell of a mess to clean up."

Chapter Thirty-Five

Kathryn Youngs knelt by the cot and held a cup up to the little boy's lips so he could take a sip. He moaned and the water trickled down the side of his face.

"It's all right, it's all right," she whispered. The boy could not see her because of the bandages covering his eyes. Her words probably meant nothing either. She wished she'd paid more attention to those Spanish classes in high school.

"Here, let me do that." A nurse squatted down beside Kay.

"It's all right. I can do it," protested Kay. The woman firmly took the cup out of her hands.

"Marshal Youngs, if you don't take a break, you'll end up on one of these cots, yourself! I've been watching you here all day. At least go outside for a while!"

Kay nodded and got to her feet. She walked shakily past the endless rows of cots in the field hospital tent until she found an exit. She stumbled out into the blazing heat of the Mexican summer. There were a number of awnings outside and she went under one to find the shade. For once, there was plenty of room and as she stared out she realized why. Several enormous objects were settling in for a landing about a kilometer away and the crowds of refugees were heading toward them. She recognized one of them as *Terra*. The ship still bore all the scars of battle. Huge gashes in her hull told a stark tale of the fury she had endured.

But there had been no time for any but the most urgent repairs. The *Brak-Shar* attack had left millions dead, but millions more were injured and in desperate need of help. The Fleet had been pressed into service to transport food, medicine, supplies, and volunteers. *Terra* alone could carry more supplies in one trip than a hundred cargo planes, and land them virtually anywhere. The converted subs were not well designed as cargo carriers, but huge containers could be strapped to their sides and transported that way.

A week had passed and Kay had been shuttling to the various camps that had been set up. Mexico and India had been the hardest hit, but she had made stops in Russia and the Mideast as well.

And the United States, too. She had saved her sisters' children, but far too many others had died.

It was really very hot. She sat down in the shade. Maybe a little rest would be a good...

"Kay? Kay? Are you all right?"

She started awake and looked around in confusion. Bob was standing over her. To her surprise, Jonathan was beside him.

"Jonathan! What are you doing here? I thought you were still in the hospital."

"They kicked me out to make room for others, ma'am. I'm fine now."

"Fine?! Don't give me that! Three cracked vertebrae do not heal in a week's time!"

"Well, they do have me strapped together pretty tight," admitted her aide.

"Somehow I doubt your doctors would approve of this. So what are you doing here?"

"I've come to collect you, ma'am."

"What?"

"We need you back in New York. In case you've forgotten, there's a rather important meeting coming up."

"That's not for four more days."

"Just enough time to let you rest up beforehand, ma'am."

"I…I'll be fine."

"Marshal, you were asleep sitting up just now! How much farther do you think you can push yourself?"

"As far as I have to…"

"Commander," said Hancock, breaking in, "would you excuse us for a moment?"

"Of course, Captain." Cresswell-Jones retreated, walking stiffly and glancing back at her.

"Kay, why are you doing this to yourself?"

"I don't know what you mean."

"You know perfectly well what I mean!" He waved his arm. "Going from camp to camp like this. Trying to personally help each and every survivor. You're killing yourself!"

"They need help," she whispered.

"Yes they do, and they're getting it. As fast as we can provide it. It's wonderful that you are helping, too, but we both know that's not why you're doing this."

"Oh? Why am I doing it, Captain?" She was so tired she couldn't even sound angry.

"I don't need to tell you. And don't try to deny it. I was there on the bridge of *Terra* with you. I saw your face. Every time one of our ships was destroyed, every time a city was hit, it was like someone was carving a piece out of you. It hurt all of us, but you act like every single death was your fault!"

"I…I was in charge, Bob," she whispered. "I was responsible. If it wasn't my fault, then whose was it?"

"It was war, dammit! We didn't start it, but we had to fight it! If it hadn't been for you, the whole damn planet would look like this now—if we were lucky! You did everything you possibly could."

"Did I? Oh Bob, I know I'm being stupid here, but we were *so close*! We almost won without all this mess! Just another few months and we would have had a real fleet. Those bastards wouldn't have even gotten near Earth. All these people didn't have to die." She stepped away and then pointed to a nearby tent where a woman was holding a small child that was wrapped in bandages.

"I keep asking myself how many hours I wasted in the last nine months. If all those hours were added up, and all the hours everyone else involved wasted were added up, how many more subs could we have converted? How many more fighters built? Enough to have prevented this? I can't sleep, Bob. It's driving me crazy."

"Kay, Kay," said Bob. He stepped close and put his arms around her. She tried to pull away, tried to deny herself even the smallest comfort, but he would not let her go. She gave up and sobbed against his shoulder. Once she started she couldn't stop. He didn't say anything, he just held her.

"Maybe we all could have done more, Kay," he said after a while. "Time is unforgiving. It won't give anyone a break. But we have to give ourselves a break,

Kay. We're not machines. Look, look at those kids over there."

She turned her head and saw a half-dozen children, maybe ten years old, chasing each other through the camp. They were laughing despite the tragedy all around them.

"They're old enough to work. They could have been digging bomb shelters these last nine months. Should they have? And there will be more *Brak-Shar* coming eventually. Shouldn't those kids be in the mines, digging up raw materials for the fabricators?

"We all have responsibilities, Kay. But we have a responsibility to be human, too. Yes, maybe we all could have done more to prepare. But how much can we do without losing everything we're trying to save? You did everything duty demanded of you and more. Now it's time to give yourself a break."

She continued to cry, but she nodded and leaned against him.

"Come on. I'll take you home on my next trip."

* * * * *

Expedition Leader Keeradoth stood in the recreation chamber aboard *Seeker of Truth* and sadly regarded the withered vegetation. The damage from the battle had opened this compartment to space and all the plants had died in the vacuum. The ship's chief environmental technician and the botanist were working on replacing everything, but it would take quite some time. At the moment it was a dreary and desolate place.

Keeradoth walked stiffly over to the viewport, mindful of the not-quite-healed injuries suffered during the battle. The view out the port was considerably more pleasant than the view inside. The planet turning below was still blue and green and brown with dazzlingly white clouds. The damage it had suffered was scarcely even noticeable from this altitude. The studies Keeradoth had ordered indicated that the environmental and climatological damage from the *Brak-Shar* weapons should be minimal.

The effects of the *psychological* damage to the planet's inhabitants were harder to measure. The casualties had come as a shock, even to the warlike beings who lived here. Rough estimates put the dead at around eighty million. Not the most costly war in these people's history, but to take them all in *one day* was certainly unprecedented. Keeradoth had a surprising amount of sympathy for the Terrans. *Have they indeed become 'people' to me at last?*

But the expedition leader's feelings did not obscure the facts. *We have won the battle, but what about the war?* Some of the Terrans were blaming the Race for their losses and, in truth, there was some justice in that. But others were pointing to the dead as a warning of the danger that remained. These Terrans placed so much importance in their dead 'not having died in vain' and that might well be the case here. The dead, the blasted cities, would be memorialized if the past actions of these Terrans were any guide. They would be constant reminders to the survivors of what happened. They would be a lesson to generations yet to come. Keeradoth had hope that when the next attack came, these Terrans—no, these *humans*—would be ready for it.

"Honored One, the shuttle is waiting."

Keeradoth turned and saw Hablajin standing in the entrance to the chamber. Keeradoth was glad the xeniologist had survived the battle. Three-twelves of the crew had not. The loss of Tandalin had been especially painful.

"Yes, I am ready," said Keeradoth.

They walked through the corridors of *Seeker of Truth* to the hanger bay. There was another meeting with the Terrans scheduled; the first since the battle. Much had happened within the convoluted political systems of the humans recently. Keeradoth was not entirely sure what to expect of this meeting.

"The Terrans have been acting in a very gratifying manner of late, Honored One," said Hablajin as they boarded the shuttle.

"I suppose they have," said Keeradoth. "Space Marshal Youngs has managed to hold the Earth Defense Forces together—at least for now."

"Yes, and they have begun to make real strides in distributing the new technology. There are still those who oppose, but I hope that as the standard of living rises worldwide, the opponents will find they have less and less support."

"That is a possibility. And already some of them are looking outward. There are plans to begin asteroid mining and orbital manufacturing. My hope is that the EDF can base its future expansion on space-based facilities. That would be much less affected by the changing politics down on Earth."

"That would be excellent," said Hablajin. "But what do they plan to do in regards to their relations with the Race?"

"An excellent question! I believe we may find that out shortly."

The shuttle left the hanger bay and headed for the planet below. It was not long before New York City was growing in the viewport. One of the city's tallest spires was lying in ruins. Keeradoth could see where work was being done to repair nearby buildings. One was apparently being dismantled—perhaps the damage had been too severe for repairs?

A short time later the shuttle landed and Keeradoth and Hablajin debarked. They were met by Marshal Youngs and Doctor Vasthare. Nalorom was with them. Keeradoth was amazed at how much time Nalorom seemed to spend with Doctor Vasthare. Keeradoth was also slightly surprised at how pleasant it was to see Youngs…

"Commander, it is good to see you again," said the Terran. "I can't begin to tell you how happy I was when we heard that you and your ship had survived. I really feared the worst."

"Thank you, Marshal. It was 'a near run thing' as your saying goes, I believe. The damage to the ship was extensive."

"And your casualties, too. My condolences."

"Thank you, again."

"How do the repairs on your ship go?"

"Slowly. But there is no great need for haste. We shall be remaining here for some time."

Youngs nodded. "Yes, your future plans are what we need to discuss today. If you'll follow me, we can get started."

The Terran woman led them inside the building that was becoming almost familiar to Keeradoth. Fortunately, they did not go to the enormous assembly hall, but to a smaller conference room. For once, there were no chairs waiting for them. Keeradoth, Hablajin, and Nalorom stood before their spots and waited while the usual preliminaries were dealt with. The Terrans present included Youngs and some of her staff, the Secretary General, and ambassadors from a number of important countries. Lars Sjolander stood up.

"Commander Keeradoth, we have asked you here because we wish to formalize the relations between your people and ours." Keeradoth was suddenly alert. Formalize? That certainly sounded hopeful—they would not 'formalize' an order to leave!

"That would be excellent, Mister Secretary. I assume you have some detailed proposals?"

"Yes, we do. But before I go into them, I'd like to briefly bring you up to date on our own activities. As I'm sure you are aware, there has been considerable debate on what our future course should be."

"Yes, I understand there is a certain amount of disagreement." An understatement for certain!

"Indeed there has, and unfortunately much disagreement remains. However, a great deal of progress has also been made. We have established an acceptable chain of command for the Earth Defense Forces, the national space navies, and the planetary defenses we plan to build. It is a delicate juggling act, but we have come up with a balance of authority and responsibility that have satisfied the majority of our peoples."

"That sounds very good, Mr. Secretary," said Keeradoth. "May I ask how my people fit into your plans?"

"How would you like to fit into them?"

A direct question. How to answer?

"Our original intent was to have you as allies in our fight against the *Brak-Shar*. We would still like this to happen. However, we would understand if you are reluctant."

"Yes, there are still many people angry at your past actions. Others blame you for the losses in the battle. At the moment, there is considerable sentiment against any *offensive* alliance with your people."

"Offensive?" A glimmer of hope. Marshal Youngs now took over from Sjolander.

"From the information you have given us before, it was obvious you looked at us as an advanced base to carry out offensive operations against the *Brak-Shar*. I do not believe that will be agreeable at this time. Of course, at the moment, it is entirely academic," added Youngs with a grin. "We won't have any offensive capability for many years and it will be decades before we can complete a star portal and allow your ships to move through here. I'm hoping that by the time it becomes more than academic, we can re-think the matter."

"You plan to build a star portal?" asked Keeradoth eagerly.

"With your assistance, of course. I understand that the next ships of yours will have the specialized equipment to begin construction."

"Indeed, yes. Marshal, this is very encouraging. From what you have said, I take it you are willing to enter into some sort of defensive agreement?"

"That was the idea. I think that most people would accept that. Most realize that there will be more, much heavier, attacks by the *Brak-Shar* in the future. Having your fleet available to back us up would be a very prudent move. It would also allow us to seriously contemplate colonization of other systems without leaving ourselves open to attack."

"That would be entirely agreeable to us, Marshal."

"Well, don't sign on the dotted line until you've read the contract, Commander!" Youngs made that strange sound the humans used for laughter. "I'll let Mister Sjolander explain what we have in mind."

The meeting went on for some time and, as Marshal Youngs had hinted, there were many, many details that had to be discussed and settled. Keeradoth was relieved to learn that the Race would not be held accountable for the damage done in either of the battles. The lawsuits had been totaling several trillion US dollars and Keeradoth had feared they would need to hire a human lawyer...

Finally, the meeting began to wind down. Keeradoth was certain that there would have to be more meetings and debates in the General Assembly before anything became official, but the major issues had been solved. A feeling of great satisfaction coursed through the expedition leader. After the early disasters and setbacks this was a greater success than ever could have been expected.

When the next ship comes I can turn over command with a clear conscience. And then I can finally go home.

"I think we have accomplished all we can today," said Sjolander. "Are all the...human...members in agreement?" Everyone looked around the room, but all that could be seen was heads nodding.

"Commander? Any problems?"

"None."

"Very well then, I believe we have reached a consensus."

Expedition Leader Keeradoth carefully curled up the corners of its mouth in approximation of a human smile.

"Yes, Mister Secretary, I believe we have."

* * * * *

A short time later, Kay Youngs walked out the front doors of the UN building. There was a large crowd of people staring at five enormous objects floating over the East River. *Terra* was immediately recognizable by her battle scars, but she now had four sisters. Kay shook her head. If they had only had those ships for the battle! But she knew that even now they were not battle-worthy. Their reactors were not operational and many other vital systems were offline. They were running off their batteries and only here for this ceremony. She had only been told this was going to happen a few hours earlier.

Kay was met by her staff and then she joined a large group of VIPs in a roped off area. A number of speeches were made praising Earth's gallant defenders and then the four new ships were formally turned over to the EDF. It was all very nice, but Kay scarcely paid attention. She was very tired. Eventually it was over. It was only when a shuttle detached itself from *Terra* that she perked up.

The shuttle landed a short distance away. She immediately spotted Bob Hancock, but she was delighted when she saw that Melissa and Steve Sokol were with him.

"Hello, Captain, Ensign, Lieutenant," she said when they approached. "Glad to see you, and welcome back."

They all greeted her in return. "We're glad to be back," said Melissa.

"Yeah, too many mosquitoes up there," said Sokol.

"So I assume you all knew about this little surprise but didn't see fit to tell me about it," said Kay accusingly.

"Yup, and I don't feel the least bit guilty," said Bob. They all laughed.

"Ed Osborne is commanding the second one from the right," continued Hancock, indicating one of the ships. "It's just temporary, but he asked me to tell you that he'd be interested in a permanent position, if it's open."

"I think something can be arranged," said Kay. She smiled at him and their eyes met and locked.

Kay reached out and took Bob's hand. She was sure that a dozen newsmen were watching, but she didn't care. She noticed Melissa and Steve were holding hands, too. She also noticed that Melissa had a ring on her finger.

"So when are you going to get me one of those?" she said to Bob.

He raised an eyebrow. "I don't have any taste in jewelry. Want to pick one out together?"

"Okay. When?"

"Tomorrow soon enough?"

"That should do."

They stood in silence, oblivious to the crowds around them. Kay Youngs held the hand of the man she loved. He would be a huge part of her life now. But she stared out at the leviathans floating over the East River. Those things would demand at least as much from her. She knew it and she knew he knew it. And they both accepted it.

She turned her head as Jonathan came up beside her. Nisima was standing very close to him, although they weren't holding hands.

"Quite a thing, isn't it, ma'am?" he said, indicating the ships. "Having these in the EDF's possession changes the situation considerably."

She pondered Jonathan's words. The debate over the future role—or continued existence—of the EDF had been hotter and a more 'near run thing' than they had admitted to the aliens. There had been real fear that the nations building these ships would keep them for themselves. A lot of people would like to see the EDF—and Kay Youngs—quietly vanish. But, at least for the time being, the world was still stuck with both. "Yes, I suppose it does," she answered at last. "It gives me some hope for the future. But you realize that we still have a tiger by the tail."

"Oh, yes, ma'am, that I do."

Bob Hancock laughed and said to Kay: "Well, you know what you have to do when you have a tiger by the tail, don't you?" She smiled.

"Yes, I do: hang on! Hang on tight!"

The End

ABOUT THE AUTHOR

Scott Washburn is an architectural designer by profession, an avid reader of military history as well as long time re-enactor and wargamer. He has written several SF&F books that are being published by Zmok Books

Zmok Books – Action, Adventure and Imagination

Zmok Books offers science fiction and fantasy books in the classic tradition as well as the new and different takes on the genre.

Winged Hussar Publishing, LLC is the parent company of Zmok Publishing, focused on military history from ancient times to the modern day.

Follow all the latest news on Winged Hussar and Zmok Books at www.wingedhussarpublishing.com

Other great reads from Zmok Books

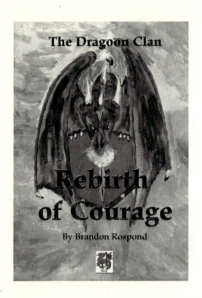

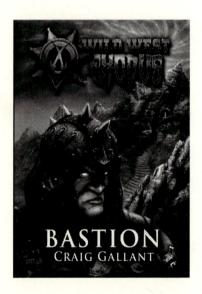

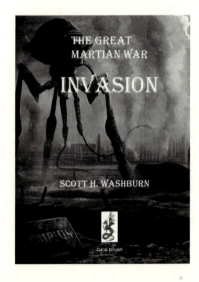